That Prince is Mine

ALSO BY JAYCI LEE

BOOKED ON A FEELING

THE DATING DARE

A SWEET MESS

That Prince is Mine

A NOVEL

JAYCI LEE

ST. MARTIN'S GRIFFIN
NEW YORK

First published in the United States by St. Martin's Griffin, an imprint of St. Martin's Publishing Group

THAT PRINCE IS MINE. Copyright © 2024 by Judith J. Yi. All rights reserved. Printed in the United States of America. For information, address St. Martin's Publishing Group, 120 Broadway, New York, NY 10271.

www.stmartins.com

Designed by Devan Norman

The Library of Congress Cataloging-in-Publication Data is available upon request.

ISBN 978-1-250-90776-9 (trade paperback)
ISBN 978-1-250-90777-6 (ebook)

Our books may be purchased in bulk for promotional, educational, or business use. Please contact your local bookseller or the Macmillan Corporate and Premium Sales Department at 1-800-221-7945, extension 5442, or by email at MacmillanSpecialMarkets@macmillan.com.

First Edition: 2024

10 9 8 7 6 5 4 3 2 1

To Gwen—thank you for staying by my side
through the darkest years of my life.
I hope you'll still be by my side through
the brightest times to come.

QUICK AND DIRTY
GUIDE TO KOREAN

For the word nerds . . .

Pronouncing romanized Korean words is really hard even for someone who is fluent in Korean like I am. In *That Prince is Mine*, I try my best to be consistent in romanizing Korean words, following the Revised Romanization of Korean system used in South Korea.

The consonants are pretty straightforward (until you get into the double "dd," "ss," and "kk," etc., but let's not worry about that for now). How you sound out the consonants in your head will be close enough to how it should sound without tripping you up.

But there are a few tricky vowels until you get used to them. I think these are the most helpful ones to note.

- "u" is pronounced "oo"
- "eo" is pronounced "uh"
- "a" is pronounced "ah"
- "ae" is pronounced "eh"

The cool thing is that those vowels will always sound like that, no matter with what consonants you combine them. So the word "gujeolpan" is pronounced *goo-juhl-pahn*, "gungjung" is pronounced *goong-joong*, "jaebeol" is pronounced *jeh-buhl*, so on, so forth.

Now, if I haven't confused you more, go forth and read *That Prince is Mine* with confidence. I hope you love Emma and Michel as much as I do.

That Prince is Mine

CHAPTER ONE

♥

Emma Yoon tucked her feet under her and tilted her face toward the midday sun. The window seat overlooking the garden was her favorite spot in the house. Well, the garden had been transformed into a veritable organic farm since her dad retired, but it still provided her with a lovely view. Exhaling a happy hum, she sipped her tea from a delicate porcelain teacup dotted with pink blossoms.

With her morning lesson finished, she had a couple of hours to herself before her next client arrived, but her thoughts had already drifted to the recipe she planned to teach. Gujeolpan, platter of nine delicacies, consisted of colorful julienned meat and vegetables circling a stack of small, delicate crepes. Each of the dish's nine components took time and effort to prepare, but the end result was visually stunning and absolutely delicious, which made it the perfect introduction to Korean royal court cuisine. Anyone could add beauty and harmony to their lives with a little loving care. With jeongseong.

Jeongseong wasn't a cheeky sentiment like a "sprinkle of love." It meant working hard with a generous heart. It was a pure and true intent to do your very best—to imbue the best of yourself into something. Korean royal court cuisine would be nothing without jeongseong. As a matter of fact, Emma was a firm believer that life itself would be meaningless without it.

When her mother left, Emma built a warm, loving home for her dad and herself with jeongseong. All the meaningful relationships in her life were sustained through it. Everything that was beautiful and worthwhile required jeongseong. It might not come conveniently bottled, but jeongseong might truly be the secret ingredient to a happy, secure life.

As Emma swung her legs to the floor to go check on some ingredients, her cell phone rang in the pocket of her favorite floral maxi dress—the pocket being a major contributor to why the dress was her everyday go-to. Setting down her empty teacup beside her, she glanced at the screen before answering with a smile.

"Hi, Imo."

"Hello." Her godmother's voice sounded uncharacteristically hesitant and her heart gave an involuntary lurch. "How are you, my dear?"

"I'm doing great, thanks to you," Emma said, smoothing out the frown gathering between her brows. It was probably nothing. "The new clients you referred to me are all so sweet and eager to learn. They're a pleasure to teach. And with my business growing, I'll be able to put a down payment on a commercial kitchen space soon."

Auntie Soo was a renowned Madame Ddu, a Korean matchmaker, with a coveted Black Book that made her unbeatable at the game. She'd not only successfully matched countless couples in the US, but her reputation had reached the rich and powerful jaebeol families of Korea, extending her business overseas. This development proved lucrative for her godmother and came with an unexpected boon for Emma's small enterprise.

Rumor had it that a bride of the pseudo-royals in Korea must possess a proficiency in Korean royal court cuisine—gungjung yori. Since Auntie Soo had an impressive line of clients hoping to marry into a jaebeol family, she directed them straight into Emma's kitchen and open arms. The implication that women belonged in the kitchen chafed. Who did these jaebeol people think they were? But if these women *chose* to be in the kitchen—as Emma had—then more power to them. Their *place* should be wherever they chose to be.

And thanks to her new clients, Emma's dream of opening a culinary school was finally within reach. Her parents disagreed on virtually everything, but the one thing they tacitly agreed on was the importance of having a profession you were passionate about. It shouldn't mean *everything* to her—her mom's career took precedence over her family—but it should be something essential to her. She wanted to do something worthwhile with her life. Something worth her jeongseong. Running her own culinary school would be just the thing.

"Those goddamned busybodies," Auntie Soo muttered.

Emma's mouth dropped open. Her godmother treated all her clients with warmth and respect. She would never call them . . . "Goddamned busybodies? Your clients?"

"No, not them." She clicked her tongue. "Why would I call them busybodies?"

"I have no idea. That's why I asked—Never mind." Emma paused for a calming breath. "Who were you calling busybodies, then?"

"The Crones, of course," Auntie Soo said.

Mrs. Chung, Mrs. Lee, and Mrs. Kim—her godmother's rival matchmakers—were not-so-affectionately nicknamed the Crones. They absolutely abhorred each other except when it came to ganging up on Auntie Soo. *Then* they became of one mind and purpose—to cause their biggest rival the most grief they could possibly conjure up. But they were pesky little gnats more than anything. Her godmother really shouldn't let them get her so worked up.

Emma padded into her bright and tidy kitchen and glanced around with a content smile. Even with tidings of the Crones, the pristine white of the subway tiles and the cool depth of the slate-gray countertop soothed her. Every small detail in the kitchen—from the sunny yellow valance over the sink to the copper rooster mold on the side wall—were lovingly handpicked by her.

"What did they do this time?" she said with studied patience as she placed her empty teacup in the sink to hand-wash later. Seeing no point in being idle, she wiped the already clean counter with a dish towel.

"Don't patronize me, child. I'm not calling to gossip," Auntie Soo said with an impatient huff. "This can impact my business, which means it can impact *your* business."

Emma's hand stilled over the spice jars she was about to rearrange. "How can they possibly hurt your business?"

"They've discovered my Achilles' heel," the older woman said in an ominous whisper.

"You have an Achilles' heel?" Thank goodness she was done with her tea. Otherwise, she would've spewed it all over her kitchen counter.

"Yes." Her godmother paused for dramatic effect. "It's you, Emma. *You* may be my downfall."

"Me?" Emma couldn't hold back her snort, but an uneasy premonition tempered her amusement. "Imo, you can't be serious."

"We should've done a video call. Then you'd be able to look into my eyes and see how serious I am."

"Fine. I believe you," Emma said with an innocent sigh. "Your eyes are full of seriousness."

"Impudent girl," Auntie Soo chided, but Emma didn't need a

video feed to see the affectionate smile on her godmother's face. "You're like a daughter to me."

"I know, Imo." She blinked away hot, sudden tears as gratitude mingled with the ache of an old wound. Her godmother was more of a mother to her than her own mom ever had been.

"Oh, sweetheart." Her godmother sniffed loudly, understanding Emma's unspoken words. "But since you are basically my daughter, the Crones are whispering in people's ears that they can't trust a matchmaker who has a spinster daughter."

"A spinster?" Emma sputtered. Focused on building her business, she hadn't given relationships much thought. Besides, she had no reason to waste time on something as unreliable as dating, since she'd always assumed her godmother would arrange a good match for her when the time came. But a spinster? "What are we? Living in a Jane Austen novel? No, wait. Are they telling people I'm *on the shelf*?"

"Be serious, Emma."

"I am, Imo. My eyes are filled to the brim with seriousness. I'm only twenty-eight." She threw her hand up, pacing back and forth in her kitchen. The Crones were making her feel like a canned good about to expire. "I'm not close to being a spinster."

"Of course, my dear," Auntie Soo readily agreed. "You still have months until you turn twenty-nine."

She shouldn't even ask. "What happens when I turn twenty-nine?"

"*Then* I will have a spinster daughter."

"Imo," Emma shrieked, smacking her palm down on the counter. It was just a number. What made twenty-nine so special? Why not thirty-five? Or twenty-seven? Or eighty? What if there were no random number *at all* to label women as this or that? Was that too much to ask?

"Oh, my poor ear." Her godmother clicked her tongue. "In

my line of work, reputation is everything. Something as inconse-quential as having an unwed, twenty-nine-year-old goddaughter could be spun into a personal failure."

"What about Jeremy oppa?" Emma was breathing so hard she probably looked like a charging bull. And she sure wanted to ram into something. "Your son is thirty-two years old and still single. Why isn't *he* your personal failure?"

"Jeremy is busy building his practice—"

"Well, I'm busy building my culinary school," Emma snapped, then closed her eyes. There was no point in berating her godmother. She wasn't responsible for the inequities of society, where a woman's worth hinged on her youth and beauty. "Just say it."

"And he's a man," Auntie Soo said with a resigned sigh. "He has at least two more years until he's considered an aging bachelor—probably longer since he has an MD."

"Ugh. Just ugh." *Fuck patriarchy.* Emma massaged her temple. "It's all so ridiculous. The Crones are just going to make them-selves look foolish."

"The problem is I deal mostly with my clients' mothers, and they tend to have thin ears."

"Thin ears?" Emma returned the spice jars to their original positions, too agitated to keep still.

"It's a Korean saying," her godmother explained. "People with thin ears are easily swayed by what others tell them. They confuse gossip at the grocery store with gospel."

"So they'll question your competence just because the Crones say so?" Emma stopped puttering around the kitchen and headed for the stairs. She needed to continue this conversation in private. Her dad was out in the garden for now, but she didn't want him to come in and overhear something that might cause him to worry.

"I'm afraid they will." Auntie Soo sighed. "If I lose clients over this, you'll lose clients as well."

Emma trudged into her pale sage bedroom, her knees feeling weak. She plopped down on the neatly made bed and smoothed her hand over its simple cream bedding with a mountain of artfully arranged pillows.

She was so close to achieving her dream. If business continued like this for a few more months, she would have enough money saved up for a down payment on a commercial kitchen. She had something special to share with the world. She could help people create moments of warmth, joy, and beauty in their lives.

The house had felt so dark and cold after her mom left, but the simple grilled cheese sandwich and tomato soup she had made for dinner had brought a smile to her dad's face—a smile that had felt like sunshine and hope. Food had the power to do that. *She* had the power to do that. Her hands curled into fists on her thighs. She wasn't about to let a group of petty, spiteful women take that away from her.

"Madame Ddu." She shot to her feet and jutted her chin. She didn't particularly feel ready, but she'd always intended on having an arranged marriage. Why not now, when it could be so helpful to her and her godmother? Emma had worked too hard to delay her dream any longer. "It's time for you to make my match."

CHAPTER TWO

♡

I don't understand why you insist on staying at a hotel." Gabriel glanced around the hotel café, then shrugged his reluctant approval. "Charming café notwithstanding."

Michel took a sip of his excellent coffee. The hotel was something of a historical monument, built more than a hundred years ago, with rich wood panels, sparkling chandeliers, and a grand double staircase. But the airy, sunlit café that sat beneath the vaulted ceilings of the lobby was the main perk of staying at this hotel.

The café was the perfect place to prepare for his lectures—and put out the occasional fires with the ministers back home—while indulging in some people watching. The hotel bustled with a variety of clientele, from tourists dressed head to toe in Mickey Mouse paraphernalia to businesspeople in somber, dark suits. Michel relished the luxury of being the one to observe others for once.

"There are many things about me you will never understand, my dear cousin," he drawled.

"Ah, yes," Gabriel said in a voice that made the Sahara Desert sound humid. "The crown prince of Rouleme is an enigma no one can decipher."

"Can you say that a little louder in case anyone missed it?" Sarcasm was a talent at which they both excelled, but Michel did feel a trickle of unease as he scanned his vicinity. If his true identity became public knowledge, then he might as well return to his country—to a reality he could not accept. He could bear the weight of the crown, but he wanted someone he loved by his side. Just as his father had his mother . . . even for a short while.

"Relax. There's no one close enough to hear." Gabriel smirked when Michel raised his royal middle finger at him. "How are the lectures going at USC?"

"There was a bit of a learning curve in the beginning—it's not exactly the same as giving a speech in front of the UN—but I'm getting the hang of it." Michel sat forward with his elbows on the table, forgetting his momentary ire. "The students seem truly interested in the importance of international relations. How it could impact this changing world. It takes me at least half an hour to get out of the lecture hall because they bombard me with questions at the end. It's fantastic."

"I'm sure they're enthusiastic about international relations . . . among other things." His cousin's lips stretched into a sly grin. "Such as—what is it the media always goes on about?—hair spun from the golden rays of the sun and a toe-curling accent that could melt the coldest hearts."

"That's rich coming from you," Michel said with a pointed look.

With his jet-black hair and piercing green eyes, Gabriel Laurent looked as though he belonged on the silver screen. No one would guess that he was an exacting philosophy professor at USC, whom his students called the Sphinx behind his back. But to Michel, Gabriel was simply his favorite cousin, childhood playmate—when they'd been allowed to be children—and someone he trusted with his life.

"I've heard good things about your class from both the faculty and the students," his cousin said with obvious pride. "For the time being, I don't regret sticking my neck out for you."

When Michel explained his fraught plan to his cousin, Gabriel didn't laugh his head off. Instead, he arranged for him to come to America as a visiting professor at the University of Southern California. While Michel assured his father that he would also be carrying out his diplomatic duties, his royal status was shared only with the president of USC, citing security reasons for the secrecy. To everyone else, he was Dr. Michel Chevalier, a European expert on international relations. He decided to borrow his mother's maiden name for anonymity, as well as for the practical reason that royal last names were a lengthy, complicated bore to recite in full.

"It's a shame I can't say the same about you." Michel crossed his arms in front of his chest. "Aunt Celine makes it a point to visit the palace nearly every week to lament the fact that her only son *abandoned* her to live in America *of all places* and never even calls her. She likes to point out how *I* convinced the king to allow you to leave Rouleme."

"Sorry, cousin." Gabriel had the grace to cringe in sympathy. "Mother can be melodramatic."

"It wouldn't hurt you to call her more often," Michel pointed out. "She just misses you."

"You mean she's hell-bent on guilt-tripping me back home," his cousin grumbled.

"That, too." Michel chuckled. "Even so, call her."

He couldn't help but envy Gabriel for his headache. The king's sister was used to getting her way, but she really did love her children. Michel would give anything to talk to his mother one last time. Maybe she would tell him the secret to finding the woman of his dreams and making her fall in love with him. Tell him what made her fall in love with his father.

"Speaking of home," Gabriel smoothly changed the subject, "do you plan on returning to Rouleme with nothing to show for your three months here? As I've said, a dating app is the way to go."

"And as *I've* said"—Michel pinched the bridge of his nose—"that is not going to happen."

"You've been in the US for over a month now and you have gone on zero dates." His cousin brought his hands together to form a circle. "*Zero.*"

"Thank you for the reminder." His middle finger twitched on top of the white tablecloth, ready to be sprung. He didn't need a reminder that he'd used up one month of his three-month reprieve and was no closer to achieving his goal. A vise was tightening around his chest with every passing day. "I would certainly have forgotten if you hadn't mentioned it."

"It's your quest. Not mine." Gabriel wiggled his fingers and crooned, "But the sands of time are running out. You can't keep relying on serendipity."

"Yes, quite." Michel arched an eyebrow. His cousin was really in touch with his inner arsehole today. "You're a tremendous help in all this."

"Jesus. You don't have to go all polite on me." Gabriel shivered. "There's no need to resort to meanness."

Drawing on the last slivers of his immaculate manners, Michel stopped himself from rolling his eyes and raised his cup to his lips. But he lowered it without taking a sip when *she* walked into the café.

This evening she wore a sleeveless cream dress that hugged her curves and ended a few inches above her knees. His eyes traveled farther down to her shapely legs before he forced them back to her face. Her skin was dewy and flawless, the pink of her cheeks and lips giving her a lovely glow. She wore her black hair in a loose updo, revealing the graceful line of her neck.

Clearing his throat, Michel tore his gaze away from her only to find his cousin studying the woman, half turned in his seat. When Gabriel faced him again with an appreciative whistle, Michel fought back a warning growl. Gripping his cup harder than necessary, he gulped down his coffee along with his unexpected reaction.

His cousin watched him in silence for a moment, then murmured, "Perhaps Lady Serendipity has already smiled down on you."

"I don't know what you're talking about." Michel didn't even know her name. He'd seen her at the café a few times in the last couple of weeks and had been scrounging up the nerve to approach her. But it was difficult since she only seemed to come here on dates.

She always sat at the same table, wearing a perfect outfit and an unflappable air, and met with a different man each time. The meeting inevitably ended with the men politely bowing and leaving her. If they were indeed dates, they were rather stilted ones. But what else could they be? All in all, it was intriguing. *She* was intriguing.

Whatever the case might be, he couldn't very well march up to her and demand to make her acquaintance right after the end of a bad date. Although it might be better than approaching her after she'd had a fantastic one. *Merde.* He had no idea what he was doing. Should he succumb to his cousin's nagging and create a profile on one or *all* of the dating apps?

No. Michel didn't want to resort to online dating. He wanted to meet his soulmate by happenstance. Fate would bring them together if they were meant to be. But maybe he was being a hopeless, old-fashioned romantic, squandering his last chance to fall in love. Or could fate have already brought them together? His gaze listed toward the woman again.

"I better head back for office hour." Gabriel glanced at his watch and got to his feet. "I don't like to keep my students waiting."

The other café-goers lingered at their tables as the sun made its leisurely descent, warming the lobby with a pinkish glow. She looked beautiful in the setting light, and it took some effort to turn his attention back to his cousin.

"Certainly. Rush right on off. I'll pay for your coffee," Michel groused.

"Well, you *are* the one with the palace," Gabriel said with an irreverent grin. "I only have a three-bedroom condo you won't deign to stay in. Although I must say, I do see the appeal of this café . . . and its clientele."

Michel pierced his cousin with a narrow-eyed glare, not taking the bait. He wasn't ready to talk about her, especially since there was nothing to talk about. But he really should remedy that. "If you blow my cover, I will throttle you. With great pleasure."

"That's dark, cousin. Even so, I thank you for the coffee." With a mocking bow of his head, Gabriel sauntered away from the table, making heads turn without effort.

As he neared the exit, his cousin caught the woman's eyes and *winked* at her. She blushed and tucked her chin, a shy smile turning up the corners of her Cupid's bow lips. Michel pushed his chair back with every intent to tackle the bastard to the ground. Luckily for both of them, Gabriel took his leave without lingering.

It took a few minutes for Michel to unclench his back teeth and realize that his cousin had delivered a swift kick to his arse to get him to stake his claim. God, was that even something people said? He had no idea how to proceed. Other than a few discreet affairs with women from his trusted circle—good women who remained his friends—Michel didn't have much experience with dating. Especially the kind that involved walking up to total strangers and asking them out. He actually had zero experience with that kind of dating.

In Rouleme, his every move was watched and scrutinized by his family, his people, and the media. It had never crossed his mind to approach a stranger with romantic intentions. In fact, approaching a stranger with any sort of intention would give his royal guards a heart attack.

Everyone knew who he was—who he was meant to be. Even if a woman agreed to go out with him, he would never know whether she said yes because she wanted to or because she was afraid to say no. Who would want to offend the future king of their country?

Back home, he had no chance of meeting someone who would see him—and love him—for the man he was. That was why he came to America. For a chance to find true love without the shadow of his crown distorting every encounter.

Even as Michel waved down the server for another cup of coffee, his attention drifted back to the beautiful woman he couldn't keep his eyes off. Her date hadn't arrived yet, and she sat staring down at her steaming mug with a pensive look on her face. What was she thinking about? Hopefully, after he finished his coffee, he would have worked out a plan to ask her.

CHAPTER THREE

♡

*I*t would be a tragedy to break her godmother's matchmaking streak. This was Emma's fifth matseon and Auntie Soo secretly prided herself in making matches within ten arranged first dates or less. The woman had a sixth sense about what similarities in the potential couple's background would lead to a successful match.

The Madame Ddu Method, as Emma called it, not only considered the couple's compatibility based on their education and profession, but also focused on their upbringing and family reputation. Based on age-old Korean beliefs and customs, an arranged marriage wasn't simply about a match between two people, but about two families coming together.

Emma considered herself a die-hard believer in the Madame Ddu Method. It made much more sense than any other way to meet your future spouse. It was worlds better than some random meet-cute where people were entirely led—or misled—by their attraction to each other. Her parents were a "love match," and look how that turned out. Their marriage fell apart once the initial high of love faded, because they had nothing in common. Because love had fooled them into ignoring their differences.

She took a soothing sip of her green tea and glanced around the café. She could see why it was Auntie Soo's favorite place to set up matseons. The hand-painted, high-vaulted ceilings and the light streaming in through the perfectly placed windows gave the café a whimsical, fairy-tale feel. Add in the sweet water fountain and live piano music, and romance seemed inevitable.

A heavy sigh escaped her when she recalled why she was sitting in the fairy-tale café. She was about to have yet another arranged first date. But just because none of the other matseons worked out didn't mean this one wouldn't. Emma sat up taller in her chair and took a deep breath. There was still a long way to go until she reached matseon number ten. She just had to trust in her godmother's magic touch.

Besides, she had high hopes for tonight's husband candidate, who seemed perfect on paper. Charles Shim was an entrepreneur like she was with a promising future ahead of him. He grew up in an upper-middle-class home and went to a respectable four-year college. His parents were well off but not so well off that they would look down on her dad. All in all, she and Charles Shim shared a very compatible background.

Auntie Soo also mentioned his parents had two adorable labradoodles, so there was a good chance he was a dog person. That was always a plus in Emma's book. And not to sound superficial or anything, but she couldn't help noticing that he was bite-your-knuckles gorgeous. If he ever entered a Hyun Bin look-alike contest, he would place second at the very least.

"Excuse me."

The warm, deep voice had her glancing over to a table tucked away in the corner. She barely stopped her mouth from falling open. The owner of the delicious voice lowered his half-raised arm when he caught the server's attention. He looked out of place sitting in a hotel café. With rich blond hair, an aristocratic nose, and a jawline sharp enough to give you a paper cut, he should be atop a black stallion, galloping down a deserted beach with his billowy white blouse fluttering in the wind.

"Yes?" Anne, the server, clasped her hands in front of her. "What can I get for you?"

"Just more coffee, please," he said with a polite smile that succeeded in unhinging Emma's jaws. She didn't want to know what a real smile from him would do to her. Actually, she very much wanted to find out. "Perhaps a glass of water as well."

God, what *was* that accent? If she had to guess, she would say it was British with a hint of French. It sounded like butter sprinkled with sugar. *Yum.* She should order some madeleines. She normally didn't order snacks for these arranged first dates, but she had a sudden craving for butter and sugar.

Even as she told herself to cut it out, she stole surreptitious peeks at the stranger. He wore his hair a smidgen long, so that it curled over his shirt collar and a wayward lock kept falling into his chocolate-brown eyes.

Emma didn't realize she was full-on staring at him until his gaze clashed with hers. Her breath caught in her throat, and the sound of her blood pounding in her ears drowned out the noise of the café. She should be embarrassed he caught her ogling him, but she couldn't look away.

When he held her eyes with his sensual, almost too-wide mouth tilting up at one corner, her tongue flicked out to wet her suddenly dry lips. His barely there smile disappeared as his gaze dropped to her mouth. She shouldn't be able to see from this distance, but she could swear his eyes darkened with an intense awareness that reflected her own.

"Are you Emma Yoon?"

She hopped an inch off her chair and glanced up at the man standing stiffly across from her. *Right.* Her prospective husband. She cleared her throat and gave her head a little shake. This was not a good time to be checking out another man.

"Um . . . yes. I'm Emma. You . . . you must be Charles."

"That is correct," he said with precise enunciation. He wore a nondescript beige suit that had been pressed to within an inch of its life, complete with a tie in the exact same shade. "I'm Charles Shim. May I sit down?"

"Please." She gestured to the seat across from her. He sat with his back so straight that she wondered if he had a military background Auntie Soo had missed. "Do you want to order a drink? I got here a little early and already ordered mine."

"I hope that is herbal tea." He looked down his nose at her drink. "Caffeine this late in the afternoon isn't a good idea. It'll throw off your circadian cycle."

Did he just lecture Emma on her choice of tea within a minute of meeting each other? Her polite smile wobbled as she fought the impulse to tell him exactly where he could shove his circadian cycle. Her imagined comeback didn't make any sense, but she was too annoyed to care. *Think of Auntie Soo. Think of your future culinary school.*

"I'll keep that in mind," she said through only slightly clenched teeth.

Charles nodded once as though satisfied with her answer. That was a wise decision on his part. If he'd persisted with his caffeine lecture, he might've ended up wearing her green tea on his starched white shirt.

After ordering his mint tea and some sweet, buttery madeleines for her, they sat in awkward silence until she blurted, "It's been so nice out."

Dear God above. She was talking about the weather. In California. Where it was basically always "nice out." Unperturbed, her matseon partner nodded, glancing at his smartwatch.

"The high today was seventy-three degrees. It's seventy degrees now," he said in a monotone that made her car navigation

system sound warm and fuzzy. "I believe that puts us in the typical range for Los Angeles at this time of year."

"Yes. Typical range. Mm-hmm." Emma was right. Charles
Shim was just like Hyun Bin . . . if he were an android.

"Do you think you'll be a good mother?" He stared unblinkingly at her as though waiting for her to spew forth her stellar
qualifications as a future mother.

"Uh . . . I hope?" Her forced smile leaned heavily toward a
cringe. He jumped right into *that* after the caffeine lecture and
the weather report? She adored babies and hoped to have children someday, but she wasn't about to share such deeply personal
thoughts with a virtual stranger. Unnerved by his creepy question, she took a stab at an awkward joke. "But in the end, I think
every parent screws up their kid one way or another."

Not even a single smiley muscle twitched at his lips. She
forced a feeble laugh and took an extra-loud slurp of her caffeinated green tea.

"That is an interesting observation." Android Hyun Bin
cocked his head five degrees to the left. She could've sworn she
heard the whirring of machinery at his stiff, precise movement.
"Would you like to hear my thoughts on my potential to become
a good father?"

"No, no, no." She waved her outstretched palms with enough
urgency to stop oncoming traffic. Sure, the whole point of an arranged marriage was to skip the romantic nonsense and choose a
spouse based on sensible, practical reasons. But jumping straight
to procreation went a little too far. "I mean . . . why don't we talk
about something . . . fun?"

"Fun?" His eyebrows shifted three millimeters in a confused
frown. She almost sagged with relief. It was the first human emotion he'd exhibited.

"Yes, fun." Emma nodded encouragingly.

His frown deepened as he considered her suggestion. It wasn't a good look for him. In fact, he grew less attractive by the second, his stuffy personality draining the handsome right out of him. As the silence lengthened, she began to worry that smoke would billow out of his ears. *Cannot compute. Cannot compute.* Fortunately, their order arrived before her prospective husband's head exploded.

Reminded of the inspiration for her madeleine, she stole a glance at the criminally gorgeous stranger. Her heart flopped around like a fish out of water. He stared intently at his laptop screen, tapping a finger lightly against his lips. Her hand rose to her throat as she imagined him studying her with the same intensity, pondering what to do with her. With a choked gasp, she tore her eyes away from him. *Oh my God. What is* wrong *with me?* Swallowing a whimper, she stuffed an entire madeleine into her mouth.

"What's your favorite movie?" Emma mumbled around her cake. Or was it a cookie? Whatever it was—a cakie!—she was secretly delighted when a crumb flew out of her mouth and landed within inches of Charles Shim's saucer.

His eyes zeroed in on the offending shrapnel as he said, "I am not a movie person, but I do enjoy an occasional documentary on the History Channel."

"Documentaries can be so interesting." He didn't bother asking her what her favorite movie was, but she told him anyway. "I love *The Lake House.* The one with Sandra Bullock and Keanu Reeves?"

"Hmm." The moist madeleine crumb still held his attention. "I'm not a fan of Keanu Reeves."

Emma barely held back her gasp. *This matseon ends now.* But how? She didn't want to do anything so horrible she would get blackballed from the matchmaking market. She also didn't want to risk embarrassing Auntie Soo. The whole point of this was to preserve her godmother's venerated reputation, right? If Emma didn't succeed, then both their businesses would suffer and her dream of opening up a cooking school might slip through her fingers. Who knew how long it would take to get it back on track?

Since slurping her tea and speaking with her mouth full hadn't been enough to put Charles off, she needed to come up with something a little more drastic. She could go for an obnoxious, nasally chortle, but she couldn't imagine him saying anything remotely funny to warrant a laugh.

She cringed when an idea popped into her head. It would definitely work, but she really didn't want to do it. But she also couldn't spend another minute with someone who *wasn't a fan* of Keanu. Steeling herself, she picked up her cloth napkin and pretended to blow her nose in it as loud as a honking goose. The stunned silence that descended between them was pretty impressive.

Wait for it. Wait for it.

"Shall we conclude this meeting?" Charles asked abruptly, not bothering to hide his shudder of disgust.

"Oh, so soon?" She bit her cheeks to stop herself from smiling.

"Yes . . . well." He straightened his already straight tie. "I promised my mother I'd be home for dinner."

"Then you should go." She stood and held out her hand. He hesitated for a full three seconds before he shook it limply. "You must never keep your mother waiting."

"Yes, of course." He practically threw her hand back at her, bowed stiffly, and speed walked out of the café. Who knew androids could move so quickly?

Once he was out of sight, Emma dropped back into her seat and cradled her forehead in her palm. Her fifth matseon had gone down in a blaze of glory. She wasn't proud of pouring lighter fluid all over it, but she just . . . couldn't.

She always figured she would marry a nice, compatible man one day. "One day" just arrived sooner than she'd expected. Ideally, she wanted her culinary school to be well established before she split her attention to start her own family. But if flipping the order of her goals could secure her dream quicker, didn't it make sense for her to get married first? Yes, it made total sense. Then what was her problem?

Am I being too picky? Am I just not ready to commit?

"These are for you." Anne placed a trio of madeleines in front of Emma. "The gentleman at that table thought you might need some more of these."

"What?" Emma followed her server's line of sight, which led straight to the man who'd inspired her sugar and butter craving in the first place. At her questioning expression, he inclined his head with a hint of a smile. "Oh."

"He also took care of your check"—Anne winked—"with a generous tip for me."

"Oh," Emma said again, her heart fluttering. Maybe not every bone in her body was as practical as she'd like. Maybe a part of her longed to experience *romantic nonsense* with a handsome stranger. Just a taste. Nothing more.

She barely heard her server say, "Let me know if you need anything else."

When she looked across the café again, the man was absorbed in whatever he was doing on his laptop. It was just an act of kindness. He felt bad for her because her "date" had ditched her without paying for their drinks. He obviously didn't want anything in return.

It was probably that last part that made Emma walk up to him.

CHAPTER FOUR

♥

Michel stared at the PowerPoint slides for his next lecture without registering a single thing. His heart created an undignified ruckus in his chest, and his hairline grew damp with sweat. How did people do this kind of stuff? Or did they? Maybe he'd made an utter fool of himself by paying for the woman's check.

But it was the gentlemanly thing to do. Her companion was well dressed and irritatingly good looking, but he had atrocious manners underneath the shiny veneer. The man abandoned her in the middle of their meeting and left without paying—not even for his own drink—which was abominably rude. Sure, the woman had deliberately chased him away by pretending to blow her nose in a cloth napkin, but it would not have been difficult to place a twenty on the table before leaving in a huff.

He forced himself to keep his gaze on his laptop screen. Her wide-eyed surprise at his gesture had been so lovely that he wanted to spend the rest of the evening stealing glances at her. But he didn't want to make her think he'd paid for her check expecting something in return. It certainly wasn't a part of any plan to woo her. He'd come up blank on how to go about doing that.

He had just acted out of instinct. She deserved to be treated with respect—not unceremoniously dumped by some ill-mannered pretty boy.

"Um . . . hello."

Michel jerked his head up at the hesitant greeting. Her voice was lower and huskier than he'd imagined, sending a jolt of awareness down his spine. The woman stood close enough for him to smell the citrus and floral notes of her perfume—crisp yet sweet. When he continued gaping at her without saying a word, she tucked a wayward strand of hair behind her ear, a pink blush staining her cheeks. Christ, she was beautiful.

"Hello." He shook himself out of his stupor.

"I hope I'm not disturbing you," she said at what must seem like his lukewarm welcome.

"Please," Michel said loudly enough to draw sideways glances from the other customers, and shot to his feet. Gabriel would laugh his arse off when he heard about this. "Please. Have a seat. If you'd like, that is."

"Yes." She met his gaze with bright, intelligent eyes, and he braced himself against the sensation of falling into them. "I'd like that."

So the first time hadn't been a fluke. When their eyes met across the café earlier, his stomach had swooped as though he'd bungee jumped off a bridge. The world around them seemed to disappear—like time and place held no meaning—which he found profoundly disconcerting.

He never forgot where he was, who he was, *why* he was. He was Prince Michel, the future king of Rouleme. He always carried the responsibility—and yes, the privilege—with him, even when it felt like a heavy winter coat in the peak of summer. But when she looked at him, he could remember nothing but the fact that he was a man. While he tried and failed to swallow, she sat down across from him.

"You didn't have to do that," she said, tilting her chin up.

"Do what?" He gingerly lowered himself back into his seat, his knees not as steady as he'd like. He couldn't decide if this was a friendly visit or not, but it thrilled him to finally speak with her.

"The check." She arched a graceful eyebrow.

"Ah, that." He ran his hand down the back of his head. Had it been presumptuous of him? God, he was so out of his depth here.

"Yes, *that*." Amusement danced in her eyes. "I wouldn't have minded paying for it myself."

"Should I also not have sent those madeleines?" He wasn't sure whether he owed her an apology for that as well.

"Who in their right mind refuses dessert?" She smiled, a tiny but deep dimple blinking at one corner of her mouth. "And I never said you *shouldn't* have paid for my check. I said you didn't have to."

"I wanted to." He sighed, relieved he hadn't offended her somehow.

Before he could think of what to say next, his gaze dropped to her dimple and stayed there. Her lips parted on an indrawn breath. He should look away. She might think he was staring at her mouth because he wanted to kiss her. He slammed a door on that thought. It was too much. Her dimple provided more than enough distraction without having to imagine what she might taste like. Perhaps if he could just explain to her . . .

"I like your dimple," he blurted. It had sounded a lot better in his head.

Her lashes fluttered as she blinked several times in quick succession. He resisted the urge to sink low into his chair. While true in essence, it was the most juvenile, asinine sentence he had ever uttered. He'd blown it even before he had a chance to figure out what *it* was.

But then something miraculous happened. Her smile

widened—and her dimple deepened—until she burst into laughter. He didn't know what he'd done to make her laugh. Chances were high she was laughing *at* him. It didn't matter. Her laughter was incandescent and joyous. She laughed with her whole body—her eyes curved into double crescent moons, her nose crinkled, and her torso bent at her waist.

Michel watched her with wonder, holding his breath so he wouldn't miss a single detail. The moment imprinted itself onto his mind—the moment a stranger's laughter made him forget the weight of his identity.

"Sorry. I . . ." She held up her hand as she caught her breath. "Thank you."

"For what?" he asked in a low, husky voice.

"For the madeleines. For taking care of my check." Lingering laughter clung to her words. "And for the compliment. That was . . . unexpected."

"Unexpected?" He cocked his head to the side.

"Let's just say you don't strike me as a man who goes around complimenting women on their dimples."

"Well, that depends on the dimple," he said with a wry smile, then curiosity got the best of him. "What kind of man *do* I strike you as?"

She glanced down at her hands as color rose to her cheeks. Her blush made him even more curious, but she said in a rush, "The kind who sends consolation madeleines to jilted women."

"So that man *was* your date? And he *jilted* you?" An unfamiliar burst of jealousy and outrage coursed through him.

"Yes and yes?" She shook her head with a rueful laugh. "It's a bit more complicated than that."

"How so?" As his head cleared, he recalled what had prompted the man to flee from her. He bit his cheek to rein in his grin. "Does it have anything to do with you using the cloth napkin as a tissue?"

She sat utterly still as though she wanted to become invisible. It was the most adorable thing he'd ever seen. After a moment, she slowly came back to life, a reluctant smile curving her lips. His mouth dried out when her dimple made a reappearance.

"I didn't actually blow my nose in the napkin." She drew little circles on the tablecloth with her finger. "I really like Anne. She's our . . ."

"I know who Anne is," he interjected. He enjoyed chatting with the friendly server.

The woman nodded approvingly, then said, "Yeah, I would never do that to her."

"I believe you." He leaned in slightly. "But why go out with someone only to chase them away fifteen minutes into the date?"

"Did I mention it was complicated?" Her teeth snagged on her bottom lip. "I . . ."

"You don't have to tell me." He held up his palm. He wouldn't cause her discomfort to satisfy his own curiosity. "We can save that story for another time."

Michel realized what he'd implied when surprise flickered across her face. He opened his mouth to retract his accidental slip. Although he hoped—more than he was ready to admit—that there might be another time, he would never make such a presumption.

"Okay." A shy smile curved her pink lips.

Was she saying there would be a next time? His face split into an enormous grin that made his cheeks ache. He might have bumbled his way into securing another chance to see the woman. Or she was just being polite. Either way, he really needed to stop thinking of her as *the woman*.

"I don't know your name," he confessed. He knew nothing about her, and that was suddenly unacceptable to him.

She huffed a laugh and stuck out her hand. "My name is Emma."

"And I'm Michel." He clasped her outstretched hand and something electric shot up his arm. It was fortunate he managed to introduce himself before his brain short-circuited. Did the slight widening of her eyes mean that she felt it, too? He reluctantly released her and cleared his throat. "It's a pleasure to meet you, Emma."

For a second, she frowned down at her open palm. Then, with an almost imperceptible shake of her head, she looked back at him with a polite smile. "Pleased to meet you, Michel."

He didn't know which he liked better—the feel of her name on his lips or the sound of his name on hers, the soft *el* clinging to the tip of her tongue. He only knew he wanted there to be many more instances of both, in many different ways. He'd been watching her from afar for much too long. It was imperative he secure a date with her as soon as possible. *Only two months left.*

"Emma, I would like to see you again." His voice came out in a low rumble.

"I would like that as well, but . . ." She looked conflicted for a second before her shoulders drooped. "I have another date here in a couple of nights."

"With the same man?" It took some effort to stop the grooves from forming between his brows.

"No, with another man," she said morosely.

Disappointment and that odd spike of jealousy flashed through him. Should he protest? Should he insist she go out with him instead? How about tomorrow? Her date was in two nights, so she should be free tomorrow. But his damn manners compelled him not to push her—not to make her uncomfortable.

"I'm sorry to hear that," he murmured. She had no idea how sorry. "But I'm here most afternoons, so I hope we will meet again."

She nodded and sighed softly. It sounded wistful like she was as disappointed as he was that she had another date. But if she wanted to see him again, then why couldn't she cancel her other date? She did say it was complicated. Perhaps she had a reason why she couldn't cancel even if she wanted to. Or it might be wishful thinking on his part. He raised his hand to catch Anne's attention. He might as well return to his suite to brood and re-search which dating sites suited him best.

"Yes?" The server glanced between Michel and Emma with a smile. "What can I do for you?"

"I'd like the check, please." He managed not to sound down-trodden.

"Um . . ." Anne's eyes flitted to Emma.

"I took care of your check." Emma's expression could only be described as smug.

"You didn't have to do that," he protested automatically.

"I wanted to." She echoed his words from before with an impish smile. "Besides, I'm Korean. We're masters at paying the check before anyone else."

He chuckled under his breath, watching her from beneath his lashes. Was he really going to let this alluring woman walk out of his life without a fight? Hell no. It didn't matter that she would be on a date with another man. When she chased the man away as she'd done with the others, he would be there to convince her that her next date should be with him.

"I'll keep that in mind," Michel murmured, leaving *until next time* unsaid.

Emma gathered her purse and stood from her seat. After a brief hesitation, she gave him a small wave. "It was nice meeting you."

Michel responded with a slight bow of his head instead of saying goodbye. Her first steps away from him seemed heavy, as though there was something holding her back, but she soon straightened her shoulders and marched out of the café without a backward glance. His gaze followed her until she disappeared from view.

Until next time, Emma.

CHAPTER FIVE

♡

*W*hat kind of man do I strike you as?

As soon as Michel had uttered those words in his rich, buttery voice, her mind had gleefully reminded her that she'd imagined him racing across a sandy beach on a dark stallion, his sculpted chest glistening with sweat from the exertion . . . *Wait.* He was wearing a billowing white shirt in her original daydream. Apparently, not anymore. The wind must have blown it off along the way.

Emma continued to stir the sauce to dissolve the brown sugar and fanned her face with her other hand. Her kitchen was unusually warm today. She sighed as man and beast galloped down the beach in her mind, his muscles shifting and bunching impressively. She had no idea if Michel actually had muscles that shifted and bunched. But from the way he'd filled out his shirt, she was fairly certain they existed.

"Emma?"

"Hmm?" she said distractedly before remembering she was in the middle of a lesson. *Oh, for God's sake.* It was as though her mind had developed a personality of its own—a remarkably lustful personality. "Yes, Sarah?"

"How can ddeokbokki be a part of royal court cuisine?" her client asked, stirring her own sauce. "It's *the* street food staple in Korea."

They stood shoulder to shoulder at the counter. Emma couldn't help but notice how cramped it felt during these lessons. This was definitely a one-person kitchen. Once she leased a commercial kitchen, she'd have plenty of room to move around and demonstrate techniques. She couldn't wait to teach group classes, filling the kitchen with all their excited energy. *Soon.*

"Well, what sets gungjung ddeokbokki apart from the spicy rice cakes sold on the streets is this sauce we're making." Emma lifted the small bowl of sauce and inhaled the sweet, salty, and nutty aroma. Her mouth watered on cue. "Korean royal court cuisine is defined by its subtle, nuanced flavors. The seasoning complements and enhances the natural flavors of the ingredients. It's all about harmony and balance."

"Ah." Sarah nodded. "So we're using soy sauce and toasted sesame oil instead of gochujang because the red chili paste can overpower the delicate flavor of the rice cakes."

"Exactly." Emma beamed at her favorite pupil.

It was such a thrill to teach someone so smart and eager to learn, especially since Sarah wasn't one of Auntie Soo's referrals. Not that there was anything wrong with the brides-in-training. It just made Emma happy that Sarah was someone who wanted to learn about Korean royal court cuisine purely for the joy of cooking.

"Today, we're using julienned beef brisket for the dish." Emma brought the meat they'd prepared earlier out from the refrigerator and gingerly balanced it on the narrow counter space beside the stove. "But when you're at home, you can use pre-marinated bulgogi in a pinch."

Emma gave Sarah shortcuts whenever possible because she worked as a teaching assistant to a demanding philosophy professor at USC while she obtained her master's degree there. Even though cooking was Sarah's happy place, she sometimes had to resort to instant noodles and fast food out of sheer necessity.

Having originated in the Joseon dynasty to nourish the royal family, Korean royal court cuisine didn't exactly make for easy, weeknight meals. So shortcuts it was. Any kind of home-cooked meal was better than fast food.

"Awesome." Sarah pumped her fist. "My mom fills my freezer with little bundles of bulgogi whenever she visits."

"Korean moms are masters at feeding their children." Her college roommate's mom used to do the same thing and always made sure that there was enough for Emma, too. She chased away the twinge of sadness—her mom's absence motivated her to learn to marinate her *own* bulgogi—and smiled brightly. "And their friends."

"I wonder if there are any other cultures where *have you eaten* is a form of greeting."

"It's the Korean *I love you.*" Emma winked.

"Oh my gosh." Sarah snorted. "That is so true."

"Okay. The gungjung ddeokbokki isn't going to cook itself." Emma turned on the front burner of her stove, setting it to medium-high heat, and watched her client mimic her on the next burner. "Add a swirl of oil to the frying pan."

"A swirl? Not a splash?" Sarah said with wide-eyed innocence. "Are you positive it isn't a drizzle?"

"A *tablespoon* of oil, smart aleck." Emma hip bumped Sarah. She gave her clients exact measurements for the recipes, but she herself never used measuring tools. She kind of *knew* how much of what her dishes needed. "One swirl around the pan usually comes out to about a tablespoon."

"I'll try it next time." Sarah measured out the oil. "I'm too chicken to eyeball something with a new recipe."

Emma added the small strips of marinated beef into the hot

pan, and Sarah did the same in her own pan. Once the meat was nicely browned, they added the sliced bell peppers, onions, and green onions.

"The rice cake goes in last because these are fresh and will take no time to cook." Emma added the ddeok into the pan. "With the dried kind, soak it in water first, then put it in once the meat is browned."

"Got it." Sarah nodded and breathed in the aroma. "I'm drooling. This smells so delicious."

"Well, it's done," Emma said after a few minutes. She plated a small portion, sprinkling some sesame seeds and chopped scallions on top. "Ready for a taste test?"

Glancing at Emma's sample, Sarah plated her ddeokbokki and garnished it. They each picked up a rice cake with their chopsticks and took a careful bite. It was soft and chewy, and sweet and savory. A perfect harmony of textures and flavors.

"Wonderful, isn't it?" Emma smiled.

"Heavenly." Her happy client sighed before taking another bite.

There. She had helped create a moment of joy for Sarah—helped her slow down and smell the . . . well, the gungjung ddeokbokki. That was the most meaningful, satisfying part of her job. And that was why Emma was so impatient to start her culinary school. She wanted to help more people nurture happiness in their lives.

"Save some for dinner." Emma opened a kitchen cabinet and reached for a reusable container. "We'll pack up the rest for you to take home."

"Oh no." Sarah palmed her forehead. "I forgot to bring back the containers from our last lesson. I have them washed and everything."

"Don't worry about it. I have plenty. You can return them next time." Emma lined up the finger-size rice cakes in the container and artfully interspersed the perfectly browned marinated meat and fragrant vegetables over them. "Here, you try packing up the rest."

Sarah placed the last of the rice cakes in the container and sprinkled scallions and toasted sesame seeds on top. "I won't be able to concentrate in class, knowing that this beauty is waiting for me at home."

"Great job today." Emma began tidying up the counter as her client packed up to leave, but her hands stilled when she heard her dad out in the hallway.

"Soo, what a lovely surprise," he said with a smile in his voice. "Come in. Come in."

"Hello, old friend." Her godmother sounded a bit distracted. "Is Emma home? She wasn't answering my texts, so I figured she must be in the middle of a lesson."

Emma swallowed and pulled out her cell phone from her apron pocket. She had silenced it for the lesson. After a calming breath, she unlocked her screen. Eleven unread texts from Auntie Soo. Her stomach dropped. It might have nothing to do with her matseon from last night. Maybe her godmother wanted to see her one and only goddaughter because she missed her.

"Yes, she should be finishing up right now," her dad said as Emma finished putting the used pans and utensils in the sink. She strained to hear their conversation in the hallway with a distracted smile at Sarah, who hefted her backpack onto one shoulder.

"Oh, good. I need a word with her." Her godmother sounded like she meant business—the ass-whooping kind.

"Is everything okay?" Her dad was probably leading Auntie Soo to the living room, because her answer was too soft to decipher.

"Ready to go?" Emma turned to her client.

"Yup." She seemed to deflate. "Time to go grade a pile of midterm papers."

"Good luck with that. And don't let the Sphinx intimidate you." The Sphinx was the not-so-affectionate nickname the students had bestowed on Sarah's supervising professor.

"Down with the Sphinx." She pumped her fist in the air and laughed. "Bye, Emma."

After closing the front door behind her, Emma pulled her shoulders back and headed for the living room. How bad could it be? She sighed. It could be bad. Like really bad. Angry Auntie Soo was so freaking scary.

"Imo"—Emma burst into the living room with a cheek-cramping smile—"what brings you here at this time of day?"

Auntie Soo looked as placid as a midnight lake, sitting on the couch with her hands folded over her thighs. Maybe she wasn't angry? But her dad met her gaze with wide, frightened eyes and gave a subtle shake of his head. A warning. Emma gulped.

"Does anyone want a snack?" Emma said with even more forced cheer. "I have some gungjung ddeokbokki in the kitchen."

"Gungjung ddeokbokki?" Her dad shot to his feet and matched her infomercial voice. "That sounds fantastic. We should all head to the kitchen and enjoy a first-rate afternoon snack."

"Jae, why don't you go ahead and start without us?" The very evenness of her godmother's voice sent a trill of fear down Emma's spine.

"I . . . I have to plate it for him," Emma squeaked.

Auntie Soo kept her gaze on Emma's dad. "You're capable of transferring some rice cakes onto a plate, right?"

"Certainly." Her dad nodded and kept nodding.

In all honesty, Emma wasn't sure her dad could plate his own ddeokbokki. At least, not properly. Plating involved more than just transferring some food onto a plate. Her godmother knew that. The fact that she acted so dismissive of the fact meant she was mad. Like really mad.

"But . . ." Emma bit her lip.

"It's just one snack, Emma." Auntie Soo's expression softened a fraction. "Your dad doesn't need to be presented with a work of art every time he sits down to eat."

"Your godmother's right." Her dad's eyes roamed her face with heartrending love and sadness. Emma didn't want to parse out what that meant. "I'll be fine, my dear."

Even so, her dad stood rooted to his spot in front of the sofa. Only when Emma nodded and mouthed *I'll be okay* did he leave her alone with her godmother. With a sigh, she sat down beside her.

All traces of softness left her godmother's face. "Would you like to hear what people are saying about you?"

"Not particularly." Emma stared down at her hands.

"The consensus is that you are beautiful but . . . gross."

"Beautiful?" Emma snorted. "I'm passably pretty on my best days."

Auntie Soo gaped at her. "But you *are* gross?"

"I didn't say . . ." She *did* pretend to blow her nose into a cloth napkin. "Maybe?"

When her godmother leveled her steely gaze on her, Emma felt like a middle schooler caught drawing little penises with capes in her spiral notebook. "Explain yourself."

"I don't know," she said with a helpless shrug. "None of the men seemed compatible with me."

"The men *I* matched you up with?" Auntie Soo pressed her hand to her chest. "They weren't *compatible* with you?"

"No, Imo. Of course they were compatible." Emma winced. The last thing she wanted was to insult her godmother's skills as a matchmaker. "I . . . I guess I just wasn't in the right frame of mind."

It might even be true. When Charles Shim showed up, her mind had been full of a certain handsome stranger. She didn't have the luxury of being distracted by something as fanciful as romance. Emma had to meet the right match to save Auntie Soo's reputation and finally open her culinary school. She'd come too far to derail her dream for some man. But oh my God, what a man.

"Emma." Her godmother sighed. "I would never push you into doing something you don't want."

"You're not pushing me to do anything." Emma took Auntie Soo's hand and squeezed. "I want to do this."

Emma had spent years of her life cultivating a warm, happy home for her and her dad. Having a family of her own, with her dad tucked into an in-law suite, had always appealed to her. It fit neatly into the things she considered important in life. With family being the most important and opening up her culinary school—sooner rather than later—a close second. Having a family and a secure job ensured stability.

"Even before those miserable Crones created havoc in my life, I wanted to see you matched with the right man." Her godmother cupped her cheek. "I understand why you have a hard time opening yourself up to relationships."

"I don't—" Emma clapped her mouth shut. This was her godmother. She would see through her lies. "You know my parents' divorce wasn't pretty. It taught me that love was something that . . . faded. I would never bet my whole life on it."

"Your dad fell in love with your mother even though they had nothing in common. I told him the two of them were too different and their differences didn't complement each other, but he wanted to marry her anyway. I think when that first flush of love faded, there was nothing left to sustain their marriage. Their love had no roots." Auntie Soo looked down at their hands. "But that's where I can help you. The men I match you up with have so much in common with you. If you give them a chance, you'll find companionship, respect, and maybe even love. Look at Uncle John and me."

Uncle John and Auntie Soo had been so happy together until he passed away five years ago. They were husband and wife but best friends, too. Even after thirty years of marriage, they never ran out of things to talk about—they always had something to laugh about. The Madame Ddu Method really was the best way to secure a healthy, lasting marriage—a shortcut to the constancy and stability Emma wanted for her future.

"Do you miss him?" she whispered.

"Every day," Auntie Soo said, her voice breaking. Then she sniffed loudly and sat up tall. "Your next matseon partner is an absolute gem."

"Ooh, is he sparkly?" she said with a cheeky grin.

"Don't sass me, child." Her godmother pinched her arm.

"Ow," Emma yelped, rubbing the poor mistreated spot.

"There is more where that came from"—Auntie Soo clacked her thumb and pointer finger together like lobster claws—"if I hear another word about you being *gross*."

"You can put those away." Emma laughed even as her heart grew heavy. If she was smart—and she was—daydreams about Michel and his stallion needed to stop. She instinctively knew the man would wreak havoc on her plans for a sensible life. "I promise to be on my best behavior for my next husband candidate."

"I certainly hope so." Her godmother sighed. "Word has it that the YogurtBerry family is in the market for a Madame Ddu for their daughter. They're one of the most influential Korean American families in California. Whoever signs them will rule the matseon market for the foreseeable future. But the Crones will do their worst to keep them from signing with me."

"Don't worry, Imo." Emma hugged Auntie Soo. "I'm sure the YogurtBerry family knows you're the best Madame Ddu out there. And I have a feeling I'll meet my perfect match soon."

CHAPTER SIX

♡

Michel unrolled the sleeves of his shirt, then rolled them back up past his elbows. Emma didn't seem to have any objections to his attire the last time they met. There was no reason to fuss over his clothes. Even so, he examined his reflection yet again in his bedroom mirror. White dress shirt open at the collar, pressed gray slacks, and simple black belt. It was his casual attire of choice.

Well, today was an important day. Emma would be at the café for her date with another man. Once she chased him away, Michel wanted to present his best self to her when he convinced her to go out with him next. And how did he plan on doing that? He'd racked his brain for the past two days to come up with a foolproof strategy. But there was no such thing.

He would just be himself and hope that she felt the same connection he felt with her. Under the circumstances, it was only reasonable to pay extra attention to his appearance . . . but he still felt quite foolish as he turned this way and that in front of the mirror.

"You look immaculate," Sophie said from the doorway. Her tone and expression didn't veer from bland professionalism, but

Michel knew his royal guard well enough to know when he was being mocked.

"You forgot to add *as always*," Michel drawled, walking toward his dresser.

"How remiss of me." She bowed her head. "Apologies, Your Highness."

"What did I do this time?" He glanced sideways at her as he fastened his watch. She never called him *Your Highness* unless she was annoyed with him.

"Do? What could you possibly have done?" Her impassive demeanor slipped minutely as she stepped into his room. "Come to America without any security? Insist on keeping your identity a secret? Spend every possible minute away from the safety of your hotel suite? I can't imagine what you could've done."

"I have security," Michel said evenly, knowing her grumbling came from a place of concern for his well-being. "You're standing right there. And I didn't come to America to hide out in my room."

A low growl came from her direction. Michel wisely ignored it. He wouldn't dare cross Captain Sophie Bellevue. With her wide eyes and glowing mahogany skin, she was undoubtedly lovely, but he never forgot that she was quite lethal. She might seem slight in stature at one hundred seventy centimeters and less than ten stone, but she was pure muscle, speed, and power. She could take out seven men twice her size in two minutes flat. Yes, he had sufficient security. No, he wouldn't mess with her.

"I see that you are going out again." By the time he turned toward her, Sophie was once more the picture of stoic capability.

"Just downstairs to the café," he said with a twinge of guilt. Being a one-woman security team had to be exhausting. "You should take the day off this Saturday. I have that monstrosity of a report from the finance minister to keep me busy. Maybe I'll invite Gabriel over. We'll order room service and stay put all day. You wouldn't have to worry about a thing."

"Gabriel?" Sophie deigned to roll her eyes. "Don't get me started with that one. Refusing *all* security. He's even worse than you."

"He's been on his own for years." Michel reflexively came to his cousin's defense even though the three of them had been friends since they were children. "No harm has come to him."

"That's because he cut all ties with Rouleme. If anyone finds out who he is—"

"No one will," he interrupted firmly. "Gabriel built a life for himself here that has nothing to do with his birth or station. His past doesn't matter anymore."

"His country, family, and"—her voice caught—"friends do not belong in his past."

Michel belatedly realized that she'd stayed hidden at her post and never once acknowledged Gabriel in the month that they'd been in America. When Gabriel left Rouleme, Michel had been too busy rooting for his cousin—and being envious of him—to feel abandoned, but he hadn't considered how others felt. He often became so wrapped up in concerns for his country as well as his own burdens that he forgot people around him didn't have it easy either. It was a failing he needed to endeavor to remedy.

"Sophie."

The punch came out of nowhere, and it was pure instinct that had him ducking to the left and spinning out of reach. Michel didn't even see Sophie move until her fist was an inch from his nose. But when she aimed a roundhouse kick to his head, he was ready for her. He blocked her kick with his forearms and swung his fist toward her solar plexus. She evaded his punch with fluid grace and closed up the space between them.

"Merde," he cursed.

He could see it happening, but there was nothing he could do to avoid being thrown to the floor. He broke his fall with one arm and rolled onto his feet without missing a beat, but Sophie already stood glaring at him with her arms crossed over her chest.

"Did you just let me take you down with osoto gari?" She scoffed. "I would laugh if it wasn't so pathetic."

"I admit I'm out of practice," Michel muttered, slightly winded.

"And that's why I can't take Saturday off."

"Be reasonable, Sophie."

Her lips pressed into a mutinous line. "I'll escort you to the café, *Your Highness*."

Michel tucked his shirt back into his pants as he followed Sophie out of his room. "I can spend an hour at the café without getting myself kidnapped."

She didn't dignify his protest with a response and led the way to the elevator. When they walked out into the lobby, she wordlessly made her way to an armchair beside a lush potted plant. A jerk of her chin told him that he was to sit himself down at his usual table, facing her. Not wanting to aggravate his stubbornly loyal friend any further, he did as he was bid.

Anne brought him his coffee as soon as he settled in his seat. He crossed his leg over his knee and scanned the café. He checked his watch when he found no sign of Emma. He'd grown impatient to see her in the last two days. Not only to see her, but to finally convince her to go on a date with him. All her prior dates seemed to have been set for six o'clock from what he'd gathered. *Strange*. She'd never been late before.

He chuckled under his breath and opened up his laptop. She wasn't late for a date with *him*. She could stand the man up for all he cared. His laughter trailed off, and he pursed his lips. But he *would* care a great deal if she didn't show up *at all*. If she didn't come tonight, there might never be a next time for them. He would never forgive himself if he'd squandered his chance to get to know her. His stomach twisted with panic.

Michel sipped his coffee as he quieted his mounting unease. She would be here. He'd mastered the art of maintaining an impassive, regal expression no matter what storm brewed inside of him. But under the table, his fingers drummed a restless beat on his knee as his eyes darted to the entrance every time someone walked into the café.

He hoped Sophie wouldn't notice anything amiss with him, but there was little to no chance of that. She never missed anything. He sighed and met her gaze across the lobby. She raised her eyebrows a couple of millimeters in question. *What's going on?* He gave her a minute shake of his head. *Nothing. I'm fine.*

Emma rushed into the café and skidded to a stop just past the entrance. Her eyes zeroed in on him and widened before they flitted away. He nearly lost his balance uncrossing his legs and wobbled on his chair. By the time he was securely upright, she was approaching a man sitting at a table on the other side of the café.

His heart thudded, heavy and thunderous in his chest, and his breath grew shallow. He'd always thought her lovely, but she was breathtaking tonight. She wore a short-sleeved dusty-rose dress that hugged her torso, then flared out at the waist, ending just above her knees. Her long black hair fell in thick waves down her back and framed her fair, heart-shaped face. His throat worked to swallow. She'd never worn her hair down before. His fingers twitched on the table as he wondered if it felt as silky as it looked.

If her attire on previous occasions conveyed neat and proper, her outfit tonight sang lush and romantic. Who was meant to hear her song? Her date, who was gaping at her with a dim-witted smile? *Or me?* Michel blew out a shaky breath.

He dragged his eyes away from Emma and focused on his laptop. He should read over his lecture notes for tomorrow. Or review the research his personal assistant had forwarded him regarding the updated agricultural subsidies program. At the very least, he should stop scrutinizing the progress of Emma's date like a nosy voyeur. Yes, he'd been desperate to see her again, but he would have his chance to look his fill once she chased her date away.

He glanced at his watch. They'd been talking for fifteen minutes. None of her other dates had lasted longer than that. Any minute now, the man was going to stand up, bow, and walk out of the café.

Anne came by to refill his coffee, and they chatted for a few minutes. Emma laughed at something her date said as he pushed a plate of madeleines closer to her. The man had been very attentive to her the entire time, his eyes rarely leaving her. Michel clenched his jaws and read the same PowerPoint slide he'd been reading for the last twenty-seven minutes.

Her date waved down Anne—rather imperiously—and paid for the check. Emma and the man finally stood from their table after close to an hour. Still smiling like a fool, he gestured toward the entrance. She shook her head and said something that made his smile falter. *There it is.* Michel bit his lips to stop himself from grinning.

At last, Emma sat alone at her table, staring down at her drink. Michel waited for her to raise her head and acknowledge him somehow. But she didn't. He waited until his smug smile faded away into nothing. Perhaps she'd forgotten about him. After a torturously long ten minutes, he rose from his seat. Well, he would remind her of his existence and make *next time* happen now.

CHAPTER SEVEN

♥

Emma stared at her empty cup as though she could read the tea leaves. Unfortunately, she didn't have the gift of divination, so she had no idea what the tea leaves were telling her to do. What was she still doing in the café? Why couldn't she make herself leave? She couldn't risk Auntie Soo's chances of signing the YogurtBerry family. *And think about how good it would feel to put a down payment on a commercial kitchen space.* But even her imagined elation—not to mention her very real guilt—couldn't force her to her feet.

She'd been late to her matseon because she couldn't decide what to wear. Then her hair wouldn't cooperate, and the perfect shade of lip gloss kept evading her. She told herself she was fussing over her appearance because she'd promised Auntie Soo that she would be on her best behavior—*not* because she'd hoped to see Michel.

She had made up her mind. She'd made the smart choice to not see Michel again. The problem was she *did* see him—the moment she stepped into the café—and it took an alarming amount of willpower for her to turn away and walk over to her prospective husband candidate, Paul Lim, instead.

While she didn't feel an immediate connection to Paul—like the connection she'd felt with Michel—Emma tried her hardest to give him and their matseon a real chance. And she was glad she did, because he turned out to be a really nice guy. His very square nails were hardly a distraction. She couldn't care less about his slightly high-pitched laugh making her ears ring. *No. Big. Deal.* What mattered was how much they had in common—which turned out to be *a lot.* Around 60 percent of their conversation consisted of *You, too? Me, too!*

Then why did she decline his dinner invitation, making excuses about preparing for tomorrow's lessons? *Why* was she sitting in the café practicing tasseography? Because . . . She tilted her cup this way and that, watching the tea dregs shift at the bottom.

Because she should at least tell Michel that she couldn't see him again. He was the wrong man for the sensible and stable future she envisioned for herself. She could already tell they would hardly have any common background. With Auntie Soo's reputation and her culinary school on the line, now was not the time to explore their unexpected attraction.

But she owed him an explanation. They were virtual strangers, but it still felt like the right thing to do. And Emma almost always tried to do the right thing.

"May I join you?"

She knew who had spoken even before she raised her head. That voice. That accent. *Heavenly butter and sugar.*

"Please," she whispered.

Please? Why couldn't she have said *yes, you may?* Or *sure?* Even *yup yup* would've been better than her breathy *please.* She'd been avoiding this moment—or had she been looking for reasons to justify it?—but seeing him again felt so good. Which was *not* good. It was *bad* how good it felt . . . how happy it made her.

Michel gracefully lowered himself onto the chair across from her and gave her a breathtaking smile. "I was hoping we'd meet again."

"Yup yup," she said. Yeah, she was wrong. *Please* definitely sounded much better than *yup yup*.

Emma squeezed her eyes shut. It was her heart. There was something wrong with it. It was doing this weird hiccuping thing—like it did when she watched a rom-com with the perfect ending. Her arteries must be clogged from all the madeleines she'd consumed in the last couple of days. All that sugar and butter could not be healthy for her.

"I'm looking for a husband," she blurted.

Michel sat up in his chair and stared at her with his mouth hanging open. He caught himself and promptly closed it, but something bright—like hope—lit up his eyes. *Hope?* She had to be misreading his expression. Why would he look hopeful about her looking for a husband?

"You're . . ." He pressed a fist to his lips, but a bark of laughter burst from him. "You're looking for a husband?"

"Yes." Mortification washed over her. He wasn't *hopeful*. He was *amused*. What did she think? That he hoped he could be her husband? She felt ashamed of her brief burst of elation. How ridiculous. She would never marry some random man she met at a hotel café. It belied everything the Madame Ddu Method stood for. A common background was the key to a stable relationship. She raised her chin. "What I mean is that I won't be seeing you again."

All traces of laughter left his face, and a smooth, impassive mask fell into place. Emma wished he would go back to laughing at her. This polite stranger felt too much like a . . . stranger. And Michel had never felt like a stranger to her. From the moment he ordered those madeleines for her, his warmth and kindness had drawn her to him. Clearing her dry throat, she raised her cup to her lips, but lowered it remembering it was empty.

Michel's gaze dropped to her cup. Even though his expression remained stoic, he immediately turned to catch the server's attention. "Anne."

She hurried to their table. "What can I get for you folks?"

"Would you like another cup of tea, Emma?" His voice and accent remained exquisite, but it no longer reminded her of sugar and butter. Now it sounded like ice cream that was too frozen to dig a spoon into.

"Yes, please," she croaked.

"Green tea, right?" The server smiled at Emma's nod and turned to Michel. "Anything for you?"

His eyes flicked to Emma before he began to shake his head. He wasn't staying. *Of course not.* But she wasn't ready to see him go, so she blurted, "He'll have the same."

A slight arch of his brow was the only sign of his surprise as he faced her again. He sat stiffly with his back pressed against his chair as though to create distance between them. At least he didn't leave.

"Android Hyun Bin chastised me for having a caffeinated drink late in the afternoon." Emma said the first thing that popped into her head to fill the silence. Even after her refusal to see him again, Michel was considerate and respectful of her needs, unlike said android.

"There's an android version of the Korean actor?" A confused frown broke through his indifferent mask.

"You know who Hyun Bin is?" Emma blinked like an astounded owl. She hadn't expected Michel to understand the reference.

"My friend Isabelle is a huge fan of his." A hint of warmth returned to his eyes.

The constriction in her chest loosened a smidgen at the same time something sharp dug into her stomach. She welcomed his warmth, but didn't like thinking that this Isabelle person might've prompted its return. When Michel cocked his head to the side, she realized he was waiting for her answer.

"My date from the other night," she said. "He looked a lot like Hyun Bin."

"I don't see it, personally." He coughed, glancing away. "But why an android?"

"This is mean"—Emma cringed—"but he had no perceivable personality."

"Is that why you . . ." He stared pointedly at her napkin, his mouth twitching suspiciously.

"I can't believe you're bringing that up again." Affronted laughter burst from her as relief rushed through her. Michel seemed like . . . Michel again. "That's so ungentlemanly of you."

"My apologies," he said with a very gentlemanly bow of his head. But the amusement crinkling the corners of his eyes didn't look apologetic at all—just ridiculously attractive.

"But yes," Emma continued before she became completely sidetracked, "I practically chased him away by being gross. He was perfect on paper but . . ."

"Perfect on paper?"

"Mm-hmm. Remember that complicated story I mentioned?" She waited until Anne finished setting down their tea in front of them. "In Korean culture, there are these arranged first dates called matseons. A matchmaker—my godmother in this instance—collects and compares loads of background data on the candidates and their families to find a match that ensures compatibility."

"So these dates you've been having . . . they were matseons?" That bland, unreadable expression settled across his features again. "Your goal is to enter into an arranged marriage? Based on a common background and compatibility? Based on *data* collected by a matchmaker?"

"Y . . . yes." She didn't like how unsure she sounded—how

unsure his questions made her feel. What happened to being a die-hard believer in the Madame Ddu Method?

"But why?" His frustration broke through his stoic façade. "What about the unquantifiable . . . the real-life connection? What about . . . about love?"

"Real-life connection? You mean attraction? Attraction only makes people illogical. It makes them ignore obvious incompatibility." She sat up straight, certain in her conviction again. "As for love, what happens when it fades? They'll have nothing to fall back on if they don't have anything in common. What began as an exciting, hopeful relationship would turn into an ugly lie they'd trapped themselves into."

Michel slowly shook his head, his eyes a little sad. "You can't really believe that."

"You might find it odd, but it's just a cultural difference—" She bristled, going on the defensive.

"I think our cultures are well aligned in this instance," he cut in with an edge to his voice. "I'm quite familiar with arranged marriages."

She snapped her mouth shut at his tone and studied his face. "And you don't approve of them."

He sighed and spoke more gently. "That hardly matters now, does it?"

"No, I guess it doesn't." She wrung her fingers under the table.

It didn't—it shouldn't—but Emma couldn't ignore the ache spreading in her chest. She wanted to know if he really believed in love. How was he so certain? And how was he familiar with arranged marriages? Why didn't he approve of them even though they were accepted in his culture like hers? She wanted to know in what other ways their cultures aligned. She wanted to know *him*.

She felt herself wavering on her decision not to see him again.

What was the harm in *one* date? Just a few hours, really. What Auntie Soo didn't know wouldn't hurt her. Even the Crones wouldn't be able to make an issue out of a single date. Not that they would ever find out. It wouldn't delay her from achieving her dream, and she certainly wouldn't be risking her heart. It would be something fun to do. A rare self-indulgence.

"Have you decided to marry the man you met today?" Michel held her eyes, willing her not to look away. "Is that why you won't see me again?"

"I . . ." She couldn't draw a full breath. Was that what she meant? She couldn't even remember what Paul Lim looked like with Michel sitting in front of her. Why was it she couldn't see him again? "I haven't decided that I'm *not* going to marry him."

"What about the other men?" He took a slow sip of his tea, watching her from under his lashes.

"I have definitely decided not to marry them." Of that, she was certain.

"So the last one had the personality of a microwave." He rubbed his jaw in thought, drawing her gaze to his five-o'clock shadow. "What was wrong with the others?"

"There was nothing *wrong* with them . . ." She trailed off, distracted by his motion. What would it feel like to scrape her fingernails along his jaw? She shifted in her seat, her fingertips tingling with phantom sensation. "I couldn't imagine going on another date with them, much less spending the rest of my life with them."

"Because?" he cajoled.

"The man at my first matseon hardly spoke at all." She couldn't even recall his name.

"Well, that must've been awkward." Michel came to her defense without hesitation. She ducked her head to hide her smile. "What about the second matseon?"

"I was hoping you wouldn't ask that." When he raised his eyebrows in question, she sighed. "He talked too much."

"Some people love to hear themselves talk." He scoffed, indignant on her behalf, but couldn't quell the telltale twitch at the corner of his mouth. "That could grow tiresome rather quickly."

"Mm-hmm." She narrowed her eyes at him, catching on to his game. He wanted to convince her the arranged first dates were hopeless. She couldn't help but feel flattered . . . and relieved . . . that her blunt refusal to see him again wasn't enough to dissuade his interest in her. "My third matseon partner loved cats. And I'm allergic."

"Yes, of course." He nodded with impressive gravitas. "Asking him to give up cats for you would've been cruel. You couldn't possibly do that to him. Or the cats."

"You're full of shit." Emma couldn't hold back her grin any longer. "You know that, right?"

His deep, rumbling laughter set off a thousand butterflies in her stomach. He propped his bare forearms on the table, his shirtsleeves rolled past his elbows. She found unmistakable evidence of rippling muscles there as his broad shoulders shook with mirth. The butterflies migrated to flutter at her throat.

"Tell me the truth." His deep, conspiratorial whisper felt hot and intimate even though amusement still crinkled his eyes. "What about your date today bothered you?"

She considered flipping him off. Or she could argue that Paul Lim was flawless. But in the end, she leaned forward, irresistibly drawn to him, and confessed, "His nails were *really* square."

"God have mercy on us all." Michel made a valiant effort to deliver the line with a straight face, but he looked positively delighted with her admission.

"You must think I'm outrageously picky." This was fun. *He* was fun. She worked hard on worthwhile endeavors—strived to make her life meaningful. But when was the last time she'd allowed herself to have fun . . . just because?

"There is nothing wrong with being picky." He held her gaze until her smile faded and her blood pounded in her ears. "You deserve someone who knows what you're truly worth. And those men had no idea."

"Are you saying you know better?" She meant to sound haughty, but her voice came out husky and unsteady.

"I do," he said with quiet certainty. "You are radiant and full of life. You are strong-willed but kind. You are . . . I have never met anyone quite like you."

She should tell him he knew nothing about her, but all she could do was stare. When he looked at her like that—with something like awe—she almost believed he really saw those things in her.

They were both bent over the table, and not even a hand's width separated their faces. He smelled like sandalwood and spice. His rich brown eyes had specks of gold in them, and they were staring at . . . her lips. Her tongue swept out to wet them, and his pupils nearly swallowed the brown of his irises.

"Go out with me." His voice dipped so low that it sounded like a growl.

A shiver went down her spine, and her toes curled in her shoes. She had to be smart. There was so much at stake. Her godmother's reputation. Her culinary school. Now was not the time to answer the wild call of attraction . . .

Oh, what the hell.

"Okay." Emma nodded to make sure he understood she was saying yes. *Sorry, Auntie Soo.* But it would be just this once. As a present to herself. One date and he would be out of her system. "I will go out with you."

CHAPTER EIGHT

M y God," Gabriel muttered. "You really are awful at this."

"I know," Michel groaned. He dropped his head back on the sofa and threw his forearm over his eyes.

"How can you not get her number?" His cousin sounded as frustrated as Michel felt.

"I panicked." He sat upright and buried all ten fingers into his hair. "She said yes and I just panicked."

"Didn't you want her to say yes? Why would you panic when you got what you wanted?"

"She got this look on her face as soon as she said it. As though she was torn. As though a part of her already regretted her decision." Michel frowned, remembering her conflicted expression. "I was terrified she might change her mind if I stayed. So I threw some bills on the table, grabbed my things, and took off."

"Took off?" Something like horror dawned on Gabriel's face. "You didn't actually run, did you?"

"I walked fast." His voice broke on the last word. "Very fast."

"I need a drink just listening to that story." His cousin stalked to the wet bar and filled two tumblers with cognac. "We both need a drink."

Michel didn't realize he'd neglected to get Emma's number until he was back in his suite. Grinning like a fool, he'd texted Gabriel to tell him why dating apps were inferior to good old-fashioned serendipity. Then he wondered whether he should text Emma to see if she'd gotten home safely. He wasn't sure whether that might seem too forward since they hadn't gone on their first date yet. He was halfway through typing his question about proper dating etiquette to his cousin when the realization hit him. It was as though someone had struck a gong in his head. Even his teeth seemed to reverberate from the enormity of his blunder.

Michel groaned again and dug the heels of his palms into his eyes. Thank God his cousin came over to get him drunk in his time of need. But there had been a tense moment when his cousin first arrived at the hotel . . .

Sophie had stepped close to Gabriel and snarled, "Do not let Prince Michel leave this suite. Understood?"

"Understood," his cousin had answered, studying her face with somber eyes.

She'd glared at him for a long moment as though she had more to say, but then she'd stormed out without another word.

"What the hell is going on with you and Sophie anyway?" Michel let the cognac burn its way down his throat.

"Absolutely nothing." His cousin tilted back his drink. "This was the first time she even looked at me since you two came to LA."

"Exactly. Why is that?"

Gabriel glared at him for a moment, his jaw clenching, then he visibly willed himself to relax. His signature sardonic smirk returned to his face when he said, "We're not here to talk about my love life. We're here to talk about yours. Or more precisely, the lack thereof."

"Wanker," Michel muttered. He needed to sort out the mess he'd made with Emma before he could give proper attention to the fact that his cousin had called the situation between him and Sophie his *love life*.

"She must be on social media." Gabriel unlocked his mobile and looked expectantly at Michel. "What's her name?"

"Emma."

"Does Emma have a last name?" His cousin employed the gentle, patient voice of an adult speaking to a lost child. *Where is your mummy?*

"Of course she has a last name," Michel said with utter disdain.

"Well, what is it?"

"I. Don't. Know." He stood from the sofa to refill his glass and returned with the entire bottle. "I never asked her."

Gabriel raised his eyes to the ceiling and sighed ponderously. "Do you know her profession, by any chance?"

"No, but that is one of the many questions I plan to ask her on our date." Michel courteously refilled his cousin's empty glass before pouring his own drink.

"What date?"

"Shut up," he said with the maturity and dignity befitting the future king of Rouleme. "I'll camp out at the café if I need to. She's bound to show up again."

"So your best chance of seeing her again is if she decides to go on another one of those arranged dates—"

"Matseons."

"—after she agreed to go on a date with you?" Gabriel doggedly finished.

"It doesn't matter," Michel mumbled, refusing to feel as foolish as he sounded. "She never likes any of those men anyway."

"But she likes you? Are you sure about that?" His cousin crossed his arms over his chest. "What happens when she discovers that your left nostril is ever so slightly wider than your right nostril?"

"I beg your pardon." Michel stalked to the gilded mirror dominating one of the walls. "My nostrils are completely symmetrical."

Gabriel laughed himself hoarse, tipping over to his side on the sofa. Michel calmly withdrew his mobile from his pocket and hit Record on the camera app.

"How undignified of you, Professor Laurent." He tsked. "Your students will be thrilled to see the great Sphinx undone like this."

His cousin shot to his feet and lunged for Michel when he realized what was happening. "Stop filming before I kick your skinny arse."

"First my nostrils and now my arse." Michel pocketed his mobile and grinned. "You really must stop insulting me, my dear cousin. Your reputation as the Sphinx will be ruined if I accidentally leak this video."

"Fuck you," Gabriel muttered, dropping back down on the sofa. "Just delete the damn thing."

"I will . . . as soon as you agree to stake out the café on the afternoons I have lectures," he bartered.

Michel wasn't about to allow this mortifying faux pas to derail his plans to get to know Emma. Not when the brief conversations he'd had with her enchanted him. She was refreshingly frank, unquestionably intelligent, and funny as hell. And the contradiction between her confidence and shyness intrigued him, enough to make him forget everything but the need to spend more time with her.

He'd never met anyone like her. She made him feel like a different man—maybe the man he would be without the weight of the crown. He had to get his first date with her. If his intuition proved correct, he would do everything in his power to secure the next date with her, then the next, until he convinced her to spend a lifetime with him.

"Christ." His cousin shook his head. "Why do I have to suffer because you're an utter failure at dating?"

"I'll make an excuse to send Sophie over to you." Michel swirled his drink, observing his cousin from the corner of his eyes.

Gabriel went eerily still for a moment, then gave him a firm nod. "I can take next Wednesday."

Sophie and Gabriel? Michel slowly lowered himself onto an armchair next to his cousin. *Very interesting.* Perhaps there was more than one happy ending on the horizon. Filled with hope and determination, he raised his glass, and his cousin mirrored his movement before they both downed their drinks.

~

Michel cracked one eye open at the insistent nudging against his arm. He promptly squeezed his eye shut when the sunlight streaming into his bedroom pierced his brain like a white-hot laser.

"The least you could have done was bring Antoine with you," Sophie said. "I am not your personal assistant. It isn't my job to wake you up for school."

Michel sat up with a start, then grabbed his head with both hands. "God. What in the . . ."

Sophie picked up the empty cognac bottle from the floor with a grimace. "You boys have outdone yourselves."

"Where is Gabriel?" he rasped.

He reached for the water decanter on his nightstand and drank straight from it. He wasn't at the palace. No one would be horrified by his poor manners. As for Sophie, she was made of sterner stuff.

"He left as soon as the sun came up." Sophie scoffed. "At least he had the sense not to leave in the dead of night."

"You don't have to worry about him." Michel gingerly swung his feet off the bed. "He's smart. He can take care of himself."

Without responding, Sophie walked out of his room and returned, pushing a room service cart. She removed the lids off the plates, revealing piles of soft scrambled eggs, bacon, and toast.

"You can pour your own coffee, Your Highness," she said, pushing a thermal carafe toward him. "If you didn't refuse the butler assigned to your suite, I wouldn't have to serve you food at all."

"And risk him catching you call me *Your Highness*?" He massaged his pounding temples. "This—my time here, my anonymity—is important to me, Sophie. More than you know."

"I do know," she said, her face softening with sympathy. With an awkward cough, she made a show of checking her watch. "If we leave here in an hour, you'll make it to your lecture on time."

"Thank you."

His royal guard responded with a grunt and stepped out to the living room with long, confident strides. Alone with his breakfast, Michel poured himself some strong, dark coffee and gulped it down like the nectar of life. Then he dug into his breakfast like he hadn't eaten in a fortnight.

Once the coffee cleared his head and the hearty food settled his stomach, Michel took a hot shower to wash off the last traces of hard drinking. Other than a faint headache behind his eyes, nothing remained of his hangover as he pulled on a white dress shirt and cinched his sleeves with the cuff links he'd tossed on the nightstand.

Dressed in a pale gray suit with a burgundy tie, Michel headed for USC with Sophie. Once they arrived on campus, she melted away into the crowd of students and staff, and he got to be just your average visiting professor—someone who blended in with everyone else. It wasn't real and it wouldn't last, but he'd be damned if he didn't enjoy every minute of his reprieve.

He smiled at some wide-eyed students who recognized him—as Professor Chevalier, of course—and nodded at a familiar faculty member as he passed her on his way to the Center for International and Public Affairs. But for the most part, he walked through the sunlit campus without notice. It was fucking glorious.

And after his lecture, Michel intended to enjoy his glorious reprieve by blending in at the hotel café until Emma showed up again.

CHAPTER NINE

♥

*E*veryone is talking about him," Sarah said, tugging Emma into the crowded auditorium. "Even the coldest cynic will be singing about global harmony by the time they leave one of his lectures."

"Are all visiting professors such big deals?" Emma managed not to get elbowed in the ribs by a group of eager college students racing for the last empty seats. As curious as she was to see what all the fuss was about, being trampled by a swarm of overexcited undergraduates wasn't her idea of a fun time.

"Not all of them. But this one is so passionate about international relations." Sarah wiggled her eyebrows.

"Is *international relations* code for something lascivious?"

"The eyebrow wiggle was to emphasize the word *passionate*, not *international relations*." Sarah affectionately rolled her eyes at her.

Emma hadn't been too surprised when her favorite client invited her out to lunch. It seemed natural that their easy rapport would lead to friendship. What *did* surprise her was that her new friend wanted to meet because she needed advice about a girl she was crushing on.

She gladly accepted the invitation. After all, she *was* the god-daughter of a renowned Madame Ddu. She knew a thing or two about compatibility and healthy relationships. And who could resist a chance to meddle in someone else's love life? She wanted to rub her hands together and cackle.

Too bad she was hopeless when it came to her own love life. She could *not* believe she didn't even get Michel's last name, much less his phone number. And what about him? Why didn't *he* ask for *her* number? It was inconceivable that he was as awful at this dating thing as she was.

When Sarah suggested heading over to USC to show Emma the object of her affection, Emma figured it would help take her mind off of her dismay over the Michel situation. Now that she'd decided on indulging in a fun evening with a handsome, sophisticated man, the thought of not getting that date disappointed her. But moping about it solved nothing.

Once she finished her friend duty, she should go camp out at the hotel café. She was bound to run into Michel sooner or later since he said he was a regular there. It might make her seem kind of desperate, but she didn't care. She wanted to see him again, so she would make it happen.

She stumbled forward a couple of steps when someone shoved her from behind. She shot a narrowed-eye glare over her shoulder, and the kid blanched. She felt a little bad, but she had to make it out of here alive. They finally managed to find seats in the very first row of the auditorium, always the least popular seats in lectures, but even those were nearly filled up.

"We're not staying for the entire lecture, are we?" Emma whispered.

"No, I'll just point her out to you, then we can leave." Sarah scanned the stage area and the seats around them. "I don't see her yet. She's probably coming in with Professor Chevalier. Jeannie is his TA."

"So your crush is an international relations major?"

"Shhh." Sarah glanced around quickly. "I'll die if she finds out."

"It's too loud in here for anyone to overhear us," Emma said with a reassuring smile. "And I promise you won't die."

"She's here." Sarah gripped Emma's arm and pointed out her crush with her eyeballs and tongue. Sure, it was less conspicuous than pointing with her finger, but her friend looked like she was impersonating a dead fish—the cute cartoon kind but a dead fish nonetheless.

Emma dutifully turned in the direction of Sarah's tongue and eyeballs, then froze in her seat. She barely registered the fresh-faced redhead juggling a stack of folders down the aisle because her focus zeroed in on the man walking beside her.

"Here, let me help you with that," he said, taking some of the folders from his TA's arms.

Butter and sugar. A long breath rushed past Emma's lips as something unknotted in her chest. She didn't have to languish away at the hotel café after all. Michel was right here. And if she'd found him handsome in the café, Michel in a well-fitted suit and tie . . . She swallowed. Well, he looked good enough to eat.

"So? What do you think?" Sarah whispered, loosening her grip on Emma's arm. "Isn't she dreamy?"

Emma tore her gaze away from Michel as Jeannie walked up the stage and arranged the folders on a rectangular foldaway table off to the side. Even in a baggy sweatshirt and tattered jeans, her translucent skin and flaming red hair—which could use a good brushing—made her hard to miss. The TA jogged down the stage and settled into a seat not far away from them. She pulled her long hair into a messy ponytail, her cheeks expanding on a heavy exhale, and promptly slouched into her chair.

"Yes, absolutely dreamy," Emma said with an indulgent smile at her friend.

She thought better of adding that the gorgeous redhead would be much improved with properly fitted clothing and good posture. But appearing professional and well put-together might not be important to Jeannie. While Emma believed in putting care and effort into her appearance, everyone had their own priorities.

Speaking of priorities, she should ask Sarah whether Jeannie's priorities were compatible with hers. Physical attraction mattered, of course, but it shouldn't be all about that. Sarah should consider the practicalities of a relationship with her crush before she did anything rash like confess her feelings. But the crowded auditorium didn't seem like the place to have that discussion.

Deciding she'd adequately carried out her friend duty for the time being, Emma returned her focus to *her* dreamy crush. Well, *crush* might be an overstatement. She barely knew the man. It was more like a mild interest. Well, *mild* might be an understatement. Would *temporary interest* work? She huffed out an impatient breath. She was being ridiculous.

But all other thoughts, ridiculous or otherwise, left her head as Michel took the stage, clipping a small mic to his lapel. A hush fell across the room. He shielded his eyes from the spotlight and glanced slowly around the packed auditorium. Emma sank low in her seat, afraid he'd spot her—she didn't want to distract him from his lecture. But when his glance skipped right over her, she guessed the bright lights hid her from view.

With a low whistle, he slid his hands into his pockets and rocked back on his heels. "Is it me or is this auditorium getting smaller by the day?"

Emma smiled when laughter rang through the lecture hall, feeling oddly proud of him. He was the visiting professor that had the whole school buzzing. And five minutes into the lecture, she could see why. He was a charismatic speaker, intelligent and articulate, but it was his passion for the topic that drew in the crowd. His fairy-tale good looks should have been a distraction, but his words held everyone captive.

"Emma?"

"Hmm?" She half turned toward Sarah.

"I asked if you wanted to leave," her friend whispered.

"Oh, no." Emma shook her head at once. Michel walked across the stage with wide, confident steps, emphasizing opposing perspectives with each hand. "It would be rude to leave in the middle of the lecture, especially since we're in the very front row."

"Okay." Sarah didn't seem to mind, as she settled back in her seat and resumed stealing glances at Jeannie.

When the lecture ended, Emma found herself clapping as enthusiastically as everyone else. Her blood pounded in her ears, and her chest rose and fell faster than sitting at a lecture warranted. It wasn't only due to her newfound enthusiasm for global harmony. It seemed Emma had a thing for gorgeous, brilliant men with sweet, buttery accents—like 80 percent of the audience.

Even as Michel's lecture had riveted her intellect, her body had hummed with awareness. She found his warm, playful side charming, but she couldn't get enough of this *competent* side to him. There was something innately sexy about a man who knew what he was doing. He commanded her attention with a natural grace and confidence that she couldn't resist. Lust wasn't an emotion Emma was overly familiar with, but something deep inside her *craved* this man.

"Shoot. I'm going to be late for my next class," Sarah said, gathering her backpack off the floor. "Will you be okay finding your way back to your car?"

"I'll be fine." Emma stood to give her friend a quick hug. "Bring extra containers to your next lesson. We're going to make a smorgasbord of jeon."

"Mmm. Pan-fried goodness." Sarah stole one last lingering glance at Jeannie. "I'll see you next week."

By the time Emma turned to face the stage again, she couldn't find Michel. In a panic, she spun around in a circle. The auditorium was emptying out quickly. Did he already leave? Frustrated tears prickled behind her eyes until she caught a glimpse of deep golden hair at the bottom of the stage. He hadn't left. He'd just been swarmed by a group of students.

Relief and bemusement coursed through her. He was like a celebrity surrounded by eager fans. She wasn't entirely sure if she could shove her way past the students to reach him. With a huff of frustration, she sat back down in her seat and trained her eyes on him, determined not to lose sight of him again.

He listened attentively to each student, his head bent forward and his brows slightly drawn, then answered their questions thoughtfully. Once in a while, his face would split into a proud smile at a bright pupil, and it was enough to get Emma's pulse fluttering. She couldn't help but wish she was the recipient of that smile. Suddenly, she could hardly wait to speak to him again, but nearly half an hour passed before he raised his hand and made placating noises as he maneuvered past his admirers.

"My brilliant TA, Jeannie McMahon, can answer the rest of your questions." Michel nodded apologetically at the redhead who stood a few paces away from the crowd.

"All right, people. Enough with the mosh pit," Jeannie called out, clapping her hands smartly to draw the students' attention. "And for those of you who look poised to chase after the professor, remember that I'll be the one making your grade recommendations at the end of the term."

With his head down, Michel took long, quick strides toward the nearest exit. Even after an hour-long lecture and being mobbed by eager students, he didn't have a single hair out of place. Slightly queasy with nerves and anticipation, Emma hurried down the aisle to catch him before he disappeared. Blowing out a calming breath, she fell into step at his side just in time to walk out into the hallway with him.

"It's Yoon, by the way," Emma said as casually as she could manage with her heart bouncing off the walls of her chest cavity.

"Emma." Michel halted so abruptly that she had to retrace a couple of steps to join him again.

"Yes." She held up her index finger. "Emma *Yoon*."

"How . . . What are you doing here?" His eyes roamed her face as though he couldn't quite believe that she was standing in front of him.

She smoothed a self-conscious hand down her hair. She wasn't dressed to impress like for her matseons, but she looked far from shabby in her rose-gold peasant blouse and formfitting jeans. Her makeup was light but flawless, and her strappy gold stilettos were to die for. She had no reason to feel self-conscious. She cleared her throat and brought her hand down to her side.

"Wrong question," she said, arching her eyebrow. "You, Michel Chevalier, should be asking me for my number."

His dumbfounded expression faded away as a broad grin overtook his face. "Ms. Emma Yoon, may I please have your number?"

"Your cell." She held out her hand, palm up. His head cocked to the side. "I need your cell phone to give you my number."

"Ah." He promptly reached inside his suit jacket and withdrew his phone. "Here you go."

She took it from him, their fingers brushing in the exchange. She questioned the wisdom of her three-inch heels when her knees went weak at the contact. Resolutely, she typed in her number and pressed Dial. When she heard her cell ring in her purse, she hung up the call.

"There." She handed him his phone, careful not to let their fingers touch, since she had to be able to walk back to her car.

"Thank *you*," he said in a low voice that sent a shiver down her spine. "Should we—"

"Call me," she cut him off, then swept past him, flipping her hair.

Her visceral reaction to watching his lecture had thrown her off her balance. Meeting him in the hotel café had already proven inconvenient, and she had no intention of losing control of the whole situation. She hoped this dramatic exit put them back on an equal footing while she figured some things out.

She couldn't resist glancing over her shoulder. Michel stood where she left him, staring after her with unmistakable yearning. She faced forward again with a happy smile tugging at her lips. *Equal footing accomplished.*

CHAPTER TEN

H ow did she know to find you here?" Sophie materialized at his side while he watched the hypnotizing sway of Emma's truly fantastic backside as she walked farther and farther away from him.

"I don't know," he murmured distractedly. Then, with a thrum of excitement, he raised the mobile he still held in his hand. "I can call and ask her."

"Now?" His friend's nose crinkled with affectionate frustration before she smoothed out her expression. "You can't call her now."

"Why not?" He couldn't keep the bounce out of his steps as they headed toward the parking structure. Adding Emma Yoon into his contacts gave him great satisfaction. "I have her number."

"Because you don't want to seem as desperate as you obviously are." Sophie nudged him with her shoulder to soften her words. Then she straightened and said in a firm tone, "Come now. Let's get you back to the hotel. I need a break from guarding you with my life."

Michel complied immediately because he knew she was only half kidding. His royal guard would throw herself in front of a bullet for him without hesitation. Following her directions not only protected him, but her as well.

"What's the proper protocol for calling a woman after you get her number?" He matched her clipped pace as they headed to his car.

"I'm not your bloody dating advisor, Your Highness." Her expression remained convincingly deferential. "Look it up on the internet."

He scoffed indignantly, but as soon as he reached the privacy of his suite, Michel typed in his pressing query. It was apparently a popular question, because the search engine completed it for him. *How long to wait to call a girl after getting her number.* Not that he would ever think of Emma as a girl. She possessed an intrinsic poise and confidence—even when she was chasing away unwanted matseon partners—that made it impossible for him to think of her as anything but a woman.

Michel scrolled through the results, then scrolled some more. He tossed his mobile on the coffee table with an exasperated flick of his wrist. The overwhelming consensus was that you needed to wait three days before calling someone. Followed by a bevy of opinions as to why you should call sooner, as well as why you should call later.

To hell with it.

He snatched his mobile from the table and texted Emma.

> **Michel:**
> I admit I'm quite beside myself with curiosity. How did you find me?

He stared at the screen as though willing her to respond immediately. Being self-aware enough to know when he was being ridiculous—an indulgence that wasn't often afforded to the prince of Rouleme—he leaned his head on the back of the sofa and closed his eyes. He didn't go so far as to put the device down, but held it loosely against his thigh.

When his mobile buzzed within a couple of minutes, Michel shot all the way up to his feet and fumbled around until he managed to unlock his screen.

> **Emma:**
> You're asking the wrong question
> again, Professor Chevalier.

Lust shot straight to his groin at her last two words. He liked the sound of that a little too much coming from her—impudent and sexy as hell. His thumbs were already typing out his response.

> **Michel:**
> Then what's the right question?

> **Emma:**
> You really are kind of hopeless
> at this. You know that? 😊

The smiley face at the end of her text took away the sting of her words. Besides, when she was right, she was right. He was absolutely hopeless at this dating business. He grinned like a sod.

> **Michel:**
> Have dinner with me tonight and
> show me how it's done.

He frowned at the screen when the ellipses didn't start scrolling for a beat too long. He reread his last message, and red-hot heat crept up his neck until it reached his hairline. *Show me how it's done?* It sounded like he was insinuating . . . He certainly didn't mean . . . *Dear God*. He made *it* sound like *sex*, didn't he? He was beyond hopeless. He was catastrophically ruinous at this.

And all he'd meant to do was ask Emma out on their first date. A perfectly innocent, absolutely appropriate, unimpeachably respectful dinner. The kind that involved food and conversation. Not *it*.

Emma:
Tonight?

He nearly dropped his mobile in his rush to reply.

Michel:
Yes. Please. If you're free.

Michel:
For dinner.

Michel:
Tonight.

He needed to stop typing.

Emma:
Okay. Does seven work?

Michel:
Yes.

And just so she understood how well seven worked, he sent another text.

Michel:
Please.

Before he could type *thank you*, a new message arrived from her.

Emma:
Where?

"Shit," he spat. Where? He had no idea. He rushed out the front door and crossed the tastefully decorated elevator bank to the only other suite on his floor. He pounded on the door with his fist. "Sophie!"

Before he could register the door opening, Sophie hauled him behind her with narrowed eyes and scanned the empty foyer with her muscles coiled tight, ready to spring into action. Regret and frustration rushed through him at the alarm he'd caused his friend.

"It's safe, Sophie," he said softly. "I'm not in danger."

It took a moment for her grip on his wrist to loosen, and she slowly turned to face him. "What. The. Fuck."

"I just needed to talk to you." Michel raked his fingers through his hair. "No one can even come up this elevator without your permission."

Her shoulders visibly relaxed, but her expression remained stony. "Fine. Talk."

"Her name is Emma Yoon," he said, swiftly changing tactics. He couldn't ask Sophie for restaurant recommendations, much less drag her out to a restaurant after scaring her like that. Since he refused to sneak out like a rebellious teenager, there was only one option. "You probably want to run a background check on her before I invite her over for dinner tonight."

"Tonight?" Sophie unknowingly mimicked Emma's question.

"Yes." It was too late to second-guess himself. It hadn't even occurred to him to postpone his date with Emma. Probably because he absolutely did not want to do that. As his cousin so helpfully reminded him, the clock was ticking. "I was thinking around seven, so that should give you a good three hours to figure out if she'll kidnap me for ransom or not."

"You're inviting her to your hotel room? On your first date?" Her eyebrow arched skeptically even as her thumbs flashed over her phone.

"Not a room. A suite. A fifteen-hundred-square-foot suite." Inviting her to his hotel—suite or not—wasn't ideal, but he didn't have much choice. "I think we'll manage not to trip over my bed."

"She won't get anywhere near your bed or even set foot on this floor until I let her—as you pointed out." She finished typing before looking up. "You'll have my answer in three hours, my prince."

She closed the door in his face. But as he turned to leave, muttering under his breath, she peeked her head out and said with a hint of a smirk, "And for your next date, I'll help you pick out a restaurant."

He returned to his suite and sat on the couch, pinching the bridge of his nose. With his identity concealed, he was in no real danger. Very few people in America would even recognize him. Their media had more than enough on their hands, covering the antics of their beloved Hollywood stars. They weren't interested in the lives of princes from small European nations.

Even so, this trip was taking a toll on Sophie, because she and she alone was responsible for his safety while they were here. But that was what he'd wanted. He couldn't risk drawing attention to himself with a brood of royal guards. It was selfish of him, but this was his only chance to take back a portion of his life and avoid an arranged marriage, which neither he nor his childhood friend Isabelle wanted.

His father, the king, was tired. When he told Michel that, his father had indeed looked exhausted . . . and old, his once-golden hair gone completely silver. The king intended to abdicate, with immediate plans to announce Michel's coronation as well as his impending engagement to Lady Isabelle Duprey. His father wanted Rouleme to celebrate their new king and future queen rather than mourn the end of his rule.

Michel begged for forbearance even though he would do anything for his father and Rouleme. The king granted him a three-month reprieve, presumably to allow him to prepare himself for the inordinate responsibility of leading a country. But Michel had been trained for that inevitability his entire life. Every facet of his upbringing had centered around that all-important goal. He still wasn't sure what kind of ruler he would be—what he could do for his people—but he intended to dedicate himself wholly to the betterment of Rouleme and his people. He would accept that responsibility with gratitude and humility, if not joy.

All he wanted was to be allowed to do so with someone he loved by his side. *That* was the true reason Michel needed the three months. There were things in his life that he had no control over, but marriage wasn't something he could let happen *to* him as he watched passively from the sidelines. He had this one chance to choose something—*someone*—for himself. He wanted to marry someone simply because he couldn't live without her and she couldn't live without him. A union of love between a man and a woman. Nothing more. Nothing less.

For this *one* thing, he wanted to be selfish. He wouldn't marry for his country and his people. Not for duty and responsibility. He didn't care about sensibility or compatibility. He would settle for nothing less than all-consuming love. For three months, he could still make that choice.

But one month had already passed, and he had no time to waste. He needed to find out if Emma was meant for him. He typed out his next message with renewed determination.

> **Michel:**
> We've already established that I'm hopeless at this dating business, right?

He inhaled through his nose and exhaled slowly, forcing himself to put down his mobile. He'd taken a while to respond to her, so he shouldn't expect an immediate response. After five minutes, he noticed his bouncing knee and gaped at it, appalled at his lack of composure. He didn't know when shock gave way to delight, but he found himself grinning. This woman stripped his royal upbringing right off him. That was an excellent sign. His mother had always said that love made fools of all men—even kings.

> **Emma:**
> Sorry. I was in the shower.
> But yes. Quite hopeless.

The more Michel told himself not to imagine Emma in the shower, naked and wet, the more vivid his mental image grew. He shifted on the sofa, adjusting his pants. He ran his hand down his face and got himself under control.

> **Michel:**
> So fully accepting that I'm likely doing this all wrong, I would like

to invite you over to my place for
dinner.

Emma:
Your place?

Michel:
Yes, I'm staying at
the hotel where we
met.

That sounded worse than he thought it would. She might
think he was inviting her to his hotel room with nowhere to sit
but on his king-size bed.

Michel:
In a two-bedroom suite. It's just
like your typical flat with a dining
room and a living room . . .

He stopped himself before he recited the entire hotel bro-
chure.

Emma:
I guess we won't be encountering
an only-one-bed scenario then.

Michel blinked. What the hell is an only-one-bed scenario?

Emma:
Haha. Never mind. Bad joke.

Emma:

But, yeah. Dinner at your place it is. At
seven.

Relief and anticipation rushed through Michel, and a huff of laughter tumbled out of him. He was about to reply saying he would meet her in the lobby, but Sophie's scowling face flashed through his mind. The best he could do was greet her at the foyer on his floor, which was as far as he could go without his royal guard. He swallowed an unexpected flash of frustration. This was his life. He came to terms with it long ago. There was no point getting worked up over it now.

Michel:

If you let the front desk know
you're here, they'll show you up
to my suite.

Emma:

Oh. Okay. See you soon.

At the risk of sounding like an eager fool, Michel tapped out what was on his mind.

Michel:

I can't wait to see you.

CHAPTER ELEVEN

♥

*E*mma had visited the hotel café a couple of times even before her series of unfortunate matseons, but she had never actually seen any of the hotel's accommodations. She had no reason to stay overnight since she only lived forty minutes away. And there was also the small matter of the hotel being a wee bit out of her price range.

When Michel invited her to dinner at his place, her heart had clamored to exit her chest. *His place?* Her mind had immediately conjured breathless, sweaty scenarios, but she'd dragged her thoughts back, instinctively knowing he didn't have ulterior motives for the invitation. She honestly couldn't say whether the little dip in her stomach had been relief or disappointment.

His next message had revealed that he was actually a guest at the hotel, and her heart had plummeted at the reminder that he didn't live here. But her heart rallied, remembering that he was a visiting professor at USC, which meant he wasn't leaving the next day or anything. By the time he revealed that he was staying in a *suite* in one of the most luxurious hotels in LA, her heart couldn't do much but lie down on a fainting couch to recover from the back-to-back acrobatics it had performed.

He was rich—really rich. Red lights had flashed through her mind as the word *incompatible* rang in her ears. Auntie Soo never would've matched Emma up with someone *that* rich. She'd stopped herself short at the thought.

Michel had asked her out on a date, not proposed marriage to her. Her date with Michel had nothing to do with marriage. She was going out on *one* date with him—for fun—because she deserved to do something nice for herself.

If Emma were to marry, and she had assured her godmother that she would, she still intended to choose her future husband through the Madame Ddu Method. A love match wasn't for her. Without a solid, common background, she would have nowhere safe to land when love faded.

Emma found Michel unbelievably attractive, which meant she shouldn't trust her instincts when it came to him. Case in point, going on this date with him was impulsive and irresponsible. But she fully recognized that, and she didn't intend for it to happen again.

She would let herself have this one date as a treat for herself, then focus on her matseons. It was actually a very clever and efficient plan. If she didn't go out with him, she would waste time wondering what it would be like. This way, she would spend one evening with him and he would be out of her system.

When Paul Lim texted her soon after their matseon, Emma hadn't outright refused his invitation to go out to lunch with him this weekend. It had more to do with not wanting to disappoint Auntie Soo than any real desire to see him again, but at least the thought of a second date with him didn't make her want to blow her nose in a cloth napkin.

Emma smiled as she pulled her car up to the valet, remembering the shared laughter with Michel over her antics. After handing over her keys, she caught a brief glimpse of her reflection on the sliding glass doors leading into the hotel lobby. She'd chosen a midnight-blue, one-shoulder dress for a confidence boost. It hugged her body in all the right places and stopped a few inches below her knees, so she felt sexy and powerful without feeling too exposed. Her strappy Manolo heels and ruby-red lipstick added to the sexy and powerful theme.

She might have overdone it. They were having dinner *at his place,* after all. He could very well be waiting for her in a pair of jeans and a T-shirt, not that he would look any less devastating. But Emma stopped second-guessing herself when the distinguished-looking gentleman at the front desk straightened to his full height as she approached.

"How may I be of service?" he asked with a formal incline of his head.

"I'm here to see Michel Chevalier." She sounded cooler than she'd intended as renewed nerves slammed into her.

"Of course." The man didn't seem to mind in the slightest as he beamed at her. "Please allow me to show you to the elevators."

"I could find . . ." Emma trailed off as he joined her at her side with lightning speed.

"This way, please." He stretched his arm forward, and she had no choice but to start walking.

When he led her past the main elevator bank to a small alcove to the side, she realized she wouldn't have been able to find her own way. He called the single elevator nestled in the private nook, and the doors opened immediately, revealing a rich, wood-paneled interior with gold trimmings. She stepped inside at his beckoning, and the man reached toward the elevator panel with a key card. Once it beeped, he pressed the button marked "PS" out of the four total buttons on the panel.

"I hope you have an exceptional evening," he said with another bow of his head.

Emma felt nervous laughter bubbling up inside her. She wanted to look good tonight, but she definitely overshot it if the hotel staff was treating her like royalty. With a brisk shake of her head, she got her nerves under control and said, "Thank you."

After a fast, dizzying ascent, the elevator opened up to a posh foyer as big as her living room, adorned with champagne-colored wallpaper and burgundy carpeting. Michel wasn't rich. He was *filthy* rich. In all honesty, she might have bolted back to the lobby if he hadn't been waiting for her on the other side of the elevator with a heart-stopping grin. She bit down on her bottom lip with a soundless whimper. He looked irresistibly gorgeous in his navy suit.

"Emma," he said in a rush of breath. A beat passed as his appreciative gaze traveled over her—making heat spread through her body—then he stretched his hand out, palm side up. "Shall we?"

She hesitated as her gaze darted to the foyer behind him, intimidated by the opulence despite herself. His smile dimmed and uncertainty crept into his expression, and a pang of regret spread through her chest. She had a feeling his unguarded grin wasn't something that often made an appearance. Taking a deep breath, she placed her hand in his and stepped out of the elevator.

"Nice place," she said in the most carefree voice she could manage. She wanted to smooth away the crease she'd put between his eyebrows.

"This is a shared foyer." He cleared his throat and waved vaguely at the two double doors on opposite sides of the hallway. Emma nodded as though having all of *two* suites on an *entire* floor was totally pedestrian. He placed a hand on her lower back, and she shivered at the light touch. "We're this way."

When he guided her through the doors, she had to clamp down on a gasp. A wall of floor-to-ceiling windows showcased the LA city lights while sparkling crystal chandeliers lit up the interior. Every piece of impeccable furniture probably cost more than her monthly mortgage, but the place was undeniably beautiful. And the soothing earth tones of the walls and the exquisite area rugs adorning the rich walnut floors added a warm, inviting feeling to the elegant suite.

"I . . . um . . ." She cringed at the slight wheezing in her voice and collected herself. It wasn't like she'd never seen a nice home before. But to stay in a suite as big as a good-size Southern California house? He belonged in a world different from hers. "Is that a grand piano?"

"I believe it's a baby grand." He tugged at his light blue tie, then dropped his hand to his side as though catching the nervous gesture. "The dining room is this way."

The dining room was as tasteful and luxurious as the living room. But Emma almost burst out laughing when she saw the twelve-person table with two place settings at opposite ends—the *long* ends. "Are we seriously going to sit this far apart? We'd have to throw the saltshaker to pass it to each other."

"I'm sorry." His flustered gaze bounced from one end of the table to the other. "I didn't realize the staff had set the table like this."

"Maybe they thought you were expecting more people," she said, eyeing the three sleek dining carts filled with at least ten covered dishes.

"I didn't know what you liked." A blush spread across the bridge of his nose as he ran a finger under the collar of his shirt. "So I ordered several different entrées for you."

Emma forgot about her flash judgment that he was different from her. All she saw now was Michel, sweet and shy, and she just wanted to enjoy his company. With a soft smile, she murmured, "I think you might've accidentally ordered the entire menu."

He didn't respond right away to her teasing, as his eyes dropped to her lips, and her breath caught in her chest. After a sharp shake of his head, he managed a slightly dazed smile. "You may be right."

She crossed over to the carts. "May I?"

"Please," he said, his gaze following her every move.

As she lifted the covers one by one, Emma studied the artful setting of each plate and inhaled the delicious scents wafting toward her. Filet mignon nestled atop a delicate mound of polenta. Chicken breast with crispy, golden skin. Fluffy little pillows of gnocchi in a trio of flavors—cream, pesto, and tomato sauce.

"Everything looks so good. I don't know which one to choose." She couldn't have asked for a more delightful dilemma. Like opening presents on Christmas morning, she uncovered even more delectable dishes. "Hmm. What are you having?"

"The Dover sole." He came to stand beside her, and the air around her seemed to heat up by ten degrees. He glanced sideways at her, and she blushed for no reason whatsoever. "And what will you be having?"

"Everything," Emma said, coming to the only possible decision. She replaced the covers on all the dishes and gave Michel a cheeky grin. "So are you."

"I am?" Amusement lit up his warm brown eyes.

"Yes. This is what we're going to do." Emma moved their place settings so they could sit facing each other without the entire length of the table separating them. "First, we'll each select a dish without peeking under the lids. Come on. Pick one."

He graciously complied with her command and waited for her to make her choice. Once they were seated across from each other, he said with a smile, "What next?"

"Second, we'll unveil the dish with a flourish." She lifted the cover and waved her free hand around the filet mignon like a game show assistant.

With a low chuckle, he followed her example and held out a dignified hand toward his—she peered closely at his dish—sea bass. "This is the most flourish I can manage."

"I'll accept it. Just this once." Her attempt at a stern glare failed miserably. "Third, we take a bite of our respective dishes, then switch."

"Switch?" His eyebrows rose.

"Yes, so we could taste each other's . . ." She trailed off with sudden self-consciousness.

Emma loved *sharing* food because she *loved* food. Sharing meant she could try more of it. And in Korean culture, family and friends ate banchan—small side dishes to accompany the rice— from the same plates, so sharing food came naturally for her.

Of course, there were people who balked at eating off other people's plates. Which was totally fine. But it just hadn't occurred to her that Michel might be one of them. She'd assumed that he was her kind of people because being with him felt so effortless.

"Brilliant," Michel said, cutting through her thoughts. He gleefully rubbed his hands together. "Then we'll repeat steps one through three until we've tried all the dishes, right?"

"Right," she said, relief flooding her veins. He *was* her kind of people. Which didn't matter at all since this was going to be their first and last date. The point of tonight was to have fun. "After we taste every entrée, we can each pick our favorite."

"What if we like the same dish?" He leaned forward, his lips curling up in one corner.

"We fight to the death . . . with rock, paper, scissors." She winked. "Or we could always share."

Unable to wait any longer, she sliced into the filet mignon, revealing a perfect, pink center, and took an eager bite. Her eyelids fluttered shut as a happy hum escaped from her. She would have to search deep for a reserve of willpower to pass her plate to Michel.

When she opened her eyes, he was staring at her with an expression she could only describe as *hungry*—as though he wanted to snatch the filet mignon out of her mouth. She hurried to swallow just to be safe.

"Wine," he said with enough urgency to make her jump. He pushed away from the table and shot to his feet. "Let me bring you some wine."

"Uh, okay."

He was halfway across the dining room when he rounded back and came to stand in front of her. His shirt stretched across his broad chest as he inhaled deeply, and his words spilled out in an embarrassed rush. "Do you prefer red or white? Do you even drink wine? I should've asked you that first."

"I drink all forms of alcoholic beverages," she murmured distractedly, absorbing how well he filled out his impeccably fitted suit. Tailor made for sure.

"I . . . see." He cupped his chin, strategically placing his fingers across his twitching mouth. If she peeled his fingers away, the mirth she could see building up inside him would spill out of him. She loved the sound of his laughter, but embarrassing herself wasn't the best way to hear it.

What possessed her to say that? It wasn't something you said on a first date. It probably wasn't something you said at all. Never mind that it was true. Her love of food extended to adult beverages. The perfect drink could elevate a meal to the next level. Korean fried chicken was a delicious meal—but Korean fried chicken with ice-cold beer was a celebration.

"Maybe you should bring a bottle of each since we haven't chosen what we're having for dinner yet," she said, deciding she wasn't humiliated enough to refuse wine.

Why just have dinner when they could have a celebration?

CHAPTER TWELVE

♥

Michel didn't remember the last time he'd laughed so much.

In the end, they skipped rock, paper, scissors to the death and decided to share three of their favorite dishes—the chicken under a brick, the tagliatelle with chantarelle mushrooms, and the Dover sole. When he reached over to refill Emma's chardonnay, she covered the top of her glass with her fingers and shook her head.

"No more for me. I'm a lightweight." She narrowed her eyes at his skeptical expression. "Just because I enjoy adult beverages doesn't mean I drink a lot. For me, it's more about how the flavors meld with the food, adding another layer to the experience."

"The experience?" He chewed thoughtfully on a morsel of mushroom.

"I think every meal has the potential to be a special experience . . . a memory," she explained, building the perfect bite of chicken on her fork—chicken, crispy skin, and a dollop of creamy mashed potato. "I haven't even told you what I do for a living, have I?"

"No, you haven't." Michel blinked in surprise.

The initial awkwardness of the evening had melted away, and the last hour had flown by as they talked and laughed. It felt as though he'd known Emma for a lifetime—their connection solid as a deeply rooted tree—but he actually didn't know anything about her.

"I'm a culinary instructor." She smiled as though just thinking about her job made her happy. "I teach people how to cook Korean royal court cuisine."

Michel choked a little at the words *royal court* but managed to pass it off as a cough. "That's fascinating. How did you know that's what you wanted to do? Did you always know?"

Never having had that choice, he found it intriguing how people decided on a profession—how some are guided by their passion while others stumble into it. Either way, he envied them the process of discovering who they were.

"Huh." Emma tilted her head to the side and studied him curiously. "That's not the first thing people usually say when I tell them that."

"Then what is?"

"Oh, I don't know. Something like, 'You're Korean? I love BTS.'" She shrugged. "Or sometimes they tell me their cousin's friend's sister's boyfriend is Korean."

"Well . . . that's strange." His eyebrows furrowed. "What does that have to do with anything?"

"Right?" She huffed an exasperated breath. "Anyway, I've always loved cooking, even as a kid. There's something reassuring about being able to create something delicious, a slice of happiness, with a little time and effort. And I wanted to teach others to do that for themselves."

"That's lovely." Warmth spread across his chest. "Why did you choose Korean royal court cuisine specifically?"

"Gungjung yori takes a bit more effort than other cuisines, but it's harmonious and beautiful, not to mention healthful and delicious. I feel like cooking and eating Korean royal court cuisine feeds the soul as well as the body."

He nodded, unable to look away from the amazing woman. Emma tucked her hair behind her ear and cleared her throat. Damn it. He was staring again.

"Where are you from, Michel?" she asked with a soft smile. "I promise not to play six degrees of separation to one of your countrymen."

"How did you know I'm not from around here?" he said after a moment to regain his composure. Hearing his name on her lips made his whole body clench with need. "Did my accent give me away?"

"No, the fact that you're living in a hotel did." She didn't have to roll her eyes. It was already implied by her tone. "And that you're a *visiting* professor at USC."

"That's right." He leaned forward, remembering his burning question about how she'd found him at USC. "Are you a student at USC? In addition to being a culinary instructor?"

"God, no." She pretended to shiver with distaste. "I went to UCLA."

"Sorry. No offense intended." Playing along, he held up his hands in swift surrender. He knew of the bitter rivalry between the two LA schools. "Then how did you end up in my class?"

"My friend is a graduate student at SC and needed my advice on . . . something." She shrugged her shoulder—the one left bare by her asymmetrical dress—drawing his eyes to its smooth curve and the delicate ridge of her collarbones. Her creamy skin caught the light and glimmered like satin. He gripped the stem of his glass tightly to prevent himself from finding out if she felt as soft as she looked.

"Fraternizing with the enemy?" he said a bit hoarsely.

"Does that make you my enemy, too?" Her dimple winked beside the mischievous curve of her lips.

"I'm anything but." He couldn't hold back the low invitation in his voice.

Her chest rose with a quick inhalation as a lovely blush blossomed on her cheeks. The air turned dense with awareness, and the space between them crackled with electricity. He grew lightheaded as all his blood rushed south. One word of encouragement from her—one glance—and he would hurl himself across the table for her. Then his lifelong discipline snapped him out of the trance, pulling him back from a place of raw need and breathless want.

"Besides, visiting professors don't count as enemies," he said to break the tension.

"Yes . . . well. Never mind, then." She flapped her hand as though to clear the air. "So where *are* you from, Michel?"

"Rouleme," he said, purring the R in the back of his throat in its proper pronunciation.

Her lips parted, and her eyelashes fluttered. His head tilted to the side. Did he surprise her? After a pause, she whispered, "I'm sorry. What was that?"

"Rouleme," he repeated. She might not have heard of it. "It's a small country that borders France and Switzerland."

"Ah, yes. I've never been, but I heard it's beautiful there." Emma ran her hand down the side of her neck. "I just never heard it pronounced that way before."

"What? The correct way?" he teased.

"I guess so." She laughed, the sound traveling across his skin like a silken caress. "So you really are from another country. I thought maybe you had a permanent position at another college in the US."

"No, Rouleme is my home." And it would always be his home. He couldn't imagine living anywhere else even if he wasn't meant to rule the country in a few short months. Would Emma be able to call Rouleme her home one day, too? He realized with a jolt he desperately wanted the answer to be *yes*.

"Like you said, it is beautiful there." He braced his forearms on the table and leaned toward her with his heart pounding. "In the capital, buildings straight out of storybook fairy tales stand amongst modern architectural masterpieces in perfect harmony. And the people . . . they are open-minded and hardworking, united in their love for Rouleme. It truly is an incredible country. I think you would like it there."

"That sounds wonderful," she said quietly, then offered him a soft smile. "Maybe I could visit someday."

"Yes." His hands were fisted on the table, and he forced them to unclench, not wanting to alarm Emma with his urgency. "Rouleme would love to have you."

"So . . ." Her eyes scattered away from his. "How long will you be here?"

"For two more months." He swallowed past his suddenly dry throat. *Only two months to find my true love.*

"Will the semester be over by then?" She took a long sip of her wine.

"Not quite. My colleagues—with the help of my TA extraordinaire—will wrap up the term for me."

"Hmm." Emma traced the rim of her glass with the tip of her index finger. "Two months, huh?"

"Yes," he croaked.

Michel didn't want his time with Emma to end—this fun, intelligent, and beautiful woman who turned a simple meal into an event. This incredible woman who made him laugh and catch fire with desire. Perhaps if they spent more time together, he might discover that she wasn't the woman of his dreams. This might turn out to be nothing more than a passing fancy . . .

But in his heart of hearts, he knew there was nothing left for him to discover that would change his mind. This was it. *She* was it. Emma was his first and last chance at love. And he only had two months to convince her to start a new life with him in Rouleme.

"I want you." He reached across the table and took her hand in his. "I want to be with you."

"You only have two months here . . ." She trailed off as her gaze roamed his face with part conflict and part yearning.

"Even if it's only for two months, I want to spend my time here with you." He ran his thumb across her knuckles, stopping himself from telling her he wanted to spend a lifetime with her. It was too soon for that. He didn't want to scare her away. And there was the small matter of telling her that he was the prince of Rouleme.

"We have nothing in common," she murmured, staring down at their entwined hands.

"Give me two months to prove you wrong." He ducked his head to catch her eyes. "I'll prove to you common upbringing and surface similarities don't dictate how well two people fit together. I'll prove to you that you don't want perfect on paper."

"I don't think I'm wrong. I know what I want and what I'm not willing to risk . . ." She didn't look away from him. "But if it's only for two months, maybe it doesn't matter which one of us is right."

"Maybe," he conceded without meaning it. She thought he was proposing a brief interlude, and that couldn't be further from the truth.

"I should go." She pulled her hand from his grasp and stood from her seat.

"Of course." He rose as his stomach plummeted to his feet. This couldn't be the end. This *could not* be the end.

Michel saw Sophie's door close discreetly as he and Emma stepped out to the foyer. Even with a secure floor, his royal guard had to stay alert while he was in the company of a nonfamily member.

As he walked Emma to the elevator, he contemplated begging her to let him see her again. His mind spun in frantic circles, looking for ways to stop this moment from being their last. *Merde alors.* Emma stepped inside the elevator, and he stood rooted to the floor of the foyer, his lips melded together. Even when she turned to face him, he couldn't find the right words. He wanted to roar with frustration. Or prostrate himself at her feet and stop the elevator doors from closing with his body.

"I'll see you soon," she said.

He lurched forward as though someone pushed him from behind. "When? How soon?"

"I'll text you." A faint smile touched her lips just as the door closed.

With his back against a wall by the elevator, he sagged to the floor. He stretched a leg out and rested his arm on his folded knee. A chuckle rose from his throat, quaking his shoulders. He shook his head, pressing a loose fist against his forehead. When the top half of Sophie's body materialized from behind her door, he lowered his fist to his lips to curb his laughter.

"Is everything all right?" she asked dutifully even as she leveled him with a stare that said he was a git.

"Everything is fine." Another huff of laughter spilled out of him. "Against all odds, I've managed not to mess this up."

"Congratulations, my prince." The rest of her made an appearance as she leaned against the doorjamb, crossing her arms. "So when is your next date?"

"I don't know yet." He pursed his lips. "She said she'll text me."

"Sounds like you still have a chance to mess this up." Sophie pushed off the door with an exasperated sigh. "Maybe you should read her file to learn more about her. It sounds like you need all the help you can get."

"Her background check was about giving *you* peace of mind." He stood up from the floor. "I have no wish to learn about her through a report. But I plan to learn every detail about Emma from the woman herself."

I plan to learn every inch of her body so I can map out her pleasure. I plan to learn all about her hopes and dreams to help them come true. I plan to learn her fears and regrets to help assuage them. I plan to learn her past hurts to help her heal—and possibly to pummel anyone who had hurt her. I plan to spend a lifetime learning everything about her so I'll know every way to make her happy.

"I don't know," she said solemnly. "I think you should learn about her porcelain clown collection before it's too late."

With an undignified snort, he turned his back on her and ambled toward his suite. If he was honest with himself, even a porcelain clown collection wouldn't be a deal-breaker. The thought was rather alarming . . . and kind of wonderful.

"Good night, Sophie." Michel waved over his shoulder, not bothering to look back. "And you're sorely mistaken if you think a collection of creepy clown figurines is going to keep me away from Emma Yoon."

CHAPTER THIRTEEN

E mma had basically been wrong about everything. She was not smart when it came to Michel Chevalier. One date with him only made her want to spend more time with him. No, her little *self-indulgence* did not get him out of her system. In fact, it did quite the opposite.

Their date had been more than fun. It had made her happy. And the way he looked at her made bubbles rise inside her, fizzy and tingly like champagne. Even though she had Auntie Soo's reputation and her culinary school to worry about, she was sorely tempted to see the sweet, considerate, and sexy-as-hell man again.

"Wrong, wrong, wrong," she sighed under her breath.

"Oh my gosh. I'm so sorry," Jiyeon said, stepping away from the cutting board. She looked like she was about to burst into tears. "I'm hopeless at this."

Startled out of her thoughts, Emma glanced at the green onions she'd instructed Jiyeon to slice thinly at an angle. The poor thing had cut them into long, fine ribbons, which had to have been a slow, painstaking process. Emma couldn't believe she didn't catch that. *Michel Chevalier.* The man was trouble . . . sweet, buttery trouble.

"That is actually an advanced technique I planned on introducing in later lessons," Emma reassured her client. "I'm very impressed you already mastered it."

"Really?" The younger woman looked at her with wide, hopeful eyes.

Jiyeon was barely out of college, and her mother was already pressuring her to marry into a jaebeol family. She was exquisite and her family was stinking rich, but Emma didn't envy her the stress of trying to live up to her mother's expectations.

"Yes, really. I can hardly believe that you've never cooked before," Emma said gently. "You'll be a fine cook of royal court cuisine once you complete your lessons. But for this dish, let's cut the green onions like this."

She demonstrated with a new stalk of green onion and watched her client mimic her movements. Satisfied with the results, she next showed Jiyeon how to cut the carrots into small, thin rectangles. With practiced ease, she continued cutting the carrots as her client followed her example. Preparing the ingredients was one of her favorite parts of cooking. There was something reassuring and therapeutic about the repetition of slicing, dicing, and chopping food. It also provided ample opportunity for her mind to wander.

Emma might not be right *all* the time, and she might not be as smart as she would like where one particular man was concerned, but she was without a doubt proficient at adapting. She was exceptionally good at taking stock of changes and adjusting her strategies to fit a new set of facts. She knew how to make the best of any situation life threw her way.

Case in point, rather than wasting her remaining five matseons—and they would be wasted while she remained so thoroughly distracted by Michel—she would put her quest for a perfect-on-paper husband on hold until she got said distraction out of her system once and for all. She would see Michel Chevalier a few more times, but only to confirm that they had nothing in common. Once she proved to herself that they shared no common background and were utterly incompatible, she could put him out of her mind forever and give her matseons her full, undivided attention.

A short reprieve wouldn't hurt anyone. Auntie Soo's reputation could withstand some more bad-mouthing by the Crones— she didn't linger on how much her godmother wanted to sign the YogurtBerry family—and Emma already had enough clients to maintain the projected growth of her business for at least another two months. Not that she had any intention of letting this little detour go on for two whole months. God, no.

To prove to herself how wholeheartedly she believed in the transient nature of their relationship, Emma hadn't even given in to the temptation of googling the filthy-rich visiting professor. But now that she thought about it, maybe looking him up on the internet would give her ample proof of how utterly different their lives were . . . No, it would be best for her to experience their incompatibility in real life. Besides, she couldn't trust everything she read on the internet.

"Is this any good?" Jiyeon asked, chewing on her bottom lip. "Or did I butcher them? My mom says I have the grace of a hippopotamus."

"What? They look fantastic." Emma kept her thoughts about her client's mother to herself.

"I don't know." The younger woman sighed, absently stacking the carrot slices on the cutting board. "I don't . . . I don't think I'm jaebeol bride material. I'm not sure I even want to be."

"My godmother is very good at her job," Emma said pragmatically rather than telling her she didn't have to be a jaebeol bride if she didn't want. "She would never match you with someone who isn't compatible with you."

"I . . . I'm sure you're right." Jiyeon nodded slowly. "Is your godmother going to find a match for you, too?"

"Um . . . yes, of course." Building a carrot tower suddenly seemed like a great idea. She focused on laying one paper-thin slice over another, then shook her head. "Let's continue to the next step."

Jiyeon did have a talent for cooking, and her dish came out beautifully. After showing her out, Emma returned to the kitchen to tidy up, only to find her dad doing the dishes.

"Appa." She tried to pull him away from the sink. "I can do that."

"I know you can." He shrugged off her hand and resumed washing the pot. "But so can I. You shouldn't have to do everything."

"But this is literally part of my job." Emma couldn't keep the exasperation out of her voice. She'd been taking care of her dad ever since her mom left them. And he'd let her because he knew it was her way of coping with their divorce. Now, they were just used to their roles. So what had gotten into him?

"Well, taking care of you is my job," he said with a stubborn jut of his jaw. "You—and sometimes I—forget that I am the parent. I should be the one taking care of you."

"You have." She leaned her head on his shoulder. "You do."

He grunted unappeased and started on the second pot, his hands slipping on the handle and spattering soapsuds on his shirt. Finally, he muttered, "I know you've been going out on matseons."

"Is that what this is about?" She straightened up and planted her fists on her hips.

"I want you to know that I can take care of myself." He heaved a ponderous sigh. "I've relied on you for too long. But you don't have to worry about me."

"Of course I don't have to worry about you." Emma rolled her eyes. "Because I'm not going anywhere without you."

"What do you mean you're not going anywhere without me?" Her dad finally gave up the ruckus and rinsed his hands.

"I told Auntie Soo not to match me up with an only child or

the eldest son." She gently maneuvered her dad away from the sink and pulled on the rubber gloves. She needed to rewash all the pots. "I didn't want there to be an issue as to whose parents my future husband and I live with."

"No man is going to want to marry you if you and I come as a set." He threw his hands up. "What are you thinking?"

"I'm *thinking* I have everything figured out." She felt her jaws jut the same way her dad's had. She was just as stubborn as he was. "I got this, Appa. You can stop worrying."

"I guess it might be okay if I lived in a detached in-law suite." His shoulders drooped in defeat—and maybe a little in relief. "I would be the father-*in-law*, after all."

"It would be more than okay, Appa. It would be *right*. Besides, I'm going to take a little break from the whole matseon thing." Emma dropped that last detail in casually even though her heart pounded at the implication of her words. Was she really doing this? "I need to focus on my business for the next few weeks. Finding a suitable commercial kitchen is turning out to be a bit of a headache."

"That makes complete sense." Her dad nodded enthusiastically. "You *should* focus on your business. There is no need to rush into marriage. No need at all. Take all the time you need."

"Okay, I will." Emma ducked her chin to hide her smile and finished rewashing the dishes.

~~~

In the quiet of her room, Emma sat on her bed and fidgeted with her phone. Spending a little time to get Michel out of her system would be worth the detour in the long run. Until she got rid of that distraction for good, forcing herself to sit through matseons would be a waste of time for everyone.

But she had to tell Auntie Soo she wanted a break from the matseons as soon as possible. It wouldn't be a long break, but her godmother needed to formulate a contingency plan in case Emma's marital status came up while she courted the Yogurt-Berry family. Hopefully, the Crones' inane chitter didn't reach them yet. Emma also needed to tell Michel that she accepted his indecent proposal to have a . . . fling?

She clapped a hand over her mouth, but a loud, unladylike snort snuck past her anyway. She didn't even have a prospective husband to chase off. *What a waste.* She promptly dissolved into giggles—part glee and part major nerves. *A fling? Me?* Pressing her lips together, she drew her eyebrows into a deep frown and swallowed her laugh.

Give me two months to prove you wrong . . . I'll prove to you that you don't want perfect on paper. Her heart swooped from the memory of his heated gaze and the conviction in his voice. *No.* She took a deep breath. He wouldn't be the one to prove anything to her. After a few dates, *she* would have proof of their hopeless incompatibility. Then she could put him out of her mind for good.

Emma nodded to herself and unlocked her phone. She'd made her decision. There was no reason to wait. She typed two messages with quick, impatient taps.

> **Emma:**
> I want a break from the matseons.

> **Emma:**
> I want to see you tonight.

There. That wasn't so hard. Before she could pat herself on the back, her phone buzzed twice in a row.

> **Michel:**
> A break? I'm not sure I understand.

Auntie Soo:
Tonight? What's wrong?

"Ahhh!" Emma buried the offending phone under her pillow, but it wasn't enough to save her from the mess she'd created. When her phone started ringing, she sat on her pillow for good measure.

"Why me?" she implored, but her ceiling gave no answer.

The ringing stopped but resumed with almost no pause in between the calls. If she didn't answer this time, Auntie Soo would just come to her house in person. With a drawn-out groan, she retrieved her phone from under her pillow.

"Hi, Imo." Emma took a deep breath, ready to dig deep for some bullshit to serve her godmother.

She couldn't tell her the real reason why she wanted a break from the arranged first dates. *I met the hottest man alive after chasing away the guys you matched me up with, and I'm going to have a fling with him.* Oh God. A fling? Was that what she wanted? Was that what Michel meant when he all but growled at her that he wanted to *be* with her?

"What's wrong?" Auntie Soo said without preamble. "Why do you need to see me tonight?"

"What? I can't just miss you?" Emma defaulted to sweet-talking. A part of her wished she could tell her godmother everything so she could help her figure things out. But it wasn't worth the worry the news might cause. "I didn't mean that I'll literally barge into your house tonight. I just meant that I missed you."

"Well, aren't you a dear," Auntie Soo cooed.

"Okay. Remember that feeling, because I actually have something to tell you." Emma cringed, closing her eyes. "I want to take a brief break from the matseons."

There was a long pause. "A break? How brief?"

"Maybe a couple of weeks? Three weeks max?" Emma braced herself for Auntie Soo's reaction.

"Three *weeks*?" her godmother all but screeched. "Why would you want to do such a thing?"

Emma held the phone away from her ear. "I'm a *dear*. Remember?"

"Dear, my ass," Auntie Soo muttered.

"Imo," Emma gasped. "*Language*."

"You still haven't answered my question. Why do you need this . . . break?"

"My dad needs some time to come to terms with his only child getting married." Emma went with the partial truth so she wouldn't have to lie more than necessary to her godmother. "And it wouldn't hurt for me to take a little time as well. I rushed headfirst into this whole matseon thing. Marriage is a huge step, and I need to be sure that I'm ready. Two, three weeks should be enough time for me and my dad to become comfortable with the idea, but it's not so long that irreparable damage will come to your reputation. I know you want to sign the YogurtBerry family . . ."

"Emma, your well-being is so much more important to me than my reputation. And don't worry about the YogurtBerry family. If they're smart—and they are based on the success of their frozen yogurt franchise—they'll sign with me," Auntie Soo reassured her. "I'm sorry if I pushed you into this, my dear."

"Please. That again? *I'm* the one who suggested this." Emma's stomach twisted with guilt. "I mean it, Imo. It's not your fault. I just have a feeling the matseons will go much smoother once I've acclimated myself to the idea that this is the right time. I've always planned on asking you to find my match for me when I was ready."

"Really?" Her godmother sounded so relieved that she had to smile.

"Yes, really." And she meant it.

Her phone dinged in her ear, and she took a quick glance at the screen.

Michel:
Emma?

She knew what her message sounded like. *You'll be my little break from matseons.* She squeezed her eyes shut. Everything was fine. She would deal with this.

"Very well then." Auntie Soo sighed. "I only want what's best for you."

"I know, Imo." Her godmother was the loveliest person alive. Emma would be ready to settle down with one of her matches after this break. That was what she'd always wanted. She ignored the queasy flutter in her stomach. "Thank you for understanding."

"So you're not coming over tonight, right? Because I have a book club meeting . . ."

"No, but I'd love to see you soon," Emma said in a rush. "Let me know when you're free to have lunch."

"I'm free as a bird all next week. Except for Tuesday . . . and Wednesday. Friday might not work either."

"Monday or Thursday, then." Emma laughed. "I'll touch base with you next week. Talk soon."

Her laugh died in her throat as she stared despairingly at her phone screen. Would it be so terrible to let him think that he would be her little break from matseons? Wasn't it kind of true? She gave herself a firm nod. He could make what he wanted out of her text message. She would focus on getting him out of her system as soon as possible. And that started by going on another date with him.

CHAPTER FOURTEEN

♡

Emma thought he wanted a brief interlude with her . . . and she was agreeable to the idea.

"Bloody hell," Michel growled as he reread her text.

I want a break from the matseons.

A part of him was thrilled to spend more time with her, but it riled him that she wasn't willing to give him a real chance. He would only be a "break" for her. She clearly intended to resume her search for her perfect-on-paper husband as soon as he returned to Rouleme—without her. What about him screamed *bad husband material*?

He was tempted to text her again—he wasn't even sure what he wanted to say—but he pushed his mobile to the far side of his desk. No matter how impatient he felt, he could wait until after office hour. It was a privilege to teach these bright minds, and they deserved his full attention.

He opened his office door and said to the first student in line, "Please come in."

"Hi, Professor Chevalier." A young man with a mop of brown

hair plopped down on a chair across from his desk. "Thank you so much for seeing me."

"Of course. That's what I'm here for." Michel tore his eyes away from his mobile and focused on his student. "What can I do for you?"

"Nothing specific, really." The kid blushed, scratching his head. "I wanted to hear more about your thoughts on the practicality of an international treaty on climate change. How can we trust so many countries to take steps to achieve carbon neutrality?"

"Sometimes trust has to be the catalyst for change. No one wants to be made to look foolish, but expecting subterfuge will paralyze the countries from taking the bold, courageous steps that the world needs right now. It can't always be about coming out on top." He threaded his fingers together on his desk when his mobile buzzed. He gripped his hands harder to stop himself from reaching for it. "May I recommend some fascinating new papers for you to read?"

It was quite possibly one of the longest hours of his life. But when the clock struck five, he invited his students to return for his next office hour and firmly closed the door on them. He all but lunged for his mobile and unlocked it.

Emma:
Hi.

The message felt a bit anticlimactic, but he gladly responded.

Michel:
Hello.

Emma:
Where are you?

Michel:
At USC. Just finished
office hour. About to
head out.

He stopped himself from adding even more details to hint
that he could see her anywhere, anytime. Preferably as soon as
possible.

Emma:
Do you like Peruvian food?

Michel:
Yes. Absolutely.

He was sure he would like it once he tried it. He enjoyed all
kinds of food.

Emma:
Can you meet me in an hour?
I'll send you the address to the
restaurant.

His thumbs felt big and clumsy in his rush to respond.

Michel:
Yes, I can. Meet you.

Emma:
I'm glad. See you soon.

Michel:
See you. In an hour.

Eloquence had been bred into him. It was a royal super-power, if you would. Then why did he become a bumbling mup-pet every time he attempted to communicate with this woman? Maybe that was why she didn't see him as husband material.

According to the address Emma sent him, the restaurant was in Old Town Pasadena, and he felt a spark of excitement at discovering a new city. He hadn't visited many places in the Los Angeles area—or anywhere, for that matter. He'd traveled the world, but he went where his duties required. This meeting and that function. Endless embassies, auditoriums, and ballrooms.

Well, he had two months to actually *see* Los Angeles, and he might get to do that with Emma by his side. With his heart thudding and a smile spreading across his face, he gathered his briefcase and rushed out of his office. Sophie appeared beside him before he stepped out of the building into the bustling campus.

"You seem to be in a rush," Sophie murmured with a sideways glance at him. "You also seem extremely happy about it. Care to share where we're headed?"

Michel bent his head over his mobile, not slowing down his pace, and forwarded her the restaurant's address. "I hope you like Peruvian food."

"I haven't had it in a long time, but I do love Peruvian. So thoughtful of you to suggest it." Sophie held her arm out in front of him as a maintenance cart rambled past them. "But there's no need to run into oncoming traffic for lomo saltado, my prince."

"That golf cart was going less than five miles per hour," Michel grumbled. "What's lomo saltado? Never mind. I'll find out soon enough."

"Other than delicious food, what awaits you in Pasadena?"

"Emma." He still loved the feel of her name on his lips. "I told you I didn't mess this up."

"Dear Lord. Did you just sigh?" Sophie arched an eyebrow

at him. "Anyway, do you have any idea how you'll explain my presence?"

"I actually hadn't thought that far ahead." He switched his briefcase to the opposite hand and rolled his shoulders. "Perhaps we could use the same arrangement we have for my visits to the hotel café."

"You mean you want me to hide behind a potted plant?" She unlocked the car and waited for him to get in to the passenger seat—since he'd forbidden her from opening the door for him— before sliding into the driver's seat.

"A fish tank or a large decorative vase would suffice," he deadpanned.

Sophie's lips twitched at one corner. "If this restaurant is a tasteless establishment with neither, I can always hide under the table."

"Quite."

Pasadena wasn't very far from USC, but the famous LA rush hours made the trip interminable. Michel drummed his fingers on his knee, growing more impatient by the mile. He checked the dashboard clock for the tenth time. He might be late for his date.

"You won't be late," Sophie said, noticing his impatience. "And she's an Angeleno. She knows what traffic is like."

"Hmm." Emma would certainly understand, but he didn't like the thought of wasting even a minute of his time with her. He needed to spend that time convincing her that he was indeed husband material. In fact, he would become boyfriend material, lover material, father material . . . He would become everything she needed him to be.

"I bet you're missing your royal helicopter right about now," his friend teased.

"Just drive," he muttered, tugging off his tie and tossing it in the back seat.

They arrived at the restaurant with three minutes to spare, and Michel stepped inside, relieved to be on time. Until he spotted Emma sitting at a table by the window. *Damn it.* She'd beaten him here.

"How many in your party?" the host asked.

"I see my friend is already seated," Michel said, tearing his gaze away from Emma. She looked so lovely. "I'll show myself to the table."

"Of course. Enjoy your evening." The host nodded with a smile, which Michel barely returned in his rush to get to Emma.

"I hope I didn't keep you waiting." He reached for the back of his chair. "May I?"

She turned her gaze away from the window and smiled up at him. "By all means. Unless you prefer to stand all night."

He sank into the seat across from her with an answering smile. "I wouldn't want to give you a crick in your neck."

"That's very thoughtful of you." Her dimple deepened and snagged his attention.

Before he could stop himself, he reached out and ran a thumb over the spot—light and quick. God, her skin felt so soft. He immediately withdrew his hand, not trusting himself to let his touch linger.

"I still like your dimple," he said huskily.

"Thank you." A blush stole across her cheeks as she tucked her hair behind her ear.

He opened up his menu to stop himself from staring at her. "I have a confession to make."

"Oh?"

"I've never actually had Peruvian food." He caught a glimpse of Sophie slipping into the restaurant. She pointed out a table at the back to the affable host. "I enjoy trying new things, but some guidance would be very much appreciated."

"Oooh. You're in for a treat, my friend." Emma hugged the

menu to her chest and leaned forward. "We'll start with Inca Kola. I normally don't drink soda, but there's something irreverent about having *golden* cola. Are you in?"

"Yes." He drew closer to her, hoping to catch a whiff of her scent, and . . . just to be closer to her. "I'm entrusting myself to your capable hands tonight."

"That's either really brave or very naïve," she said with a roguish wink.

In an instant, he grew achingly hard. *Fuck.* He felt lightheaded with lust and wanted nothing more than to put himself in her hands. He needed to pull himself together. She was talking about food, and he was behaving like a slavering beast. She *was* talking about food, right? Her voice always had that husky, breathless tone.

"I like to believe that I'm being exceptionally smart." He sounded a bit strangled but coherent. "You are a food expert, after all."

"Well then. Prepare to be impressed."

"Oh, I assure you," he said, "I already am."

Their eyes met across the table, and breathing became secondary to survival. This attraction. This connection. He'd never felt anything like it. They had found something extraordinary in each other. If Emma didn't believe it to be anything more than a passing fancy, then he would prove her wrong.

CHAPTER FIFTEEN

When Michel told her he'd never tried Peruvian food, Emma had immediately glommed on to that fact as a prime example of their differences. She loved Peruvian food. He hadn't even tried it. They were *so* different, right?

But as they left the restaurant, she grudgingly conceded to herself that it was no longer a difference, because it turned out he loved Peruvian food, too. But the fact that he wasn't afforded the chance to try it until now had to mean something. Like a difference in upbringing or the different crowd they hung out with. Was she reaching?

As they strolled through the picturesque Old Town area with its charming redbrick buildings and old-fashioned streetlamps, Emma pulled her powder-blue faux-fur jacket tighter around her. The spring evening held a hint of chill.

"Are you cold?" Michel asked, his brows furrowing.

"Just a little." She shivered. "I'll be fine."

Drawing her away from the middle of the sidewalk, he turned her toward him and buttoned up her jacket, his knuckles brushing the bare skin above the neckline of her tunic dress. Her pulse fluttered in her throat at his gentle ministration, and she surreptitiously breathed in his warm, woodsy scent.

"Better?" He ran his hands up and down her arms.

"Yes." If he kept that up, she was going to have to take the damn jacket off. "Thank you."

"Hmm." He took hold of her hand and led her a few steps back the way they'd come. "Over there. Let's get you warmed up with a hot drink."

Down a small alleyway off the main street, a round wooden sign read *Café Monde*. They walked into the atmospheric coffee shop hand in hand. Did he realize he was still holding her hand? She held her breath, hoping he wouldn't notice and let go. He absently brushed the pad of his thumb across her knuckles while reading the menu board over the counter. She tried not to melt into a puddle at his feet.

"Their tea selection is remarkable." He peered at the clear jars of tea lining the back wall. "I can see white blossoms in that jasmine tea. How does that sound to you? Some fragrant tea with *caffeine*?"

"In the evening?" She widened her eyes and gasped into her free hand. "Whatever will become of my circadian cycle?"

His chuckle traveled down her spine in a delicious shiver. "Maybe I can tire you out enough to offset the caffeine."

"Oh . . . um . . . hahaha." Emma tugged her hand free and slipped out of her jacket. She'd been wrong about Michel. He wasn't hopeless at this dating business. Not at all. He was *very* good. Too good, maybe. "Is it warm in here?"

His half-lidded glance and the sensual curve of his lips exuded enough male arrogance to make her whimper. His hand came to rest on her lower back as he guided her up to the counter, and the heat of his skin seared her through the thin material of her dress.

"Have you decided?" he murmured close to her ear. The innocuous words sounded like a seductive challenge. *Shall I tire you out?*

"I'll have the jasmine tea," she squeaked to the woman behind the counter.

"And I'll have the same." He kept his hand firmly planted on her back and withdrew his wallet from his suit jacket with his other hand.

Michel was wearing a dark gray suit minus the tie—probably because he had come straight from USC. It fit him like a glove, and he wore it so effortlessly that he didn't look overdressed for a weeknight date. He just looked sinfully handsome.

He'd left the top two buttons of his shirt undone, and she could see where the strong column of his throat met his chest. She wanted to *taste* the dip of triangle under his Adam's apple. Maybe fill it with something sweet like ice wine and drink it from there, lapping up the last drop with her tongue. And . . . she was officially out of her flipping mind.

They found a cozy love seat in the back of the café and settled there with their tea. White flowers blossomed in their mugs, and the heady scent of jasmine perfumed the air around them. She took a careful sip, savoring the hint of earthy bitterness on the back of her tongue.

"This tea is beautiful," she said, setting down her mug on the coffee table in front of them.

"So are you." Michel's eyes roamed her face with unabashed appreciation.

Her heart tripped in her chest as warmth spread low in her stomach. "And you're cheesy."

"Since when has honesty been cheesy?" His lips tipped into a lopsided grin.

"I feel like I've been hustled." She wanted to taste that cocky smile of his. "I thought you were supposed to be 'hopeless at this dating business.'"

"I am." He took a sip of his tea and placed his mug beside hers. "Utterly hopeless."

"You are so not hopeless." Her words prickled with accusation. Since she was horrible at dating, it should definitely count as an incompatibility.

"I'm glad to hear that." He picked up her hand and toyed with her fingers in the narrow space between them.

"I've never . . . The thing is . . ." Emma became fascinated with how their hands looked tangled together—the golden tan of his skin against her fairness. There was beauty and harmony there. "I don't know if I want a fling? I'm not even sure I know how to have one."

"That's not what I want either." Michel gently brushed her hair off her forehead.

"Then how do you . . . why do you want to be with me?" she asked with wide eyes.

"I want to know everything about you. Your hopes and dreams. Your favorite ice cream flavor." He cupped her cheek, and she instinctively leaned into his touch—warm and strong. "And I want you to know me as well. My most embarrassing childhood memories. My favorite song."

"I'd like that." Her voice was barely above a whisper. She wanted to learn everything about him to prove how incompatible they were, right? "I would like that very much."

"Make no mistake. I want you, Emma. Desperately." He swept his thumb across her bottom lip. When her mouth parted at his touch, he sucked in a rough breath. "But nothing will happen unless you want it to. I am . . . at your mercy."

Even as she heard his words, she was already lifting her head toward his, her eyes fluttering shut. But she couldn't kiss him. She couldn't think properly with the lure of this attraction clouding her mind. And how was kissing going to prove that they had nothing in common? Still, she didn't move away. She couldn't.

"I would definitely be at your mercy"—he brushed his lips on her temple as light as a whisper and pulled back—"if you knew the sound I make when I see a spider."

"That I *have* to hear." She smiled tremulously, grateful to him for giving her the space she needed.

"Oh, you would love it." His eyes sparkled with mischief and lingering lust. "I sound terribly manly."

"So what *is* your favorite song?"

"It's an old folk song from my country," he said quietly. "My mother used to sing it for me when I was little . . . before she passed away."

"Oh, Michel. I'm so sorry." She squeezed his hand.

"It was a long time ago." He squeezed it back. "What about you?"

"My mom left when I was ten," she said, surprising herself. She didn't talk about her mom very often. "It's been just me and my dad since then."

"That must've been hard for you." He held her gaze as though he really wanted to know.

Most people shied away from asking about her mom or brushed it off as *More than 50 percent of marriages end in divorce.* Emma really didn't need a reminder that she was just part of a statistic, so she'd gotten used to not talking about her parents' divorce. But she realized she wanted Michel to understand.

"Yes and no." She thought for a moment. "My parents fought a lot. They couldn't agree on the simplest things. So in some ways, I was relieved that they wouldn't have to fight anymore. But that also meant I wouldn't have my mom around."

He nodded slowly. "Do you keep in touch with her?"

"Apart from our annual Christmas call?" Her mom couldn't seem to bother with remembering her birthday even before the divorce. "No, not really. She's a partner at a fancy accounting firm. Her job keeps her pretty busy."

"No job is important enough to keep someone away from their family so completely." He linked his fingers through hers. "I'm sorry."

"We made it work, though—my dad and I," Emma said with a soft smile. "I wanted us to have a happy home even though my mom was gone. I started doing a lot of the cooking and discovered how much I loved it."

"Is that why you decided to become a culinary instructor?" His thumb brushed across her knuckles, drawing a shiver from her.

"Uh-huh." Her voice sounded a little breathless. "Life doesn't have to be perfect for it to be good. Food is one way to make that happen."

He stared at her for a long while without saying anything. "I think that's extraordinary. *You* are extraordinary."

She ducked her head, blushing at the reverence in his voice.

"But I was actually," he continued, "asking what your favorite song was?"

She burst out laughing and slapped his shoulder. He caught her hand and kissed it lightly.

"I don't really have a favorite song." She crinkled her nose. "Is that weird?"

"A little weird," he said with a straight face.

"Really?" She frowned, fighting a blush. He looked dead serious . . . but then he smiled. "Oh, you . . ."

She shoved his chest and found that there was absolutely no give. Was he wearing a metal plate under his shirt? She moved her fingers an inch or two to the side and pressed down tentatively.

Again, no give. When she flattened her palm on his chest, he trapped her there with his hand and tugged her close.

"May I ask what you're doing?" he asked in a low voice, his face only a few inches away from hers.

A confused frown drew her eyebrows together. "You're . . ."

"I'm . . . what?"

"I was checking to see . . . making sure that . . ." She pressed her finger into his chest, and he wrapped his hand tighter around hers.

"That?" he prodded.

She scoffed, impatient with herself. So what? The man was built like a brick wall. Maybe that should count as a difference. He was all hard muscle. And she was soft—so soft that she would give where he wouldn't, and they would fit in such delicious ways . . .

"Never mind." She tugged on her hand, flushing to her roots. God, she was so turned on.

But Michel dragged her hand across his chest, all the way to the opposite wall. "I don't mind, you know."

"You don't mind what?"

"You . . . checking." His voice was deep and growly and . . . *Shit*.

She squeezed her thighs together. She needed to kiss the damn man right this second. It was a matter of survival. Besides, kissing him wouldn't change anything. She knew not to trust this attraction—it would fade away soon—but she could still indulge in it while she had the chance. It wouldn't affect her objectivity in proving their incompatibility.

"Like this?" She brought her other hand to rest on his chest.

"Yes," he rasped.

"Are you sure you don't mind?" She pressed up against him and dipped her head until their lips were mere inches apart. She pivoted at the last second to brush her lips against his ear. "I think I'm all warmed up now."

Emma stood and strode out of the café, knowing Michel

would be hot on her heels. Rather than turning toward the main street, she walked deeper into the narrow alleyway and leaned against the brick wall, her top half-hidden in shadows. As she expected, it didn't take Michel long to join her and move toward her until the tip of his shoes nearly touched hers.

"What are we doing out here, Emma?" The teasing arrogance in his voice told her he knew exactly what they were doing out here and that he liked it.

She loved how he said her name, like he was savoring it. "Does it taste good?"

"Does what taste good?" He ran the backs of his fingers down the side of her face.

"My name . . . on your lips," she said boldly.

"It tastes fucking glorious." He bent his head until she could feel his words caress her lips. "*Emma*."

With a little whimper, she tugged his head down and crushed her mouth against his. Everything in her went slack at first contact like she'd exhaled a long-held breath. Pure relief. *At last*. Then mayhem erupted.

She must've literally exhaled, because her mouth had parted, inviting Michel in, and he accepted with a guttural groan. Their tongues slid and tangled frantically against each other as her hands resumed their exploration of his hard pecs, and his fingers, spread wide on her hips, dug into her skin and pulled her flush against him.

She pushed up onto her toes, desperate to get closer, and he growled his approval. Wanting to feel that sexy rumble against her breasts, she pressed up against him and wrapped her leg around his waist. She thought she heard someone cough in the distance, but she soon forgot about it, lost in the kiss. His palm slid down her thigh and gripped her ass under her minidress, tugging her even closer to him. They moaned in unison as her center met his hard length.

Michel suddenly went still. Growling her frustration, she thrust herself against him, and he moaned as though in pain.

"Emma." He kissed her hard like he couldn't help himself, then dropped softer kisses on the corners of her lips. "We need to slow down."

"We do?" She tried to deepen the kiss, but he pressed his forehead against hers, thwarting her efforts. Now she wanted to kick him as much as she wanted to keep kissing him. *Wow.* She never knew she was so vicious. "But why?"

"Because," he sighed, "I have to tell you something."

This time, she froze. *I have to tell you something* is literally the scariest phrase in the world, because the *something* was usually something terrible. Like your parents saying, *We lied to you about everything being okay. We're getting a divorce.* Emma absolutely hated the phrase *I have to tell you something.*

If Michel didn't have his hands wrapped around her arms, she might have run off into the night. But instead, she squeezed her eyes shut and waited for the *something* with her heart clawing to escape through her throat.

Please don't let it be something bad.

CHAPTER SIXTEEN

*E*mma went stiff and rigid in his arms—her eyes and teeth clenched tight—as though she was waiting for a ravenous lion to pounce on her.

"What's wrong?" Michel leaned back to get a better look at her expression, but it was hard to see in the shadows. He cupped her cheek and lifted her face toward him. "What's happening right now?"

"Just tell me what it is," she gritted out. "I don't like being hit with surprises. Let's get it over with."

Michel gulped. That didn't bode well for when he broke the news that he was the crown prince of Rouleme. He pushed the thought away even as dread settled in his stomach like a leaden anchor. He would worry about that when—*if*—that time came. It would be hard enough to explain to her why they weren't alone right now.

"I have a . . . bodyguard," he said in a strained voice.

"What?" Her face went blank for a moment, then she burst out laughing with obvious relief. "That's strange and unexpected but not *bad*. Oh, thank goodness the *something* isn't a bad thing."

"The something?" His eyebrows pulled together as he tried to understand what she was saying.

"You said you had something to tell me, and that *something* is usually bad news." She carefully wiped the corners of her eyes with a knuckle. "But wow. You have a bodyguard? Why? Are you a celebrity in your country or something?"

"Or something," he said in an attempt at levity.

"As long as *that* something isn't bad." Her expression grew guarded again, and that was the last thing he wanted.

"No, no. I assure you it's nothing bad." At least, he hoped she wouldn't think it was bad. His real concern was that she might like the idea of him being a prince too much—more than she liked the man underneath the crown. Even though he couldn't tell her his real identity yet, he wanted to be as honest with her as possible. "It's a simple precautionary measure to reassure my father that I'll be safe. I come from an . . . influential family, and he's rather overprotective."

"Um, okay." Emma nodded. "So where's your bodyguard right now?"

"She has actually been with us the entire evening," he said with a small cringe. He'd completely forgotten about Sophie—kissing Emma left little room for any coherent thought—until he heard her cough insistently from a few meters away. "That's why I had to stop kissing you."

"What?" Emma pushed herself off the wall so fast that she nearly butted his head with hers. "Where?"

"Do you . . . want to meet her?" Michel wasn't sure what Emma needed to become comfortable with the idea. He could only hope that he hadn't scared her off.

"Meet her?" Her head swiveled left and right down the alleyway, but Sophie had slipped into an alcove. "I can't meet her. She just saw us . . . We were . . . Oh God. I can't look her in the face right now."

"Certainly. Not a problem at all," he agreed quickly. "I'll introduce you two next time."

This time, he didn't wonder about whether there would be a next time. After a kiss like that, it would be impossible for there not to be a next time. But he swallowed thickly when Emma didn't answer right away.

"Okay. Let's do that." Her shoulders rose as she inhaled deeply and lowered as she blew out the breath in a gusty whoosh. "So what happens now?"

He didn't want their night to end, but he knew Emma needed some time to process what he'd shared and get accustomed to the idea. "May I walk you to your car?"

She worried her bottom lip, drawing his gaze back to her mouth. Even in the dark, he could tell that her lips were swollen. He felt a surge of male pride, and it was all he could do not to kiss her again.

"Yes," she said at last. "I'm not parked too far away."

He offered her his arm. "Please lead the way."

Michel shortened his stride to match hers and to make their walk last as long as possible. Emma looked over her shoulder, then faced forward again with her mouth scrunched to one side.

"Is she following us? I can't tell who she is."

"Oh, she's there." Sophie hung back farther than usual, keeping pace with a group of young women walking behind them. "She's very good at her job and very discreet. I often forget she's even there."

"Hmm."

He tugged Emma closer and placed his hand on top of hers tucked into his arm. "I'm sorry to make you uncomfortable."

"That's okay." She gave him a small but genuine smile. "I'm sure I'll get used to it soon enough. I actually think it's kind of neat that you have a woman as your bodyguard. Is she taller than you? Because . . . well, you know . . . your height and build are quite imposing. I can't imagine someone smaller bodyguarding you."

"Sophie's actually about your size. A bit broader in the shoulders maybe." He glanced sideways at Emma. "But she's a master in a number of martial arts and more than capable of taking down people much bigger than her. Besides, protecting someone is often less about brute force and more about skill, intelligence, and instinct."

"Wow. She sounds *awesome*. I totally want to meet her now." But she quickly added, "Not *now* now. But next time."

They walked quietly for a few minutes, and Michel took in the scene around him. The streets weren't overly busy, but a good number of pedestrians strolled alongside them. The people in America seemed bigger and louder than their counterparts in Europe. Not necessarily in size and volume. They seemed to take up more space around them but just as easily shared that space with others. There was something open and confident about them.

Maybe it was Los Angeles. Or it was limited to the people around him, here and now, but Michel felt as though he could breathe easier tonight. It was as though a tight fist he hadn't realized was clenched around him had loosened its hold ever so slightly. Being the prince of Rouleme was a privilege, but he was grateful for this brief taste of freedom.

"Can I ask you a question?" Emma looked at him. "Are you never alone, then?"

"It's not like Sophie watches me sleeping." Michel chuckled even though the fist around him tightened again. He was never truly alone, especially back in Rouleme. "Sophie and I each have our own suite at the hotel, so we have all the privacy we need. She's able to give me that space because no one can come up to our floor that she hasn't cleared."

"But I was able to come up to your suite." Slowly, Emma's eyes and mouth rounded. "Was I *cleared*?"

"Yes." He wasn't sure how she would take the revelation.

"She did a background check on me?" Her voice rose a fraction.

"Yes . . ." He still couldn't get a read on her reaction. "She can access certain information on people to ensure there aren't any red flags."

"So does that mean she knows my life story?" She stopped walking and withdrew her hand from his arm.

"Emma, please—" His stomach sinking, he reached for her hand, but stopped himself.

"That's so cool." She turned to face him, wearing a wide grin.

"What?" He blinked.

"It's kind of neat that someone had to clear me for *security reasons*." Her tinkling laughter felt like a balm on his frazzled nerves. "Besides, I don't have anything to hide. My life is annoyingly *normal*. She must've been bored out of her mind, doing whatever she did to background check me."

"Dieu merci," he breathed. "I'm so relieved you aren't offended."

"No, she was just doing her job." Then she pierced him with a sharp glare. "I have no reason to be offended unless *you* also read up on me."

"I would *never*." He placed his palm on his chest. "I swear. I didn't read a word of her report."

"You swear you know nothing about how my last two boyfriends went missing?"

"No, of course not . . ." He stopped and stared at her. "I beg your pardon?"

"Oh my *God*." Emma doubled over laughing, her hands pressed to her thighs. "Your face. Oh, that's priceless."

"That"—he wrapped his hands around her waist and hauled her against him—"was not very nice."

"No, I guess it wasn't." She gripped his shoulders for balance. "But it was very, *very* funny."

Michel swooped his head down and kissed her soundly on her smiling lips, pushing her back against an antique-style lamppost. When she rose to her toes and buried her fingers into his hair, he deepened the kiss like a man starved. The heady scent of jasmine lingered in her mouth. With a gasp, he drew away from her before he completely lost his head. He dropped his hands to his sides and fisted them to stop himself from grabbing her again.

He couldn't believe he had let his control slip—kissing her in the middle of the street like that. For some reason, it made him want to laugh. The pedestrians didn't seem to mind their public show of affection in the least. Most of them were involved in their own conversations as they walked past them. An older couple chuckled and smiled fondly at each other, as though remembering their younger selves.

"We should probably stop embarrassing your bodyguard," Emma said with a rosy blush on her cheeks. "Anyway, this is me."

"Here?" he asked, not taking his eyes off her.

"My chariot awaits." She pointed her thumb over her shoulder to a white compact car behind her and fiddled with the strap of her purse. "So . . . I guess this is good night."

"Yes. I guess so." But he couldn't make himself step away from her.

He wanted to kiss her again. It felt as though he might *die* if he didn't kiss her. But he didn't kiss women in the middle of the street. The dignity of the crown demanded he not make a spectacle of himself—at least not twice in one night.

But he wore no crown tonight. Prince Michel might not kiss women in public, but Michel Chevalier could kiss the hell out of Emma Yoon anywhere. He ran the backs of his fingers down the side of her face. She leaned into his touch.

"May I kiss you good night, Emma?" She looked lovely illuminated by the warm light of the streetlamp, and he tucked her hair behind her ear.

"But . . . isn't Sophie watching?" She caught the bottom of her lip in her teeth.

"I don't care." He gently freed her lip with the pad of his thumb. "The whole damn street can watch if it means I can taste you again."

Emma sucked in a sharp breath and swayed toward him. "God, you really are good at this."

"What am I good at?" He traced the line of her jaw and smiled when she shivered. She felt this attraction between them as strongly as he did. There was no question that they would be *compatible* in bed—he grew instantly hard at the thought—but he couldn't make love to her until he told her who he was.

"Being hot," she said with a petulant pout. "It makes rational thought very difficult."

Incredulous laughter huffed out of him. As the desire pushing against his skin became something warm and tender, he leaned his forehead against hers and sighed. Emma made it clear that she felt uncomfortable kissing in front of Sophie. He couldn't coerce her to kiss him by . . . *being hot* . . . no matter how much he wanted her.

He gently pushed her hair away and kissed her on the temple, then brushed his lips down the side of her face and kissed her impossibly soft cheek. "Good night, Emma."

"Good night, Michel." She offered him a sweet smile. "And tell Sophie good night for me."

"I will." He hesitated for a second, unsure whether he was being too familiar. *To hell with dating protocol.* "Will you text me when you get to your house? I just want to know you got home safely."

"I'll also text you if my car breaks down in the middle of the road." Her smile widened until her dimple appeared, and Michel questioned the wisdom of his decision not to kiss her again. "Maybe Sophie could come rescue me, all badass."

"Don't get stranded." Before all his good intentions came to naught, Michel carefully turned Emma away from him and nudged her toward her car. "Get home safe. Text me."

Michel was still watching Emma's car disappear down the street when Sophie came to stand next to him.

Looking out onto the street, she crossed her arms over her chest and said with an approving nod, "I like her."

"That's only because she thinks you're badass." He arched his eyebrow at her.

"Don't be jealous, my prince," she deadpanned. "I promise to tone down my badassery when I'm around her."

Michel scoffed with royal disdain but was secretly grateful for his friend's promise. It would be hard enough capturing Emma's heart in two months without her being distracted with a girl crush on Sophie. He shook his head at his own foolishness.

"Let us head back to the hotel, Captain Bellevue"—he grinned—"where you can rest your badassery for the evening."

"Of course, Your Highness." Sophie rolled her eyes deferentially.

"I like her, too," he said as they walked to their car.

"I know." She stared straight ahead, but he felt a featherlight nudge of her elbow on his arm. "And she likes you."

Michel didn't even know what it felt like to have true privacy, but if anyone had to invade his privacy, he was glad that it was his badass friend.

CHAPTER SEVENTEEN

♡

I have a confession to make," Michel said close to her ear as the lights dimmed for the previews. "I've never been to a movie theater."

"What?" Emma spun in her seat to stare at him. "Never? Not even once?"

She added *Never been to the movies* to the list of their outrageous incompatibility. *Filthy rich, Lives in another country,* and *Has a bodyguard* were the other items on the list. *Never had Peruvian food* and *Has a hard body* didn't make the list for obvious reasons. Since she couldn't gather enough evidence on their last date, she'd had to come on another date with him. Hopefully, this would be their last.

The fact that Michel had a bodyguard because he was from an "influential family" made her succumb to the temptation to google him. But the only Michel Chevaliers she found—who were alive—were older, white-haired men. None of them from Rouleme. She wasn't too surprised to find nothing on her Michel, though. If his father was so overprotective that he needed a bodyguard, it didn't make sense for him to risk exposure with an online presence.

Speaking of bodyguards . . . she turned and waved at Sophie two rows behind them. The badass bodyguard gave her a regal nod of acknowledgment. They barely had time to say hello before taking their seats, but Emma already liked her. She wouldn't play high-stakes poker with the woman, but Sophie Bellevue had kind eyes.

"Never, ever." Michel closed the three inches of space between them with a soft kiss and leaned back with a lazy grin.

"Do you not like movies?" She swept her tongue across her still-tingling lips.

"No, I quite enjoy them." He reached over and grabbed some of her popcorn. "When I have time to watch a movie, I usually do so in our . . . home theater."

"Well, that's convenient," she quipped, and mentally added *Has a home theater* to the list. "I bet you don't have movie theater popcorn at your house."

"No, we don't." He chewed thoughtfully, then swallowed. "Did you say this isn't real butter?"

"Nope." She munched on some popcorn saturated with fake butter. "It's some sort of mysterious butter-like substance. Kind of icky but oh so delicious."

"I've been missing out." With a broad grin, he nabbed another oily handful from her popcorn bucket. There was no doubt he was from a different world, but she couldn't help but notice that he seemed enthralled by hers.

"You know it." Smiling back at him, she offered him some of her blue raspberry slushie.

Emma watched mesmerized as he leaned close and took the straw between his lips. It was indecent how sexy he made everything look. Or she might just be hyper horny for him. She definitely did not recognize this side of herself.

"That's quite interesting." He coughed into his fist and

smoothed his expression to hide his utter disgust at the syrupy drink.

"Nah, it's gross." She giggled at the relief on his face. "But it's a nostalgia thing. Even though my taste buds have outgrown it, I still get slushies whenever I come to the theater because it made me so happy when I was a kid."

"Gross or not, I like things that make you happy," he murmured before turning his gaze to the screen.

Her heart fluttered wildly in her chest. *God, the things he says.* But she couldn't let herself get distracted. She had to compile a bulletproof list of why they were incompatible so she could return to the matseon circuit as soon as possible. Every day she spent dating this man meant more time for the Crones to sully Auntie Soo's reputation. Her godmother didn't deserve that, and Emma couldn't afford to lose any clients to their smear campaign.

She shook her head. There was nothing she could do about that right now. She might as well enjoy the movie as well as her date. She saw no reason not to have fun while compiling her incompatibility list.

Emma sighed and leaned back in her seat. She loved watching previews. They were the best morsels of a movie stitched together to hook you in mere minutes. Unfortunately, she didn't catch a single one, because she couldn't take her eyes off Michel, the lights of the silver screen playing across his handsome face.

But she pulled herself together—unwilling to waste the fortune it cost to watch a movie—and laid her head on Michel's shoulder to make herself stop ogling him. He wrapped his arm around her shoulders and tucked her close to him. With a happy sigh, she turned her attention to the feature film. A space opera with major Jane Austen vibes. It was excellent.

They took their time getting out of their seats and filing out of the theater. As they stepped out into the night, Emma realized she had to cross out *Never been to the movies* from her list. This was going to be harder than she thought.

"So how did you like your first time at the movies?" She linked her arm through his.

"Other than the sticky floors?" he deadpanned.

She bumped him with her shoulder. "Haha."

"It was fantastic." With a broad smile, he tugged her closer to his side as they made their way to her car. "The company might have had something to do with it."

"Careful with the compliments." She ducked her head to hide her blush. "I might get used to it."

"I see no problem with that," he said, dropping a kiss on her temple.

She stiffened, because she saw major problems with getting used to his warmth and affection. But he might be someone who opened up easily to other people—someone who wasn't afraid to let people into his life. She bet he was this sweet and charming to everyone around him. She shouldn't take things so seriously. It didn't mean anything.

"So what else haven't you done?" she asked with an overly bright smile.

"There's so much . . ." His shrug looked a little lonely.

"Like?" she softly prompted.

"Like . . . I've never run a marathon before."

She gave him the side-eye. "No, I mean stuff that normal people do."

"Normal people *do* run marathons." Michel returned her side-eye.

"Now you're just talking nonsense." She scrunched her lips to the side as she considered the options. "Have you ever gone bowling?"

"No, I haven't." He didn't sound *quite* appalled.

"Fine. Putting on stinky shoes worn by the masses was more torture than leisure for me, too." They arrived at her car, and she pressed her key to unlock it.

"May I drive?" Michel asked with a touch of eagerness.

"You've never driven before?" Her mouth fell open.

"Of course I've driven before." He rubbed the back of his head. "I just don't get to do it very often."

"What's *not very often?*" She squinted at him and added *Doesn't get to drive very often* to the list. Living in LA, she had to drive every day.

"It's been a couple of years," he mumbled, picking invisible lint off his slacks. "Perhaps several years."

"I feel for you"—several years was a long time—"but I also love my car."

"I assure you I'm an excellent driver." Milk-chocolate puppy-dog eyes implored her.

"Are you sure this is a good idea?" Sophie said sternly from behind Michel.

"You could follow us in my car." His lips quirked. "I promise I won't try to lose you."

"Oh, you could try." His bodyguard arched an eyebrow. She was so badass that Emma wanted to squeal.

"Emma?" The puppy-dog eyes returned full force.

"Okay, okay," she grumbled, but had to laugh at the look of boyish delight on Michel's face. "Where do you want to go?"

"I have absolutely no idea." He sounded incredibly excited about the prospect of having no destination in mind.

"I know." If driving was a special treat for Michel, then Emma would show him one of the best drives in Los Angeles. "We'll head to Mulholland Drive."

"Mulholland Drive?" he asked, opening the passenger-side door for her. "I've never heard of it."

"Well, aren't you lucky I'm a local." She winked at him before sliding into her seat. She was so excited to share the experience with him that she almost forgot to add *Never been to Mulholland Drive* to the list.

"Indeed I am." He flashed her a grin that made her heart trip.

While Michel rounded the front of her car to get into the driver's seat, she pulled up the directions on her cell. She rolled down the window and shared it with Sophie. With one last bemused look at Michel—which he studiously avoided—his bodyguard went to retrieve his car parked a few spaces away.

"Shall we?" he asked after adjusting the seat and the mirrors to fit his much taller frame.

"Sure." She wasn't anywhere close to sure. "I'll be your navigator."

Michel backed out of the parking spot in a smooth arc and maneuvered her car out into the street. She guided him through a few turns until they were headed in the right direction. He couldn't seem to stop grinning. While he drove a bit on the fast side, it was with enough confidence that Emma soon relaxed her death grip on her armrest. If he wasn't so well mannered, he would be sticking his head out the window and whooping up a storm.

"I hope you're not regretting this." He glanced at her, then quickly turned his gaze back to the road.

"Not at all." Emma couldn't stop smiling back at him. "You really are an excellent driver."

"Thank you." He reached for her hand and gently squeezed it. "We make a good team."

"We do," she murmured, squeezing his hand back. "Have you visited LA before?"

"Yes, on a few occasions." He peered at the directions on her cell phone, which she'd stuck on the magnetic mount on her dashboard.

"We still have a few miles to go before our exit." She hadn't forgotten about her navigator duties. "Did you do much sightseeing when you were last here?"

"Unfortunately, no." He shrugged. "I came here for . . . business, so there wasn't much time for anything else."

"I had a feeling that might be the case." She snuck a peek at Michel's profile but quickly turned away before she lost her train of thought. He was much too gorgeous for her to stare at him and talk at the same time. "Let's do the LA version of 'What haven't you done before?'"

"As sad as it sounds, I don't even know what I've been missing out on." His low chuckle made goose bumps prickle across her arms. "Why don't you tell me some of your favorite things to do in Los Angeles, and I'll tell you whether I've done them or not."

Michel looked at the rearview mirror and frowned. Emma turned to look outside the rear window and said, "She's two cars behind us. Oh, she's making a lane change . . . Damn, did she just cut that car off? And . . . she's right behind us now."

"That's Sophie for you." He shook his head but couldn't keep the fond smile off his face.

Not for the first time, Emma noticed that their rapport didn't seem purely professional. "You guys seem close."

"We are," he said. "We grew up together."

She wasn't exactly jealous. Emma felt . . . envious that Sophie had known Michel for so much longer than she had—so much longer than she would ever know him. She doggedly pushed the thought away.

"Okay. Back to things to do in LA." She cleared her throat and adjusted her seat belt. "Have you ever been to the Griffith Observatory?"

"No, I haven't," he said without hesitation.

She tapped her chin with her index finger. "How about the Hollywood Bowl?"

"Can't say that I have."

"No? Hmm. Let's see." She pursed her lips. This was almost too easy. She might have to bind the list into a book at this rate. "You must've been to the beach."

"I've been to the French Riviera, which is known for their pristine beaches." He paused. "But I haven't actually *been* to the beach in the traditional sense."

"What's the traditional way to go to the beach?" Her eyebrows drew together.

"Probably to walk on the sand. Maybe even go in the water?"

"Wait." She put her hand on his arm. "I was actually talking about LA beaches. Are you telling me you've never been to a *single* beach?"

"Like I said, not in the traditional sense." He sounded aggravatingly nonchalant about never having experienced the joy of going to the beach. "I believe I've had drinks or perhaps even dined at beachside restaurants or residences."

"There's only one way to go to the beach," she nearly shouted. "To actually *go* to the beach."

"Then, no. I've never been." He glanced at the navigation. "We get off at the next exit?"

"Yes, sorry. In half a mile." Emma sighed. "I don't know if I want to play this game anymore."

"Why not?" Checking that Sophie was right behind them, Michel exited the freeway with some harrowing lane changes.

"I don't know." She should be happy she got further confirmation that they'd led completely different lives. But Michel seemed to have missed out on so many of life's simple pleasures that her heart ached a little. "I think it's safe to assume that you haven't tried anything I've done in LA."

"Well, isn't that a good thing? We have so much to experience together for the first time. People who've led similar lives with similar experiences miss out on the thrill of discovering new things together—experiencing each other's firsts together." He sent a meaningful glance her way as they turned onto Mulholland Drive.

She'd never thought of it that way. That a shared experience could be more memorable. That a different background could sometimes be a good thing. Unwilling to concede the point, she mumbled, "Hmm."

After a stretch of silence, Michel asked hesitantly, "May I ask why . . . why you want a perfect-on-paper husband? Why common background and data-based compatibility are so important to you?"

"I don't want what happened to my parents to happen to me." She tried to sound matter-of-fact, but her voice shook a little. "They fell in love and got married even though they were incompatible in many ways. When they fell out of love, their marriage just . . . crumbled. They became strangers to each other."

"But there are people—"

"I know some people find love and happily ever after. But not everyone." She sighed and looked unseeingly out her window. "I'm just not willing to take that risk with my heart. I don't need a broken heart to set me back from achieving my dreams."

Michel's hands clenched on the steering wheel, then relaxed as he exhaled a long breath. "And what dreams are those?"

"I want to open up a culinary school." She smiled, glad to move on from the uncomfortable topic. "I can't take many clients, because I can only teach one-on-one lessons in my home kitchen. But if I lease a commercial kitchen space and start a culinary school, then I could take so many more students. Touch so many more lives."

"You really love what you do, don't you?" His voice sounded faraway, as though he was deep in thought.

"Yes, I really do." If she meant that, she should try harder to prove their incompatibility. She should be impatient to return to her arranged first dates so she could ensure that she could open her culinary school as soon as possible. But even that reminder wasn't enough to fire up the necessary urgency.

"I'm sure I've done things that you haven't tried." Michel spoke up suddenly with boyish excitement. "Not specific to Los Angeles, of course."

"Like what?" Her ears and curiosity perked up.

He seemed distracted by the winding road for a moment. "Have you ever done archery?"

"Archery?" He had her there, but she wasn't ready to admit it. "I dressed up as Legolas for Halloween when I was in eighth grade. Does that count?"

"Legolas?"

"Oh God." She grabbed her forehead. "Please don't tell me you haven't read and/or watched *The Lord of the Rings*."

"Okay. I won't tell you." He smirked. "But we're talking about things *you* haven't done, remember?"

"Fine, I haven't done archery before." This wasn't as fun when he was the one pointing out the things she'd missed out on.

"How about horseback riding? Wait." His eyebrows furrowed. "Is there anywhere to go horseback riding in Los Angeles?"

"Of course there is." She had a friend who grew up in a house in Rolling Hills with an actual stable. "There's a city about twenty miles south of LA that has a famous bridle trail."

"And?"

"And what?" she stalled, but he pressured her with his silence. "Okay, okay. I haven't gone horseback riding either. Wait! I rode on a pony when I was in preschool. I don't remember it very well, but there's a picture of me riding one, with a cowboy hat and everything. That counts, right?"

"Hmm." He pretended to consider her question. "Did the pony move at any point you were on it?"

"As a matter of fact, it did," she said triumphantly. "The handler walked the pony in a little circle around the playground."

"All right. Let's say that counts." He shot her a playful grin.

"There's no *let's say* about it." She crossed her arms. She didn't know why she was adamantly arguing something that proved they had something in common. "That totally counts."

"But I do think you would enjoy a real ride." Before she could think of a smart-ass response, Michel inhaled sharply. "Mon Dieu. This is stunning."

Too busy winning the argument, Emma hadn't noticed the view outside. When she looked out the window, she remembered exactly why she loved this drive so much. The dark, winding roads took them higher up into the hills, and the city spread out below them like a silky black blanket with a million pinpricks of starlight in them.

"It is, isn't it?" she whispered.

"Absolutely stunning," he repeated, his expression soft with wonder.

He slowed the car to a crawl to keep the city lights in sight longer. She bit her bottom lip and dragged her teeth over the tender flesh. God, he was so sweet.

"There's a lookout point." She sounded like a Marilyn Monroe impersonator. "Turn into that parking lot."

Michel parked the car and killed the lights, bringing the sparkling city below into sharp relief. The dimly lit lot was dotted with cars here and there, but it wasn't crowded being a weeknight. Still gripping the steering wheel, he leaned toward the windshield to get a better look. "I never knew that Los Angeles was so beautiful."

"It's an amazing place." She smiled fondly. "Once you look past the superficial glamour, there is so much beauty to be discovered."

They sat in companionable silence as they took in the view. He might be onto something about experiencing each other's firsts together—how it was a good thing. Sharing his first time on Mulholland Drive made the experience feel brand new to her as well. Not only that, this experience was now *theirs*—a newly forged common ground. The beginnings of somewhere that they could both put down their roots.

Whoa. What was she even thinking? No one was putting their roots down anywhere. But she wanted to kiss him. She wanted to shake him. Why did he have to come into her life right now? Why did he have to make everything so complicated? Why did he have to be so wonderful?

"Sophie's parked a few spots away," she said to remind herself that they weren't alone—to dislodge the contentment cocooning her.

Michel nodded at his bodyguard, and she nodded back, then turned her attention to the view. They weren't strictly alone, but Sophie was pointedly giving them privacy. *Dang it*. Emma worried her bottom lip as her pulse quickened with anticipation. Kissing Michel was exciting and frankly addicting, but she had to focus on gathering evidence so she could stop seeing him. An ache burrowed into her chest at the thought.

"Is it hard?" she blurted. "Being from your family."

"It could be challenging at times, but every family has their issues." Her question wasn't well thought out, but Michel seemed to understand her meaning. "I don't want to claim that my life is more difficult than anyone else's."

"I don't know." She studied his face in the muted glow of the city lights below. "It seems like you missed out on so many experiences. Simple things that give . . . regular people moments of joy. But I can see that those experiences wouldn't be *simple* for you. I mean, you can't even leave your hotel room without your bodyguard. It must be suffocating at times."

"At times," he murmured, looking out at the view. "But most times, I'm grateful for the opportunities I have. Being in my family means my life is governed by more restrictions than most, but I also have experienced things that I otherwise would never have."

"Do you ever wish that things were different?" she said in a near whisper. Why was she asking him this? Was she the one who wished that they weren't so different? "Do you ever wish you had a 'normal' life?"

"No, I don't wish for a different life." He finally turned to face her, and she met his eyes. "I sometimes envy the freedom others enjoy, but those moments are fleeting. I'm grateful for my life and look forward to doing my part to make a difference in the world."

"I want to make a difference in the world, too. A culinary instructor probably won't make as big an impact as an international relations expert"—she waved his protest away—"but I want to do my part to help people find happiness. In my own way."

"That's an admirable goal." The intensity of his gaze made her hold her breath. "And I know you will be amazing at it."

The sincerity of his words brought tears to her eyes, and all she could do was nod. How could being with someone so different from her feel so easy . . . so right? Emma sat up with a start. *No, not right.*

"It's too dark now, but during the day, you can see the Hollywood Bowl and the Griffith Observatory just up those stairs." She swept her hand across the view, shaking off her disquiet. "We could've checked three things off your list all in one shot."

"Where's the fun in that?" He captured her hand from the air and linked their fingers together. "We'll take our time and enjoy every one of them together."

"But time is the one thing we don't have." Emma wished she could snatch the words back as soon as they left her mouth.

"Maybe it doesn't have to be that way." Michel lifted their hands and kissed the backs of hers, soft and lingering. "Emma . . ."

What could he mean? Her heart pounded against her rib cage like it was trying to burst free and run away into the night. It didn't matter. She didn't want to know. Before her conscience could tell her what a liar she was, Emma closed the distance between them and kissed Michel until she couldn't think about anything at all.

CHAPTER EIGHTEEN

♥

Have you told her?" Gabriel demanded as he pulled out a chair across from Michel at his usual table at the hotel café.

"Why don't you order a drink first?" Michel said with exaggerated solicitude. "You might get parched from lecturing me."

"Cut the bullshit." Gabriel's anti-bullshit glare transformed into a charming smile when their server came over to their table. "Hello, Anne. I'll have a double espresso."

"You got it," she said with a cheeky wink.

While the two of them flirted shamelessly, Michel sipped his green tea—he was a sentimental fool—and enjoyed his brief reprieve. As anticipated, the smile melted off his cousin's face as soon as their server walked away.

"Don't bother telling me you're not head over heels for her." Gabriel resumed berating him as though there was no interruption.

"Anne is an excellent server, but head over heels might be an overstatement." Michel adjusted the cuffs of his shirt.

"You're not as witty as you think." Gabriel narrowed his eyes. "People just feel obliged to laugh at your jokes."

"What people? You're the only person I joke around with," he muttered.

The comment hit too close to home. Other than with his family and a select few friends, Michel could never be sure how genuine people were being—never know what effect his crown was having on their interaction. Which was precisely why he needed more time with Emma before he told her the truth. He needed to know what she felt for him was for *him* and not the crown.

"By people, I mean *me*," his cousin clarified—taking the sting away from his comment—and promptly blew out a frustrated breath. "Goddamn it, Michel. I can't believe you put me in this position. I hate being the voice of reason. It's unbearably boring and frustrating."

"We've only been on three dates." Three incredible, unforgettable dates. But even so. He wanted *more* before he risked losing it all. "I still have much to consider."

"You've been talking my ears off—nonstop—about this woman." Gabriel threw his hands up. "What more do you need to know?"

"For one, I haven't even met her family." All he knew was that Emma was an only child and she lived with her father. He wanted to meet the man who had brought up such an amazing woman. "Maybe I should meet some of her friends as well."

"Since when did any of that matter to you? If you're going to start considering her family background and standing in society, you might as well marry Isabelle."

"I had no idea the voice of reason was so irritating." Michel pinched the bridge of his nose. He couldn't care less about background and standing. He just wanted to find out everything about Emma while he was simply Michel Chevalier. He ignored the small voice telling him that he was being selfish. And he didn't want to listen to his cousin's wise counsel either. "Please do shut up."

"Fine. I'll stop." Gabriel ran his hand through his perfectly styled hair, making it perfectly mussed. "But don't come crawling back to me when this whole thing blows up in your pretty face."

"Pretty? That's just blatant flattery."

"Fuck you."

"You mean 'Fuck you, *Your Royal Highness*,'" Michel whispered even though the tables near them were unoccupied. "America has done a number on your manners, my dear cousin."

"Pulling rank on me at a time like this is a sign of weakness." Gabriel smirked, relaxing into his seat at last. Officially relinquishing his role as the reasonable cousin, he scanned the lobby, taking care to look extra bored, and failed spectacularly at pretending to *not* search for Sophie.

"She's on the other side of the lobby today," Michel said with a smug grin. "Want to go say hello?"

"That's the last thing she'd want me to do." Something vulnerable crossed his cousin's face before his mask of cynical ennui returned. "Besides, I don't want to distract the woman while on duty. That would be tantamount to putting your royal arse on the line."

"My royal arse would be fine for five minutes." Michel huffed a frustrated sigh. "Are you ever going to tell me what the hell is going on between you two?"

"Sophie might be under the impression that I abandoned her when I left Rouleme without asking her to come with me," Gabriel said blandly as though he was remarking on the weather.

"What?" Michel had no idea what he was expecting, but that was not it. "What?"

"Which is completely unfair, since she never would've agreed," Gabriel muttered, warming up to the topic. "She always made it clear that her loyalty lay with the crown."

"You two were together all those years ago?" He floundered to wrap his head around the idea.

"Nothing clear-cut like that. It was new. We were young." His cousin gave him a pointed look. "We'd only gone out on a few dates."

Michel ignored the dig and leaned into his indignation. "I can't believe you didn't tell me, all these years."

"Of course." Gabriel managed to look chic and sophisticated while rolling his eyes. "Because it's all about you."

Michel didn't bother flipping off his cousin. He should've been there for him. "I could've helped you."

"There was nothing you could've done." Gabriel raked his fingers through his hair again, and this time a strand of hair dared to stick up out of place. "Like I said, she would never have come to the US with me."

"How do you know when you didn't ask?" Michel prodded gently, seeing that the conversation wasn't easy for his cousin.

"Because I know her. I was in love with her since we were ten." Gabriel huffed a humorless laugh. "Do you know how hard I had to work to get her to go out with me? She wouldn't have uprooted her entire life to start anew here. Besides, I couldn't ask that of her. It would've been too selfish of me."

"I'm sorry," Michel said sincerely, even as he fought to not see the similarity between his cousin's past choice and the one he would have to make in less than two months. But leaving one's home for an uncertain future was different from leaving to become a queen. Who wouldn't want to be a queen? The thought didn't sit right with him, but he resolutely returned his attention to their conversation. They were talking about Sophie right now, not Emma.

"It all happened a long time ago." His cousin waved aside his apology.

Michel couldn't help but ask, "Do you still love her?"

"It broke my heart to lose her"—Gabriel swallowed—"but Sophie and I are living the lives we were meant to live."

Michel nodded. That was the closest thing to an answer he

would get from his cousin. He had to respect that. Even though he wished he could do more for him. Even though Gabriel and Sophie deserved so much better.

"How are you enjoying your sightseeing adventures?" His cousin changed the topic as he drained the espresso Anne had brought him earlier.

"Let's just say I'm beginning to understand why you chose to put your roots down in Los Angeles."

"*Of all places.*" Gabriel grinned, the shadows beginning to recede from his eyes. "It's a gem with endless facets to discover and experience."

"And you get to be *you* here." The familiar envy tugged at Michel.

"I'd be me anywhere I am." His cousin held his gaze. "The crown doesn't erase who you are, Michel. I wish you could see that."

"Perhaps my problem is that I don't really know who I am, with or without the crown." Michel straightened his teacup, staring down at his lukewarm drink. "Am I the sum of my father's and my country's expectations? Is that all I could ever be?"

"Most days, I don't know whether to pity you or envy you. But make no mistake. You are in a position that gives you the power to make real change in Rouleme—in the world."

"I thought you were tired of being the voice of reason." Michel smiled, grateful to have his cousin by his side.

"I wasn't being the voice of reason. I was just being your wiseass cousin."

"Thank you for being a wiseass." He raised his teacup in wry salute.

"Anytime." Gabriel inclined his head like true royalty.

Michel's pulse jumped when his phone vibrated in his pocket, and he pulled it out in record time. His shoulders slumped when he saw who it was.

"Yes, Antoine," he responded with an apologetic look at his cousin. "Is this something urgent? This isn't a good time to talk."

"I wouldn't have called if it wasn't urgent, Your Highness." His assistant used the formal address without irony, but Michel was conditioned to feel chastised by it from all the time he'd spent with Sophie lately.

"I apologize for doubting you," Michel said, switching to French. "What is it?"

"The ministers are balking at the social services addendum you proposed."

"That addendum was passed last winter." He stood from his seat and nodded his goodbye to Gabriel. "It was meant to go into effect next month."

"Go." Knowing the drill, his cousin shooed him off with his hand. "I got the check."

Michel walked away from the table, clapping Gabriel on the shoulder. Sophie appeared by his side as he headed toward their elevator. She arched an eyebrow in question, and he shook his head.

"They're claiming that there is a discrepancy in the proposed budget." Antoine sighed. "It's an obvious delaying tactic. They're taking advantage of your absence, Your Highness."

"But Toulouse gave me his word." Michel cursed under his breath as the elevator shot up to their floor.

"And the minister is trying to keep it," his assistant said. "But the old-timers are ganging up on him."

"I want to see this alleged discrepancy in the budget." Sophie wordlessly followed him to his door and held it open for him. "And set up a call with Toulouse."

"For when?"

"Right this damn minute," Michel snapped as the door closed behind him.

"Of course, my prince," Antoine said with calm efficiency.

"I've emailed you the documents already, and I'll track down the minister in person if I have to."

"Good." Michel inhaled through his nose and got control of his temper. "Thank you."

"It's my honor, Your Highness. I will update you as soon as I have the call scheduled."

Michel threw his mobile on a side table and walked to the window overlooking Downtown Los Angeles. His time in America was not a vacation. It came with a price he couldn't ignore. Would all this be worth it if he couldn't win Emma? He wouldn't trade a single moment he'd shared with her for the world, but that wasn't enough. His people needed him—especially the single mothers and their children that the addendum was supposed to benefit. He clenched his fists. He had to make his time away from Rouleme count.

CHAPTER NINETEEN

♡

*W*ho needs Disneyland when you have H Mart?

Well, there was no rule that Emma had to choose between the two. All she meant was that H Mart was *amazing*. It was her happy place. She could easily spend two hours just browsing the Korean market, picking out the freshest whatever-she-needed and trying all the yummy samples offered by the nice ajummas scattered around the store. And it was beyond awesome that shopping at H Mart was part of her job.

Midmorning was her favorite time to shop. It was less crowded, and there was a better chance that everything would be freshly stocked. She pulled out a crumpled piece of paper from the pocket of her wide-legged pants. Her grocery list. It was old-school, but it worked. She liked writing out her list in the order of the market layout and seeing the whole list at one glance. The apps on her cell were fine, but they all required scrolling up and down, which meant she could easily miss an item on the list. She didn't have the luxury of running out to buy a forgotten item during her lessons.

Today, she needed every texture of tofu offered—firm, medium, soft, and extra soft. Her favorite brand of medium-firm tofu had been fully restocked. She didn't bother holding back her smug smile. But when she reached for a package, another hand grabbed the same one. She was too polite to say *What the hell?* but seriously. What the hell?

She turned to her supermarket rival to courteously ask them to remove their grabby paw from her tofu, but burst out laughing instead.

"Oppa." Emma pressed a hand to her chest. "What are you doing here?"

"What else? I'm stalking you." Jeremy enveloped her in a bear hug and lifted her off her feet.

"How did you know I was here?" She hugged him back, then wiggled to be released.

"You're a creature of habit." He stepped back, grinning ear to ear. "And my mom has your weekly routine memorized. I'd be a little creeped out by that if I were you."

"Auntie Soo loves collecting data. Call it an occupational hazard. It's what makes her such a great matchmaker." Emma loaded sixteen packs of tofu into her shopping cart. "Besides, I like having her keep tabs on me. It's her love language."

"I'm a little concerned about your relationship." Her god-brother scratched his jaw. "It isn't entirely healthy."

"You're a pediatrician." Emma patted his shoulder. "Leave psychology to the professionals."

"God, I missed you, brat." He ruffled her hair, and she slapped his hand away.

"You still haven't told me what you're doing here." She pushed her cart toward the produce aisle. "I thought you were busy setting up your new practice in San Jose."

"My partners and I had the brilliant idea to take turns with some much-needed vacation before we officially opened the doors." Jeremy kept pace with her as she browsed. She usually liked to stick to her planned menu, but the napa cabbage looked too good to pass up. "It's my turn to take the week off while they cover for me."

"Auntie Soo must be thrilled to have you home." She grinned happily at Jeremy.

"Just look at that dimple," he cooed, tapping her cheek with his index finger.

"Cut it out, dingus." She shoved him half-heartedly. He'd been teasing her about her dimple ever since she could remember. "I can't believe parents trust you with their children."

Emma called him her godbrother because he was her godmother's son, but he was basically a real brother to her. They grew up together—the best of friends and the worst of enemies like any other self-respecting siblings. She loved him to death, but he annoyed the hell out of her.

"My mom wants you and your dad to come over for dinner tonight." Jeremy gently bumped her out of the way and commandeered the quickly filling cart.

"Um, I can't." She cleared her throat. "I already have dinner plans."

She and Michel had been spending almost every evening together—creating a bulletproof list of incompatibility took a lot of work—but he'd had to cancel last night because of an emergency at work. She wasn't sure what kind of emergencies arose for international relations professors—did a country need his expertise in a diplomatic nightmare?—but she felt more disappointed than she'd thought possible. She didn't want to cancel their date tonight. Because postponing the date meant spending another day away from the matseon market. Obviously. She had Auntie Soo's reputation and her culinary school to think of . . . Guilt twisted in her stomach at the lie.

"Oh?" Jeremy wiggled his eyebrows. "What kind of dinner plans?"

"Stop being weird." Emma willed herself not to blush. "I'm just meeting up with a friend."

"What kind of friend?" The eyebrows continued to wiggle.

"Ugh. You're such a dork." Then panic pierced her. "Don't tell your mom."

"Don't tell my mom what?" His eyes widened with surprise. "Are you really seeing someone? I was just messing with you."

"No. It's nothing. Just . . . don't." She stopped in the middle of the spice aisle. "Please, oppa. I don't want to upset Auntie Soo."

"Okay. Here's the plan, kiddo." Concern replaced the mischief on his face. "When you're finished with your shopping, we're going to drop everything off at your house, then have a nice long lunch."

"But—"

"This isn't a negotiation," he said firmly. "I want to know everything I'm not supposed to tell my mom."

"Just . . . ugh." The last thing Emma wanted to do was talk about her . . . whatever . . . with Michel. It was hard enough ignoring her own mind's attempts to talk some sense into her. "Promise you won't pull some big brother bullshit on me."

"Nope. Not making that promise." Jeremy shook his head. "I one hundred percent reserve my right to pull all the big brother bullshit I see fit."

"Fine, but we're not going to have a nice long chat over lunch." She pointed toward the meat section. She didn't want to wait an hour, agonizing over what her godbrother would say. Time to rip the bandage off. "I told your mom I'd marry a perfect-on-paper man she matches me up with, but I'm secretly dating this guy I met at a hotel café."

"You agreed to what?" He almost hit her with the shopping cart as he spun to gape at her.

"There was a thing with the Crones and Auntie Soo's Achilles' heel and . . ." Emma waved her hands in front of her face. "Never mind all that. That's not important. The point is I'm going to date the man from the café until I convince myself that we are utterly incompatible. It shouldn't take long. Then I'll resume the matseons to marry a nice Korean American man from a middle- to upper-middle-class family that I have loads in common with. There is absolutely no need to worry Auntie Soo over any of this."

Jeremy dug the heels of his hands into his eyes. "Are you done with your shopping?"

"Almost." She gave him a wary sideways glance. "Why?"

"Because H Mart doesn't feel like the most appropriate place for my big brother bullshit," he said through gritted teeth.

Emma opened and then closed her mouth. Talking right now might not be to her advantage. Her godbrother would calm down once everything sank in. He would realize that it was *not* a big deal. They would laugh about it together.

She finished shopping with a very serious and very silent Jeremy by her side—two adjectives that she never thought she would use to describe him. With his jaw clenched hard enough to crack a molar, he loaded her trunk with all her shopping bags and turned to her.

"Is Samchon home?" he asked.

"My dad's having lunch with some of his old coworkers." She peeked at her phone. "He probably left by now."

"Good." He nodded curtly. "I'll follow you."

That didn't sound good at all. If she didn't have a trunk full of food that needed refrigeration, she would've made a run for it. Instead, she drove docilely home, with her godbrother on her tail.

Emma was hoping her dad's lunch got canceled or something, but his car wasn't in the driveway when she got home. With a sigh, she popped her trunk, gathered her shopping bags with Jeremy, and headed to the front door. She felt like a prisoner walking to the gallows as she led him into the house. Waving a weary hand toward the kitchen stools for him to take a seat, she put away the groceries.

Even with trepidation dogging her, Emma enjoyed putting everything away in its proper place, nice and tidy. She finished sooner than she wanted and turned to face her godbrother.

"Do you want some tea before you start your interrogation?" she grumbled.

"You've never mentioned wanting to get married," he said with uncharacteristic sternness. She guessed he didn't want any tea. "Not once."

"I was never against marriage. I think there's a certain charm about building a life with someone and creating a happy home together." She went to stand across the island from him. "And I always assumed that your mom will find me my ideal match eventually."

"How did *eventually* become *now*?" Jeremy's voice softened a smidgen. "What changed?"

"Well, it provided an efficient solution to a problem." She shrugged with more nonchalance than she felt. "Never mind that part. It doesn't really matter *when* I get married. I was going to do it someday anyway."

"Marriage should be about love and happiness." He huffed an impatient sigh. "You talk about it like it's some inconsequential checkbox to tick off before continuing with your life."

"You're exaggerating. I know it's an important decision." She rubbed at a stain on the quartz counter before she realized it was part of the pattern. "I just don't think marriage has to mean *everything*."

"So is that what you want? To marry some *nice* man my mom matches you up with?"

"Someone who's compatible to me in every way." She raised

her index finger for emphasis. Compatibility was *key*. Love and attraction faded, but you could always fall back on a common background. "Someone who has so much in common with me that we would never drift too far apart."

"And who is this *guy* you met at the hotel café? What the hell do you mean you'll date him until you convince yourself that you two are incompatible?" Jeremy's voice rose along with his obvious frustration. "What did you say before? That you wanted to marry some 'nice Korean American man from a middle- to upper-middle-class family'? Why can't *he* be that someone?"

"Because he's a filthy-rich European man who I plan to prove has absolutely nothing in common with me." She blinked away the sudden tears that threatened to fall. What was wrong with her? Jeremy was just aggravating her. That was all. "But he *is* very nice."

"Fine. There's something very wrong with your logic in all this. But fine." Her godbrother scrubbed his face with both hands like it wasn't fine at all. "Then why are you dating the guy in the first place? Why do you have to prove to yourself that he has nothing in common with you?"

"Because he was becoming an unwelcome distraction to my efforts to find a perfect-on-paper husband." She smoothed out her shirt to avoid her godbrother's bewildered gaze. Explaining her reasons out loud made them sound less than logical. "I figured once I went out on a few dates with him and proved that we were hopelessly incompatible, he would be out of my system and I could focus on my matseons."

"Why draw a line in the sand like that?" Jeremy tilted his head to the side.

"Because." Emma threw her hands up, dangerously close to tears again. "He's a visiting professor at USC. He's going back to his country in a couple of months."

"Even knowing he won't be around for long, he wanted to . . .

what . . . have a fling with you?" Her godbrother's mouth twisted with distaste.

"No, he's not like that," she countered, automatically defending Michel. "What I mean is . . . he wanted to spend time with me even if it's only for a short while. And . . . I like him, oppa. I really like him."

"Then why can't you leave all the options open? That's what I don't get." He dragged a hand through his hair.

"What options? Leave my life here and follow him to Rouleme? What about my business? What about my dad? I can't abandon him." She wrapped her arms around her midriff. "Besides, didn't you hear a single word I said? He and I have *nothing* in common. I'm not going to make the foolish mistake of 'following my heart' like my parents did."

"Oh, Emma."

"Don't." She held up her palm. She did not need his sympathy. "Don't you dare venture into psychology again. I know what I'm doing and why I'm doing it. The only reason I told you any of this was because you're like a brother to me and I badly needed to vent. I don't need your permission, and I don't want your advice."

After a pause, Jeremy arched an eyebrow and said, "I thought you were trying to buy my silence."

"That, too." She shot him a grateful smile. He wasn't going to push her any further.

"I assume that means you're going to whip up something droolworthy for me."

"You assumed right." Emma rubbed her hands together. Their talk had drained her emotionally, and she needed to recharge with some comfort food. "Kalguksu?"

"Hand-cut noodle soup?" Jeremy pursed his lips. "I was hoping for lunch, not dinner."

"Give me forty-five minutes."

"I knew you were good"—he whistled under his breath, shaking his head—"but not that good."

"What can I say? It's a gift," she said primly.

Her godbrother chuckled and stood from his stool. "How can I help?"

"You can help knead the dough in a second." She pulled out a mixing bowl and a bag of flour. She added a sprinkle of salt and splashes of ice water until a rough dough formed. "Here. I need you to knead this until it's smooth and stretchy. Put some elbow grease in it. It'll make the noodles chewier."

Jeremy rolled up his sleeves and did as he was instructed. Satisfied with his progress, she filled a pot with water for the broth. She pinched her lips to the side. Seafood broth would be best. It was rich, flavorful, and quick. Her shoulders fell away from her ears and the knot in her chest disappeared as she relaxed into the cooking.

"Just so we're clear," he said, "I need to meet this fancy European guy of yours."

Annnnnd . . . her shoulders stiffened right back up. But how bad could it be? Michel was a nice guy. Jeremy was a nice guy. It would be fun.

CHAPTER TWENTY

This Jeremy bloke was something else. If he glared any harder at Michel, Sophie might have to jump in front of him to bodily block the death ray. But Prince Michel had years of practice at civility and propriety. If he could smile and play nice with greedy, conniving foreign officials who wanted to take advantage of Rouleme, Michel could endure an hour or two of Jeremy and his homicidal eyes. For Emma.

Even in the smoky, raucous Korean barbecue restaurant—the last one in Los Angeles permitted to use lump charcoal indoors, per Sophie's research—Emma looked impeccably poised and beautiful in her white off-the-shoulder jumper and black jeans. But she still fit in seamlessly at the no-frills restaurant.

When the server came to grill the meat for them at the table, Emma politely waved her away. "That's all right. I'll cook for our table."

"You just can't help yourself, can you?" Jeremy grinned when the server left with a shrug. The murderous light evaporated from his eyes when he looked at Emma. "You need to relinquish control sometimes. The servers are professionals. You can trust them with cooking our meat."

Michel's eyes narrowed at the easy way the other man teased Emma. They were undoubtedly close, but how close?

"It's not that I don't trust them." She placed long strips of marinated boneless beef rib onto the sizzling grill. "I just enjoy doing this."

Jeremy rolled his eyes, and she elbowed him in the ribs, then went right back to grilling the galbi. Michel's eyebrows furrowed into a faint frown at their antics. He was being ridiculous. They were friends. That was how close friends acted with each other. Right? Impatient with himself, Michel turned his focus on Emma as she laughed and talked while expertly flipping the meat and cutting it into bite-size strips with a pair of kitchen shears. *Fascinating.*

Emma caught his eyes and smiled a little shyly at him. His answering grin was full blown and ridiculous. Her lashes fluttered down as she returned her focus to dinner, but Michel couldn't look away. His gaze slid to her creamy bare shoulders and lingered. Suddenly, the delicious grilled meat in front of them didn't tempt him. All he wanted to do was bite the soft curve of her shoulder and lick away the sting. His mouth watered with the hunger to taste every inch of her.

"Okay." Emma sat back and spread her hands toward the grill. "Help yourselves. We need to get it off the grill before it burns."

Without stuffy decorum, she and Jeremy began piling the meat onto their plates. After a couple of seconds, he and Sophie followed their example. His friend was a more accomplished chopstick wielder, but Michel managed not to drop any meat on the table. He carefully picked up a perfectly cooked piece with his chopsticks and popped it in his mouth. It was a literal flavor explosion. The sweet and savory marinade added to the richness of the generously marbled beef, and the meat melted in his mouth with hardly any assistance from his teeth.

"This is fantastic." He reached for another piece of galbi. "What's in the marinade?"

"I don't know their exact recipe, but it's generally soy sauce based with sugar or honey—sometimes people use grated Asian pears or apples—garlic, onions, and toasted sesame oil," Emma said. "Do you really like it?"

"How could I not?" And he liked every minute he spent with her—he liked *her* more every minute. His gaze lingered on her face until she blushed, but he couldn't look away.

The side of his face prickled with some sort of premonition—or perhaps a sense of self-preservation—and he reluctantly broke eye contact with Emma to meet Jeremy's stinging gaze. The death ray had intensified into a weapon worthy of Armageddon. Michel swallowed his annoyance at the other man's antagonism and prepared to offer his best diplomatic smile, but it died on his lips when Jeremy gave the barest shake of his head. Was he warning Michel off Emma? Something snapped in him at that.

"Tell me, Jeremy," he drawled. "How exactly do you know Emma?"

"My mother is her godmother." It was impressive how Jeremy managed to enunciate with his jaws clenched so tight.

Emma glanced warily between them as though sensing a storm brewing.

"So, you're a family friend of sorts," Michel said blandly.

"I'm basically her older brother." The other man's nostrils flared like those of a bull being taunted by a matador.

"*Basically* is a far cry from *actually*." Michel bared his teeth at him in a not-so-diplomatic smile.

An angry flush rose up Jeremy's neck, but he seemed to check himself and leaned back in his seat, slinging an arm across the back of Emma's chair. "In some ways, *basically* is much better than *actually*."

It was Michel's turn to see red. His hands clenched into fists, and he leaned forward. He wasn't sure what he could do with an open-fire grill between them. Perhaps he could cautiously reach across the table to smack the smirk off the other man's face—anything to get him to drop his arm from Emma's chair.

"Michel." Sophie placed a firm hand on his forearm.

"Are you guys for real?" Emma snapped at the same time. With an impatient huff, she shoved a too-big piece of galbi into her godbrother's mouth. "Eat, dingus."

Jeremy dropped his arm from her chair and chewed his meat with a sullen scowl. Michel lowered his eyes to his plate, bemused by his own behavior, and took a deep, calming breath.

Deliberately ignoring the two chastised men, Emma smiled at Sophie. "How are you enjoying dinner?"

"I've had Korean barbecue before, but this is exceptional," Michel's royal guard said as she slowly withdrew her hand from his arm.

"It's the lump charcoal—sutbul." Michel loved how Emma's eyes lit up when she talked about food, especially Korean food. "There's nothing quite like the smooth, smoky flavor it adds to the meat."

Michel opened his mouth to speak, but Sophie shot him a look that told him he hadn't earned his right to talk yet. She turned her attention back to Emma. "I read in my research—sorry, I'm a bit of a nerd—that Korea has the greatest number of distinct cuts of beef in the world."

"That's right." Emma beamed at Sophie like she was her star pupil. "Each cut of beef has such different textures and flavors, especially when they are flash grilled at the table like this. It's an art and a science that Koreans pursue relentlessly."

Sophie raised her shot glass filled with fiery soju. "I have to salute that."

"Hear, hear." Emma clinked her glass to Sophie's and tilted back the potent liquor, and Michel's royal guard followed suit.

When Sophie gasped, blinking back tears, Jeremy laughed as he refilled her empty glass. "If you're not accustomed to soju, I would take it easy the first time around. It hits you fast and hard."

"A little late for the warning," Sophie said hoarsely, drinking ice water to soothe the burn.

"Take it easy, my ass. Don't listen to him, Sophie." Emma grinned slyly. "Michel can be your designated driver for tonight."

"I'd be happy to drive," he offered without hesitation. His friend could use a real night out. Even if she didn't show it, being his one-woman security team was a tremendous strain on her.

"That won't be necessary." Sophie shot him a cutting glare that rivaled Jeremy's. Her narrowed eyes seemed to say, *You dare question my professionalism?* "I'll be drinking water for the rest of the evening."

"So how do you guys know each other?" Jeremy asked.

"They're childhood friends," Emma rushed to answer for them. "They happened to come to LA at the same time."

Michel glanced at Sophie, who shrugged. Emma had quietly insisted on Sophie sitting with the rest of them when they'd arrived at the restaurant. It made sense. It was easier to have Sophie just be his friend than to discomfit Jeremy by telling him she was his bodyguard.

Across the table, Emma snickered at something Jeremy said. They seemed exceptionally close. They even had their own unique vocabulary for bickering and teasing each other. Michel wasn't at all sure he liked it, since Jeremy was *basically* but not *actually* her brother, as the other man had so helpfully pointed out.

Michel's index finger tapped restlessly on the table as he watched their interaction with growing ire. Was he jealous? He *was* jealous. He'd never considered himself a possessive man, but his body shook with the raging need to shove Jeremy away from Emma. *She is mine.*

"Please excuse me for a moment." He stood abruptly from the table and bolted for the lavatory.

What was the matter with him? Staring at himself in the mirror over the sink, Michel raked his fingers through his hair and tugged on a handful. He had to snap out of this. Did love make a thoroughly reasonable man lose his shit? *Was* he in love? He paced the small space of the men's lavatory.

This was beyond forgetting himself in the moment like kissing Emma in the middle of the street. His control was truly slipping, and it terrified him. He'd arrogantly believed that he would be spontaneous and let love *happen*, all the while having full control of his emotions and actions. He'd been an absolute fool. He wasn't even sure he was in love with Emma, but he already felt well and truly wrecked.

As he continued pacing, he caught a glimpse of himself in the mirror and started. He was smiling. As his mind caught up with his heart, Michel felt a reckless calm settle over him. A woman who made him feel this way had to be worth it. He was still terrified, but he welcomed the feeling—he embraced the uncertainty—because no one ever said love would be easy. After splashing some cold water on his face, he walked out of the lavatory.

Jeremy stood guard in the hallway. "I thought you were pretending to go to the restroom to pay the check."

"Why would I go behind everyone's backs like that?" Michel blinked. "I would've offered to pay when they brought out the check."

"Because it's the oldest trick in the book." Jeremy scoffed in disbelief. "Paying for the meal is a matter of honor for Koreans, and we're not above engaging in subterfuge to have that honor."

"I apologize for not understanding the seriousness of the matter." Michel chuckled, remembering what Emma had said to him the first time they met at the café. *We're masters at paying the check before anyone else.* "But it would be *my* great honor to treat everyone to dinner."

"Too late, my friend." Jeremy's grin was all savage glee. "*I* paid while you were in the restroom."

"Thank you for holding back your evil cackle," Michel said dryly. When he turned to go back to the table, the other man placed a hand on his shoulder.

"What are your intentions toward Emma?" he asked solemnly.

Michel was taken aback, but he didn't hesitate before answering, "The most honorable."

"How honorable can it be if you're planning to leave her in two months?" Jeremy sounded exasperated. And genuinely concerned.

"I'll be leaving *America* in two months. Not Emma," he said fiercely. "Temporary is the last thing I want."

"That's not what Emma thinks." Jeremy held his gaze a moment longer, then sighed. "At least, that's not what she wants to believe."

Michel blocked the other man's path as he made to walk out of the corridor. "What do you mean?"

"Unbelievable." Jeremy smirked. "You're going to have to work a lot harder to earn my trust. Until then, you're not getting any more intel on Emma from me."

The insufferable git. He had not been trying to get intel out of him. The man had offered the enigmatic statement on his own and Michel merely sought clarification. He still couldn't decide whether Jeremy was being a good friend or if he was jealously guarding Emma.

"Were you two fighting over the check?" She gave them a stern frown when they returned to their seats.

"Nah." Jeremy leaned back in his chair and flicked imaginary dust off his shoulder. "I wouldn't call that a fight. He didn't even realize I'd paid for everything when he saw me standing by the cash register."

This bloke was too much. And he was standing outside the lavatory, not beside the cash register, when Michel saw him. What a pompous, juvenile piece of—Emma's laughter brought his train of thought to a halt. Was she laughing at him? With Jeremy? Something inside him curled in on itself.

"You know what would really be funny, oppa?" She examined her fingernails for a second, then looked Jeremy in the eyes. "If Michel said, 'Well, actually, I bought the entire restaurant.' *That* would be funny. Because he *can*."

Michel blinked. Jeremy blinked. Sophie . . . snorted? Michel didn't feel triumphant that Emma stood up for him and put the other man in his place. Instead, something warm and aching spread through his chest. He had always been protected from physical threats, but people believed him to be invulnerable to petty hurts. The equanimity and . . . yes, the arrogance . . . instilled in him stopped him from expressing his true feelings, especially soft and frivolous feelings such as hurt and disappointment.

But that wasn't how Emma saw him. All she saw was Michel Chevalier—someone human enough to feel the dig of insults, someone human enough to deserve her protection. Gratitude and greed filled him. *This.* This was what he stood to lose the moment he told Emma that he was the crown prince of Rouleme.

Everything would change once he became Prince Michel to her. She might be angry at first, but he wasn't too worried about that. She would come to understand his reasons for the secrecy soon enough. But she would never look at him the same way again. People looked at Prince Michel with fascination and calculation—a mixture of awe and avarice. They saw him as someone they could gain something from.

To Emma—at least for now—he was just Michel. A person with vulnerabilities and insecurities like everyone else. He was starved for the kind of genuine affection that she offered. He didn't want to let this go. He wanted . . . no, needed . . . to stay Michel for as long as possible.

"What is it you Americans say?" Sophie couldn't hold back her smirk as she held out a fist to Emma, who bumped it with relish. "Burn."

"Ladies"—Jeremy put a theatrical hand to his chest—"you wound me."

"Nobody likes a bully, oppa." Emma grinned and gave his shoulder a light punch.

"Yeah, sure. Your boyfriend's rich, and I'm just a lowly pediatrician. You sure put me in my place." Her godbrother tousled her hair. "I apologize for flaunting my prowess at paying for dinner on the sly. I admit he was an unsuspecting opponent."

Michel found Jeremy slightly less irritating when he took being ganged up on by the two women with good humor. But something Emma said niggled at the back of his mind. Oppa? Was that some kind of nickname she had for him? And Jeremy became thoroughly irritating again.

"What does 'oppa' mean?" Michel asked casually. Or attempted to. The slight arch of Sophie's eyebrow told him that he'd failed miserably.

"It literally means 'older brother,' but it's also just what you call someone who's older than you," Emma explained, her head quirking to the side. "Well, what a younger girl calls an older boy. But not a lot older, because then you would call him 'ajeossi.' Ugh. It's a little complicated."

"Oh? How old are you?" He assumed she was in her midtwenties, which put him squarely in the *older male* category—but hopefully not old enough to render him an ajeossi.

"Twenty-eight." Suspicion narrowed her eyes.

"I'm thirty-four," he said meaningfully.

Jeremy burst out laughing. "It's a Korean thing, man."

"Well, I'm learning more about your culture"—he spread his hands—"such as the honor of paying for your party's meal, so I don't see how this is any different."

"You want me to call you 'oppa'?" Mischief swiftly replaced the surprise on Emma's face. "I'll call you 'oppa' when you're being an exasperating ass . . . oppa."

"Fair enough." Michel chuckled, jealousy at last loosening its grip on him.

"But it'll be a shame." She glanced up at him from underneath her lashes. "Because I like saying your name, *Michel*."

His sheepish laughter died in his throat, and his mouth dried up. He was suddenly done with this meet and greet. He wanted Emma alone.

"Then I'll take great care not to be an exasperating arse, because nothing's sweeter than hearing you say my name," he murmured in a low voice.

Emma's lips parted on a quick intake of breath, and a blush blossomed on her cheeks. Their gazes locked, and their surroundings seemed to melt away. His throat worked to swallow as the urge to touch her became nearly unbearable.

"For Christ's sake," Jeremy hissed.

"My sentiments exactly," Sophie said dryly.

Michel gave his head a sharp shake in an attempt to regain his composure. They were in the middle of a crowded restaurant with Jeremy and Sophie at their sides. He shouldn't be giving serious consideration to reaching across the table to kiss Emma senseless over burning charcoal. But she held his eyes, ignoring their friends. When her lips curved into a soft smile, full of promise, Michel gave up trying to break free of her hold. It was a losing battle from the start.

With a long, heavy sigh, Sophie said, "Thank you so much for dinner, Jeremy."

"My pleasure," he replied with smooth charm. "I hope to see you again soon."

"Your—" Sophie swallowed the *Highness* that nearly slipped and came to stand at his side. "Michel."

He got to his feet and held out his hand to Emma. When she stood and placed her hand in his, he pulled her to his side and looked at Jeremy.

"Thank you for dinner. I'll see Emma home." His tone brooked no argument, but Jeremy didn't seem like a person who took note of such things. Even so, the other man folded his arms across his chest and gave Michel a curt nod without further argument. The concerned glance he shot Emma eased much of the wariness Michel felt toward him. "It was nice meeting you."

"Same here." After a pause, Jeremy added, "Maybe next time, I'll let you grill me for more intel."

"I wasn't trying to grill . . ." Michel trailed off as he noticed Jeremy's grin. "You know what? I might take you up on that."

"That intel better have nothing to do with me," Emma warned, tugging on her hand. He tightened his grip and tucked her close to him. "Besides, I wouldn't trust that guy if I were you."

"What? Nonsense." Jeremy walked out into the street with them past the crowd of people waiting for an open table. "I'm the most trustworthy man you'll ever meet."

"Only an *un*trustworthy man would say something like that." Emma grinned until her dimple winked. "Good night, oppa. Thanks for dinner."

Jeremy waved over his shoulder as he sauntered to his car. Michel led Emma in the opposite direction, where they had parked his car.

"Do you want to come over for a drink?" He wasn't ready to

say good night to her. The desire that flared between them was banked to quiet embers, but it still burned in his blood.

But he sobered at the stern warning in his head. *You need to tell her before this goes any further.* His hand tightened unconsciously around hers. He couldn't wait until she fell in love with him—*if* she ever did. Besides, how true would that love be if she fell for him, knowing only a part of him? And how true could he claim his own affections to be if he kept his identity a secret any longer? It didn't matter how much he longed to remain just Michel Chevalier. He needed to stop being selfish. She deserved to know.

"Just for a drink?" Emma looked up at him.

God, he hoped for so much more, but he made himself say, "Maybe some dessert?"

"I can't say no to dessert." That sultry smile curled her lips again.

"Good," he said thickly.

She leaned close and whispered in his ear, "We can do *other stuff* after dessert."

He tripped over his own foot. If it wasn't for her hold on his hand, he might have fallen flat on his face. Once he regained his balance, he made a run for his car, tugging a laughing Emma along his side.

Sophie caught up with them. "What's the hurry?"

Looking down at Emma, Michel answered, "I might die if I don't get some dessert as soon as humanly possible."

CHAPTER TWENTY-ONE

♥

Emma wanted Michel. She thought a few dates would be enough for her to get him out of her system—enough to convince her that their attraction was fleeting. She thought with no common background, she wouldn't enjoy his company after the first spark of interest faded—that every new difference she discovered between them would dull his charm.

Well, she thought wrong. Every day she spent with him, experiencing his *first times* together, made her crave more, and her desire for him only grew stronger.

Maybe she wouldn't be able to get him out of her system until she gave in to their attraction. Sharing *that* first time with him might be the only way she could move on. She had never felt this way about another man. And there was no guarantee that she would ever feel this way again. What were the chances she would have this kind of white-hot chemistry with her perfect-on-paper husband? An arranged match was not based on passion after all.

There was a certain grace to going with the flow. She didn't want to be left to wonder what it would be like—to be left with regrets. She wanted to surrender to the desire and see where it led. Emma prided herself in leading her life with purpose and effort—her every choice well thought out and deliberate—but in this instance, she wanted to stop thinking and weighing. She wanted the mess, imperfection, and freedom of letting go. Just this once.

With her mind made up, she deserved a medal for not jumping Michel in the back seat of the car. She liked Sophie too much to force her to sit through that. But Emma was relieved when her new friend bid them good night in the foyer and headed for her suite.

"Shall we?" Michel's voice was low and intimate as he held open the door for her.

Even though it wasn't her first visit, the elegance and opulence of the presidential suite awed her anew. The expansive view of the city lights drew her to the floor-to-ceiling windows wrapped around the living room. As she stared into the night, she ran her hand down the thick ivory curtain pulled to one side, which was as heavy and soft as she'd imagined.

Michel came to stand behind her—not so close that he crowded her but close enough for her to feel the heat coming off his body. She reached her hand behind her until he clasped it, and she tugged him closer to her. Then she leaned the rest of the way so the back of her body was pressed against the front of him and dropped her head against his shoulder. His free hand curved around her waist, his touch firm enough to feel possessive, and her breathing grew shallow.

"Do you ever get tired of this view?" she asked to distract herself from the nerves quaking in her stomach.

"Not tired"—his eyes met hers through their reflection in the window—"but it pales in comparison to the view I'm beholding now."

She didn't even try to fight the blush rushing to her cheeks. Too shy to speak, she pulled his arms tighter around her and laid her hands on top of his. He lowered his head—his jaw and then cheek brushing against her temple—until his lips traced the curve of her ear.

"Ready for your dessert?" His warm breath made her shiver. She turned around in his arms to claim his lips, but he stepped back from her and tucked her hand into the crook of his elbow. When she blinked up at him, he said with a boyish grin, "This way."

Emma gasped as they walked into the dining room. The table was lined from end to end with gorgeous desserts of all kinds—from perfectly ripe strawberries to Sachertorte—and a bottle of champagne sat chilling on ice.

"How did you manage this?" she whispered.

"Sophie's a good friend." Michel cleared his throat. "I asked her to make a quick call before we headed back to the hotel."

"She's an *amazing* friend." Emma smiled up at him, placing her hand on his chest. "It's a shame this isn't the kind of dessert I'm craving right now."

"Wait. I want you . . . more than you can know . . . but I need to tell you something first. The *something* isn't bad, but it might change things between us." He raked his fingers through his hair. "God, I don't want things to change."

Emma didn't want things to change either, especially not now. She slid her palms up his torso and wound her arms around his neck. His eyes darkened, and his tongue flicked out to wet his lips. The practical side of her brain told her to hear him out, but her body only wanted him. She felt intoxicated with lust, and she liked it. But he tucked his hands into his pockets and held himself stiffly away from her.

"Emma, please. If I kiss you now, I won't be able to stop. I—"

"Perfect." She rose to her tiptoes and drew his head down until they shared each other's breath. Whatever he had to tell her could wait until she satisfied this roiling need inside her. He said it wasn't *bad*, right?

Michel gave in with a helpless groan. His mouth claimed her as he spun them around and pushed her back against the wall. When she parted her lips to invite him in, he didn't hesitate, and plunged his tongue into her mouth. She moaned, digging her fingers into the thick softness of his hair. His hands finally escaped the confines of his pockets and roamed her body like he wanted to touch her everywhere all at once.

No hint of his polished demeanor remained as he wrapped her leg around his waist and ground his hips against her, pinning her to the wall. He growled his pleasure against her lips, and she grew a little wild, her hands fisting in his hair. An affronted gasp escaped her when he broke the kiss, but he moved his mouth down the length of her neck, and her skin heated from his hot breath. His fingers dug into her waist when his lips arrived at the soft curve of her shoulders.

"God, what is this . . . jumper?" he rasped, sounding tortured. "These shoulders have been driving me out of my mind all night."

He none too gently scraped his teeth along one shoulder, making her hiss and writhe against him. He licked away the sting with leisurely strokes of his tongue. Then with one rough tug, he pulled her top down to her waist, trapping her arms by her sides and exposing the lacy strapless bra cupping her breasts. Slowly, too slowly, he trailed hot, open-mouthed kisses down her chest until he reached the mound of her breast.

"Michel," she breathed. "Please."

"What do you need?" He dipped his tongue under the top of her bra and swept it across her breast. So close but not close enough to the aching tip. "This?"

"More."

Emma arched her back and thrust her chest into his face. She whimpered with relief and anticipation as he hooked his finger into the cup of her bra and tugged it down. Just as his lips brushed the hard tip of her breast, someone pounded on the door loudly enough to rattle its frame.

The pounding was soon accompanied by a booming voice. "Michel. Open the fucking door. I need to speak to you."

Michel straightened and ran a hand down his face, muttering a string of curses. When his fingers grazed her sensitive skin as he straightened her clothes, she sucked in a sharp breath. His lips curved into a crooked smile even though he was clearly frustrated with the interruption.

"I'm sorry." He placed a lingering kiss on her forehead. "I'll be right back."

He walked out of the dining room at a clipped pace, and she heard him throw open the door. "This had better be—"

"Mother's coming," the other man said, cutting him off.

"Aunt Celine? Coming? To Los Angeles?" Michel's voice rose with each question.

"Yes, yes, yes." The door clicked shut, and footsteps clacked across the hardwood floor.

"But why?" Michel said. "She hates Los Angeles."

"I don't know. She suddenly decided I don't visit Rouleme often enough, so she is coming to me."

"Christ, Gabriel." Michel's voice had returned to its normal decibel, but the panic remained. "She could . . . complicate things."

"For both of us."

"You still should've come back another time like I asked you," Sophie said stiffly. Emma didn't realize she'd come, too. *Great.* Was anyone else coming? Right, Aunt Celine. She leaned her head against the wall, blowing out a frustrated breath. "This conversation could've waited."

"Waited?" the man called Gabriel roared. "She is going to board the plane in less than three hours."

"Three hours?" Michel croaked. "Why wasn't I informed of this? If the king—"

"Michel." Sophie spoke over him as Emma tried to remember whether Rouleme was a monarchy. "Perhaps you two should have this conversation in private."

"What? This *is* private." Gabriel sounded confused. "And like I said, this can't wait."

Emma sighed, shoulders drooping in disappointment. It didn't sound like Michel's guests were going to leave anytime soon. And she couldn't hide out in the dining room forever, listening to what was meant to be a private conversation. So, after running her hands down her hair and making sure all her clothes were in order, she stepped out into the living room.

She cleared her throat to alert them to her presence. Michel spun around to face her as though he'd forgotten she was there. Not very flattering, considering where they'd left things, but he still wore a panicked expression. This Aunt Celine must be a force of nature to shake him up so much. Emma forgot about her frustration at the interruption. She wanted to pull him into her arms to ease his anxiety about whatever was happening.

"You know my mother will . . ." The tall, raven-haired man trailed off as his green eyes landed on Emma and widened. She stared right back. He was ridiculously attractive. "That is . . . she . . ."

Silence descended in the room as everyone collectively scratched their heads as though they had no idea what to make of her. *Awkward.*

"Hi, I'm Emma." As she took an uncertain step toward the trio, the gorgeous newcomer blinked awake and a warm smile spread across his face.

"It's a pleasure to finally meet you. I've heard so much about you." He walked the rest of the way to her and held out his hand. "I'm Gabriel."

"Nice to meet you, too." Emma shook his hand, feeling a bit

dazed by the brilliant flash of his white teeth and the piercing green of his eyes.

"He's my cousin." Michel came to stand beside her and planted a hand on her lower back. Gabriel noticed his possessive touch, and his grin broadened. With mischief glinting in his eyes, he held on to her hand a second longer than necessary until Michel continued in a clipped tone, "He's also a professor at USC. He teaches philosophy."

"Wait, you're not . . . Are you Professor *Gabriel* Laurent?" Emma gaped at him. Michel shot her a surprised glance. "You're the . . . *Sphinx*?"

"You know who I am?" His cousin's eyebrows furrowed in confusion.

"My friend Sarah Bae is your TA." Maybe she shouldn't have called him the Sphinx to his face, considering her friend was the source of that information. "She . . . she speaks very highly of you."

"Is that so?" Gabriel said with a bemused twist of his lips.

"Uh-huh." Emma nodded enthusiastically, hoping to smooth over her faux pas. "She said she was learning so much from you. Sarah loves being your TA."

"Hmm." The Sphinx didn't seem sold.

"Don't mind him. He isn't *all* that petty," Michel said in a stage whisper. "He just likes to speak in impossible riddles."

"That will be all, wanker," Gabriel retorted with an imperious wave of his hand. "Now, leave me in peace to get to know the lovely Miss Emma."

Michel shook his head in feigned disgust, even as a smile tugged at his lips. An incredulous laugh huffed out of Emma. With their wry humor and irreverence, she could tell the two men would be trouble together. It was yet another side of Michel that she was discovering for the first time. She should probably be worried that she liked each new side of him better than the last, but she couldn't stop the affection stealing into her heart.

"I'm surprised you have time to flirt, Gabriel." Something sharp lined Sophie's voice, and her poker face took on a hard edge. "I thought you had an urgent matter to discuss with the . . . with Michel."

"It's called avoidance." Gabriel winked at Sophie, which made her narrow her eyes into slits. Emma had the good sense to be terrified, but his smile only grew wider. "Knowing my mother, she won't be up for another hour. I'll call her then and have a heart-to-heart with her. For now, I'd like to have a nice visit with Emma."

"Thank you so much for the dessert, Sophie," Emma blurted, desperate to disperse the tension in the room. "Speaking of which, why don't we go have some now? There's plenty for all of us."

"I don't want to intrude," the other woman said stiffly.

"Come now, Sophie. What's the harm in having dessert with us?" Gabriel's voice was a velvety purr. "I promise I won't bite."

"No, you won't"—her hands fisted at her sides—"because I'll knock every one of your pretty teeth out if you do."

Gabriel didn't even flinch. "Are they?"

"Are they what?" Sophie spat.

"My teeth. Are they pretty?" He practically fluttered his eyelashes. Growling in disgust, Sophie spun on her heels to leave, but he caught her arm and said in an abruptly subdued voice, "Don't leave. I'll behave."

Sophie looked poised to shake his hand off and walk away, but she heaved a deep breath and turned around instead. Not looking at Gabriel, she headed for the dining room and announced to no one in particular, "I'm staying for the crème brûlée."

Emma raised her eyebrows at Michel, curious to death about the vibes between Sophie and Gabriel. He shrugged and shook his head in a way that said *I don't have the faintest clue*. He was no help. How could he not know what was going on between his cousin and his bodyguard? Well, she would go straight to the source.

She caught up with Sophie and linked her arm through hers. "I'll share my sticky toffee pudding if you share your crème brûlée."

The other woman offered her a rare smile. "Deal."

Emma hadn't forgotten what she and Michel had started in the dining room. But if she couldn't satisfy *that* craving tonight, she might as well nose around the intriguing dynamic between Michel's rakish cousin and his stoic bodyguard. She might even have some choice relationship advice for Sophie. After all, Emma was a relationship expert by proxy.

CHAPTER TWENTY-TWO

Y ou need a better plan, Gabriel," Michel murmured quietly.
"A heart-to-heart with your mother isn't going to stop her
from boarding that plane."

Even as he spoke to his cousin, he couldn't help glancing at
Emma across the table. Her head was bent close to Sophie's, her
dimple winking in and out as she laughed. His heart seemed to
melt and break at the same time. He couldn't believe how close
he'd come to making love to her in the very room where they all
sat right now.

He was betraying her trust by keeping his identity a secret
from her. He couldn't betray her further by sleeping with her
before telling her who he really was. But was his title what made
him who he really was? *No.* He was his truest self with her—in
ways that he could not be with anyone else. He liked who he was
with her.

Wasn't it the whole point to allow her to get to know him
without the inevitable complications his title wrought? Didn't
they deserve to see where this led without those obstacles? He
wanted to hold on to the simplicity of their budding romance—to
hold on to being just Michel Chevalier for as long as possible.

But regardless of what he wanted, Emma deserved to know the truth before their relationship went any further. That was what mattered the most.

"I'll figure it out." Gabriel didn't sound particularly confident.

"You'll figure it out?" Michel scoffed. "You were ready to break down my door half an hour ago."

"That was before I knew you had more pressing concerns," his cousin said with a subtle tilt of his head toward Emma. "I apologize for the interruption, by the way."

"I'd rather be interrupted by you than Aunt Celine," Michel muttered. "Which brings me back to my point. You need a better plan."

"What I need is a miracle." Gabriel dragged a hand through his hair. "Once my mother makes up her mind, no one could dissuade her."

"We'll find a miracle worker, then." Michel lowered his voice. "If she comes to Los Angeles, you and I will be outed in a matter of hours."

"You underestimate my mother." His cousin laughed with doomsday humor. "It'll happen in a matter of minutes."

Michel felt Emma watching him and met her gaze. She offered him a sweet smile while nodding at something Sophie said. His gaze snagged on the plush curve of her lips, and he remembered how she'd caught fire in his arms. For a wild moment, he contemplated kicking everyone out to resume what they had started. But he nipped that thought before it could take root. He couldn't make love to her until he told her the truth. Even as he steeled his resolve, his body yearned for her, and he shifted uncomfortably in his seat.

"Would anyone like some champagne?" He needed to distract himself. "Emma?"

"I'll take a glass." Her cheek dimpled again. God, he really

liked her dimple. As he gaped at her like a fool, the champagne
bottle hung limply from his hand.

"Why don't I get that?" His cousin took the bottle and opened
it with a soft pop. He poured Emma a glass first. "Sophie?"

"No, thank you." She shook her head. "I'm not off duty yet."

"Still as dedicated as ever," Gabriel said, pouring two flutes
of champagne and handing one to Michel.

If he didn't know his cousin inside and out, he wouldn't have
caught the slight edge in his words. Sophie stiffened in her seat.
It seemed she knew Gabriel as well as he did.

When Emma rose from her seat after taking a sip of her
champagne, he and his cousin shot to their feet with manners
ingrained in them.

Her eyes widened in surprise. "I just . . . um . . . where's the
bathroom?"

"Let me show you." With a hand on her back, Michel led her
out of the dining room. They walked wordlessly across the living
room to the hallway. He stopped just outside of the bathroom
and cleared his throat. "Emma, I apologize—"

She opened the door and shoved him inside before launch-
ing herself at him, her lips crushed against his. He backed into
the wall to stabilize himself and cupped her face to kiss her back
as electric heat combusted between them. If a single kiss could
make him feel this way, what would it be like to claim all of her?
He wanted her—all of her—right now.

He grabbed her arse and hauled her up against him. She
moaned and ground her hips against him, making him growl
low in his throat. Their teeth clacked as their kiss grew desperate
and clumsy. It wasn't until her trembling hands fumbled with his
belt buckle that he came to his senses. He was past the point of
caring about Gabriel's and Sophie's presence across the suite, but
he refused to make love to Emma for the first time in a bloody
bathroom. And not before he told her the truth.

Michel gripped her wrists even as he continued kissing her hungrily. But with the last of his willpower, he slowed the kiss down. If he didn't, he would lose the little bit of sense he had left and bury himself inside her next to the toilet. *Fucking hell.*

"Emma," he rasped when she tugged his head back with a whimper. He gave in and kissed her hard once before pulling away again. "Emma, I will never forgive myself if I make love to you for the first time in the damn loo."

"This is a fine little room," Emma countered, quite out of breath. "Fine enough to take afternoon tea in."

He chuckled and pressed his forehead against hers. They stayed that way until their breathing slowed. He dropped a kiss on top of her head and let his hands trail down her arms before turning away from her. But Emma grabbed his hand before he could walk out.

"Soon," he rasped, doggedly facing the door.

Michel wasn't sure if he was relieved or disappointed when she released his hand. He didn't linger to ponder the matter, and stepped into the hallway, closing the door behind him for good measure. He had to put as much distance as possible between Emma and himself before he barged back into the bathroom. He made a mad dash for the dining room and burst in there like his salvation lay inside. But he skidded to a halt when Gabriel and Sophie jumped at his sudden appearance. His cousin dropped his hand from Sophie's cheek, and her half-closed eyes snapped wide open.

"What . . . Were you . . . Should I . . ." He jerked his thumb toward the living room. The tension between the two felt palpable. What the hell had he walked into? They weren't kissing . . . Were they about to?

"My prince. I mean . . . Michel." His royal guard scrambled to her feet. "I . . . I will stand guard outside in case you need any further assistance."

Sophie rushed past Michel before he could respond. He wasn't sure if he *could* respond. He had never seen his friend lose her composure. With his mouth still gaping, he turned to his cousin.

"I guess we're even now." Gabriel's cheeks were flushed, but his sardonic smirk was back in place.

"So I *did* interrupt something," Michel murmured, almost to himself.

"Yes . . . no . . ." His cousin plowed his fingers through his hair. "Hell if I know."

As Michel moved to step deeper into the room, he felt a hand on his arm. He turned to find Emma standing behind him just outside the dining room. Her lips still looked swollen from their kiss, but she had fixed her makeup and tidied up her clothing. She looked flawless. His eyes dropped to those lips, and he had the urge to muss her up again.

"Michel," she said quietly. "I should head home."

"Yes, of course." He walked her to the front door, keeping a respectable distance between them. He didn't trust himself to touch her right now. "Should I call a car for you?"

"There are such things as rideshare apps, you know." She held up her mobile and gave him a cheeky grin.

"I apologize again for the . . . interruption." He lowered his voice as they stopped at the door. "And I'm sorry I can't see you home."

"No worries." She gave him a featherlight kiss and echoed his earlier promise. "I'll see you . . . soon."

He longed to pull her body flush against his and claim a proper kiss. Instead, he forced himself to hold the door open for her, because *soon* was much more complicated than what he'd led Emma to believe.

Sophie stood outside his suite, her unshakable professionalism restored. He nodded at her. She nodded back, then addressed Emma. "Let me get the elevator."

"Thank you, Sophie," Emma said before looking up at him. "Good night, Michel."

"Good night, Emma." He clenched his hands at his sides so he wouldn't reach out for her.

Michel watched her walk to the elevator and give Sophie a warm hug, whispering something to her. Then she waved at him once and got in the elevator. His royal guard had a smile on her face as she returned to his side.

"Have I mentioned that I like her?" Sophie said, still grinning.

"Once or twice," he replied dryly. "What were you guys talking about?"

"None of your business"—she bowed her head with utmost respect—"my prince."

He smirked. "So you'll tell me all about it later?"

Sophie didn't dignify his teasing with a response as she opened the door to his suite. "Do you need me to stay and help strategize about Princess Celine's visit?"

"Christ, yes. Stay, please." Michel marched into his living room and bellowed, "Come on, Gabriel. We can't let Aunt Celine loose in Los Angeles."

"Why, cousin, you make my mother sound like Godzilla," Gabriel drawled as he walked out of the dining room, spooning chocolate mousse into his mouth. "But I must admit it *is* a rather apt comparison."

Michel snorted, and Sophie ducked her head to hide her smile. A dopey grin spread across Gabriel's face as he stared at her. His cousin was completely besotted with his royal guard. It was so obvious. How could he not have seen it before? He and Gabriel needed to have a nice chat once they put out this fire.

"There is one person who could convince Aunt Celine to

stay," Michel said as the three of them settled around the large sectional.

"Obviously, yes." His cousin dragged a weary hand down his face, his half-eaten mousse forgotten on the coffee table. "But the king has a hard time saying no to his little sister. I don't know if he would intercede on my behalf."

"You know who he has a harder time saying no to?" Michel paused meaningfully. "*Your* little sister."

"Marion?" Gabriel grimaced. "That brat wouldn't help me out of the goodness of her heart."

"No, but she'll do it for a price," Sophie countered.

"You mean like a bribe?" His cousin's eyebrows shot up before his face split into a slow grin. "Now you're talking."

"She's always idolized you, Sophie." Michel leaned back on the sofa and crossed his legs. "Coax her to name her price."

"It won't be cheap." She pulled out her mobile as she got to her feet.

"That's what my dear cousin here is for." Gabriel thumped Michel's back. "I just hope Marion asks for something that Antoine can procure."

Michel cocked his head and glanced blandly at his cousin. "I'm glad you're so comfortable spending my money."

"I wouldn't go as far as *comfortable*, but *untroubled* would be an apt description." Gabriel quickly sobered as Sophie headed to a quiet corner of the living room with her mobile to her ear. "Do you think this will work?"

"It has to. I can't have Aunt Celine descend upon us and blow everything wide open." Michel's eyes rounded in dismay when another thought occurred to him. "God, if your mother catches scent that I'm trying to get out of my engagement to Isabelle, my father will be the first to hear of it, and my time here will be over."

His time with Emma would be over. *Emma.* His breath caught in his throat, and panic lodged itself in his chest. Had he done enough to convince her that they belonged together? No, he needed more time. The thought of leaving without her gutted him. He pressed the heel of his hand into his chest. What was wrong with him? He wasn't even sure if she was the one.

But that wasn't true, was it? He smiled like a fool whenever he thought of her. When she was near, his heart pounded against his ribs as though it wanted to jump into her arms. And when he touched her . . . held her . . . he felt as though he was truly home. If he wasn't in love with her already, he knew he could fall in love with her. She *was* the one. Hadn't he known since their first date?

"Breathe, cousin." Gabriel unfurled himself from the sofa and headed for the wet bar. He returned with two tumblers filled with amber liquid. "This is going to work."

Michel accepted his drink and took a long sip. "Yes, it will."

He would tell Emma the truth and do everything in his power to win her heart. Because life without Emma wasn't an option anymore.

CHAPTER TWENTY-THREE

S o what happened with your aunt's visit?" Emma asked, setting out the food on the table they'd snagged under the shade of a tree. It was a perfect spring day, and a picnic lunch on the beautiful USC campus felt like a treat.

"She decided it'll be best to have Gabriel visit *her* in the summer instead," Michel said, watching her progress. "Did you really make all of this? These dishes look like something out of a cookbook."

She arched an eyebrow at him. "You do remember that I'm a culinary instructor, right?"

"Even so." His boyish grin made her heart trip. "I'm impressed."

"It's nothing." Emma blushed at the compliment and joked, "Just a meal fit for royalty."

Michel made a choking noise beside her and started coughing.

"You okay?" She patted his back. "Do you need something to drink?"

"I'm fine," he wheezed. "Thank you."

Emma clicked her tongue and poured him some warm

cassia-seed tea from the thermos. He took it with a grateful nod. While he caught his breath, she studied the spread in front of them with a critical eye. It wasn't really a meal fit for royalty—she would need three tables and over thirty dishes for a true surasang—but it was healthful and pleasing to the eyes. She gave a nod of approval.

"Here." She handed Michel a small, deep bowl when he set aside his tea. "Start with this."

"What is it?" He brought the bowl to his nose. "It's fragrant."

"It's pine nut porridge," she said, taking a bite of her jatjuk. "It's rich and creamy but also soothing. It's a nice way to ease into a meal."

"It's delicious." His eyes slid closed for a moment. "I could eat a big bowl of this alone."

"You have to save room for the rest of the food." She cleared the empty porridge bowls to the side.

"That's true, since you've brought enough food for five people." He peered at the noodle dish and said, "I think I recognize this one. It's japchae, isn't it?"

"Yes." She beamed at him. The vermicelli with beef and colorful julienned vegetables was a well-known Korean dish, but she was still delighted that he knew what it was called. "You can find it at most Korean restaurants, but I made some for you because it's one of my favorites."

"May I?" He waited with his chopsticks poised over the noodles.

"Of course." She watched him take a bite, holding her breath.

"I've been missing out if this is what japchae is really supposed to taste like." He took another bite and chewed slowly. "It's savory with just the right hint of sweet. And the texture—the soft, chewy noodles with the crisp vegetables—is so satisfying. I could eat this every day."

"Me, too, but it's usually only eaten on special occasions because of all the work that goes into it." She placed a hwayangjeok on his plate. It kind of looked like a two-by-three-inch flag with multicolored stripes and a skewer at the end holding it all together. "Now try this."

"This I've never seen before." He turned the meat-and-vegetable skewer this way and that.

"It's a perfect bite built onto a skewer." She pointed out each of the six ingredients that made up the stripes in the miniature flag. "That's egg yolk, egg white, marinated beef, cucumber, shiitake mushroom, and carrot. Everything is cooked and seasoned separately but made to complement one another's flavors."

"That's like a symphony in my mouth," Michel said after he swallowed. "I don't know if I want to inhale all the food or savor every bite."

"I vote for savoring, but let me point out the rest of the dishes in case you can't control yourself. I'll be quick." Emma laughed. "This is fish jeon, which is bite-size fish fillet battered with flour and egg wash, then pan-fried to a golden brown. Use the soy sauce dip with it. And that's blanched soybean sprouts with toasted sesame oil and green onions, a staple in Korean meals. Oh, and you should have some of this shredded white radish with vinegar and mustard sauce to refresh your palate between the heavier dishes."

She looked expectantly at him, with every intention of watching him eat, but he didn't pick up his chopsticks. Instead, he held her gaze for a moment, then leaned in to kiss her lightly on the lips. "Thank you for all of this. It means a lot to me."

"You're welcome." Her eyes widened as a thought occurred to her. "Does . . . does anyone cook for you at home . . . in Rouleme?"

"We have a chef, but . . ." He shrugged with an elegant lift of his shoulders, but the gesture felt forlorn.

"But this is different," she finished for him.

"When my mother was alive, she used to make crepes with butter and sugar on some nights. We would eat them in the kitchen, and she'd let me stay up way past my bedtime, talking about our day," he said with a faraway smile. "She led a busy life, so it didn't happen often, but I remember those moments so clearly."

"When did she pass away?" Emma linked her fingers through his, resting their hands on his thigh.

"I was nine." His fingers tightened around hers, and she heard all his unspoken words. He might be rich and successful, but no one—other than someone paid to do so—had cooked for him since he was nine years old.

"Eat." She smiled past the tears blurring her vision. "The food's getting cold."

He held her eyes a moment longer, then he plated some japchae for her. "You should eat, too, before I finish all this by myself."

Suddenly, this beautiful man by her side didn't feel like someone from a different world. It didn't feel as though they had nothing in common. The connection between them shone brightly in her heart, strong and tautly tethered.

Somewhere along the line, she'd forgotten about proving their incompatibility . . . too happy to be with him to notice any jarring differences. And she acknowledged for the first time that it would cost her something to lose him. But how much would it cost her? Was this time with him worth the cost?

Sitting side by side beneath a tree heavy with springtime leaves, they enjoyed their picnic lunch with quiet happiness. She couldn't imagine trading this time with him for anything in the world. *And there's my answer.* So practical and smart Emma made the impractical and not-so-smart decision to be with Michel for the remainder of the two months even if it meant it would cost her more to lose him—even if it meant her heart would get broken. He was worth the risk.

As for her godmother's reputation, how much difference could a few weeks make? She hadn't said anything yet about losing clients over the Crones' smear campaign. And even if they ended up losing clients here and there, how much would it affect Emma's goal of leasing a commercial kitchen in the long run?

Her profession was important to her, but she didn't want it to be her everything like for her mom. This time with Michel meant something to Emma. *He* meant something to her. He was worth a bit of delay in opening up her culinary school.

Besides, a few weeks was a very short time in the grand scheme of things. She would enjoy every moment of their time together even though she knew exactly when and how things would end between them. She pressed the heel of her hand into her aching chest. This was enough. It had to be enough.

When they finished eating, she picked up a second thermos filled with ice-cold sujeonggwa—a sweet drink flavored with fresh ginger and cinnamon sticks. "This is dessert."

"It's delicious," Michel said after taking a sip of the translucent burgundy drink. "Everything was delicious."

"Thank you," she said, her cheeks growing warm.

He linked his fingers through hers and dropped a kiss on each of her knuckles. "Will I see you tonight?"

The warm intimacy of his words left little doubt as to what he meant. He wanted to know if she wanted to finish what they'd started last night. God, did she ever. She'd hardly slept the night before because she couldn't stop thinking about the feel of his lips and hands on her.

"I can't tonight," she said with heartfelt regret. "My godmother invited me and my father over for dinner."

"It probably won't kill me to wait to see you until tomorrow. Probably." He groaned, pressing his forehead against the back of her hand. After a moment, he lifted his head with a rueful laugh "If you don't hear from me first thing tomorrow morning, know that I have perished from the wait."

Her huff of laughter turned into a gasp as he brushed his lips against hers. She curled her hand around the nape of his neck in case he got the foolish idea of pulling away from her. He wisely deepened the kiss, cupping her jaw with one hand and tugging her closer with the other. She slid her tongue into the warmth of his mouth, and he suckled gently on it before swirling his own around it.

"You taste like cinnamon. So sweet." His teeth scraped on her bottom lip. "I can't wait to taste the rest of you."

How was she expected to keep her clothes on when he whispered things like that to her? She whimpered and pressed herself closer to him. She wanted to climb onto his lap and grind her hips against him to relieve the pressure building in her core. Without thinking, she tugged his shirt out of his slacks and slid her hands up his sculpted torso. He definitely had muscles that would ripple as he rode a horse bare-chested across a deserted beach.

Emma broke the kiss and snatched her hands out of his shirt before things went too far. Michel stared at her with dazed eyes, his lips wet and swollen from their kiss. He leaned in as though to resume their kiss, and she pressed her hands against his chest. On top of his shirt.

"Michel," she said, ridiculously out of breath. "People might see us. Your *students* might see us."

"I don't . . ." He blinked rapidly with a sharp shake of his head. "Hell."

"I'm sorry. I shouldn't have . . ." She fluttered her fingers toward his disheveled shirt. "You should fix your clothes."

Michel quickly tucked his shirt in and adjusted his slacks against his straining . . . She jerked her eyes away and stared at the leaves above them until she was certain she wasn't going to jump him.

"Emma."

"Yes?" She met his eyes.

"Never apologize for touching me." A corner of his lips quirked up. "And thank you for reminding me about where we were. I seem to lose my mind every time I kiss you."

Her pulse fluttered in her throat. "You're welcome."

"And thank you again for this beautiful picnic." He brushed a soft kiss against her cheek. "It was the best meal I've ever had."

"I guess I overshot it a bit," she teased, crinkling her nose. "I wanted to show off a little, not make it impossible to top myself."

"So we'll do this . . . again?" he asked shyly.

"Yes, Michel." She cupped his face in her hands, her chest clenching into an achy knot. "We don't have a lot of time left, but I intend to feed you well and often while I can."

An expression she couldn't read flickered in his eyes. "Emma—"

"You guys had a picnic without me?" Gabriel Laurent plopped down on the bench across from them, earning a dark glower from Michel. "Well, that's not very nice."

"Oh my gosh. I didn't even think . . ." Emma flushed deeply. "I'm so sorry."

"Good Lord, Emma. Don't feel bad. I was only joking." Gabriel reached for a fish jeon, and she slapped his hand away without thinking. He glanced up, startled.

"Sorry. I'm sorry," she said even as she surreptitiously dragged the plate of food away from him. "But I saved that plate for Sophie since she wouldn't eat with us."

"Wow, was I really the only one not invited to this picnic?" Before she could answer, Gabriel snatched the plate from her and got to his feet. He winked and said, "Since I'm such a nice guy,

I'll take this plate over to Sophie for you. Who knows? Maybe she'll take pity on me and share. Enjoy the rest of your picnic, cousin."

Michel heaved an exasperated sigh in response and waved his cousin off. Without delay, Gabriel made a beeline for Sophie, which impressed Emma. She hadn't been able to spot her even though she knew the royal guard was close by. The fact that being with Michel made everything else fade into the background might have had something to do with it as well.

Grinning like a mischievous boy, Gabriel tugged Sophie toward a bench within view of their picnic table. Emma craned her neck to see them better. Their heads bent close together as Gabriel whispered something in Sophie's ear.

"You really don't know what's going on between them?" she asked Michel, annoyed that she couldn't hear what they were talking about.

"All I know is that it's complicated," he supplied unhelpfully.

"Sophie told me as much last night." They caught her watching them, so she smiled and waved.

Her friend pointed at the plate and gave Emma a big thumbs-up. Gabriel grabbed a fish jeon off her plate while she was distracted and popped it in his mouth. Sophie caught him stealing and punched him in the arm, but he just smiled happily at her.

"She told you that?" Michel's eyes widened.

"Uh-huh." Emma gave him a distracted nod and continued spying on the striking couple. "But not much else."

"Well, that's more than what she told me," he said glumly.

"You focus on your cousin." She patted his thigh with a sympathetic smile. "I'll talk to Sophie."

"Do you think it might be better if we minded our own business?" He sipped the last of his sujeonggwa.

"Where's the fun in that?" She took the cup from him, tucking it into the picnic basket along with the other empty containers. "And who knows? Maybe we can help them, since it's complicated and all."

"Are you suggesting we play matchmakers?" He raised his eyebrows.

"Nah." She bumped her shoulder to his. "You just get me intel from Gabriel. *I'll* be the matchmaker."

CHAPTER TWENTY-FOUR

A untie Soo claimed she wasn't much of a cook, but she made the best lasagna. When they were teenagers, Emma and Jeremy would clean out a whole pan between the two of them, so her godmother had to make two pans if the grown-ups wanted to eat, too.

"This is way too much food, Imo," Emma protested, setting out a teetering pile of thick garlic toast on the table. She paused to inhale the delicious aroma of toasted bread, garlic, and butter before she continued, "Oppa and I are well past our growth spurts."

"Hey, speak for yourself." Jeremy placed a giant bowl of Caesar salad next to the bread. "I have at least another inch left to grow."

When Auntie Soo rolled her eyes at her son, Emma taunted him with a bratty smirk. She switched to an innocent smile as her godmother turned to her. "Old habits die hard, my dear. I'll freeze the second pan for Jeremy to take with him when he leaves."

"Yesss." Jeremy pumped his fist.

"Ugh." Emma grimaced. "Again, I can't believe parents actually pay you to care for their children."

"I'm sure the children love his playful nature," her dad said as he took his seat.

"Samchon *sees* me." Her godbrother placed his hand over his heart. "Unlike you, brat."

"Silly boy." Auntie Soo slapped her son none too gently on his back. "Quit insulting our guest."

"Guest? Who, Emma?" He backed away from his mother when she raised her hand again. "Miss Yoon, please have a seat whilst I serve you some lasagna."

Emma stuck her tongue out at him but sat down and held out her plate to him. "I want a corner piece."

Jeremy scoffed but only said, "Anything for our guest."

"I still can't believe you won't share your salad dressing recipe with me," Emma said around a mouth full of tart and creamy salad.

"I told you it's nothing special," her godmother mumbled and quickly stuffed half a slice of toast into her mouth.

"She's just embarrassed to tell you because it's actually store-bought." Jeremy winked, then almost dropped his fork at his mother's outraged shriek.

"How did you know?" Auntie Soo buried her face in her hands.

"I *didn't* know, Umma." He wrapped his arm around his distraught mother's shoulders. "I was just kidding."

"Well, now you all know." She sat up and said with calm dignity, "I just add some fresh lemon rind and Kewpie mayonnaise to a store-bought brand. You know, the one in the fancy glass bottle?"

Emma couldn't help it. She burst out laughing. She clapped her hand over her mouth, but a snort escaped her nose.

"Oh my God. I'm so sorry, Imo. I promise I'm not laughing at you. It's just—" She dissolved into another bout of laughter. "Oppa accidentally revealed your deep, dark secret by being a jackass."

One by one, everyone at the table joined in—even Auntie Soo—and they laughed until they had stitches in their sides. Emma sighed, dabbing at her eyes. "It's still my favorite Caesar salad dressing. And I've tried that brand, so I know your secret ingredients make the dressing."

After a hurricane of eating, catching up, and reminiscing, their conversation dwindled as they sat in a carb, cheese, and Chianti–induced stupor. Stifling a yawn, Emma decided it was long past time to switch to water. When Jeremy clinked his fork against his wineglass, she turned to him with sluggish curiosity, which sharpened into concern when she saw the terrified expression on her godbrother's face. *What in the world?*

"I . . . have an announcement to make," Jeremy said in an uncharacteristically small voice, fidgeting in his chair.

Emma wanted to ask him what was wrong, but she was afraid if she interrupted him, he might bolt from the table. She glanced at Auntie Soo and her dad, who both sat still and silent with their eyes glued to Jeremy. Clasping her hands tightly on her lap, Emma waited for her godbrother to continue.

"You guys are my family and I love you, and I know that you all love me, but there's something you should know about me." He drew in a long, tremulous breath, then words tumbled out of his mouth like water rushing past a broken dam. "I'm gay. I know it must come as a shock, but I hope you can accept me for who I am."

There was a long, awkward silence at the table until the blood drained out of her godbrother's face. Before he panicked in earnest, Emma rushed to explain. "We all know, oppa. Of course we accept you and love you. We always have. We just thought you knew that we knew. That's why we're so surprised by your announcement."

Auntie Soo and her dad nodded in confirmation, soft, warm smiles lighting their faces.

Jeremy's eyes rounded. "You guys really knew?"

"Of course I knew. I'm your umma." Her godmother sniffled and squeezed her son's hand. "I love you and I'm here for you. You know that, right?"

"I do," her godbrother said, voice hoarse with emotion. "On that note, I also want to share that I met the most wonderful man in the world, and we . . . we're engaged."

"Oh my gosh. Congratulations, oppa." Emma clasped her hands together in front of her chest. It put new light on his lecture that marriage should be about love and happiness. Even though her perspective on marriage remained unchanged, she sincerely hoped that was what he'd found.

"What fantastic news," her dad said, beaming. "Congratulations, son."

"How *could* you?" Auntie Soo whispered through pale, trembling lips.

"Umma?" Jeremy blinked.

"How could you keep such an important relationship a secret from me until you got *engaged*?" Her godmother blinked back tears.

"I . . . I . . ." Jeremy shot a panicked glance at Emma's dad, who always had his back.

"Now, Soo." He laid a calming hand on Auntie Soo's arm, but she shook it off.

"Does his family know? Did . . . did you meet them?" At the guilty expression on Jeremy's face, her hurt morphed into anger, and her fists clenched on the table. "You hid the man you loved from me—my future son-in-law—because . . . what?"

"I know you support the LGBTQ community, but I thought . . . it might be different when it's your own kid." Her godbrother shot a beseeching look in Emma's direction.

"Imo, it must be terrifying to come out as gay, especially to the people you love most . . ." She understood and sympathized with both sides, but she mostly wanted to hide under the table until the conflict was resolved.

"And you always said that you wanted to match me up with the perfect partner. I guess I didn't want to disappoint you," Jeremy continued. "I'm sorry. If . . . if it helps, we only got engaged last week. I wanted to tell you in person. I'm *so* sorry."

Auntie Soo took a breath and opened her mouth, her expression turning stony. *Oh no. Oh no.* She was about to say something hurtful that she would regret later. *No, no, no.*

"Speaking of relationships," Emma blurted in a brittle, chipper voice, "I'm seeing someone."

All eyes at the table slowly turned to her. Jeremy mouthed, *No, Emma.* But it was already too late.

"Since we're all being honest here," she squeaked, terrified of her godmother's reaction. Did Auntie Soo feel betrayed that Emma had kept it a secret from her? That she put her reputation at risk?

Her dad's eyebrows drew together in confusion. "But you're not gay."

"No, Appa. I'm not."

"Okay." He absently patted her hand. "I just wanted to make sure I'm following everything."

"Jeremy, what is your fiancé's name, age, and occupation?" Auntie Soo was back to her formidable self, her hurt and anger under control. Emma breathed a sigh of relief.

"Steven Kim. Thirty-six. Pediatric neurologist," Jeremy answered with military precision minus a salute. "He's actually one of my partners."

"And you." Auntie Soo turned to Emma. "Did you also think I would oppose you dating someone you chose? Do you kids not understand that all I want is your happiness?"

"But the Crones . . ." Emma said, chastised for doubting the depth of Auntie Soo's love for her.

"I will handle the Crones." The icy determination in her

godmother's tone made her believe her. Emma had no idea how, but the Crones had better watch out. Auntie Soo was coming to handle them. When her godmother snapped her finger at her, Emma remembered she wasn't off the hook yet. "What is your suitor's name, age, and occupation?"

Emma straightened in her chair. "Michel Chevalier. Thirty-four. Professor of international relations at USC."

"Is he the reason you're taking a break from the matseons?" Auntie Soo demanded.

"Yes?" Emma croaked, casting a furtive glance at her dad. She didn't want him to know she'd been worried about how he was taking the news of her matseons. "But also, because of what I told you that day."

"Humph." Her godmother studied her with shrewd eyes but didn't continue with the interrogation.

"Is Michel good to you, sweetheart?" her dad asked with a gentle squeeze of her hand.

"Yes, Appa." She blinked away sudden tears. "He is very good to me."

"Well, that settles it." Auntie Soo stood abruptly from the table and began gathering the empty dishes. "Invite Steven and Michel to dinner this Saturday."

"But Steven is in San Jose—" Jeremy made a valiant attempt to take back some control of the situation.

"He will take an hour flight to LA on Saturday and drive back up with you on Sunday." Auntie Soo didn't pause in clearing the table, and her son knew better than to contradict her a second time.

"Imo." Emma went to Auntie Soo's side and placed a hand on her arm. "I'm sorry I didn't tell you about Michel sooner, but . . . I didn't plan for any of this to happen. And I'm so sorry if my actions are hurting your chances of signing the YogurtBerry—"

"I already signed the YogurtBerry family," her godmother

blurted. She placed the empty plates back on the table and sandwiched Emma's hand between hers. "I'm sorry I didn't tell you. It
only happened last week. And . . . I thought it would help moti-
vate you to resume your matseons if you had that added pressure
hanging over your head. I . . . I'm a no-good meddling ajumma.
But I thought I was helping you find happiness."

"That's okay. We'll call it even." Emma patted Auntie Soo's
hand with her free one, her relief trumping her indignation. "Besides, meddling is what aunties do best."

"You're a sweetheart." Her godmother side-eyed her. "But I'm
not sure about the even part . . ."

"Congratulations on signing with the YogurtBerry family. I'm
so happy for you," Emma gushed, stepping on her godmother's
words. "How did you do it?"

Auntie Soo gave her a conspiratorial wink. "Their daughter is
also on the brink of turning twenty-nine. We commiserated over
our failings as parents."

"Imo!" Emma tugged her hands back and stomped her foot.
Her dad gave her a startled glance, then shrugged, resuming his
trek to the kitchen with an armful of dishes. "I told you that's an
antiquated way of thinking . . ."

"Oh, pishposh." Auntie Soo stacked some empty dishes on
the table, glancing at her son, who was stealing bites of lasagna
directly from the pan. She cleared her throat raucously until she
got his attention. "Jeremy, you and I will have a long talk tonight.
I . . . I'm sorry I didn't make you feel safe enough to tell me about
Steven sooner."

"It's okay, Umma." He walked around the table and pulled
his mom into a tight hug. "You've always made me feel safe. I just
needed to do it in my own time."

Emma sighed in relief, wiping away a tear. Harsh words and
hurt feelings were successfully avoided. Everything was going
to be okay. But now she had to introduce Michel to her family

and somehow deal with the fallout when he left in a month and a half. Her chest tightened at the reminder that Michel would leave soon, and she couldn't draw a proper breath.

With a mumbled excuse, she escaped to Auntie Soo's living room and covered her mouth to muffle her sob. She couldn't fall apart. She'd made her decision to be with Michel until he left. It wasn't fair that a month and a half was all she got, but she would make every day count.

CHAPTER TWENTY-FIVE

Michel jumped when Emma dove into the back seat and yelled, "Drive!"

"Sophie." He nodded at his royal guard, who squealed out of the driveway without further prompting.

It wasn't the most auspicious start to their long-awaited date. They hadn't seen each other since the picnic, because of Emma's dinner with her godmother, and Michel had to cancel their date last night to deal with a situation back in Rouleme. Two days might not seem long to others, but his time with Emma was precious, and the wait had felt like an eternity to him.

Emma wordlessly stared out the rear window until her house was out of sight. Then she sat forward with a sigh of relief and gave Michel a rueful smile.

"My dad." When he arched a quizzical eyebrow, she elaborated, "I didn't want either of you to deal with an awkward interrogation. He would feel obligated to grill you as my father, but he really isn't much of a griller. Besides, Auntie Soo will do that at dinner tonight. She's very thorough. My dad will get all the answers he wants and more."

Michel swallowed and resisted the urge to tug at his suddenly tight collar. "I appreciate that."

"Sorry for yelling at you, Sophie." Emma reached across and patted her on the shoulder.

"Not a problem," the royal guard said with a smiling glance. Emma could do no wrong in Sophie's eyes. "So where to?"

"We're going to The Last Bookstore." The squeal—though unvoiced—was evident in every line of Emma's posture.

"The very last one in Los Angeles?" Michel widened his eyes. "And here I thought all that talk of Angelenos being shallow was a spurious stereotype."

"It's the name of a famous bookstore, smart aleck." Emma slapped his arm playfully, and he couldn't hold back his grin. "We'll go there right when it opens before it gets too crowded, then head over to Little Tokyo for lunch at my favorite udon restaurant."

"That sounds perfect." Anticipation coursed through him. He couldn't remember the last time he'd walked into a bookstore. Did she know how much these simple, everyday experiences meant to him?

While Michel was grateful to Emma for introducing him to the charms of Los Angeles, he felt guilty she'd planned most of their dates. There had to be something she hadn't tried before that he could surprise her with . . . He would love to see her beautiful eyes round with wonder and her dimple wink from delight. He would figure something out.

"I have a favorite bookstore in my hometown that I don't get to visit often enough," he said, feeling a little homesick. But Rouleme wouldn't feel like home without Emma by his side. He couldn't be sure, but something had changed since their picnic at USC. He felt her opening up to him—letting him in. Maybe she was giving him a real chance to prove that he was perfect husband material. "It's enchanting. I would like to take you there."

"I would love to visit Rouleme one day." Her smile looked a little sad, but she hadn't balked at the idea. He would take that as a good sign. He would have to push harder soon—time was running out—but for today, that would do.

He lifted her hand and kissed the inside of her wrist. She made a small breathy noise that set his heart pounding. He carefully set down her hand before he succumbed to the urge to wrap his mouth around the elegant length of her finger to see what kind of noise she made then.

With great willpower, he managed to keep his hands and mouth to himself until they arrived at the bookstore. The three of them—with Sophie trailing a few feet behind—walked inside just as a smiling employee turned the sign to "Open." Michel had to agree with his friend's low whistle of appreciation as he took in the store.

The Last Bookstore had the cluttered charm of a vast, old library but with an enchanting whimsy all its own. It was a two-level labyrinth of a store with Greek columns in the main hall. But with every space utilized to accommodate their innumerable books, it managed to feel quite welcoming and cozy.

"Do you want a tour? Or would you like to get lost in all this fabulousness?" Emma asked, grabbing hold of his hand.

He linked his fingers through hers. "How about a tour so I don't miss anything important, but with the option to linger if something feels magical?"

Her expression turned soft and dreamy. "You say the most perfect things. You know that?"

"I do?" His brows climbed to his forehead.

"What am I going to do with you?" Emma whispered. Before he could wonder at the tenderness that stole into her expression, she turned away from him and waved for him to follow. "For now, I'll give you a tour of this gem."

She led them upstairs, then through a zigzagging path of

bookshelves so tightly packed that only one of them could pass at a time. They made very little progress, stopping every few feet to finger through a book that caught their fancy.

"Oh no." Emma spun around and nearly bumped into his chest.

He steadied her by her shoulders. "What's wrong?"

"We'll never make it out of here in time for lunch—who am I kidding?—in time for dinner if I'm let loose in the cookbook section."

He scanned the vicinity and pointed with his chin. "Is that it over there?"

"Yes." She squeezed her eyes shut. "I'll hold your arm. Just guide me past it, then we'll be fine."

He took the opportunity to stare at her lovely face, memorizing every precious inch of it. Then he led her down the path with his arm around her waist and said close to her ear, "Open your eyes."

"Are you sure? It doesn't seem like we went far enough . . ." Her jaw went slack as she eyed the books surrounding her. "Michel, this is the cookbook section."

"I know," he said.

"But—"

"I'm not going to let you rush past a section you love just for the sake of sticking to a schedule . . ."

Emma was already lost. Some books she flipped through quickly while some she lingered over a bit longer. But when he noticed that she was reading a cookbook page by page, he carefully led her to an alcove with an armchair. Since there was just the one chair, he sat down first and settled her on his lap. She barely glanced up as she pored over the book.

After nearly half an hour, Michel shifted his leg, just by an inch to get some circulation back, but the motion jolted Emma out of her trance. It was still early and hardly anyone had passed by them.

"Oh my gosh." Her hand flew up to her mouth, and she scrambled to get up from his lap. "Your poor legs."

"Shh." He tugged her back down and rearranged his legs, all the while holding her tight against him by her waist. "This is worth it."

"Michel." She huffed a resigned sigh, then she licked the pad of her index finger and dabbed it on the tip of her nose. "Do this."

"I beg your pardon?"

"I'm serious. Do it several times and it'll help with the pins and needles in your legs." When he continued staring dumbfounded at her, she rolled her eyes and tapped his nose with her own dampened finger. He refused to put his own saliva on his nose, but he didn't mind it at all when Emma did it. "It's a trick my grandmother taught me when I was little."

The tip of his nose felt disconcertingly cold. It might've been due to the distraction of having a damp nose, but the pinpricks of blood rushing into his legs seemed to ease a bit. When proper circulation resumed in his legs and his nose was once again dry, Michel got preoccupied with the feel of having Emma in his arms.

He traced the lines of her fingers and the faint blue veins on the back of her hand. She pressed herself to him, burrowing her face into the side of his neck. The warmth of her breath sent a shiver down his spine. He shifted in his seat and tucked her closer until every curve of her fit against him. Her shoulders rose and fell on a sigh as he breathed in the scent of her hair.

"Come with me." Emma got to her feet and held out her hand before his legs could fall asleep again. A part of him wanted to stay in that armchair forever. But he took her outstretched hand and rose to his feet—simply because she wanted him to.

Emma tugged him down another labyrinth of bookshelves until they arrived at the most improbable and wonderful place—a cavernous tunnel made of books. And they had it all to themselves. He chuckled with awe and joy as his gaze wandered over the books surrounding him. This made getting up from the armchair worth it. Maybe.

She maneuvered him so gently, so slowly that he didn't realize what she'd done until he was backed up against the wall of books. Then she rose to her toes and pressed her lips against his in a sweet, lingering kiss that he felt down to his soul. Her touch was chaste, with barely parted lips, but he felt as though she was offering a part of herself that she kept closely guarded. His heart clenched in his chest, overwhelmed by a rush of emotions he couldn't parse out.

When she broke the kiss, a tremulous breath left him, and he could only stare at her for a moment. She held his gaze, her eyes shining with unshed tears. He pushed her hair away from her face with unsteady fingers and tucked it behind her ear.

"Why the tears, darling Emma?" The husky voice that emerged from him didn't sound like his own.

Her eyelashes fluttered, and a tear rolled down her cheek. "I don't know."

Michel wiped the moisture away with the pad of his thumb and brushed his lips across her temple. The back of his throat burned with his own tears, and the ache in his chest spread, making it difficult to breathe. He gathered her into his arms and pressed his cheek against hers. He held on to her for much too long and not nearly long enough as he prayed fervently in his head. *Please.*

"We should finish the tour," Emma whispered, tears still clinging to her lashes like morning dew on soft petals.

He nodded and took her hand as more people wandered into the tunnel. With their fingers laced together, they walked silently through the book tunnel and explored the rest of the bookstore. There were no words adequate to express what had happened, so they didn't try to talk about it. But they were different now. Everything was different. He had to tell her who he was. He had to ask her to come to Rouleme with him.

Back at the car, he brushed his thumb across her silken bottom lip and asked, "Hungry?"

"No." She shook her head and offered him a soft smile, the corners of her lips trembling.

Unable to look away from Emma, he managed to rasp, "We'll head back to the hotel, Sophie."

CHAPTER TWENTY-SIX

It was terrible and beautiful . . . heartbreaking and glorious. They were falling for each other. Emma didn't see the changing scenery outside the car as emotions overwhelmed and engulfed her. She felt . . . Michel was . . . God, she was going to combust into flames. She *wanted* to be consumed by it.

But she retained enough of her senses to remember not to trust her heart. He was leaving in a month and a half. She swallowed a sob before it could escape her. Even so, Michel's hand tightened around hers as though instinct moved him to comfort her. She turned away from the window and met his gaze. The gold specks in his warm brown eyes sparkled in the sunlight. Before she could fall into them, he brushed his lips across her knuckles, and her eyelashes fluttered shut.

They arrived at the hotel, and Sophie led them through the lobby. No one spoke as the elevator carried them up the floors. The tempest inside Emma calmed as though the worst had passed—then again, she might be in the eye of the storm—and she found some clarity. When Michel left, everything would return to the way it used to be. The way it *should* be. She would resume her orderly, meaningful life.

With that being the case, she could give in now. This terrible, beautiful thing between them would end before it could change—before it could become an ugly, disappointing lie. She could let herself fall. She would still be safe. It wouldn't be all of her. Never all of her.

Michel held open the door, and Emma stepped inside his suite. Other than a quiet goodbye to Sophie, neither one of them had spoken since they left the bookstore. She listlessly walked over to the piano and tinkled a few notes on it.

"Do you play?" Michel said at her side.

"No, I never had a chance to learn." Her smile was wistful. "But I've always loved the sound of the piano."

He reached around her and played a string of notes that came together in a poignant and haunting melody. Her eyes snapped to his face as a shy smile curved his lips. "Do you want me to play something for you?"

God, this man. "Yes . . . please."

Pulling out the piano bench, he sat down and gestured for her to sit next to him. Once she settled beside him, he gave her another small smile and raised his hands over the piano. Then like magic, music filled the air. His fingers moved in a gentle rhythm, gliding gracefully across the keys, but his playing was strong and masterful.

The music wove through her—the bass notes reverberating in her stomach—in slow, heart-wrenching waves. Tears welled in her eyes and flowed soundlessly down her cheeks. She bit her bottom lip and sucked in a shuddering breath, then exhaled quietly, not wanting to interrupt him. But Michel played on with his eyes closed, deeply immersed in the music.

His fingers hovered over the keys as the last notes faded away. When he finally looked at her, his eyebrows rose in alarm, and he reached out to wipe away her tears. She shook her head and brought his hands down between them.

"That was breathtaking." She flashed a watery smile at him. "What is it called?"

"Prelude in E Minor." His eyes flickered over her face as though to reassure himself that she was okay. "By Chopin."

She squeezed his hand. "How long have you played the piano?"

"Since I was five." He huffed a rueful laugh. "I'm grateful that my parents forced me to take lessons. Playing the piano is a great solace at times."

"You play beautifully." Her heart wrenched at another hint of his loneliness. She reached out and cupped his cheek, smoothing her thumb across his cheekbone. "I think you might be worth keeping around."

"Is that so?" His lips quirked into a grin, as she'd hoped. "Well, I'd better practice every day to keep my skills sharp."

"What else are you good at?" she asked coyly, her fingers tiptoeing up his thigh.

"I'm told I'm quite good at . . . many things." His smile turned wolfish as he leaned close. "Should I demonstrate some of my skill set for you?"

"Only if you think I would find it interesting," she breathed against his lips. His low chuckle sent a shiver down her spine, and anticipation swelled low in her stomach.

As though sensing that she was dying for him to kiss her, Michel cruelly denied her and brushed his lips down her neck instead. She wanted to drag his lips to her mouth and kiss him until neither of them could breathe, but she moaned when his tongue found the indentation at the base of her throat.

"Do tell me if I bore you at any point," he drawled.

"Actually, I'm a little bo—" Her breath hitched as he scraped his teeth over her collarbone.

She trembled and grabbed a fistful of his shirt. The only reason she wasn't annoyed at his arrogance was because his voice wasn't at all steady. He wouldn't be able to hold out much longer. He made his way back up the other side of her neck and dropped a lingering kiss just beneath her ear. Her back arched as another moan escaped her.

"God, Emma." Michel's control seemed to snap, and his mouth claimed hers with the desperation of a starving man.

Her triumphant smile was short-lived as his tongue delved inside and demanded her surrender. She gave in with a helpless whimper. His hands were hot and rough as they moved up her back, then down her sides before digging into her hips. With a growl of frustration, he lifted her onto the piano in a burst of discordant notes and stepped between her spread thighs.

She pulled his shirt free from his slacks and drove her hands up his torso. He shivered and groaned his approval as his mouth moved frantically against hers. Her palms and fingers traveled over the hard, rippling contours of his abs and chest, reveling in the hot, smooth feel of him. She returned his demanding kisses, growing hungrier by the minute. She wrapped her legs around his ass and tilted her hips to press her aching center against him.

He hissed against her lips, then ground himself against her, wrenching a sharp cry from her. Her hands crashed onto the keys as she sought purchase, and her back arched with a primal need to get closer to him. Her head fell back when he swerved his hips again and again. The delicious friction made her toes curl and her stomach tighten with desire.

"Michel," she breathed.

With a muttered curse, he lifted her into his arms and carried her to his bedroom with long, impatient strides. Nerves skittered through her stomach, but she wanted this. She wanted him. As soon as he set her down on her feet beside the bed, he crushed his lips against hers as though the brief separation had been unbearable. He found the zipper behind her dress and opened it in one rough tug, making her gasp. His shoulders heaved beneath her hands as he took a deep breath, then he stepped back from her.

He slowly pulled the dress down her body. The soft scrape of the fabric against her sensitive skin made her dig her teeth into her bottom lip as a shudder coursed through her. As though he couldn't stop himself, he claimed another hard, searing kiss, then fell to his knees and helped her step out of the dress on her trembling legs.

He grew still in front of her as he wordlessly took in her body, his hands clenched by his sides. When he looked up at her face, the naked adoration in his expression made her feel powerful and seductive. She reached behind her back and unclasped her bra, then tossed it to the side. His eyes darkened, turning almost completely black.

"You are so beautiful," he said in an awed whisper.

He brushed his thumbs across the lower curve of her full, heavy breasts. Then he smoothed his unsteady hands down her sides until they rested on the curves of her waist. Holding her eyes, he dipped his fingers into her panties, drew them past her hips and down her thighs. Gently clasping one ankle and then the next, he removed the last barrier from her body.

He pressed his cheek against her navel, holding her by the hips. She ran her hand down the soft, thick waves of his hair, and his breath left him in a rough, jagged exhale.

"Are you okay?" she asked, tenderness filling her. He seemed as nervous as she felt. "You're trembling."

"I just need a moment." He turned his head and spoke against her stomach, his lips brushing against her sensitive skin. "It's been a while for me, and . . . and I don't want to rush this. I want to take my time with you."

"It's been a long time for me, too." She shivered at his words even as her body heated from the touch of his hands and lips. "I actually haven't done this . . . that many times."

Michel leaned back and looked up at her. She bit her lip, embarrassed by her confession—by her inexperience—and he carefully maneuvered her until she was perched on the edge of the bed. "Tell me, what is not that many times for you?"

"There . . . there was this guy in college. He was nice and smart . . . and I wasn't overly enamored with him, so he seemed like a very sensible choice . . ." She trailed off, realizing that she was rambling.

"Emma," he enunciated slowly. "Are you telling me there was *one* man in *college?*"

"Yes?" He should know this wasn't something she took lightly. She was opening herself up to him like she seldom did. She was offering him her trust. Blushing to the roots of her hair, she added, "That one time."

Michel's breath left him in a whoosh, and he sat down on his haunches. He ran his hand down his face and over his mouth.

"Are you . . . disappointed that I'm so inexperienced?" Mortified, she glanced around for something to cover herself with. Come to think of it, why was she the only one naked? Michel was still fully dressed.

"Never." He rose on his knees again and held her chin so she would look at him. "Nothing about you could ever disappoint me, Emma."

"Then . . . I don't understand why you're upset." She hated how her voice trembled. Was she making a mistake? No. Even confused and worried, she knew she wasn't. It felt too right to be wrong.

"I'm not upset," he whispered. "Not even close."

He wrapped his hands around her knees, and she clamped her legs together. He leaned over and trailed hot, lingering kisses from her shoulder up the curve of her neck, and she sighed, desire sweeping her up again. When he spread her knees apart, she opened up for him without resistance. Running his hands up and down her thighs, he stepped between them and kissed her with tightly reined hunger.

"No, darling Emma." He brushed his lips up her jaw and said against her ear, "I'm shamefully pleased about your inexperience and . . . bewildered by the part of me that wishes *I* was your first."

"That's not so bewildering. I loved sharing so many of your firsts with you because you'll never forget them—you'll never forget me. Maybe that's what you want, too." She drew back just far enough to cup his cheek and hold his eyes. "If it helps any, that one time wasn't very good. It was entirely forgettable."

His chuckle was low and husky as he pressed his forehead against hers. "I *desperately* want to make this unforgettable for you."

"You will," she murmured, threading her fingers through his hair at the nape of his neck.

When his lips met hers once more, she forgot her insecurities—she very likely forgot her own name—as liquid lust spread through her. She became a creature of need and hunger. She wanted this man. She wanted to make him hers.

She squirmed on her perch on the bed when his hands found her breasts. She couldn't even be embarrassed at how loudly she moaned when his thumbs circled the hard peaks in excruciatingly slow circles. Especially since he groaned equally loud when she thrust her chest in his face, demanding more.

He sucked her aching nipple into his mouth, and her back arched hard enough to lift her ass off the bed. He pushed her back down, his fingers digging into her hips. After lavishing equal attention on her other breast, he licked and nipped his way down her stomach. He spread her legs apart farther and dropped wet, open-mouthed kisses on the inside of her thighs.

"Michel—"

"Shh." He didn't lift his head. "Let me taste you, Emma."

Her hips jerked wildly at the first lick of his tongue. His thumbs parted her, and he lapped at her center like she was rich, decadent ice cream. Her head fell back, and she gripped the sheets in her fists.

"I knew you'd taste like heaven," he murmured against her, drawing a shiver with the vibration of his words.

Pressure built up in her lower stomach and her center ached unbearably, but the rest of her body felt limp like a wilted flower. When his teeth scraped across her throbbing nub, she gave up and fell onto her back with a whimper.

"Good girl." He rewarded her with another delicious scrape of teeth.

"Michel." She wanted. She needed. Moaning and writhing, she lifted her hips off the bed and pulled his head deeper between her legs. "Please."

The good man that he was, Michel obligingly pushed a finger deep inside her as his talented tongue continued to swerve maddening circles around her clit. She groaned, fisting her hands in his hair—he was delusional if he thought he was going anywhere— and ground her hips into his face.

"I want . . ." With greedy, mindless lust, she sought her finish. "Michel, I need . . ."

He pushed a second finger inside her and sucked her clit into his mouth with a low groan, and she was gone. Her back arched as she screamed. His fingers and mouth slowed and gentled but didn't stop as her orgasm crashed into her in waves. He kept going as she jerked, twitched, and shivered, hissing and moaning her approval.

At last, she lay still—her legs spread wantonly and her fingers tangled in his hair—utterly spent. For a moment, the only sound in the room was the pant of their harsh breaths. But an exceptional accomplishment like this shouldn't go unpraised.

"That was definitely a first," she slurred.

"What?" Michel paused in the middle of impatiently ripping off his shirt.

Her eyes widened, and she rose onto her elbows. She might feel like an overboiled noodle, but she wasn't missing this unveiling for the world. But he stood frustratingly still with his shirt pulled down from one shoulder. Even so, her gaze greedily took in the peek of washboard abs and smooth, hard chest.

"Emma, what was a first?" he prompted.

"The orgasm." She blinked and tried to focus. "I've never had an orgasm. Not counting the ones I've given myself."

"The ones you've . . ." To her deep and utter relief, he resumed stripping off his shirt with jerky, impatient moves. "God, Emma."

She crawled to the edge of the bed on her hands and knees and unbuckled his belt. It would go faster with two people on the job. At last, he kicked off his pants and boxer briefs and stood before her in all his naked glory. Oh, and what *glory*. He. Was. Perfection.

He prowled toward her onto the bed, and she scooted back until her back hit the headboard. *God.* He looked intimidatingly big and muscular without his clothes on—like his tailored, dressy clothes somehow civilized the brute power of his body. Her hand flitted to her throat as she wondered if they would fit at all.

"What's wrong? Is this too fast?" He scanned her face, a little wild-eyed but genuinely concerned. "We could stop, if you want."

"We're not stopping anything, you silly man." Her momentary nervousness melted away. This strong, powerful epitome of male perfection was still her kind, sweet Michel, who cared more about her comfort than his raging hard-on. "Come here. Don't make me hurt you."

He sat back against the headboard beside her, leaving a few inches of space between them—like he was trying to give her some room. She rolled her eyes and promptly straddled him. Her ultra-sensitive, post-orgasmic nerve endings shouted hallelujah when they brushed against his hard length. Michel groaned as though he were in pain. Her eyes widened and she made to move off him, but he held her in place with a firm grip on her waist.

"Don't go," he rasped. "Just give me a minute."

"Oh, okay." Not the most eloquent of responses, but it was the best she could manage while straddling Michel's naked thighs.

Exhaling a shuddering breath, he pulled her head down and kissed her hungrily. She smoothed her hands over his broad shoulders and let them drift down to his chest, spreading her fingers wide to feel more of him. He tugged her bottom lip between his teeth, making her shiver in his arms. On pure instinct, she pivoted her hips to grind against his erection.

"God." Michel made that edge-of-pain sound again. "I want you so much."

Emma barely stopped herself from saying, *You can have all of me.* Because if she gave all of herself to him, then there would be nothing left of her when he went back to Rouleme. She would hold on to her heart but give him her passion and her vulnerability—more than she'd ever shared with anyone.

"Then take me, Michel," she whispered against his lips. In this moment, they would belong to no one but each other. She would be content with that.

CHAPTER TWENTY-SEVEN

E mma's husky whisper nearly undid him.

"Not yet." He wanted to see her face when she fell apart, but he didn't know how long he could last inside her. He brought his hands between them and kneaded her breasts. "You're going to come for me again before I take you."

He sucked and nipped his way down her long, graceful neck, a little rougher than he should but not as rough as he wanted. A primal thrill shot through him, knowing that he would leave his mark on her.

"Michel." She squirmed in his lap, frustrated and *wanting*.

"Fuck, Emma."

With his hands cupping her round arse, he pulled her tight against him, trapping his throbbing cock between their bodies. Then he pivoted his hips, guiding her to rub her swollen clit against his erection. They groaned in unison. Hesitantly, she glided herself over him as he'd shown her, up and down. Then again. Finding her rhythm, she rose up on her knees and ground herself against him, losing herself in the pleasure.

God, she was wild and beautiful. His eyes nearly rolled back in his head as her movements grew frantic, her wet folds slippery against his hardness.

"That's it, sweetheart," he growled in a voice he hardly recognized. "Use me."

Their ragged panting filled the room. Her fingernails dug into his shoulders hard enough to break skin, and he hissed with pleasure. She was close. So close. He pinched her nipple hard between his thumb and forefinger, and surged up to meet her, grinding himself harder against her.

She moaned as she climaxed for a second time, jerking wildly against his length. *Just fucking glorious.* He ran his hands down her back in slow, soothing strokes as he watched, mesmerized. She looked magnificent in her pleasure with her head thrown back and her teeth sinking into her swollen lip.

When she slumped limply against him, he carefully laid her down on her back. He was shaking with need and couldn't hold out any longer. Her gaze followed his movements as he grabbed a condom from his nightstand and sheathed himself with shaking hands. Then he covered her body with his, bracing his arms on either side of her head.

"Are you all right?" he asked, brushing his nose against hers.

"More than all right," she said with a breathless giggle.

"Good." He slid his hand between their bodies and circled his thumb over her clit. When she moaned and pushed into his touch—the insatiable wench—he readied himself at her entrance. "I need to be inside you."

"I need you, too." She caressed his cheek, her eyes roaming his face with tenderness and desire. Then she rose up on one elbow to press her lips against his and whispered, "Now, please."

He gritted his teeth to fight the need to bury himself inside her to the hilt. She had been with one man in college. He needed to be very gentle with her. So he rocked slowly in and out of her, inch by agonizing inch. She was so tight, and he was terrified of hurting her. He blew a shaky breath out of his mouth. But after a moment, she squirmed beneath him with an impatient whimper.

"Shh." He held himself still over her and kissed her hard on the lips. "We need to go slow."

"Goddamn it, Michel." She wiggled some more, and he felt the veins in his forehead bulge as he fought for control. "I'm not going to break."

"Even so." He eased himself out and pushed in just a little deeper. He moaned faintly, his arms starting to tremble in earnest.

He should've known what she was planning when that dimple appeared at her cheek—when she braced her feet against the mattress. Digging her fingers into his arse, she pivoted her hips off the bed hard enough to throw him aside if he hadn't been half inside her. His body reacted without thinking, and he met her thrust—and the tug of her hands—burying himself to the hilt in her warmth. He groaned so loudly that he almost didn't hear her sharp gasp.

"Fuck. I'm so sorry." He made to pull out of her, but her legs snaked around his hips and held him tight.

"Give me a minute," she said in a winded voice.

He brushed her hair away from her face. "Do you want to stop?"

"No." She pressed her lips into a mutinous line. "Quit offering to stop."

"Of course," he said automatically.

"Good." Her lips softened and quirked at the corners. Exhaling through her mouth, she pulled away from him, then slowly took him back in. Her eyelashes fluttered, and she did it again, out a little more, then in a bit farther. "Oh my."

For the life of him, he couldn't hold himself back any longer. He pulled out almost all the way and pushed back in to the hilt. They moaned together. She felt so fucking good, wrapped around him tight and hot.

"God, you're going to be the death of me," he panted as he set a careful, controlled rhythm that might very well kill him.

Urgency built up inside him. He dropped to his forearms because his arms were threatening to give out on him. He almost wept with relief when Emma began thrashing her head back and forth, her black hair spread out like silk around her.

"Faster, Michel. Faster. Please," she begged as though she didn't know that every cell in his body wanted nothing more than to comply with her request.

He pumped in and out of her with fast, steady strokes, sweat sliding down his forehead and off the tip of his nose. Nothing had ever felt so good. Nothing had ever felt so right. His climax was building inside him like a volcano about to erupt.

"Harder . . . I need . . . harder." Emma bucked against him, urgent and demanding.

At last, his control broke well and good. He lost all rhythm as he pounded into her with desperate, erratic movements, answering the call of the feral hunger inside him. He reached out to grip the top of the headboard with one hand and tilted her hip up with the other, driving into her harder and deeper.

"Yes," she hissed. "Don't stop."

Michel kept up the relentless pace until her back arched and she came with his name on her lips. He joined her climax with a guttural shout as she tightened around him again and again, stretching out his orgasm until he was shivering uncontrollably from the pleasure. Afraid he would collapse on top of her, he rolled over to his side, taking her with him. He wanted to stay inside her just a while longer.

"Ssmmphavvt," Emma mumbled against his chest.

"What was that, sweetheart?" He drew back and tipped her chin up with his index finger.

"Sex is my *favorite*." Her smile was wide, sleepy, and radiant. "Again?"

"Soon." He chuckled and kissed her damp forehead. "I need to go clean up, and you need a little nap."

"Naps are for wimps," she said as her eyes fluttered closed.

He dropped tender kisses on each of her eyelids. She was asleep even before he rolled away from her. Tearing his gaze away from her naked body, he tugged the covers up to her chin and headed to the bathroom. Once he was beneath the hot stream of the shower, he stretched out his pleasantly sore muscles. He took his time washing up because he didn't trust himself not to wake Emma up as soon as he got back in bed.

After drying himself off, he slung a towel low on his hips and stepped out of the bathroom. Emma was sleeping with one hand tucked under her chin, looking absolutely precious. He dropped his towel beside the bed and gingerly stretched out next to her under the covers. He folded his arm under his head and watched her sleep. He almost reached out to touch her but held himself back. She needed to rest . . . so he could wear her out again. They had a few hours before dinner at her godmother's house.

His eyelids grew heavy, and he struggled to keep them open. He wanted to study her just a bit longer . . . He was halfway asleep when his eyes shot open and his skin, still damp from the shower, chilled with sudden realization. He hadn't told her. He crossed the line he'd vowed not to cross until he told her the truth about his identity. It was a betrayal of her trust.

Michel got out of bed and pulled on a pair of black sweatpants and a gray Henley. He couldn't have the conversation they needed to have without clothes on. In fact, he couldn't talk to Emma if she was still naked. He went over to the walk-in closet and unhooked a French terry robe from its hanger. He laid it out on the foot of the bed, where it would be easy for her to reach without getting out of bed. Naked.

He settled himself on an armchair in the sitting area by the bedroom window. He leaned his elbows on his knees and steepled his fingers, tapping them nervously against his lips. Unable to sit still, he shot up to his feet and paced the length of the room, casting fleeting glances at Emma's sleeping form. He wished she would wake up soon. He wished she would sleep till the next morning.

Prince Michel didn't make mistakes, because the consequences would be too great. Apparently, Michel Chevalier made mistakes like a fool. But no matter how he wanted to pretend otherwise, this wasn't the ordinary mistake of an ordinary man. The consequences of his mistake could be catastrophic. He could have blown his last chance at love. He took a deep breath. He had to think this through.

Sure, she would be angry at first that he'd kept something so important a secret from her. But being a prince wasn't a *crime*. In the end, it might even help convince her to come to Rouleme with him. Wasn't that the exact outcome he wanted? Not if she only came because of some fantasy of becoming a princess—a queen. The claws of his insecurities dug into him. Would he ever know if Michel the man, not the prince, would've been good enough for her?

But she wanted him just as he was. Wasn't this afternoon proof of that? What they'd shared was more than sex—so much more than satisfying a physical need. They'd opened up to each other—given freely to each other. He'd never done that with anyone else. And he was certain the same was true for her.

Michel trusted Emma. He trusted what they'd shared. He would tell her the truth and trust that it wouldn't ruin everything.

CHAPTER TWENTY-EIGHT

Emma felt funny. She was sore and achy in places that she would usually not be sore or achy. And her limbs felt heavy and limp—she thought for a minute—in a not unpleasant way. She actually really liked how her body felt at the moment. Her eyes were slow to open, as heavy as the rest of her body, but as soon as they were open, she sat up fast enough to make her dizzy.

It was disorienting to wake up in someone else's bed, but her brain quickly and thoroughly reminded her whose bed she was in and why. What puzzled her, however, was why Michel was sitting fully dressed at the other side of the room, staring at her naked breasts with his mouth hanging open—she squeaked and pulled up the bedsheets to cover herself—and not naked beside her in bed. Something was wrong, and all the oxygen seemed to leave her body.

She tried to swallow, but her mouth was too dry. Somehow sensing what she needed, Michel got to his feet and poured her a glass of water from a carafe on his nightstand. After a split second's hesitation, he slowly approached her side of the bed and held out the glass to her. She took it from him and sipped at it until she was certain her voice would work.

"Thank you," she said, setting the half-full glass on the night-stand closest to her.

"Of course. My pleasure." His good manners were fully functional despite the odd tension in the room.

Michel didn't seem to know what to do with his hands as he stood an arm's length away, until he gestured awkwardly at the bathrobe at the foot of the bed. Had he laid that out for her? It was considerate, yet . . . disappointing. She'd hoped that she wouldn't need to put on any clothes for another few hours.

She noted again that he was fully dressed—in the most casual clothes that she'd ever seen him in, but still dressed. Uncomfortable with being the underdressed one, Emma hurriedly pulled on the white terry bathrobe. *Oh my God.* It was the softest thing she had ever felt against her skin. She shook off her momentary distraction and turned her attention back to Michel.

"Is . . . is something wrong?" She hated how hesitant and unsure she sounded. Was the *after* always supposed to be this awkward? Because the *before* and the *during* had been perfection. She didn't understand why the *after* had to be this way.

"No, no, no." He shook his head and hands vigorously. "No. Of course not. Nothing is wrong. I . . . I just need to tell you something. Something I wish I'd told you before we . . ."

I need to tell you something was her all-time most hated sentence, but the last time Michel said that, he'd just told her that he had a bodyguard. It was unexpected but not *bad*. He probably looked like he wanted to bolt from the room rather than tell her this *something* because he was conscientious and considerate. She shouldn't panic. It couldn't be that bad.

"Shall we take a seat over there?" He gestured toward the sitting area by the windows.

When she nodded, he offered her his hand and helped her out of bed. They both pretended to ignore the jolt that passed between them at the innocuous touch. But when she got to her feet, she found herself standing closer to him than she'd expected, and her heart hammered in her chest.

Without thinking, she took a step closer to him, eliminating the space between them. Her breath hitched as his heated gaze bored into her and he wrapped his hands around her waist. She might have pushed herself onto her toes. He might've dipped his head toward her. Maybe they'd moved at the same time. Who knew? All that mattered was that they were kissing each other like there was an apocalypse approaching and this was the last kiss they would ever experience.

Suddenly, Michel tore his mouth away from hers and held her away from him with a firm grip on her arms. They stared wordlessly at each other, their breathless pants the only sound in the room. Her confusion became indignation, which quickly morphed into . . . she settled on anger, because anger was safer than fear. She couldn't give in to her fear that something was very wrong.

"What the hell, Michel?" she squawked in outrage. She left the *How dare you stop kissing me* unsaid.

"Sorry. I'm sorry." He gently but insistently ushered her to the armchairs. "Please sit. Would you like more water?"

"No." Emma plopped down on the chair and crossed her arms over her chest. "Talk."

"Talk? Yes, well." Michel settled himself across from her and cleared his throat with a fist pressed over his mouth. "Of course."

Then he proceeded to not talk for a full minute. Her anger fizzled out, and fear edged in at last. She chewed her bottom lip, her legs bouncing nervously. After a moment, he reached out with the pad of his thumb and tugged her lip free from her teeth.

"Have you ever wondered what I do in Rouleme?" He laced his fingers together on his lap and not quite fidgeted in his seat. It was more of an uncomfortable shift. Even so, it wasn't like him. And the fact that he was nervous made her even more afraid.

"Do? As in a job?" She grabbed fistfuls of her bathrobe over her thighs and squeezed until her knuckles turned white. She'd wondered about a lot of things he did in Rouleme, but she never let her thoughts linger on those questions. She didn't want to think about him at home—away from her. "I assumed you were a professor there as well."

"No." He seemed to gather himself, and quiet determination replaced his nervousness. "I'm actually not a professor back home."

"Oh, I see." She didn't really see, but her panic eased a fraction. If this was about his job, she couldn't care less. It didn't matter what Michel did for a living. That wasn't what made him who he was. "Then what *do* you do?"

He barely moved, but his posture changed somehow and he seemed taller—bigger. She found herself straightening up in her chair for some reason. The set of his lips turned solemn and stern, and she didn't know if she liked it. It was very un-Michel-like but made him kind of imposing, which was hot. So maybe she liked it?

"Well?" she prompted. He'd taken advantage of her distraction to not talk again. She needed to focus.

"Emma."

"Yes?" The suspense was killing her a little bit.

"I am the crown prince of Rouleme."

She tucked her chin against her chest and gave him the side-eye. Then a low, incredulous giggle trickled out of her. "Shut the front door."

"You want me to . . ." Michel briefly looked uncertain, then he huffed something resembling a laugh. "Oh, you don't mean that literally."

Emma laughed again. But when he didn't join in and profess to being a huge dork for making such a silly joke—*Come on, the crown prince of Rouleme?*—she stopped laughing. He stilled in his seat. He might've even stopped breathing. She could only stare at him. And he stared back. So far, this conversation consisted mostly of staring and not talking.

As the silence stretched on, she considered the possibility that he might *not* be a huge dork. He might *not* be making a silly joke.

"Oh my God." Her breath rushed out in a whoosh. "You're serious."

"Yes." And there he went again, looking taller and bigger.

"You can't be the actual prince of Rouleme." She sprang up from her chair and paced back and forth—in sharp, two-step intervals—which made her a little dizzy. "You can't."

"Why not?" His eyebrows drew together. *Oh no.* His earnest, perplexed face was one of her favorite Michel faces.

"Because," she roared, throwing her hands up. Because she couldn't deal with it. Because they were too different to begin with. Because it would truly mean that there was no future for them. But the last reason didn't count, because she already knew that there was no future for them. Right? She forced her voice into an even, reasonable tone. "Because it would be ridiculous."

"Ridiculous? How so?" His face became extra earnest and perplexed. *Goddamn it.* Now was not the time to melt into a gooey pink puddle.

"Because"—she stopped pacing in front of his chair—"things like this don't happen in real life, Michel."

"Oh, I assure you they do." He rose to his feet and loomed over her. "This is real. This is *my life* no matter how *ridiculous* it seems to you."

"Wait." She poked her index finger into his chest, annoyed to find that there was no give. She obstinately pressed a smidgen harder but had to stop because her finger hurt. "Are *you* getting angry with *me*? Because I don't think you have *any* right—NONE!—to be angry with *me* right now."

His shoulders rose on a sharp inhale, then drooped back down—but not by much, because his shoulders didn't seem capable of truly drooping. "No. I'm not angry."

"Good." She jabbed his rock-hard chest once more out of principle. "Because I think *I* should be angry."

"You *should* be?" One corner of his mouth twitched suspiciously. "Does that mean you aren't *actually* angry?"

"You do not"—she glared at him *angrily*—"get to be cute right now."

His lips definitely quirked up at that. She glared harder because she *was* angry. Wasn't she? She was fairly certain she was, but she felt something calm and unconcerned beneath her anger. He'd lied to her—yes, *lied to her* by omission—and allowed her to think that he was just a *regular* handsome, ultra-rich man from an *influential* European family. As opposed to a *royal* handsome, ultra-rich man from a *royal* European family? But wasn't that just semantics?

Michel had always been someone from a world different than her own. She had made a conscious decision that their differences didn't matter, because he would be gone soon. In some ways, it almost seemed fitting that he was a prince. What they had was a fairy tale—wonderful and fleeting. Her chest tightened into a painful knot. She exhaled slowly and hardened her resolve. *We aren't meant to last.*

So was she angry that he hadn't been 100 percent forthright with her? Sure, she was. Did it matter that he was the crown prince of Rouleme? Emma resumed pacing because she couldn't think clearly with Michel so close. *No.* In the grand scheme of things, him being a prince didn't change a single thing. They had always been too different to belong together. He would still leave in a month and a half, and she would resume her real life. No matter how much that hurt, that was the way it was supposed to be.

"Sit," she ordered, arranging herself back into the armchair.

Even if his princely status didn't change anything, she wasn't about to let him off the hook that easily. He took a seat across from her and watched her with a wary expression. "You must have a reason."

"Pardon?"

"I want to hear your reason for lying to me." She held his gaze.

"Yes, of course." He got points for not trying to argue that he *technically* hadn't lied. "I wanted you to get to know me—just me—without the influence of my title."

"You think things would've been different between us if I'd known you were a prince?" She drew back, hurt and indignant.

"How could they not?" he implored, hands spread out in front of him. "Would you have come over to my table at the café if I'd been wearing a crown?"

Her eyelashes fluttered against her cheek. "I don't know."

"And if I'd been wearing my crown—if I had been Prince Michel—I don't know if I would've sent over those madeleines and paid for your check." When she sat hesitant and torn, he reached over and took her hand. "The only reason I had the courage to do that was because I was just Michel Chevalier."

"With or without the crown, you will never be *just* anything." She didn't pull her hand away. "The Michel I know is kind, generous, and funny. He's someone who finds joy in the simplest things. Someone who is good down to his bones. The Michel I know is a wonderful man."

"That is all I ever wanted." He tucked a strand of hair behind her ear, then gently cupped her cheek. "I wanted you to see me—*want* me—for the man I am without my crown interfering."

"I see you." Emma leaned into his touch. She was still angry with him, but it was imperative that he understood he was more than his title. He was wanted for who he was. He was enough. "I want you."

"Thank you," he said huskily, and pressed his forehead against hers. "I'm sorry I deceived you. I know it was wrong of me, no matter my reasons."

"You bet it was wrong of you." She drew away from him. "I don't like secrets and half-truths, Michel. Promise me you won't lie to me again."

"I promise." His warm brown eyes were open and vulnerable. "Never again."

She felt the last of her anger melt away. But she crossed her arms and narrowed her eyes. It wouldn't hurt for him to grovel a little more.

"Do you forgive me, darling Emma?" She melted a little at the endearment. It made her feel cherished. She ducked her chin because she couldn't hold on to her frown for obvious reasons. He came to kneel at her feet to hold her gaze. "Please?"

Oh, what the hell.

"Yes." Her heart fluttered like a silly thing. "I forgive you."

With a smile like starlight streaking across his face, Michel lunged forward until his lips were a mere whisper away from hers. "May I kiss you?"

"So polite," she teased breathlessly. "Kiss me alrea—"

He closed the gap between their lips before she could finish her sentence. Emma couldn't say she minded at all. She had questions—so many—but they could wait. For now, this kiss was enough. They were together, and that meant . . . everything.

CHAPTER TWENTY-NINE

♥

H ere's the game plan," Emma said on their drive over to her godmother's place. "Jeremy is infuriating at times but undeniably charming. His fiancé, Steven, is supposed to be an absolute sweetheart according to my infuriating but charming godbrother. So they'll be double-teaming to charm the hell out of Auntie Soo."

"Mm-hmm." Michel nodded so he appeared to be paying full attention to the words coming out of her mouth—instead of remembering how that mouth had been wrapped around his cock just an hour ago. "I see."

"All we have to do is deflect most of the attention to them and quietly coast through dinner." Her eyes narrowed as she studied his face. "Michel, are you listening?"

"Absolutely." He pinched his chin and pursed his lips to show how invested he was in the game plan. Sophie scoffed in the driver's seat. He ignored her.

Emma's makeup was immaculate, and there wasn't a single strand of hair out of place. She did not look like a woman who'd been thoroughly ravished three times in the course of one afternoon. She presented this perfectly put-together version of herself to the rest of the world, but he got to see her completely undone. He loved that.

"I can barely see any brown left in your eyes." She leaned close and whispered in his ear, "You're either very turned on by our game plan or your mind is elsewhere."

"The game plan is extremely scintillating." He trailed the tip of his nose down her cheek and breathed in her intoxicating scent where her neck curved into her shoulders. When she shivered, he met her gaze with a cocky grin. "And don't worry. I'm well versed in dealing with even the most difficult people with utmost diplomacy. I doubt your godmother is an exception."

"Oh, you poor, poor man." Emma shook her head with a sad pout. God, he wanted to kiss that pouty mouth of hers. But he'd promised not to ruin her makeup. "My godmother will eat you alive if you don't go in prepared."

His royal bodyguard covered her laugh with a cough. She and Emma shared a grin through the rearview mirror.

"You have my attention." He felt a frisson of alarm run down his spine. "What should I do?"

"Auntie Soo is shrewd and doesn't miss a thing, but there are two ways you could soften her up," Emma said, all business. "One, she's a Korean mom, which means she loves feeding people, so make sure you eat well. No nibbling. Full plates and big bites."

"I can do that." He was starving, actually. He'd ordered room service for their lunch, but they got too distracted to eat much of it. And they had expended quite a bit of energy in their non-lunch-related activities.

"Two, my godmother loves me. Whenever you feel cornered, change the subject to wax poetic about my many virtues."

"That also won't be difficult. Gabriel will be the first to tell you how very accomplished I am at singing your praises. Although . . ." He arched an eyebrow and lowered his voice. "I'm not sure *virtuous* is the adjective I would use to describe you."

Her dimple flashed with wicked depth by her mouth. "I doubt you'll earn many points from Auntie Soo by listing all the ways I'm a bad, bad girl."

His blood rushed south fast enough to make him dizzy. "Are you trying to kill me?"

"What?" She widened her eyes. "Am I being naughty?"

"Please have mercy," he groaned.

"That's what you get for not paying attention." She smirked. "This game plan is the only way we'll survive the night."

"What about your father?" he said with a resigned sigh. "How does he fit into the game plan?"

"My dad . . ." Her smile turned a shade crestfallen. "He's a sweet, kind man. Just be yourself with him. He'll like you no matter what."

"He will?" Michel couldn't hide his surprise.

"I told him you were good to me." Her voice grew husky. "That's all that matters to him."

"He sounds like a good man." He ran his knuckles down the side of her cheek.

"He is." She leaned into his touch, covering his hand with her own. "I'm so lucky to be his daughter."

"I'm sure he feels just as lucky to be your father." Something hitched in his chest. Emma and her father seemed so close . . . like they were essential to each other's lives.

Before he could parse out his emotions, Sophie parked next to the sidewalk of a tidy residential area with rows of quaint, two-story houses. He didn't know which one belonged to Emma's godmother, but it was probably across the street, a few houses down. His royal guard would want a good line of vision to the house, while remaining discreetly out of sight.

As Michel reached for the door handle, Emma tugged on his arm and said in a rush, "I think it goes without saying that we won't mention that you're a prince."

He stiffened in his seat. They hadn't talked much about his revelation. In some ways, he'd wanted to move past it and go back to the way things had been between them—effortless and wonderful. But he realized Emma had been awfully quiet about it as well. Why was that? Did she care so little about his title? Or was she avoiding the topic because it bothered her more than she let on? He abruptly heaved himself out of the car, needing to get some air.

"Michel?" A frown drew twin ridges between her eyebrows.

"Of course," he forced himself to answer, not quite meeting her eyes. He shook himself out of his momentary panic. "I'll be your average USC professor tonight."

"There's nothing *average* about being a professor at a prestigious university." She dimpled at him and followed him out of the car.

"Enjoy your evening," Sophie said with an encouraging smile, standing by the driver's side door.

"Are you sure you don't want to join us for dinner?" Emma asked for the third time since Sophie declined to join them.

"Yes, I'm sure." Her eyebrow quirked in indulgent amusement. "It would seem odd to bring his *friend* to a family dinner."

Sophie made a valid point. They had already introduced her to Jeremy as Michel's friend. It would complicate things to explain her presence tonight.

"I'll see you in a couple of hours." Michel nodded to his royal guard and took Emma's hand. "Shall we?"

"Wait." Sophie flagged him down before they crossed the street, holding out an elegantly wrapped box. Emma had helped him pick out the gift—a Korean red ginseng set. She assured him that it would help him make a good first impression. His friend clucked her tongue at him as he accepted the box. "I can't believe you almost forgot the hostess present."

Michel grimaced. That would've been a huge faux pas, especially when you were visiting your girlfriend's godmother for the first time. *Girlfriend*. The term felt too frivolous for what Emma meant to him. Then what would be the right word to describe her? He tucked away the thought to revisit later. He needed all his focus to win over Emma's family tonight.

"Thank you, Sophie," he said, taking the box from his friend.

"Good luck, Your Highness," she said in a low voice. "Sounds like you'll need it."

After waving goodbye to Sophie, Emma led the way toward her godmother's house, a dove-gray Craftsman home with black trimmings and a small but immaculate front yard. But instead of heading for the front door, she headed to the side gate.

When Michel glanced quizzically at her, she explained with a smile, "You're in for a treat, Professor Chevalier. We're having a Southern California backyard party. Another first for you, I'm sure."

His blood heated at her playful use of *Professor Chevalier*, but his curiosity was piqued. "What distinguishes a Southern California backyard party from those of another region?"

"The food, of course."

Before Emma could elaborate, a handsome woman who looked to be in her late forties approached them with her arms spread wide. "Emma, my dear."

"Hi, Imo." She hugged the older woman warmly before stepping back. "Michel, say hello to my godmother, Soohee Kang."

"Your godmother?" His eyebrows rose into his hairline. "You're Jeremy's *mother*? You look like you could be his sister."

The esteemed Soohee Kang snorted and rolled her eyes, but she smiled broadly at him. "Flattery isn't going to get you anywhere, young man."

"I apologize for hollering at you. I didn't mean to blurt that out like that." Michel placed a hand to his chest and cast a bewildered glance at Emma. "But I am genuinely astounded."

"Auntie Soo doesn't look anywhere near her age." She laughed at his side. "Imo, Michel isn't capable of false flattery."

"Well then." Her godmother patted her perfectly coiffed bob.

Emma nudged him with an elbow and pointedly eyed the box in his hands. *Christ.* He'd forgotten again. He cleared his throat and held out his gift to their hostess. "Thank you so much for having me, Ms. Kang."

"Oh, you shouldn't have. This is just a casual dinner with family and friends." She promptly relieved him of the gift box. "And call me Auntie Soo. There's no need to stand on ceremony."

Some of the tension left his shoulders as she hurried away to oversee their dinner. The cozy backyard had a grassy section with a picnic table and a larger paved sitting area shaded by a redwood pergola. String lights zigzagged above the backyard, connected to a long awning covering the patio at the side of the house. The lights would look lovely when the sun set and the evening settled in.

Auntie Soo spoke with a young man with broad shoulders and a trim beard. He stood over a portable grill set up on the patio, wearing a white apron around his waist. Three different piles of chopped meat sizzled on the steaming grill. Michel breathed in the air. Whatever it was, the backyard was filled with the delicious smell of food.

"Look at you," Emma said, dusting imaginary lint off his shoulder. "You've charmed your way right into Auntie Soo's heart."

"I have?" When he turned his surprised gaze to her upturned face, he forgot everything but how beautiful she looked in the light of the setting sun. He leaned down toward her, and her eyes fluttered closed.

"There you are, baby girl." The cheerful greeting had Michel jerking away from Emma.

A handsome gentleman in a cream polo shirt tucked into a pair of khakis strolled over to them with an openly curious glance at Michel. He had kind eyes that reminded him of Emma.

"Appa." Emma blushed, taking half a step away from Michel. "Um, hi. This is Michel Chevalier. Michel, this is my dad, Jaewon Yoon."

"It's nice to meet you, Michel." Her father held out his hand with a warm smile. Thankfully, he showed no signs of displeasure at their almost kiss.

"Pleased to meet you, sir." Michel took her father's hand in both of his and bowed from his waist.

Sophie had helped him research Korean customs and the proper manner of greeting an elder. Prince Michel was accustomed to receiving deference, but Michel Chevalier was honored to pay his respects to the man who raised Emma.

The older man chuckled as he shook his hand and glanced at his daughter. "Did you teach him how to do this?"

"No, I didn't." Emma's eyes were wide with surprise.

"Well, enough of the formalities." Her father clapped Michel on the shoulder. "I'm going to find Soo and hustle up some tacos. Oh, you two should go find Jeremy. He's been waiting to show off his young man."

"Welcome, friends." Jeremy waved with a bottle of beer in his hand, his free arm wrapped around the shoulders of a slender, clean-cut man. "Come say hello to my fiancé."

They were lounging on a love seat beneath the pergola. They were both dressed casually in T-shirts and shorts, but Steven still managed to look effortlessly stylish, while Jeremy looked a little rumpled.

When her father went to join their hostess, Michel and Emma made their way toward the seating area. As soon as they each took a seat in an armchair across from the happy, glowing couple, Jeremy began a boisterous round of introductions. Steven Kim patiently stared up at his fiancé with a fond smile until he finished.

"I'm going to give Emma a proper hello." He patted Jeremy on the shoulder and came around to stand in front of her. Laughing, she rose to her feet and promptly got pulled into a hug. "Hello, the little sister I've always wanted. I hope we can be friends."

"I can already tell you're too good for my godbrother," Emma joked as she stepped back.

"Watch it, brat," Jeremy warned.

Steven turned to Michel next and held out his hand. "It's nice to meet you."

"Likewise." He already liked the man.

It only took some light conversation to reveal that Steven was as softspoken and gentle-mannered as Jeremy was . . . not. Jeremy wasn't as irritating as he'd been that night at the Korean barbecue restaurant, but Michel wouldn't go so far as to say he was *undeniably charming*, as Emma claimed.

"He grows on you," Steven said as though he'd read his mind. He and Michel stood off to the side watching Emma and Jeremy bicker.

Michel smiled sheepishly. "I'll take your word for it."

"I couldn't stand him at first," the other man confided with perfect serenity, taking a sip from his sweating bottle of beer. "But now I can't imagine life without him."

"Congratulations." He felt an unexpected stab of envy at Steven's certainty—certainty that he wouldn't have to imagine a life without Jeremy. But for Michel, there were still so many what-ifs. Maybe it was time he changed that. "Your fiancé is a lucky man."

"Yes, he is." Steven grinned. "Thank you."

They watched in amicable silence as Jeremy and Emma snarled insults at each other with ruthless affection. The two pseudo-siblings reminded Michel of himself and his cousin—but without any modicum of civility. God, he even loved this alarmingly vicious side to Emma. She was—His breath got lodged between his throat and lungs. When he couldn't inhale, he tried exhaling, but that didn't work either.

I love her.

It shouldn't have come as a surprise, but the realization slammed into him with the force of a wrecking ball. He was in love with Emma—the kind of earth-shattering, life-altering love that he'd always dreamed about. The kind of love he'd hoped to find—a love more important than duty. But it also terrified him. What if Emma didn't love him the way he loved her? What if she wouldn't have him? He was in love with her, and it rendered him utterly helpless.

"If you don't behave, Steven's going to find out all about your emo phase." Emma walked away from her godbrother, wagging a warning finger at him. "Come on, Michel. Let's go get some food."

She grabbed his hand and sprinted toward the taco cart before Steven finished saying, "What emo phase?"

"Aren't you afraid of reprisal?" Michel teased, tucking away his epiphany to a corner of his mind. It was too new, too bright, too overwhelming to face right now.

"Not at all." Panic flashed across her pretty face, and she gulped audibly. "My life's an open book."

"I'm *sure* you have nothing to worry about," Michel said dubiously, which earned him a pinch on the arm. He laughed. "You were right, by the way."

"Of course I was." Her shoulders relaxed at the change of subject. "About what?"

"We're having tacos, right?" He brushed his thumb across the dimple by her mouth. "It'll be a first for me."

"You'll love it. Just follow my lead." She winked at him before going up to the grill. She greeted the busy chef with easy familiarity. "Hey, Jorge. How are the kids?"

"Getting big. Too big," the young man said with a wide grin. His hands didn't stop moving as he manned the grill with two metal spatulas. "The usual for you?"

"You know it." Emma held out her plate as the chef filled palm-size tortillas with mounds of chopped meat. The aroma of grilled meat and spices made Michel's mouth water. "And how's your sister doing?"

"Busy with the restaurant." Jorge lined her plate with three tacos. "We don't do too many parties these days, but anything for Soo, you know?"

"You guys are absolute gems," Emma said with an earnest smile, her eyebrows drawing together. "We're lucky to have you."

Following her lead, Michel asked Jorge for *one of each*—which turned out to be three street tacos with carne asada, al pastor, and chicken. Emma translated that carne asada was skirt steak, al pastor was pork, and chicken was well . . . chicken, all marinated and grilled to perfection.

"How are you with heat?" At a side table lined with condiments, Emma paused with her spoon poised over an ominous-looking red sauce with flecks of black inside.

"Define *heat*." He let his eyes drop suggestively to her lips.

"If you don't behave, I'm not helping you anymore." She stuck her nose in the air even as she blushed.

Michel chuckled. "I don't eat spicy food often, but I think I can tolerate quite a bit of heat."

"Hmm." She pulled her mouth to the side as she thought. "Well, okay. The red salsa is the spiciest, and I like it with my carne asada. The green sauce is spicy, but not nuclear level, and it's good with both the al pastor and the chicken."

After drizzling her tacos with salsa, she sprinkled some chopped onion and cilantro on top and piled some sliced radishes and marinated jalapeños on the side of the plate. She was a born teacher, guiding him every step of the way. Glancing at her plate from time to time, he dressed his tacos, if not with confidence, with curiosity and excitement.

"Last but not least, the beverages." Emma flourished her hands toward two coolers. It looked as though one held iced tea and the other milk but with ice. "We have tamarindo and horchata."

When Michel stared blankly at her, she laughed and said, "Tamarindo is a sweet and tart drink—it tastes a little bit like plum to me—and horchata is basically rice milk with sugar and cinnamon."

"Don't forget to tell him we offer adult versions." Jeremy came up from behind and draped his arms around their shoulders. "I make a mean tamarindo margarita and hard horchata."

"He basically adds tequila or rum to the drinks." Emma rolled her eyes at her godbrother.

"It's called mixology, brat." Jeremy mussed Emma's hair. "So what will it be, Michel?"

"I'll start with a tamarindo margarita," Michel said as they walked to the picnic table on the grass. Everyone else had already started eating. "Followed quickly by a hard horchata."

"That's a good man." Jeremy pounded his back a bit harder than necessary. "And the same for you, Emma?"

"Yup." She held a finger up. "With a Tajin rim, please."

"Always so demanding." He backed away before she could slap his arm. "Two tamarindo margaritas *with Tajin rims* coming right up."

"Tajin rim?" Michel murmured to Emma as they took a seat at the table.

"It's this delicious chili-lime seasoning," she said. "It takes the margaritas to the next level."

"She's right," Steven said from across the table. "But I would take it easy on them. Jeremy is *very* generous with his pours."

With that warning, the other man turned his attention to Emma's dad and godmother, who were chatting in between bites of taco. He soon had them enthralled with anecdotes from his practice, while taking neat, practiced bites out of his own taco. Michel glanced down at his plate with a twinge of nervousness.

"Don't be afraid to get a little messy. Watch." Emma squirted some lime onto her taco and folded the tortilla in half as she lifted it off her plate. "The trick is to turn your head, not the taco."

Keeping her taco perfectly horizontal, she tipped her head to the side and took a big bite, getting a drop of salsa on the corner of her mouth. Without thinking, Michel wiped it off with the pad of his thumb. Emma stopped mid-chew when he sucked the sauce off his finger, her eyes dropping to his lips.

Before he could get properly turned on, fiery heat spread across his tongue where the drop of salsa had touched it. He choked and coughed as Emma rubbed a soothing hand down his back. Jeremy delivered the margaritas with perfect timing, and Michel gulped half of his down.

"Easy, cowboy," Jeremy cautioned as he slid onto the bench beside his fiancé.

Michel coughed into his fist, fighting the urge to stick his tongue out and pant. Anything to stop the torture of the red salsa. He took another, more moderate gulp of the icy margarita and surreptitiously held it in his mouth before he swallowed it. He willed his eyes to stop watering, but to no avail.

"I . . ." He cleared his throat. "I might need to stay away from the red salsa."

"Not to worry. I'll relieve you of your carne asada taco." Emma's dad reached across the table and took the terrifying taco off Michel's plate.

"I am in your debt, sir." He would eternally be grateful for his act of kindness.

"I imagine Sir Lancelot to sound a lot like him," Steven murmured to his fiancé.

"Ding, ding, ding." Jeremy tapped the tip of his nose with one index finger and pointed the other at Steven. "He *does* sound like Lancelot, doesn't he? With his part-British, part-French accent and his ridiculously correct use of the English language. He would make a good knight of the Round Table."

"Well, only if he knows how to handle a lance," Steven pointed out.

Michel nearly groaned when Jeremy's grin transformed into a leer. But before he could make a highly inappropriate joke, his fiancé clapped a hand over his mouth.

"Stop teasing the poor man," Auntie Soo chided her son. "But I do think his accent is rather dashing."

Not knowing how to respond, Michel picked up his al pastor taco like Emma showed him and took a healthy bite with his head tilted to the side. Having his mouth full gave him an excuse not to talk and also made Auntie Soo nod with approval. And, *God*, it was *delicious*. He turned wide eyes to Emma.

"Good, huh? Backyard taco party." She grinned and made a check mark in the air. "Check."

As the late afternoon shifted into evening—good conversation and laughter flowing freely along with the delicious tacos and drinks—Michel wished that his three-month reprieve wasn't halfway over. He leaned close to Emma until their shoulders brushed and their thighs pressed together. When her shining eyes met his with sweet affection, he wished it would never end.

But these happy moments *would* never end if he had Emma by his side. He had to do everything in his power to convince her that forever and happily ever after could be theirs. Her parents' marriage had ended in heartbreak for them . . . and for Emma . . . but if she'd let him, Michel would love her until his dying breath.

CHAPTER THIRTY

Emma flipped through the hotel's coffee table book with its black-and-white pictures of bridges, bridges, and more bridges. She listlessly untucked her feet from the sofa and thumped the hefty book back in its place. She glanced toward the bedroom, where Michel had sequestered himself.

"Reaching carbon neutrality in fifteen years is not an improbable goal for a country such as ours . . ." She could make out some of his conversation on the phone with a minister from Rouleme. "Our people are conscientious and dedicated to environmental protection . . ."

Our country . . . our people . . .

She assiduously avoided the topic of his royal status when they were together to prove to him that it made no difference—that he would always be Michel Chevalier to her. Even so, she couldn't help but google "Prince Michel of Rouleme."

He was . . . amazing. He worked so hard for the betterment of his people and his country, including the environmental reform he was fighting for on the phone right this moment. And the recently passed social services addendum he spearheaded was receiving worldwide praise. What he did . . . he made a real difference. Because he was Crown Prince Michel of Rouleme.

And it was becoming more and more difficult to ignore who he was, as urgent matters from Rouleme arose with increasing frequency. He was their prince, and he was needed back in his country. Emma's stomach twisted with panic at the thought of him leaving. She squeezed her eyes shut until her heart rate returned to normal.

For the first time, she allowed the question that had been simmering at the back of her mind to come to the forefront. *Why is he here?* Why in the world was the prince of Rouleme in LA as a visiting professor at USC? It shouldn't matter. He was here, and he was leaving in a few weeks. The why shouldn't matter to her. Not really.

But why?!?! Did she even want to know? What if it was some top secret mission and the future of his country depended on it? Then again, he was a prince, not a secret agent. She worried her bottom lip. Honestly, she was afraid to ask. She was scared of getting more confirmation of how different they were—more reminders that he belonged in his country.

Tired of being alone with her thoughts, Emma walked to the front door and flung it open. Sophie shot up from her seat by the open door of her suite.

"Hey, Sophie," Emma said from across the foyer. "Can you keep me company while Michel puts out another fire?"

"Bien sûr." Her friend's lips quirked in a half grin.

They settled down on the opposite ends of the sofa—Emma with her back against the arm of the sofa, her knees drawn up to her chest, and Sophie with her back ramrod straight and her feet firmly planted on the floor.

"So how are things going with Gabriel?" Emma asked, remembering her self-imposed matchmaking duties.

"I have no idea." Sophie shook her head. She'd shared that

she and Gabriel had dated briefly before he moved to the US, but Emma had read between the lines and gathered that her friend's heart was broken when he left. Even so, there might be lingering feelings on both sides. "At any rate, he's a terrible flirt and a distraction."

"And you like that?" Emma wiggled her eyebrows. Sophie and Gabriel would certainly make a striking couple.

"Yes." Her friend barked out something between a sob and a laugh. "And it's a damned inconvenience."

"Oh, honey." Emma rushed to her side and wrapped her arm around her shoulders. This might be more serious than she'd thought. "I'm so sorry. How can I help?"

"It's pointless." Her friend's head drooped. "Nothing has changed. His place is here, but my duty lies with the prince and Rouleme. It could never work."

Emma's heart constricted painfully at the similarities of their plight. The only difference was that she had accepted the fleeting nature of her relationship with Michel while Sophie seemed torn.

"Have you thought about just enjoying the time you have with him?" Emma squeezed Sophie's shoulders once and dropped her arm.

"I . . . I fell apart when Gabriel left ten years ago." She shivered and wrapped her arms around her stomach. Emma had never seen her look so vulnerable. "If I let him close again . . . I don't know what it would do to me."

Encouraging her to hold on to false hope might be the worst advice Emma could give. Sophie and Gabriel were like water and oil. They were unlikely to last even if circumstances had been different. No, Sophie didn't need a matchmaker. She needed a friend with a good head on her shoulders.

"Then you have to protect your heart," Emma said softly. "You have to tell Gabriel to stop flirting with you. It's obviously tearing you apart. Your heart wants to give in, but your mind is telling you no. Listen to your mind. Draw a clear line he can't cross. I know it's hard, but it's the only way to stop yourself from getting hurt."

"You're right." Sophie sat up tall. "That's exactly what I need to do."

"Once you're back in Rouleme, everything will be back to normal." Emma wasn't sure who she was trying to convince— herself or her friend. It was true for both of them. Once Michel returned to his country and his duties, she would resume her life where she'd left off. She and Sophie were both going to be fine.

And Emma didn't need to know why Michel came to LA. All she had to remember was that he would be leaving soon. Whatever brought him here had allowed them to have this time together. She would always be grateful for that. And that gratitude would help her hold herself together when he left. No matter how much it hurt, she would have no regrets.

"I apologize for the interruption." Emerging from his bedroom at last, Michel took long-legged strides to reach her side. "I see Sophie's been keeping you company."

"Now that you're back, I'll return to my post." Sophie addressed Michel formally and said as a quiet aside, "Thank you, Emma."

"Anytime," she murmured, hoping her friend would find her peace soon.

"What was that about?" Michel sat down beside her and tucked her into his side. He dropped a kiss on the top of her head, unwaveringly affectionate.

"Just some girl talk." She snuggled closer to him. "Is everything okay?"

"'Okay' might be an overstatement." He wiped a weary hand down his face. "But yes. Everything is fine. For now."

"I could leave if you need more time to work." Emma tried to pull away, but Michel tightened his arm around her shoulders.

"You're not going anywhere." Michel tipped her chin up, and she shivered at the heat in his eyes. "I think we were in the middle of something very important before we were so rudely interrupted."

"Were we? I'm not sure if I remember . . ." She dragged a finger down the front of his shirt. "You're going to have to remind me."

Michel arched an eyebrow and leaned toward her. She licked her lips in anticipation, but he shifted at the last minute and kissed a trail down her jawline. Her gasp of indignation quickly morphed into a hiss when he lightly scraped his teeth on the tender skin of her neck.

"Do you remember now?" His low voice rumbled deep in his chest and vibrated against her body.

She shivered and wiggled in her seat but said, "You're going to have to try harder than that."

Despite her taunt, Michel didn't quicken his pace. He languidly drew his lips back up the length of her neck and licked a spot right behind her earlobe. She moaned and clenched her thighs together.

"Are you absolutely sure you don't recall?" He slid his hand up her torso and cupped her breast over her shirt, his thumb grazing the hardened peak. "Because I get the sense that you do."

"Vaguely," she breathed, burying her fingers in his hair to drag his mouth to hers. "Tell me if I've got it right."

She crushed her lips against his, demanding entry. He opened up with a guttural growl. Without hesitation, she plunged her tongue into the heat of his mouth. When his tongue tangled with hers, hungry and wild, she climbed onto his lap.

"So?" She bit his bottom lip, then let go to allow him to speak.

"You got it spot-on." His words sounded muffled because she was busy licking away the sting of her bite.

"I'm so pleased." She shifted on his lap to straddle him. "Do I get a reward?"

He pivoted his hips off the sofa, digging his hardness against her center. "Oh, I think you should get multiple."

Her first reward came deliriously fast as she shamelessly ground herself against him, both of them still fully dressed. Her second reward came with his beautiful golden head between her thighs. Her third reward undid her with him deep inside her, perfect and whole. And they didn't even leave the living room sofa.

"I'm sorry. Can you repeat that?" she said as she lay draped over Michel, his hand running up and down her bare back. "I got distracted at the end."

CHAPTER THIRTY-ONE

♡

I don't know how Antoine managed to snag a front-row seat and a VIP pass to a concert that sold out a year ago." Gabriel raised his water bottle in a mock toast. "But I don't care as long as the brat is appeased."

"Hear, hear." Michel clinked his mug against his cousin's bottle. "And Marion kept her end of the bargain beautifully."

Thank God for that. If Aunt Celine had come to Los Angeles, his time here might have been cut short. That would have been a disaster. If he asked Emma to come to Rouleme with him right now, he would surely scare her off.

He had yet to confess his love to Emma, but he *showed* her how much he loved her every moment they spent together. He would give her the words as soon as he figured out how to prove to her that they were perfect for each other despite—perhaps even *because of*—their differences and that his love for her would never change. Once he convinced her, she had to come to Rouleme with him, wouldn't she? He only wished he had more than one month to win her over.

"The thought of my mother in LA . . ." Gabriel gave an exaggerated shiver.

"Is Marion stopping by Los Angeles?" His personal assistant extraordinaire had mentioned that the concert was in San Francisco.

"Next Sunday." Gabriel tried for a grimace, but he couldn't hide his excitement at the prospect of seeing his baby sister. "She wanted to helicopter down Saturday night, but I put my foot down."

"You mean you begged," Michel said with a smirk.

"We can't have her drawing unnecessary attention to herself like that," Gabriel continued as though he hadn't spoken.

Michel shrugged. "A helicopter arrival is hardly noteworthy in Los Angeles."

"I'm not risking it," Gabriel said with a stubborn set of his jaws. "I worked too hard—gave up too much—to be where I am."

"Professor Chevalier," said a small voice. Gabriel started and spun in his seat. An eye and a part of a nose peeped through the small gap in his office door. "I was wondering—"

"How curious," Gabriel interrupted, his voice icy and hard. "Am I mistaken, or did his office hour end more than half an hour ago?"

"I know but . . . I thought . . ." The eye and the tip of the nose turned red. "I'm so sorry for disturbing you."

The disembodied face disappeared with a scuffling of trainer bottoms. Michel frowned when his cousin turned to face him again. "The Sphinx strikes again. Why do you do that?"

"Knee-jerk reaction?" Gabriel pinched the bridge of his nose. "I need the Sphinx persona to teach philosophy effectively. If my students ever got a whiff of the twit I truly am, my chances of convincing them to respect philosophy will fly right out the door. I don't want myself to get in the way of showing my students how incredible and essential philosophy is to humanity."

"Christ, you are such a nerd," Michel teased affectionately, touched by his cousin's earnest explanation. And there was more

to Gabriel's preoccupation with coming across as a serious academic. "I can't believe the people of Rouleme actually believed
what the tabloids were feeding them. You were never the empty-
headed playboy they made you out to be."

"My unparalleled good looks are a blessing and a curse." His
smile held a bitter edge that said it was more of a curse. "Besides,
I didn't help matters, did I? It was just easier in some ways to play
into that role."

"You should be proud of the life you built here, Gabriel."
Michel understood why his cousin had to leave Rouleme behind.
No matter what he did back home, he would never have been
more than a pretty face. He needed a fresh start. "But might I
remind you that was *my* student you just scared away."

"Like I said, knee-jerk reaction." Gabriel shrugged with a
rueful smile. "Besides, you need to learn to set boundaries for
yourself, too."

Michel couldn't hold back a harsh bark of laughter. "Easier
said than done, my dear cousin."

"I never implied that it would be easy." His cousin watched
him with quiet sympathy. Neither of them was speaking about
his role as a professor. "Look at the extremes I've had to go to for
my profession."

Being a king wasn't a profession. It would soon be his life.
Setting boundaries would be impossible. In fact, there might be
no Michel left, only the king, if he didn't have Emma by his side.
All the more reason he had to convince her that they were meant
for each other.

But . . . what about Emma? Would she be happy by his side
in Rouleme? Would leaving her life behind be the best thing
for her? He pushed the thoughts aside and quelled the gnawing
anxiety in his stomach.

"Should we start heading for the Town and Gown?" Michel
stood from his chair with a determined grin.

Gabriel groaned but rose to his feet. "The Sphinx does not enjoy interdepartmental mixers."

Michel rolled down the sleeves of his dress shirt and refastened his cuff links before adjusting the tie he'd loosened earlier. Then he retrieved his navy suit jacket from the coatrack and shrugged into it. "Perhaps I should've brought a change of clothes."

"Are you fishing for compliments? Well, I think you look very pretty, cousin dear." Gabriel grinned, just begging to be smacked on the side of his head. "And there's no need to fuss. It's not a ball. It's just a get-together for the faculty and their TAs to mingle with people outside their departments."

"You're making the event sound like happy hour." Michel watched Gabriel button up his light gray suit jacket. His cousin would look like an A-lister in a potato sack. "Even if it's not a ball, it is being held in the Town and Gown *Ballroom* with a plus-one. It sounds like a proper fête to me."

"I suppose you're right." Gabriel scratched the side of his jaw. "Especially with the open bar and dancing."

As Michel hurried out of his office, the thought of dancing with Emma placed a ridiculous smile on his face. She had agreed to meet him at the party after a late-afternoon lesson. Even though they'd gone out just last night, he couldn't wait to see her again. He quickened his pace while his cousin dragged his feet.

"Could you stop walking like an octogenarian? It would be rude to be late." When his cousin effectively flipped him off by an expressive tilt of his head and a narrowing of his eyes, Michel shrugged and rushed ahead to USC's famed ballroom.

He belatedly realized that Gabriel was slowing down to keep pace with Sophie, who had a talent for materializing out of thin air. She stared straight ahead and didn't deign to acknowledge his cousin. *Hmm.* They had seemed to be on better terms of late.

What changed? From the questioning looks Gabriel shot Sophie, he had no idea what was going on either.

When they got to the Town and Gown Ballroom, Sophie slipped into the shadows of the alcoves, and Gabriel joined Michel at his side. The ballroom wasn't as opulent as the ones that Michel was accustomed to, but it was immaculate and welcoming, especially with the gold-and-cardinal theme of the event decor. *Go, Trojans!* Many faculty and their aides had beat them to the event, their clinking glasses and laughter ringing through the room.

Michel scanned the fast-filling space for Emma but couldn't find her. He was relieved he'd arrived first. He didn't want her to step into a room full of strangers by herself. Even though it was often unavoidable for him, he never got accustomed to the nerve-racking nature of the experience.

"I need a drink," his cousin said in ominous tones beside him.

"Did something happen between you two?" Michel frowned, recalling the stilted interaction between Gabriel and Sophie.

"Hell if I know." Gabriel huffed a sigh and raked his fingers through his hair. "She was finally letting me back in—smiling more, laughing at my jokes, even. I thought there might be another chance for us . . ."

"There is," Michel reassured his obviously distraught cousin. "You just need to talk to her."

Sophie and Gabriel had been the best of friends as children even though they were as different as night and day. Their friendship confounded the elders, but Michel had always known that they understood each other better than anyone else. Their differences complemented one another in the best possible way. He had never imagined that their feelings went beyond friendship, but now that he knew, they made perfect sense together.

Gabriel was already stalking away but stopped to ask over his shoulder, "Do you want anything?"

"No, thank you." Michel would talk to his cousin later. For now, he needed to keep an eye out for Emma. "I'll get something once Emma arrives."

Thankfully, he didn't have to wait long. She glided into the ballroom with her head held high and shoulders thrown back, self-assured and confident even in the midst of strangers. He froze to the spot, his jaw going slack. She was breathtaking in a black off-the-shoulder cocktail dress. He already knew those shoulders would drive him to distraction all evening, especially with her hair up in a loose knot that left the silky skin tantalizingly bare. Her dress hugged her slim curves in all the right places, and his body tightened with desire. He shook himself out of his momentary stupor and rushed to her side.

"Emma," he said in a low, husky voice. When she smiled at him with her eyes glowing—like he was the best thing she'd seen all day—the lust thrumming in his veins dissolved into heart-wrenching affection. He couldn't help but run the backs of his fingers down her cheek. "You look beautiful."

"Thank you." Her eyelashes fluttered as she ducked her head shyly.

Michel fought the urge to kiss her senseless in a room full of faculty and graduate students. After taking a calming breath, he tucked her hand in his arm and led her toward a secluded section along the wall by a tall potted plant. He needed a few moments to gather himself. But more importantly, he wasn't ready to share Emma with anyone yet.

"How did your lesson go?" He wrapped a loose strand of her hair around his finger.

"It was so much fun." She slid one hand beneath his jacket and pressed it possessively against his chest. His heart beat out a

frantic rhythm in response. "We made hwayangjeok. Those little
striped flags we had at the picnic?"

"Ah, yes. The perfect bite." He covered her hand with his
own lest she withdraw it. He needed her touch.

"Oh, you remembered. That makes me so happy." She
pushed up to her toes and placed a chaste kiss on his lips. "That's
your reward."

She smelled so good—the warm floral note in her scent was
stronger than the citrus tonight. He took a step closer and angled
his body to hide her from the rest of the ballroom. "I think I deserve a little more than that."

Before she could answer, he dipped his head and captured
her parted lips. When she whimpered and opened wider for
him, he deepened the kiss and pulled her flush against his body.
His hands wrapped around her naked shoulders, and all rational
thought flew out of his mind. He needed to taste her soft, warm
skin . . .

"Cool it, Romeo," Gabriel said from behind him.

Emma started—even though Gabriel had spoken very
softly—and pulled away from Michel. His hands instinctively
tightened around her in protest before he forced himself to take
a step back.

"For you, my lady." His cousin handed her a flute of pink, ef-
fervescent champagne with a smile that was strained around the
edges. He was obviously torn up about Sophie, but he still had
come to stop Michel from making a spectacle out of himself. He
pushed a glass toward Michel, urging him back to stop towering
over her. "Let's put some space between you two. There. That
wasn't so hard, was it?"

Michel took his drink and clapped Gabriel on the shoulder.
As he sipped his cold champagne, he took a quick glance around
the ballroom. Thankfully, no one seemed to have noticed his

lapse in judgment. *Bloody hell*. Forget the dignity of the crown. Making out with his girlfriend at a work function was inappropriate even for Professor Michel Chevalier—for any responsible adult.

Good God. He'd just failed to behave like a responsible adult. He suppressed the incredulous laughter that rose to his throat. But his mirth quickly died away at the realization that he might have embarrassed Emma. He ducked his head and whispered in her ear, "Sorry."

She shivered and glanced briefly at his lips. *Christ, have mercy*. "That's okay. I technically started it."

"Will you kids be able to behave yourselves while I go top off my drink?" Gabriel crossed his arms over his chest, mischief fluttering just below his stern frown. He seemed to be doing a bit better.

"Fuck off." Michel offered his cousin an affectionate grin.

Emma coughed to cover her laugh and said, "Now, now, boys. Be nice."

"He started it." Gabriel winked at her. Michel scowled when she blushed. Gabriel raised his hands. "I'm going. I'm going."

"I like Gabriel," Emma said with a little sigh that grated on Michel's nerves.

"I can tell," he grumbled unhappily, even though he had no reason to be jealous. Except that he happened to have a Greek god incarnate as his cousin.

"Are you *jealous*, Professor Chevalier?" She dimpled enchantingly at him. "I hope your students don't know what a silly man you are."

Before he could formulate a comeback for her saucy comment, Emma became distracted by something on the dance floor. She gasped, then clicked her tongue. When Michel followed her line of sight, he discovered Jeannie locked in a passion-

ate embrace with a dark-haired young man. Even though he had
no right to be scandalized—since he had nearly found himself
in a similar situation moments before—he felt a tad scandalized.
He would never have expected this from his quietly awkward and
hardworking TA.

"Oh no. Poor Sarah," Emma murmured under her breath.

"Is something the matter?" he asked, but she didn't get a
chance to respond as a train wreck unfolded before their eyes.

"Um . . . excuse me." A pretty Asian woman stepped in
front of Gabriel, who had been on his way back to them. Her
eyes were shining with adoration or . . . tears. She looked familiar. *Ah, yes.* Sarah Bae was a graduate student in the philosophy department—his cousin's TA and Emma's friend. "Professor
Laurent . . . I . . . would you like to dance?"

Merde alors. Michel tensed, knowing what Gabriel—no, the
Sphinx—would do.

"Sarah?" Gabriel blinked in surprise before his features hardened into a stony façade. "Would I like to dance? With my own
TA? You can't be serious. That is quite possibly the last thing I
would want to do. Surely you know me better than that."

Knee-jerk reaction. His cousin's sheepish expression from earlier flashed before Michel's eyes.

"I'm so . . . so . . ." Sarah's apology broke on a sob, and her
lower lip trembled dangerously.

"Excuse me," Michel said to Emma with a quick squeeze of
her hand, and hurried over to his panicked cousin and the poor
young woman. "Hello, Ms. Bae. I've been wanting to meet you."

"Professor Chevalier?" The young woman sniffed as her eyes
widened.

"Oh, you know who I am?" Michel offered her a warm smile.
"I have heard such wonderful things about you from Professor
Laurent. He said you were such a hard worker and that you were
invaluable to his teaching."

"He did?" She peeked at Gabriel but quickly glanced away.

"He certainly did." It was true. His cousin had also mentioned how tempting it was to tease her about her last name, but the Sphinx would never do that. Gabriel would feel awful about this later if Michel couldn't salvage the situation. "Between you and me, the man is a brilliant academic, but he unfortunately has two left feet. Would you care to dance with me instead?"

While Sarah stood with her mouth opening and closing, Gabriel gave her a curt nod, then shot Michel a grateful glance before escaping out the side doors to the balcony. Michel offered Sarah his hand with a bow of his head, and she took it with a shy smile.

As he led the young woman out to the dance floor, he realized he'd abandoned Emma without any explanation. Surely she would understand, especially since it had been her friend in peril. When he glanced over his shoulder at her, she waved him off with a blinding smile on her face.

CHAPTER THIRTY-TWO

Emma dabbed away the tears pooling in her eyes. Her friend had been pale and withdrawn at first, but Michel coaxed Sarah out of her shell and had her giggling by the middle of the song. Emma scanned the dance floor and was relieved that the redheaded beauty—Sarah's *dreamy* crush—was nowhere to be seen. Perhaps Jeannie had found somewhere private to stick her tongue down the guy's throat.

Poor Sarah. She must've been heartbroken and desperate to have scrounged up the nerve to ask the Sphinx to dance with her. What was Gabriel's problem anyway? He was such a charming, easygoing man. But by all accounts, he turned into an absolute asshole when he assumed his role as Professor Laurent. Like tonight with Sarah. Emma pushed aside her anger. That wasn't important right now.

All that mattered was that Michel had charged in like a knight in shining armor and rescued Sarah from further humiliation. Emma dug the heel of her hand into her chest as her heart ping-ponged against her rib cage. She remembered from her high school French that *chevalier* meant "knight." It was so perfectly fitting. She sighed and leaned back against the wall. She was acting like a starstruck teenager, but she didn't care.

Michel was wonderful. He was loyal, kind, strong, and generous. And he made her laugh. He made her feel safe. He made her feel complete in a way she didn't know was possible. Her dreamy smile froze in place and slowly melted away.

Oh God. Emma released a shuddering breath, hot tears blinding her eyes. She was in love with him. She loved him so much. *What have I done?* How could she fall in love with him knowing that he would soon be gone?

She thought her time with Michel would be worth the risk of heartbreak. But now that her heart was truly on the line, she didn't feel so brave anymore. How could she bear it when he left? What was she going to do? All her life, she'd done everything in her power to protect herself from heartbreak. She never wanted any of this. Why now? Why him?

Because he was Michel. Because he looked at her like she was the most precious person in the world. Because he forgot his perfect manners and kissed her in the middle of a ballroom like he couldn't help himself—like she was irresistible. Because he stepped in to dance with a forlorn girl and make her laugh past her tears. Emma loved Michel with all her heart because he was him.

And she had to *stop*. Emma could do anything once she set her mind to it. She could do this, too. She could stop loving Michel. If she could lock away the pain and loneliness of being abandoned by her mom, she could lock away her love for Michel.

When the song ended, she stepped closer to the tall, leafy plant by her side in a subconscious attempt to hide. Michel gestured toward her, and Sarah's eyes widened. Emma hadn't had a chance to tell her friend that she was dating the famed visiting professor. The two of them walked toward her, and she took a brave step out of her hiding place.

"Allow me to replenish your drinks, while you ladies catch up," Michel said with a crooked smile that turned her knees to Jell-O. She watched as he walked away with the grace of a runway model, then turned to her friend.

"Oh my gosh," Sarah squealed, clasping Emma's hands. "I didn't know you were dating Professor Chevalier."

"It's only been a few weeks." She squashed the flare of panic along with the small voice that whimpered, *You have less than four weeks left with him.* "It's not that serious."

"Yeah, right." Her friend snorted. "Have you *seen* the way he looks at you?"

"How . . ." Emma cleared her throat. "How does he look at me?"

Sarah blushed and giggled into her hand. "Like he can't decide whether to fall on his knees and worship you at your feet, or to throw you over his shoulder to ravish you in a dark corner."

"You discerned all that from one look?" Emma said with a wry grin, even as her blood pounded in her ears.

"Here we are." Michel returned with two flutes of champagne and looked at Emma, and God help her, his eyes gleamed with lust and adoration. She took the champagne from his hand and gulped it down so fast that her throat stung from the bubbles.

"Thank you, Professor Chevalier." Sarah accepted her drink with far better manners and shot a sly glance toward Emma. She seemed to have shaken off the incident with Gabriel and was back to her sassy self. "I have to go mingle now. Have a nice evening, you two."

When Sarah disappeared into the crowd, Michel retrieved the empty flute from Emma's limp fingers and set it down on a nearby cocktail table. He leaned close to her ear and murmured, "Would you dance with me? I need to hold you."

Emma nodded wordlessly and let him lead her to the dance

floor. As if on cue, the song transitioned into Billie Holiday's "Solitude," and Michel gathered her in his arms. She clung helplessly to him as she fell deeper in love with each sway of their bodies—the strong, reassuring beat of his heart thumping against her palm.

"You're quiet." His breath fluttered against her temple. "Is anything the matter?"

She closed her eyes and pressed her body closer to his. She was drowning in the realization of love, but she couldn't tell him that. What if he told her he loved her, too? She wanted that with such desperation that it terrified her. Would she perish from heartbreak if he didn't love her back?

But what difference did it make if they loved each other? It would never last. It didn't seem possible right now, but her love for Michel would eventually fade, and there would be nothing left to hold them together. Besides, he had to go back to rule a country and her life was here—her dad, her godmother, her work—everything she loved was here. Well, not everything. Not anymore.

"I'm just a little tired." She had to say something. "It's been a long day."

"Shall I take you home?" He tried to pull back to look at her, but she held fast, afraid of what he'd see on her face.

"No. Let's just . . ." She sighed. "Let's just dance."

Emma breathed in the windswept, woodsy scent of him and let herself *be*. She'd spent her life trying to cultivate the perfect home, and she had found it in this man's arms at last. It didn't need to have just the right wall color and furniture arrangement. It didn't need to be filled with beautiful, delicious food at every meal. Being with Michel *was* home. Her feet stopped moving, weighed down by all that she had to lose. It was so unfair.

"You know what?" She abruptly stepped back from Michel. "I think I'd like to go home."

Surprise flashed across his face, but concern swiftly replaced it. "Of course. Let me drive you home."

"I drove here, remember?" She was already hurrying toward the exit.

"I could ask Sophie to follow us with my car . . ."

"Don't be silly," she snapped, and Michel's steps faltered beside her. Eyes round with regret, she reached out to squeeze his hand. "I don't want to bother her. I'll be fine going home on my own."

A shadow of a frown darkened his face before he shook his head. "As you wish. I'll just walk you to your car."

"Thank you," she said with a distracted smile.

The cool evening air greeted them as they stepped out of the Town and Gown, and she took a deep breath. The USC campus looked beautiful after sunset, with elegant streetlamps casting a warm glow on the tree-lined walkways and cardinal brick buildings.

"I . . . I haven't thanked you. For what you did for Sarah," she said suddenly. She'd forgotten all about it when he took her in his arms on the dance floor. "She has—or had—a crush on your TA, Jeannie, and it suddenly became clear that she didn't reciprocate Sarah's feelings . . ."

"Yes." Michel scratched the back of his head with a rueful smile. "I saw Jeannie on the dance floor being very . . . affectionate with someone else. Is that why Sarah asked Gabriel to dance?"

"That's my guess. I think Sarah was humiliated—even though Jeannie had no idea about her crush—and wanted to seem totally unaffected by the . . . scene." Emma's temper flashed red at the reminder. "Then Gabriel had to go and humiliate her further. What is wrong with him?"

"It wasn't his best moment, but . . . he had his reasons," Michel said diplomatically.

"What reasons?" Emma stopped in her tracks and spun to face him. "Are you *defending* him?"

"No, not exactly." His eyebrows rose. "I agree that his conduct cannot be excused, but there *are* extenuating circumstances."

"I can't believe you." She was overreacting because her love for Michel terrified her, but she couldn't seem to stop. "I'm glad Sophie won't be risking her heart for that jerk."

Michel grew unnervingly still next to her. "What do you mean? Did *you* tell Sophie to shut Gabriel out?"

"She's my friend, and I wanted to help. I couldn't just sit by and watch her twist herself into a knot." Emma crossed her arms, annoyed at how defensive she felt. She'd done the right thing. "I have never met two people more unlike each other. And they live on different *continents*. Besides, he broke her heart. It'd be foolish of her to give him the opportunity to break it a second time."

"He is a good man." Michel didn't raise his voice, but Emma suddenly realized how *big* he was.

He'd become cold and hard in his anger—someone she didn't know—and she wanted her Michel back. All her anger drained out of her. They only had four weeks left with each other. They couldn't waste their time fighting.

"Why are we arguing?" Emma touched his arm, but Michel stepped away from her to pace with short, clipped turns. "This isn't our fight to have."

"You made it our fight when you interfered in my cousin and my friend's relationship," he bit out. "I've known them all my life. You've known them for . . . What? A few weeks?"

"Yes . . . as long as I've known you." She let her words hang between them. What did she really know about Michel? *He makes you happy. He feels like home. You love him.* She bit the inside of her cheek. *He is leaving.*

"That's not what I . . . Emma . . ." He stopped in front of her and searched her face. His voice was haggard but softer when he said, "What I meant was that they are good people. They deserve a chance at happiness."

"I know Sophie and Gabriel are good people, but they're incompatible." *Just like us.* She couldn't let herself forget that. Things would never work out between them even if he didn't have to leave. She wouldn't be able to stand watching Michel turn into a stranger when their love inevitably faded. It would destroy her. It was for the best that he was leaving . . . but her soul still railed against it. "They won't be happy together in the long run, so why invite heartache?"

"Because love is *worth the risk.*" Michel held out his hands, palms up, as his eyes implored her. "And having things in common isn't what makes people compatible. Sometimes it's how their differences complement one another that makes them perfect for each other."

"So *what* if their differences make them perfectly compatible?" she asked in a near whisper. Somewhere along the way, they'd stopped arguing about the other couple. She didn't want to hear this. She didn't want to hope. She was terrified she'd already started hoping. "Sophie's life is in Rouleme. Gabriel's life is here. Compatibility isn't going to bridge the ocean between them."

Michel opened his mouth on a sharp inhale, but the retort died on his lips. She held his gaze. *See? You know I'm right.* Even if she allowed herself to ignore that they came from different worlds—even if she followed her heart knowing that it would be shattered in the end—there was no chance for them. He knew that, and it hurt him as much as it hurt her. So much so that he didn't go after her when she walked off on her own.

CHAPTER THIRTY-THREE

M ichel stared wordlessly out the window as Sophie drove them back to the hotel. She must have heard them arguing about her and Gabriel—he and Emma certainly hadn't been discreet with their argument—but he didn't have the capacity to worry about his friend's feelings at the moment.

It had gutted him to watch Emma walk away from him, but he needed time to think. Who was he to tell Emma that love was worth the risk? He'd been avoiding confessing his love to her because he'd been afraid. All his excuses—that he had to first figure out how to convince her they were meant for each other and to show her that his love would never fade—were just that. Excuses. He'd been too afraid to tell her he loved her because he didn't want to risk ruining the four remaining weeks he had with her. Perhaps . . . he had been wise in his cowardice.

All this time, Michel had thought his greatest obstacle in winning Emma would be convincing her that despite their differences they *fit* perfectly. That it didn't matter they weren't perfect for each other on paper, because they were as compatible as two people could be in real life. How could he have been so wrong?

Emma's parting words rang in his ears. *Compatibility isn't going to bridge the ocean between them.* She was right, and they had more than the physical ocean between them. She was a culinary instructor in Los Angeles, living with a single father who depended on her love and her company. He was the crown prince and future king of Rouleme, duty bound to his country and his people.

He had blithely believed that if he could get her to fall in love with him, then she would uproot her life and leave behind everything she knew—everyone she loved—just to be with him. She would have to give up her dream of opening up a culinary school. But beyond that, she would have to give up her privacy and be bound to a life of duty like him. A duty that sometimes weighed so heavily on him that he could hardly breathe.

By asking her to become his wife, he would also be asking her to bear part of the blame for breaking a long-standing engagement. While Isabelle would be thrilled to be freed from an arranged marriage, the fallout would cause unwanted tension between the families, and his father would *not* be thrilled. He would ultimately accept Emma as his daughter-in-law and learn to love her, but she would have to endure a rocky start.

And the people of Rouleme were progressive and open-minded, but a vocal minority might denounce Emma as an outsider—even take issue with her race. He would protect her in every way he could, but those insidious voices would hurt her. If he loved her, how could he push her into a perilous, uncertain future? How could he ask her to sacrifice so much?

Shame rolled through him at how utterly selfish he'd been. Emma didn't harbor secret hopes of becoming Cinderella. She believed in creating her own happiness through every meal she prepared, through every friendship she nurtured, through all the beauty she found in the world around her.

What did he have to offer her but pain and loss? Title, wealth, and power could never replace the things she would have to leave behind . . . the things she would have to endure. All he had to offer was himself and his love. But was his love even real if he wanted to have her by his side knowing that she would be unhappy?

Sophie shot him a concerned glance as they silently rode the elevator to their floor. "My prince, are you . . ."

"Please." Michel held up his hand. "Not now."

She bowed curtly with her lips pressed into a firm line. As soon as the elevator doors opened, he strode toward his suite, eager to be alone. His hand stilled halfway to the door handle when his friend spoke from across the foyer.

"I am a grown woman, Michel. My decisions are my own. You cannot blame Emma for her well-intentioned counsel."

"I know," he said quietly and stepped into his suite.

He unknotted his tie and threw it on an armchair, followed by his suit jacket. He sloshed whiskey into a tumbler and gulped down the fiery liquid, then poured himself another. Not bothering to walk over to the sitting area just a few steps away, he slid down to the floor next to the drink cart.

He rested his wrist on a raised knee and swirled the drink in the cup. What had that fight really been about? Yes, he'd felt a flash of anger at Emma's meddling, but that was not why he'd lost his temper. He'd been worried—even a little scared—by the solemn, distant look on Emma's face when she pulled away from him on the dance floor. Something was bothering her, and it made him nervous that he didn't know what it was.

Michel had let his fear and frustration get the best of him. He'd already been on edge since realizing he was in love with her—afraid of truly facing what that meant. So, like a fool and a coward, he'd picked a fight with the woman he loved. *Christ.* He didn't know what was the right thing to do. Whether loving her meant he should keep his true feelings to himself and leave Los Angeles—and Emma—when the time came. Or whether he should confess his love to her and beg her to be with him—to be his—no matter how selfish that felt.

He pushed up to his feet and set his untouched whiskey on the drink cart. He didn't know what to do for his future—for their future. But he knew exactly what he needed to do in this moment. No matter which route he chose to take, the next few weeks were theirs. And no one—least of all himself—would take that from them. He had to go to Emma.

He slipped out of his suite and down the stairs, not wanting to alert Sophie by calling the elevator. When he finally reached the lobby, he realized he didn't have the keys to the car. He strode out into the night and flagged down a taxi that had just dropped someone off at the hotel.

Fortunately, he had his wallet on him—unlike his mobile—to pay the taxi driver as he got out in front of Emma's house. He glanced at his watch. It was just past ten o'clock. She wouldn't be asleep yet, but her father might be, so he couldn't very well knock on her front door. He stood on the sidewalk feeling decidedly foolish, wondering what he should do next. He only knew he needed her in his arms. Everything else he would figure out later.

Michel skulked down a path at the side of the house, hoping that it led into their backyard. Emma had mentioned that her bedroom was on the second floor, facing the garden in the back. Holding his breath, he tried the latch to the gate at the end of the path and exhaled with relief when it opened. Even in the silvery moonlight, he could see that the garden was lovingly maintained with fragrant flowers along the outer edges and a vegetable garden—perhaps a small farm was a better description— that took up most of the yard.

On the second floor, there were two larger windows at the opposite ends of the house—one lit, one dark—with a couple of smaller windows in between. He had to guess that the larger windows belonged to the bedrooms and one of them was Emma's. He picked up several thumbnail-size pebbles and threw one, aiming for the lit window. He didn't pause to think that he might very well be summoning her father.

He used up all his pebbles, but no one came to the window. Maybe she couldn't hear the clack of the small stones. Perhaps he should use slightly larger stones at the risk of breaking the glass. He would, of course, reimburse them for any damage. A nervous chuckle escaped his lips. He might be losing his mind.

"Michel?" Emma whisper shouted from the window. *Ha!* He'd chosen the right window to pellet. "What are you doing down there?"

"Trying to get your attention," he said through cupped hands.

"Shh." She glanced behind her as though her father might walk through her door. "Stay right there. I'm coming down."

Heart pounding, he dusted his hands off and clasped them in front of him. Long minutes passed without any sign of Emma, and he began to pace, wondering if a phone call might've been wiser. When she finally stepped through the french doors with a thick cardigan over her long nightgown, he reached her in three hurried strides and pulled her into his arms. *Home.* His heart belonged to her, and no place on earth would ever feel like home again without her by his side.

"I'm sorry," he whispered into her hair. "I'm so sorry."

"I'm sorry, too." Her voice was thick with tears.

"Please don't cry, darling Emma." He leaned back to wipe her damp cheeks with his thumbs. Her tears gutted him, especially since he'd caused them. He never wanted to make her cry again. "I can't bear it."

"Okay. I'll stop." She sniffed and offered him a wobbly smile. "See? No more crying."

New tears seeped out of the corners of her eyes, and he caught them with his lips and tongue. Her breath caught, and he tried to step back with his heart in a vise, thinking she wasn't ready to be touched like that. But she buried her fingers in his hair and rose on her tiptoes to press her soft, sweet lips against his. With a broken groan, he plundered her mouth with desperate, hungry kisses. He should slow down. This wasn't why he came.

But he dragged her to the side of the house and pushed her up against the rough, cold wall, kissing and licking his way down the side of her neck. Her back arched off the wall, and his fingers gripped the soft flesh of her hips. He wanted to look at her face—to make sure she wanted this, too—but even the moon didn't cast its light into the dark alcove. He held on to his control by a single, shredded string and dropped featherlight kisses along her jaw and on her cheeks. He hoped she needed him as much as he needed her but gave her time to pull away.

When her mouth captured his with hunger to match his own, the last of his control snapped. Something flickered at the back of his mind. He tasted desperation mingled with desire in her kiss . . . like she was trying to forget something. But she raked her fingernails down his scalp, and rational thought became impossible. He hiked her leg around his waist and ground his hard length against her core. Pushing aside her nightgown, he ran his hand up her thigh.

"Fuck. Are you not—" He swept his hand over her bare arse. "Fuck."

"You already said that." Her voice was husky and dark as she unbuckled his belt and reached for his aching erection. "Panties are a nuisance."

"When—"

"I slipped them off before I ran down to meet you." She took his hand and slipped it between their bodies. He groaned when his fingers slid into her hot, wet folds. She was ready for him. "Any more questions, or are you going to fuck me?"

His eyes nearly rolled back in his head as lust singed through him. He gritted through his clenched teeth, "Condom."

"I'm on birth control." She pulled him free from his boxer briefs.

"And I'm . . ." He couldn't find the words to explain his regular blood test results as he prepared to bury himself inside her. "You're safe. I would never hurt you."

"Me . . ." She gasped and wrapped her other leg around his waist. ". . . too."

Unable to hold back a moment longer, he plunged inside her with a low groan. He hiked her up higher and pressed her back into the wall—pulling himself in and out of her tight warmth with rough, jerky movements. When she cried out, he covered her mouth with his hand, unable to stop pounding into her even for a moment. She bit down into the side of his hand to muffle her next scream, and he didn't even feel it. All he felt was her, riding him like a wild goddess, as pressure built at his spine.

"I need you to come for me, sweetheart," he growled.

He ducked his head and sucked her nipple into his mouth through her thin nightgown. Their hips bucked and slammed into each other, desperately seeking the sweet crest of release. When her back arched and a strangled cry tore from her throat, he rammed into her once, then twice as his climax claimed him.

For a while, there was no sound except for the harsh rasp of their panting breaths. His eyes had adjusted to the dark, and he could make out her wide gaze holding his. The hint of sadness in her expression made his stomach clench. It was just a foolish argument. They had to be all right. He pressed a kiss to her forehead and lowered her to the ground. He barely finished zipping up his pants when her knees buckled, and he scooped her up into his arms and strode over to a sitting area beneath a small pergola.

He settled her on an Adirondack chair in front of an unlit firepit and sat down on its twin. She shivered, and he automatically went to remove his jacket but realized that he'd left it at the hotel. He didn't want to leave her yet, but he forced himself to say, "You're cold. I should head back."

"Don't." She smiled shyly. "Not yet."

At Michel's frown, she leaned forward and fiddled with the firepit until blue flames licked the night air.

"There. I'm not cold anymore." She arched a brow. "Satisfied?"

"Quite," he said with a wolfish grin. He had to decide what the best way was for him to love her. But for now, he needed this—this warm, intimate moment with the love of his life. Another memory that would stay with him forever. "Yet, I seem to be insatiable when it comes to you."

She rolled her eyes at him, but he could see a blush rise to her cheeks in the light of the fire. Pulling her cardigan close around her, she raised her bare feet toward the flames and wiggled her toes. Then she bolted up in her seat and looked frantically around her garden.

"Oh my God." She covered her mouth with both her hands. "Sophie."

"She's back at the hotel." He reached over and pulled her hands down. "No one witnessed our . . . indiscretion."

"Thank goodness." Emma sagged with relief, then straightened again. "Wait. Did you *sneak out*?"

"I did not sneak out." The tips of his ears grew hot. "I'm not a wayward adolescent. I merely left my suite without notifying her."

"You totally snuck out." She laughed with such glee that he couldn't help but join her. "No, this isn't funny. She's going to freak out. You have to call her."

"I left my mobile at the hotel." He scratched the back of his head. "That's why I had to resort to pebbles to get your attention."

"Well, you could borrow mine." She patted down her sides, then sighed. "Wait here. Let me go grab it."

He leaned back in his chair with a sigh and looked up at the sky through the slats of the pergola. In the quiet peace of the moment, Michel knew that everything would be all right. He loved Emma with everything in him. All he had to do was follow his heart.

"Here," she said, reclaiming her seat next to him. "Call."

"Thank you." He took her mobile and dialed Sophie's number. She answered on the first ring.

"Sophie, it's me. I—"

"Don't bother," his friend snapped. He could hear her take deep, calming breaths on the other end. "I'm parked in front of Emma's house. I'll escort you back when you're ready, *Your Highness.*"

"I—" he tried again, but she'd already hung up.

"Are you in trouble?" Emma looked so worried that he pressed a kiss to her lips.

"Don't worry." He picked up her hand and dropped kisses on her knuckles. "I won't get grounded."

She linked her fingers through his and leaned back in her chair. He rested his head on the back of his chair and returned her steady gaze, their contentment forming a warm cocoon around them. Sometimes, words were unnecessary . . . inadequate. How could he describe the perfection of their shared exhalation—their souls aligned, utterly at ease? If this was his last moment on earth, he would die entirely fulfilled.

CHAPTER THIRTY-FOUR

♥

Michel stood by the side gate repeating *good night* and *I should go* for about twenty minutes, all the while holding Emma tightly in his arms and dropping kisses on her temples, eyes, and the corners of her lips. She didn't want the night to end either, but she had a morning class she should at least be semi-awake for, and he no doubt had a mountain of reports to review, calls to make, and other princely duties to deal with before his lecture in the afternoon.

Fisting his shirt in her hands, she rose to her tiptoes and kissed him soundly on the lips. When he made a growly noise deep in his chest, she was tempted to keep going, but she needed to be strong for both of them. She disengaged her lips from his and pushed him away firmly by his shoulders.

"You need to go." She was going for stern but sounded much too breathless.

"I know." When Michel stood rooted to the spot, giving her a woebegone puppy-dog stare, she spun him around and pushed him out the side gate. "I'm leaving. I'm leaving."

"Good." She didn't even try to sound like she meant it. "Shoo."

Halfway across the front lawn, he looked over his shoulder and nearly stopped her heart with that crooked grin of his. It gave her a glimpse of the mischievous little boy he must've been and the fun-loving and joyful man he hid behind a wall of civility and decorum. With her, he dropped his protective armor and let her see him—all of him. Sudden tears blurred her vision.

Emma was grateful he came to her tonight. That they didn't waste another minute being angry with each other. After their fight earlier, she couldn't avoid facing her feelings any longer. She'd let it wash over her and infuse her soul. She loved him so much it hurt. It felt as though she would burst from the enormity of that love. But that was that.

She couldn't change the fact that she fell in love with a man she could never have. Pain as sharp as nails scraped down her heart, drawing blood. *No, Emma. You can do this.* She would love him with all her heart for the remainder of the time they had together. That was all she could do.

But what would happen to him when he returned to Rouleme? Would there be someone else he could be himself with? She had made certain not to read any articles about his love life, but there were hardly any to avoid. If there had been anyone else in his life, he had been very discreet about it. A part of her—a small, jealous part—never wanted him to find what he had with her. But another part of her—the part that loved him more than anything—hoped that he would find someone to share himself with. For his sake.

She wanted to run after him and never let him leave. But she swallowed the lump in her throat and forced herself to wave at him, not quite managing to smile back. Before she could change her mind, she walked through the side gate and latched it closed behind her. With heavy steps, she let herself back in the house and headed for the kitchen. She should make herself some hot chocolate. She was too wired to sleep.

Emma turned on the soft under-cabinet lights and pattered over to the fridge. After grabbing a half-empty carton of milk, she closed the refrigerator door and screamed, long and loud. The milk carton went flying, and her hands grappled at her throat as though she was trying to rein back her bloodcurdling scream. Her unsuspecting dad shouted in alarm and plastered himself to the kitchen wall.

"Where did you come from?" she cried.

"I didn't mean to startle you." He peeled himself off the wall with a shaky chuckle. "But you scared the bejesus out of me, too."

"I'm not the one who snuck up on you." She went to retrieve the milk from the floor, which thankfully hadn't exploded on impact. "What are you doing up anyway?"

Wait. Oh, shit. Michel and she . . . They did . . . things . . . Just on the other side of the kitchen wall. *Shit, shit, shit.*

"I got up to use the restroom and remembered that there was leftover bean sprouts and spinach . . ."

"Say no more." Emma smiled with relief and affection. "I'll fry the eggs. You get the veggies and gochujang."

Impromptu midnight bibimbap was *the* best midnight snack and comfort food. And she had worked up quite an appetite . . . She flushed and cut her thoughts short. She could not think about what she and Michel did against the wall—*outside*—with her dad standing in the same room with her.

Carefully smoothing out her expression, she focused on making the perfect sunny-side-up eggs with crisp golden edges. She turned the stove off a few seconds early to let them sit in the pan while she took out a giant mixing bowl and dumped the cold rice left over from dinner into the bowl. Knowing the drill, her dad dumped all the banchan from the fridge over the rice. She eyeballed the chili paste needed and scraped it off her spoon with her finger and drizzled a generous amount of toasted sesame seed oil into the bowl.

"Will you do the honors?" she asked her dad once she added the eggs on top of the concoction.

"It would be my pleasure." Her dad swallowed audibly and mixed everything together with his spoon until the nutty, spicy smell of bibimbap permeated the air.

They placed the mixing bowl on the floor and sat cross-legged on opposite sides with their spoons poised over it.

"Ladies first," her dad said graciously.

"Ha!" She snorted. "You raised this Korean kid right, Appa. *Elders* first."

"That's my girl." With a proud smile, he scooped up a towering spoonful and maneuvered the whole thing into his mouth until he had chipmunk cheeks.

She followed his lead and stuffed her face with a fist-size mound. That was the only way to eat this kind of everything-but-the-kitchen-sink bibimbap. The sticky short-grain rice was red and shiny with gochujang and sesame oil, and the seasoned bean sprouts and spinach were salty and crunchy with just enough moisture to prevent the bibimbap from being too dry. Even though her stomach felt stretched to the max, she couldn't stop eating. When her dad offered her the last bite at the bottom of the mixing bowl, she took it.

"I'm just going to lie down here and go to sleep," she slurred, patting her full, happy tummy.

Her dad stood with the empty bowl and spoons and washed them at the sink, humming tunelessly. She didn't even have the energy to object to him doing the dishes. She had to remember that he wanted to take care of her, too. It was okay to let him sometimes.

"I was going to wait till tomorrow to tell you," her dad began.

"Tell me what?" She leaned her head against the cupboard, the ups and downs of the long day catching up with her. Her words echoed back to her. *Compatibility isn't going to bridge the ocean.* The dormant ache in her chest resurfaced.

"You remember Mr. Goo?"

"Of course I remember him." He was an old friend of her dad's who owned several successful Korean restaurants. "He asks me to come work at one of his restaurants every time he sees me."

"I told him a million times that you prefer teaching, but the man is stubborn." Her dad shook his head. "Anyway, he mentioned a commercial kitchen space he came across in Culver City."

Emma scrambled to her feet. "What commercial kitchen space?"

"Now, don't get too excited." He wiped his hands on a towel, watching her with a fond smile as she screeched and jumped up and down. "But he said that it might be coming up for lease. At a reasonable rate."

"How?" she gasped.

"Well, he had an opportunity to purchase it with a mind to start a banchan delivery service, but I mentioned you and . . ." Her dad shrugged like he didn't just hand her the whole world on a platter. "Mr. Goo said you could come take a look anytime."

"Tomorrow." She glanced at the clock. It was past one. "I mean today. But I can wait till the sun is up."

"I'm sure Mr. Goo would appreciate that." He smiled at her like she was so adorable he could barely stand it.

She smiled back at him, studying his beloved face. With a jolt of fear and sadness, she realized her dad was getting old. The laugh lines around his eyes and mouth had branched out and deepened, and his hair seemed grayer than she remembered. She walked up to him and wrapped him in a tight hug. Her dad chuckled and returned her hug, swaying back and forth as though soothing a baby. She would always be his little girl.

"I love you, Daddy."

"I love you, too, baby girl," he said, squeezing her tight one last time before releasing her. "You have a big day tomorrow. You should go to bed . . . Come to think of it, what were you doing up so late?"

"Time for bed. Big day tomorrow." She hurried out of the kitchen, hoping he'd think she didn't hear his question. "Good night, Appa."

Emma clipped her hair away from her neck and took a quick shower. Smothering a yawn, she pulled on a fresh pair of panties and trudged over to her bed. But as soon as she lay down, she burst into giddy laughter. She turned her head to smother her laugh in her pillow, squealing while she was at it. *Semi-public sex. Check.* And that had never even been on her list of things to do.

She wondered if this was a first for Michel as well. She had a feeling it was, considering how buttoned-up and proper he tended to be. *Double check.* But seeing him lose control like that was . . . so hot. She flopped onto her back and threw the covers off her suddenly heated body. God, she wanted him again. And she missed him even though she'd been with him an hour ago.

Not allowing herself to overthink things, she grabbed her cell phone from her nightstand.

Emma:
I miss you.

Before she could wonder if he was asleep, three little dots started tripping across the screen.

Michel:
I miss you, too.

Her eyes stung, and she could taste salt at the back of her throat, but she stubbornly put a smile on her face and into her words.

> **Emma:**
> Guess what? I have exciting news!

> **Michel:**
> What is it?

> **Emma:**
> I might be able to open up my culinary school sooner than I thought!

This time, the ellipses rolled and rolled for quite a while, making her smile slip.

> **Michel:**
> What wonderful news!

That was it? She worried her bottom lip, disappointed by his generic response. She thought he'd be more excited for her. And why did it take him so long to type that out? He must've written and erased his words multiple times to end up with that . . .

> **Michel:**
> How did that come about?

Her stomach dropped. Was he . . . Did he . . . No, it couldn't be. It was probably nothing.

Emma:

My dad's friend is a restaurateur
and somehow came to own a
commercial kitchen space and
he might be willing to lease it to
me for a reasonable price. I don't
know the details but I'm going to
go check out the place tomorrow.
I mean today but later when the
sun is up.

Michel:

😂😂😂 ☀ ☀ ☀

Her heart pounded as she frowned at the message. Michel
wasn't much of an emoji person. Was he . . . Did he change
his mind about their relationship? Did he hope for something
more permanent than the two months he'd proposed? But he
never hinted that he wanted something more with her . . . She
scrunched her eyes shut and shook her head as though she could
stop her thoughts from running away from her.

Michel:

Let me know how it goes. I hope it
is to your liking.

Her shoulders sagged, and she huffed a little scornful laugh
at herself. He would've told her if he wanted something more
out of their relationship. *See how silly being in love makes you?*
Besides, *she* didn't want anything more than what they had now.
No matter how much it hurt, she had to be realistic. *More* wasn't
possible.

Emma:
Okay.

Emma:
Good night.

Michel:
Good night.

He was probably just tired. She yawned. So was she. He would probably be more excited for her when she had more to share tomorrow. Whatever the case, Emma needed this. Now more than ever. Focusing on opening up her culinary school might be the only thing that could save her from falling apart after Michel returned to Rouleme. She hoped the kitchen would be perfect for her vision so she could pour what was left of her soul into it when she lost him.

CHAPTER THIRTY-FIVE

♡

Michel caught Jeannie's eyes, signaling that he was ready to leave the lecture hall. The enthusiasm of his students wasn't enough to distract him from his bleak mood today.

"All right, people." She clapped her hands to get their attention. When that didn't work, she brought her fingers to her lips and whistled loudly enough to make his ears ring. "Please let the professor through. I'll be happy to answer any questions you have. Or you could save them for his office hour."

Nodding his thanks to his TA, Michel slipped out through the back door and away from the clamor of questions. Ever since Emma texted him last night, he'd been running away from questions of his own. He couldn't ignore them any longer.

Why had he been so shocked that she was continuing to pursue opening up a culinary school? It was her dream, after all. But he'd hoped—even though he hadn't admitted it to himself until now—that she might be thinking about coming to Rouleme with him. Had the thought never crossed her mind? Was she so ready to be done with him?

Perhaps he should have expounded on the merits of his country more. Should he have been more blatant about his wish to have her come back with him? He'd been so preoccupied with not scaring her away, he might not have expressed how much he wanted to be with her.

From the beginning, she'd incorrectly assumed that he only wanted a brief fling. But hadn't everything they had shared in the last month shown her that a fling was the last thing he wanted? How could she not see that he wanted forever with her? *Because you didn't tell her. You didn't give her the words.*

He lengthened his strides toward his office, barely noticing the curious gazes of students as he stormed past them. He was grateful that Sophie kept her distance, knowing him well enough to see that he needed space.

Michel slammed his office door behind him and leaned his head against it. He felt like a goddamn prince in a fairy tale— forbidden from revealing his love for the fair maiden until she broke the curse by falling in love with him. He couldn't ask Emma to come to Rouleme with him—he wouldn't ask her to sacrifice so much. That would be too selfish, and love should never be selfish, right? But if she *wanted* to come with him, then who was he to deny her? He huffed a humorless laugh. And *there* was the loophole out of this cruel joke of a situation. Michel hated that he'd thought of a loophole. He was no better than the politicians circling him like vultures.

He dragged a hand down his face and pushed himself away from the door. He hated that a part of him wanted to manipulate Emma into offering to come to Rouleme with him—how he'd calculated that if she believed it was her idea, then she couldn't resent him for it later. It was quite possibly the most despicable thought he'd ever had.

Michel slumped into one of the guest chairs and let his head loll back. He closed his eyes and pressed his fingers against his eyelids in a futile effort to forestall the headache building be- hind them. His heart clenched with the phantom pain of losing

Emma. He pushed himself upright. *No.* Losing her wasn't an option. He would be selfish—he would be despicable—if it meant he could have her in his life.

Someone knocked, then opened the door without waiting for a response. Michel had a good guess who it was.

"Hello, Gabriel." He waved without bothering to turn around. "I'm a selfish, greedy cad."

"I can't believe you started wallowing in self-pity without me." His cousin dropped into the other guest chair.

"You won't have trouble catching up." Michel smirked despite his turmoil. "I believe in you."

"Why, that might be the nicest thing you've ever said to me." Gabriel opened his messenger bag and rummaged around in it until a bottle of bourbon emerged. He held it up triumphantly.

"It's three in the afternoon," Michel objected half-heartedly.

"And we're two distinguished professors at our place of work," Gabriel pointed out while pouring bourbon into two mugs. "This kind of conduct would be frowned upon. With good reason."

Michel accepted his mug and clinked it with his cousin's. "Welcome to the shit show."

"*Language,* Your Highness." Gabriel tilted back his drink and grimaced at the bitter heat. "Now then. Tell me what troubles you."

"I'm in love with Emma," he said miserably.

His cousin looked dashing even with a *duh* expression on his face. "Should I pretend to be shocked?"

"I love her too much to ask her to marry me." Michel waved his mug in the air for a refill. "But I'm a horrible human being because I still want to marry her even if it means she has to sacrifice everything for me."

"Ah." Gabriel poured him a generous amount and topped off his own drink. "That is a more complex dilemma. In fact, it is a profound philosophical question."

"Please." Michel grabbed the bottle from the table, as he'd already emptied his mug. "I need my cousin. Not the Sphinx."

"Fine. Be a superficial arsehole," his cousin said with a wry curl of his lips.

"As opposed to what?" He snickered and sloshed bourbon on his hand. "A *deep* ars—"

"Don't finish that sentence." Gabriel snatched the bottle from him. "And slow down. Since when have you been such a lightweight?"

"It might have something to do with the fact that I hardly slept last night," Michel slurred, "and haven't eaten all day."

"Christ." A flash of concern crossed Gabriel's face. "The plan was to *sip* bourbon like civilized people and have a bit of philosophical discussion."

"Sounds like you fucked up." Michel drew his brows down into a worried frown and patted Gabriel's back in a rush of sympathy. "Sorry, mate."

"D'accord." His cousin pinched the bridge of his nose. "Let me just tell you what I came to say before I lose you completely."

"Bien sûr." He had trouble crossing his arms while drinking from his mug, so he crossed his legs instead. "Poursuis, mon cousin."

"Forget about being a man of honor and all that bullshit. Be desperate, needy, selfish, greedy. Do *whatever* you need to hold on to Emma." The intensity of Gabriel's tone made Michel sit up straighter. "If you don't, you'll regret it for the rest of your life."

"Gabriel . . . I'm sorry." His cousin didn't need to add *like me* for Michel to understand that he spoke from experience. "But this is your second chance. Don't give up now."

"I'm not here to talk about me." He glanced away, his shoulders drooping.

"Oh, Sophie," Michel sang loudly as he stumbled to his feet and jerked open the door. "Soph—"

A small but strong hand clapped over his mouth and pushed him back into his office. Sophie closed the door behind her before she snapped at Gabriel, "I wanted you to check in on him, not get him piss drunk."

"How was I supposed to know the man had been starving himself all day?" Gabriel grumbled even as his eyes roamed hungrily over her.

Sophie noticed and blushed but didn't back down. "How am I supposed to get him out of here without creating a scene?"

"What do you want me to do?" Gabriel smirked. "Run through the campus naked to create a diversion?"

"I . . ." She cleared her throat as her blush deepened. "Better you than me."

Gabriel froze for a second before he burst out laughing, and Sophie soon joined in. Michel didn't quite follow everything, but he laughed, too, for the hell of it. He stopped to pull out his mobile when it buzzed in his pocket.

Emma:
Where are you? Can I see
you tonight?

He had enough sense left to realize that he was in no condition to see her right now. But God, he missed her. He blinked down at the screen and typed carefully.

Michel:
Tu me manques

The English translation wasn't sufficient to convey what he felt. She was missing from him. She was an inseparable part of him, and he was incomplete without her. But she didn't speak French.

Michel:
Tu me manques

There. He said it twice, so that should make it clearer.

Emma:
Aww. I miss you, too.

His shoulders sagged. She only missed him. He wasn't missing *from* her. That was the problem, wasn't it? She could imagine life without him while he . . . couldn't. She could plan for her future—visit commercial kitchen spaces to lease when he was gone—and he couldn't bear to *exist* without her.

Emma:
I had to use Google Translate.
My high school French failed me.

Then he realized that the meaning of his words was lost in translation. Perhaps he, too, was missing from her. *But wait.*

Michel:
You took French in high school?

Emma:
Yup. For four years. But they never
taught us how to say I miss you.
I know how to say grapefruit,
though. Le pamplemousse.

Emma:
I know. Very useful.

Emma:
Anyway, when can I see you?

He lifted his wrist and glared at his watch, willing the numbers to stop moving around. It was somewhere in the vicinity of three to five—he glanced out his window—in the afternoon. He could probably sober up by—he counted the numbers off on his fingers—eight o'clock?

Michel:
Eight clock clock

Emma:
Umm . . . eight o'clock?

Michel:
Yup

He'd never typed *yup* in his entire life. He'd never used the word *yup* before. But it was so adorable when Emma did, he hoped she thought he was adorable, too.

Michel:
Now am I missing from you?

The ellipses rolled and rolled, making his eyes cross.

Emma:
Michel? Are you okay?

Michel:
Yup

"Hey," he cried as his mobile was taken out of his hand.

"Are you drunk texting?" Sophie took a quick look at the screen, then arched an eyebrow at him. The eyebrow was telling him to feel embarrassed, so he obediently glanced down at his shoes.

"Let me see." Gabriel peered over her shoulder. "Who was he texting? What did he say?"

Sophie quickly pocketed the mobile and gave Gabriel a withering look. "You will not invade the prince's privacy."

"But you just read it," Gabriel pointed out.

"It's my duty to protect the prince," she said icily.

"Come on." Gabriel wielded his smile like a weapon—a weapon of irresistible charm. "Just tell me one thing he said. He must've said *something* hilarious."

"Oh, fine. He said . . ." She snorted. "He said *yup*."

"What?" Michel frowned as his cousin and his friend dissolved into laughter. "*Yup* is adorable."

And they laughed harder. He didn't join in this time. He wasn't that drunk. Maybe he should remedy that. He grabbed the bottle and slugged a mouthful before it was roughly snatched out of his hand. A trail of bourbon dribbled down his chin. *How undignified.* He withdrew his handkerchief and dabbed at his chin with precise, dignified movements.

"I'm going to text Emma and tell her that you won't be able to see her tonight," Sophie announced.

"Don't tell her I'm dru . . . drunk." He shook his finger at his friend.

"What should I tell her, then?" She was already texting, which made him nervous.

"Tell her . . . tell her that Gabby drugged me." He nodded at his brilliant idea.

"Gabby?" Gabriel sputtered.

"You're okay with me saying that you drugged him, though?" Sophie cocked her head to the side.

Gabriel shrugged. "Better than being called *Gabby*."

"Let's compromise. I'll just tell her the truth." She read off her text to Emma: "'Hi, Emma. This is Sophie. Michel won't be able to see you tonight. *Gabriel* thought it would be a great idea to pour bourbon down his throat at three in the afternoon.'"

"Okay." Gabriel shrugged. "That's fair."

"Not fair." Michel pouted. "I want to see Emma tonight."

"You'll thank me tomorrow, Your Highness." Sophie lowered him back into his chair.

"Uh-oh," Michel whispered to Gabriel. "She called me *Your Highness*. That means I'm in trouble."

"God, he really is a mess. Isn't he?" his cousin said to Sophie, rudely ignoring Michel.

"He is." She shrugged. "But to be honest, he's in better shape than he was before you came."

"Poor chap." Gabriel affectionately ruffled Michel's hair, but Michel was too sleepy to slap his hand away. "He's really torn up about Emma."

"What did you tell him?"

"I told him to do whatever it takes to hold on to her"—Gabriel hesitated for a moment—"or else he'll regret it for the rest of his life."

Sophie was quiet for a very long time. Michel was halfway asleep when she said, "If you regret anything, you should regret not asking me what *I* wanted instead of deciding what was best for me all by your egotistical self."

Gabriel sucked in a sharp breath. "Sophie . . ."

Michel didn't hear anything else except for the click of the door closing. He had a feeling that there was something very important for him to understand—something Sophie had said. But sleep claimed him before he could understand a thing.

CHAPTER THIRTY-SIX

♥

The commercial kitchen space was pretty much perfect. Twelve pristine cooking stations with the master station at the head of the class. State-of-the-art flat-screens between every two cooking stations to show any detailed demonstrations. They would come in handy when Emma had to teach her students how to peel and slice dried jujubes, for example—fiddly little suckers.

Opening up her own cooking school had been her dream for as long as she could remember. And it was about to finally come true. Then what was this cold, hollow ache in her chest all about?

"This is wonderful, Mr. Goo." Her smile felt forced. "I love it."

"Don't tell him that," her dad said, ribbing his friend. "It's kind of like buying a used car. You can't tell him you love it."

"This is why you could never match wits with me, Jae." Mr. Goo grinned. "The special rate I'm offering Emma is actually a bribe. She'll owe me one, so she'll have to agree to open that gungjung yori restaurant with me someday."

"Still, I wouldn't sign anything until you've had a test run." Her dad rubbed his jaw. "Let her use the kitchen for a night,

Byoung. Maybe she could hold a group class here. What do you think, my dear?"

"Um . . . I . . ." Emma shook off her melancholy and nodded with some enthusiasm. "That actually sounds like a great idea. I could invite my friends here for a cooking party and give all the stations a workout. That is . . . if you're okay with that, Mr. Goo."

"I see no problem with it as long as you clean up after yourselves," Mr. Goo said magnanimously, but he had the expression of a man who had hooked his prize fish. "This kitchen will perform like a dream. I'll just go and prepare the leasing papers now."

"Cocky bastard." Her dad chuckled and slapped his friend on the back.

"I'll let you know the date and time as soon as I put the party together." Emma bowed from her waist. "Thank you, Mr. Goo."

"No need for that." He waved aside her gratitude. "I told you this was purely for selfish reasons."

Emma didn't believe that. Mr. Goo was a generous man and a good friend to her dad. She was very fortunate. She felt guilty that she wasn't giddy with excitement. Maybe she was just worried about Michel after Sophie's texts earlier. Yes, that must be it.

She said goodbye to her dad and Mr. Goo, who needed to hurry to make their tee time, and walked to her car. Instead of driving home, she took out her cell phone. It wasn't like Michel to get plastered in the middle of the day. She hoped he was okay.

Emma:
How are you feeling?

No dots scrolled along the screen. She pulled into the afternoon traffic and headed home, unease gnawing at her insides.

She didn't have any lessons this evening, so she was on her own for the first time in a long while. The prospect of being alone with her thoughts made her brittle with nerves.

Emma dropped her purse on the entryway console and automatically headed toward the kitchen on slippered feet. It was past five o'clock, so she should start prepping for dinner, but the thought of cooking didn't tempt her tonight. Her stomach lurched with a sense of wrongness. She waved aside her panic. She didn't *have* to want to cook every night—even though she always wanted to cook, especially when something was bothering her.

Refusing to overthink her odd mood, she retrieved her purse and trudged up the stairs to her room. She checked her phone—no reply from Michel—and dropped it on top of her dresser. Her lack of sleep from the night before must be catching up with her.

She got a bath started, sprinkling in a generous amount of her favorite jasmine bubble bath, and went back to her room to change into a robe. The water was almost ready when she returned to the bathroom. She lit the votive candles around the tub, then blew out the long match, watching the smoke curl around the blackened tip.

Emma soaked in her bath until all the bubbles disappeared and the water turned lukewarm. She dried off listlessly and found herself rushing back to her bedroom. She'd left her cell phone in her room on purpose so she wouldn't spend her entire bath staring at the screen, willing a text to arrive from Michel. But she lunged for her phone as soon as she walked into her bedroom, hands scrambling. *Nothing.*

Why would Michel get drunk in the middle of the day? Something had to be wrong, right? Was it her? Was it them? Suddenly, she was ticked off. What the hell was wrong with him? *Forget it.* She wasn't doing this. Tonight, she decided, was going to be all about self-care.

First, she needed comfort food, but she didn't feel like making anything elaborate, so ramyeon it was. Using the spiciest gochugaru she had stored in the freezer, she rendered the chili powder in some avocado oil. Next, she cut two cloves of garlic into paper-thin slices and chopped a stalk of green onion. Preparation complete, she boiled a packet of Shin Ramyeon with a poached egg, adding the sliced garlic to the broth. When the noodles were cooked to al dente perfection and the egg was just hard enough to still be runny in the middle, she turned off the stove and finished the ramyeon with a drizzle of chili oil and a handful of chopped green onions.

She ate her ramyeon with her eyes watering from the heat, slurping the noodles fast and loud. She didn't even think she was hungry, but she picked up her bowl and drank the last drop of the soup within ten minutes.

"Ahh." She leaned back in her chair and closed her eyes. Eating spicy food was the best stress buster.

Her mouth still tingled from the heat even after she finished washing the dishes, so Emma scooped herself a giant bowl of vanilla ice cream before heading to the living room. She sank down on the couch and clicked on the TV. She planned to top off the evening by rewatching *Coco*. She was going to cry like a baby when Miguel sang "Remember Me" to Mama Coco. There was no better self-care than a nice, long cry.

Emma was lost in Mama Imelda's soulful rendition of "La Llorona" when her cell phone dinged from the coffee table. She almost didn't check her phone, but she paused the movie with an aggrieved groan.

Michel:
I'm feeling mortified but otherwise fine.

All her forgotten worries rushed back to her.

Emma:
Is everything okay?

Michel:
Yes, of course.

His response was suspiciously fast.

Emma:
I thought something was
wrong . . .

Michel:
What could be wrong?

She wanted to call him and scream, *I don't know! You tell me!*
But in the end, she texted back, Haha. Nothing, I guess.

Except for the fact that he was leaving in less than a month
and she loved him so much it hurt to breathe. Michel obviously
didn't have the same problem. *What could be wrong?* That clue-
less dingus. Her eyes and nose stung with impending tears. She
sniffed them loudly away. Everything was okay. He'd just partied
away the afternoon with his cousin. It didn't seem like him, but
she'd only known him for a little over a month. How would she
know if he liked to let loose occasionally?

Emma:
The commercial kitchen
was fantastic by the way. It's
everything I could've hoped for. I
think I'm going to sign the lease
agreement as soon as humanly
possible.

She actually had no idea what she was going to do. She didn't know what she wanted anymore. It terrified her. The one thing she could always count on was knowing what she wanted in life. She had everything figured out. Or so she'd thought. She wasn't certain of anything anymore.

Michel:
👍 👍 👍

She stared at his flippant response and grew more furious by the minute. He couldn't pretend to care a tiny bit more about her freaking future? Didn't he have any follow-up questions? Wasn't he going to beg her not to sign the lease agreement and to come to Rouleme with him?

Emma gasped so loudly that she clapped a hand over her mouth even though she was alone. *Go to Rouleme with him?* Where the hell did that ludicrous thought come from? But if he asked . . . would she go with him? And then what? Become a *princess*? What about her dad? *No.* This line of thought could only lead to trouble.

She had to remember her original plan. Once Michel went back to Rouleme, she would marry the perfect-on-paper husband to protect Auntie Soo's reputation and ensure the security of her own business. Emma would create a warm, secure home with her impeccably compatible match and make sure that her dad was well taken care of. That was the future she had decided on for herself.

Her godmother hadn't mentioned once that Emma had promised to marry a man she matched her up with—that her matchmaking business depended on it. Auntie Soo just seemed genuinely happy that Emma had found someone. She couldn't repay her godmother's love and loyalty by scampering off to some foreign country to play princess. Not that Michel had ever implied that there could be a future for them.

A jagged fissure opened up in her heart. *Enough is enough.* She had to stick to her plan. That was the only way she was going to survive this.

> Emma:
>
> I'm planning a little cooking party to test out the kitchen. Will you, Sophie, and Gabriel come?

> Michel:
>
> I'll ask them. As for me, it goes without saying that I'll be there. I can't wait to see your future cooking school. I know it's going to be amazing.

The tight knot in Emma's chest loosened a little. Of course he cared about her future. He cared about her. She would make sure that their remaining time together would be filled with enough happiness to last them a lifetime.

CHAPTER THIRTY-SEVEN

♥

Michel had racked his brain and the internet to figure out what quintessential Los Angeles experience he could offer to a lifetime Angeleno. He had devoted his every free minute to planning a date to surprise Emma—and preferably sweep her off her feet—but he'd hit dead end after dead end until . . .

The Magic Castle.

It was a private clubhouse in Hollywood for members of the Academy of Magical Arts. Only members of the exclusive club and their invited guests were allowed access. After Sophie discreetly obtained intel that Emma had never been to the Magic Castle, Antoine had worked his *magic* to get a club board member to extend an invitation. While his assistant offered the option of simply buying out the club for the evening, Michel knew that Emma would prefer to experience the place with the hustle and bustle of other guests.

She had been intrigued when he invited her on a surprise date and decidedly thrilled when he informed her that the dress code for the night was "When in doubt, OVERDRESS!" Michel couldn't help but smile as he walked up to her front door in his tuxedo. She always looked impeccable whatever the occasion. How would she look when she decided to overdress?

He rang the doorbell and rocked back on his heels as nerves and anticipation coursed through him. His mouth dropped open when Emma opened the door looking like a mermaid wrapped in shimmering gold. Even a lifetime of grooming couldn't stop him from gaping at her like a complete fool. His only saving grace was that she looked equally dazed as she took him in, her eyes traveling from the top of his head to his toes, then back up again.

Michel managed to break free of his stupor long enough to whisper, "You look stunning."

"And *you* need to wear that more often." Emma bit her bottom lip. "Like every day."

"Gabriel already gives me a hard time for overdressing to work." Michel chuckled, his gaze traveling over her again. He couldn't get over how beautiful she was. "He would have a field day if I showed up to lecture in a tuxedo."

"That would be a bit over the top, I guess." Her impish dimple jolted his heart into a gallop, and he considered taking her straight back to his hotel.

"As for you," he growled, wrapping his arm around her waist and tugging her against him, "you cannot wear that dress unless you're with me. It's far too alluring."

She arched a disapproving eyebrow at him even as she smoothed her hands over his chest and shoulders. "I *cannot*?"

"I implore you not to," he quickly amended, realizing his inner caveman had gotten the best of him for a moment.

"Hmm." She took a step back after a lingering kiss on his cheek. "I'll take it into consideration."

"Thank you." He tucked her hand in his arm and led her to his car.

"Oh my God. You look gorgeous." Sophie glanced over from the driver's seat and gasped as Michel helped Emma into the car.

"Aww, thank you, Sophie." Emma blushed charmingly, tucking a strand of hair behind her ear. She wore her hair down tonight in a curtain of luscious waves. "I kind of took it literally when Michel said I could overdress to my heart's desire."

"I think you in that dress is his heart's desire." Sophie couldn't hold back her snort. "Perhaps you might want to close your mouth, my prince."

Emma seemed to startle at the reminder that he was a prince. Michel studied her from the corner of his eye. Did she truly forget that he was a prince from time to time? Her sweet smiles and tender touches were all for him—not his crown. He was still Michel to her.

Until he met Emma, he didn't know who he was apart from his title and duty. But she showed him that he was a regular guy who found joy in everyday things and loved to laugh—even at himself—especially with her by his side. And he never wanted to forget how good it felt to be that guy.

Once he dedicated his life to the people of Rouleme as their new king, he would lose that part of himself without her. But with her by his side, he could continue finding joy in the everyday and build a life that was meant just for them—for Emma and Michel. When they were alone, he would still get to be the man who loved her more than life—the man who was happiest when he was with her.

But what about Emma? What did *she* need?

Michel remembered his cousin's fervent words. *Be desperate, needy, selfish, greedy. Do* whatever *you need to hold on to Emma.* He had to stop second-guessing himself. When he chose to come to America, he'd decided to put himself ahead of duty and responsibility—to be selfish for once. He had vowed not to settle for anything less than all-consuming love. Now that he found it, he would choose to be selfish again. He would fight for her heart, everything else be damned.

Suddenly, the love inside him felt too big, too *alive* to keep hidden. If he declared his love for her and asked for her hand in marriage—and she rejected him—then he could lose the three weeks he had left with her. But he couldn't wait any longer. He needed her to know. Tonight. He would ask her tonight after an evening filled with magic. Maybe it would help her see that anything was possible—that she could be happy with him even if it meant leaving her life in America behind.

Michel reached out and linked his fingers through hers. She glanced his way with a soft smile. He picked up her hand and brushed his lips across her knuckles before placing a lingering kiss over them. Her breath escaped her in a rush, and he grinned smugly.

She leaned close with her hand on his thigh, her fingers drifting daringly close to his hardening cock. "I suggest you behave or this drive could become *unbearable* for you."

"Are you trying to dissuade me?" he said in a rough whisper. "Or tempt me?"

When Sophie surreptitiously raised the volume on the radio, they jumped apart and scooted to their sides of the car. He didn't even make eye contact with Emma until his pulse evened out and he was certain he could behave for his poor friend's sake.

"Are you going to tell me where you're taking me?" Emma asked with her composure restored. She glanced outside the window. "It looks like we're headed to the Westside."

"Patience, Emma," he teased. "You don't want to ruin the surprise, do you?"

"Maybe we're going to watch a show." She scrunched her mouth to one side, obviously not ready to give up. "But we're a bit overdressed for a musical or a play. Maybe an opera?"

"I'm afraid we're not re-creating a scene from *Pretty Woman*." He smiled, enjoying himself immensely.

"Well, that's a shame. I love that movie." She gave him an exaggerated wink. "I especially love the Rodeo Drive scene. Hint, hint."

Michel chuckled. "I'll remember that for next time."

"Ugh, I give up." Emma slumped in her seat with a pout. "Do with me as you will."

"I like the sound of that." He gave her a pointed glance, and she blushed. Before things got out of hand again, he continued, "You'll like this surprise."

He certainly hoped he was correct. She turned even simple meals into events and celebrations. The theatrics and whimsy of the Magic Castle had to catch Emma's fancy. Before they rounded the bend and the surprise was revealed, Michel urged, "Quick. Close your eyes."

Emma closed her eyes even as she said, "What? Are you serious?"

"Yes." He placed his hand over her eyes just to make sure she didn't peek.

When the Magic Castle came into view, Michel realized that it was really more of a magic château, charming and quaint rather than opulent. But even he felt a thrill of excitement as they neared their destination, certain there was magic in the air. After reminding her to keep her eyes closed, he shot out of the car and waved aside the valet reaching for Emma's door.

He wrapped his arm around her waist as he helped her step out of the car. "Open your eyes."

"Shut. The. Front door," Emma breathed as soon as she opened her eyes, then slapped his arm. "The Magic Castle?"

"Yes?" He wasn't quite sure how to interpret her reaction. Then she squealed and threw herself into his arms. He sighed with relief as he held her tightly against him. "Surprise."

Her round eyes bounced around the exterior of the Victorian mansion as he guided her toward the entrance. Emma was tickled pink to say the magic words that granted them entry to the exclusive club.

"Open sesame," she said with gusto. She promptly dissolved into giggles as the doors opened for them.

Dark wood panels and black carpet with gold brocade greeted them as they stepped inside. A dizzying amount of artwork and photos decorated the walls, nearly obscuring the burgundy wallpaper of the corridor. The decor felt like a cross between the glamour of old Hollywood and the opulence of the *Titanic* with generous sprinklings of the outlandish.

"This is so *fun.*" She tugged him along by his hand with a manic gleam in her eyes. "We have to see every nook and cranny. Watch every show. Try all the bars. We're having dinner here, right?" At his indulgent nod—he would give her anything she asked for—she continued, "We might have to find a broom closet to hide in later so they won't kick us out when it's closing time."

"Anything for you, darling Emma," he said, cupping her face.

"Thank you for tonight." She leaned into his hand, her eyes soft with affection. Before he could steal a kiss from her, she straightened and clapped her hands twice. "Okay. We have to hustle now."

Even as they watched shows that defied logic as well as the laws of physics, he couldn't look away from her. She was radiant. It made him unbelievably proud he put that smile on her face.

"Watch." She nudged him with her elbow. "You're going to miss it."

The magic of the illusionists and mentalists sucked him in at last—he was simultaneously enthralled and a little alarmed—and the evening flew by in a blur. The cocktails they had consumed at the various bars probably contributed to the whirlwind effect.

"How do you think she made that—"

"Shh." Emma pressed a finger to his lips. "Don't try to analyze it. Just *believe*."

With a chuckle, he captured her hand in his and led her to the restaurant for their dinner reservation. The plentiful and hearty meal of beef Wellington and prime rib—they shared everything, of course—was a welcome reprieve, but brief, thanks to the efficient, well-oiled service.

"Would you like some dessert?" Michel suggested to linger a bit longer. "Or a digestif?"

"Ordinarily, you *know* I would *never* pass up dessert." She folded her napkin and placed it on the table. "But tonight is *extraordinary*. We have too many things left to see."

"I thought we watched all the featured shows." His brows drew down.

"We did, but there are so many side shows. There are literally magicians in every corner." She stood and tugged at his arm. "Come on. Let's go."

Unable to deny her anything, he followed her out of the restaurant. Michel was relieved when the crowd thinned out as the evening drew to a close. He had to get Emma alone. He had to tell her he loved her or his heart might explode. He'd waited long enough. No more second-guessing. No more being cautious. He wrapped his arm around her waist and pulled her close. This would be the night he made her his.

Before he could coax her out of the castle, a portion of the wall seemed to split open, and a staff member stepped outside with a broom and a dustpan. They had passed by the seamless hidden panel in the corridor throughout the evening, none the wiser.

"Oh my gosh. The *broom closet*," Emma whispered, squirming with excitement beside him. When the member of staff rounded the corner, she shoved Michel inside the clean but spartan storage closet and clicked the door shut.

"Emma," he said, unable to hide his alarm, "you don't truly intend to hide in here until everyone leaves?"

"Of course not." She rolled her eyes. "I've just been wanting to do this all night."

Then she launched herself at him hard enough to make him stumble into a metal shelf. But even the clattering of falling objects didn't deter him from kissing her back with abandon, his arms circling her waist to hold her close to him. The shelving dug into his back and arse, but he couldn't have cared less. *God.* The feel of her . . . the taste of her . . . He couldn't get enough.

The gold sequins of her dress felt cold against his hands, and he growled in frustration. He needed to touch her skin—her silken, bare skin. But he had a sliver of rational thought left in his head to know that this wasn't the place. Still, he couldn't stop kissing her.

"Ahhh!" someone yelped from the doorway. "I'm sorry. I mean, you shouldn't be in here. But . . . ugh."

"It seems we took a wrong turn." Michel pushed Emma behind him and arched a cool brow at the flustered staff member with the broom and dustpan. "Would you be so kind as to point us toward the front entrance?"

The staff member sighed with resignation. "Go all the way down this corridor and hook a left."

Michel nodded with more dignity than he felt and rushed past the poor man with Emma tucked to his side. They were halfway down the corridor when he heard the staff member mutter, "Why is it always the broom closet?"

As soon as they turned left at the corner, they burst out laughing hard enough to need to lean on the wall for support.

"That"—he wiped the corner of his eyes with his knuckle—"was not my finest moment."

"I've had worse." She grabbed her side, fighting for her breath. "You have to grow a thick skin when you have Jeremy for a godbrother."

With a wry shake of his head, Michel led Emma toward the main entrance. She shivered when they stepped out into the night, and he ran his hand up and down her bare arm. He wanted to get her out of the cold, but he was equally impatient to get her alone. He mentally recalled the combination to the safe in his bedroom that held his mother's ring. He'd felt like an optimistic fool bringing the ring with him, but now he was relieved he had it with him. He couldn't propose to Emma without it.

"My prince," Sophie said in a low voice, materializing at his side. "I have some news—"

"Not now." He cringed at how terse that came out. "Sorry, Sophie. We'll talk later."

"But . . ." His friend sighed. "Of course. I had the car brought over. Right this way."

He had no idea how Sophie had known when they would be out, but he was grateful for the waiting car. He ushered Emma in first, then got in beside her. He tugged off his jacket and wrapped it around her. She watched with exasperated affection as he buckled her seat belt for her.

"You don't need to coddle me, Michel," she admonished with a small smile.

"Let me." He held her gaze and ran the back of his hand down her cheek. "I want to."

Once Michel secured his own seat belt, Sophie pulled smoothly away from the curb and glanced at him through the rearview mirror. "Where to?"

"Do you mind coming over to the hotel for a short while?" He swallowed. "I wanted to talk to you about something."

"Oh?" Her eyes went wide with curiosity. "What about?"

"I'll tell you when we're alone." His voice came out in a husky croak.

"Ah." Her lips curved into a knowing smile that shot straight to his groin. For once, that wasn't at the forefront of his mind, but he couldn't say it was far behind. "I'm looking forward to our *talk*."

Even though Sophie had probably heard everything, he belatedly answered her question, "To the hotel, please."

He thought his friend muttered something under her breath. But when he shot a questioning glance at her, she merely said, "Of course, Your Highness."

Michel's brows furrowed at her terse response, and he had an unwelcome premonition that the night might not go as he'd planned.

CHAPTER THIRTY-EIGHT

♥

Emma loved that Michel was more relaxed and easygoing in her presence, but he was still buttoned-up and proper in public—which made complete sense since he was a prince who'd been groomed to be king one day. Well, she still floundered with the fact that he was a prince, but it did help her understand him a little better.

But tonight, as they walked through the hotel lobby, he was positively brimming with tension, his hand gripping hers tightly. Sophie tried to get his attention a few times, looking uncharacteristically flustered, but he remained lost in thought. Emma studied him silently, hoping to figure out what was bothering him.

When they got off the elevator, Sophie didn't head to her suite for an evening of across-the-foyer surveillance. She hovered nearby, going as far as to wring her hands once or twice. Michel seemed to notice none of it. Clicking her tongue, the royal guard finally pulled him aside by his arm and whispered something in his ear.

"She's here?" He pointed to his suite. "Now?"

"Yes," Sophie said tightly. "That is what I needed to speak to you about."

With a long sigh, Michel unlocked his door and held it open for Emma. Before she could walk in, he quietly informed her, "I'm sorry, but it seems I have a guest tonight."

"Cousin Michel," a high, childlike voice declared from the living room. "You're here at last."

He had a smile on his face as he strode toward the raven-haired beauty and Gabriel, who sat on one of the settees with his head in his hand.

"Marion," Michel said smoothly, "I wasn't expecting you until tomorrow."

"If I may." Gabriel raised his hand. "I am apparently a *party pooper*. My suggestion that she spend the night in San Francisco and fly down tomorrow morning was deemed *asinine* by my dear sister. So she helicoptered in like a spoiled brat—"

"Hey." Marion—who apparently was Gabriel's sister—pouted her pillowy pink lips. "You know I hate being called that. It was much more reasonable for me to join you sooner than to spend a night alone in a strange city. Wouldn't you agree, Sophie? For my safety and all that?"

"Yes." Sophie's voice was as dry as an overcooked Thanksgiving turkey. "So very reasonable. I'm sure your security team was thrilled you needed to rush here to feel safe."

"See?" Marion beamed at Michel, completely missing the other woman's sarcasm.

"Sorry for letting ourselves in while you were out." Gabriel stood and clapped a hand on Michel's shoulder. "It seemed prudent to remove her from the helipad and into a more private setting as soon as humanly possible."

"You did the right thing." Michel shot his cousin a half smile, but he quickly seemed at a loss for words. If he hadn't seemed so bemused, Emma would've been a little hurt that he hadn't made the introductions.

"Who's that?" Marion crossed her legs on the sofa, twirling a strand of gleaming hair, and eyed Emma as though she expected her to curtsy.

"That, little sister, is Emma. Michel's girlfriend," Gabriel answered in a strained voice, his eyes nearly bulging with warning at his sister. *A warning about what?*

"Ooooooh, intriguing." Marion got to her feet with the fluid grace of a dancer and extended her hand to Emma. "Pleased to meet you."

Intriguing? What could she mean?

"Nice meeting you as well." Emma shook the other woman's perfectly manicured hand. She didn't particularly like her entitled, haughty manner, but she was Michel's cousin so Emma intended to be as pleasant as possible. "So how long will you be in LA, Marion?"

"Oh, I don't know." She dropped Emma's hand after the briefest touch and sashayed over to the drink cart. "I prefer to let my spirit guide me rather than caging myself into a schedule."

"A week," Gabriel gritted through his teeth. "Max."

"Cousin Michel." Marion ignored her scowling older brother and waved her hand toward four giant Louis Vuitton suitcases by the door. "Could you have someone deliver my things to your spare bedroom?"

"Marion." Sophie stepped in at last, her hand outstretched toward the younger woman. "Why don't you come stay in my suite? We can catch up. It's been ages."

"Aww, that's sweet, Feefee." Marion's expression softened even as Emma crinkled her nose. *Feefee?* "But I doubt you have views as nice as this suite. And I need to be somewhere with a piano. That's why I can't stay with my brother at his condo. I'll miss my music too much."

"You hated piano lessons," Gabriel squawked.

"That was before I learned to appreciate the restorative power of music." She turned her nose up. "Now I make it a point to

play at least thirty minutes a day. I'm sure Cousin Michel under-
stands. He plays beautifully."

Sophie and Gabriel exchanged a horrified glance, then
looked back and forth between Marion and Michel. It was out
of their hands now. Emma belatedly realized what Michel's surprise houseguest could mean for their privacy. God, why now?
They only had three weeks left. Every minute was precious.

"I'd be happy to have you." A muscle twitched in Michel's
jaw. He hid it admirably, but Emma knew him well enough to
recognize his displeasure. She also knew he was too kind to kick
his young cousin out of his suite. "I'm sure Gabriel and I can
handle your luggage."

"I'll help with the bags," Sophie volunteered, and jerked her
head at Gabriel. "Come on. We don't have all night."

That had been the perfect moment for one of Gabriel's flir-
tatious quips, but he didn't so much as smirk. Instead, he joined
her by the luggage at once. Things seemed tense between them
as they walked off toward the spare bedroom with a rolling bag
in each hand.

Emma remembered her argument with Michel and worried
her bottom lip. Had her advice to Sophie the other day put a
wedge between her and Gabriel? Well, that had been the point.
But her friend didn't seem any happier for it.

"Would you like a drink?" Michel asked with a hand on her
back.

"Just some water, please." Emma had a feeling she would
need all her wits about her to survive an encounter with Marion.

The other woman dropped back down on the sofa with a
glass of red wine, and Emma situated herself on a love seat a
safe distance away. Michel sat down next to her and handed her
a glass of water. His thigh didn't quite touch hers, but she could
feel the heat coming off him. She suddenly remembered their
kiss in the broom closet, and frustration bloomed inside her. She

couldn't imagine finishing what they'd started with a stranger in the same suite.

"So . . . how did you two meet?" Marion eyed the two of them over the rim of her glass. The expression on her face was uncannily like a cat toying with a cornered mouse. Emma had a sinking feeling in her stomach. There was something she was missing. "I'm *dying* to hear everything."

"We met downstairs at the hotel café," Michel offered, sounding preoccupied. "Nothing you would find interesting."

"You're quite mistaken." Marion moued her lips. "I am terribly interested."

Michel plowed a hand through his hair, his patience noticeably running thin. It wasn't like him to be so easily flustered.

"Well, Marion." Emma decided it was time to divert the conversation. "If you're available next Saturday, I'd love for you to come to a small gathering I'm hosting. It's going to be a cooking party."

"Oh?" The other woman looked down her perfect, pert nose at Emma. "Will you be selling plastic containers to your guests? I believe I've seen such . . . occurrences in American movies."

There was nothing wrong with Tupperware parties, but Emma had a feeling she'd just been insulted. "No, it's not that kind of party. I'm a culinary instructor, and I'll actually be teaching my guests how to cook a gourmet Korean dish."

"A culinary instructor? Of Korean food?" Genuine interest flashed in her eyes. "That's brilliant. I will make it a point to be here for your party."

Michel made a choking noise beside her, but Emma decided that Marion might not be all bad. "I'm glad to hear that."

"You must be tired, Marion." Michel got abruptly to his feet as Sophie and Gabriel returned to the living room.

"Yes. Why don't you get situated in your room?" Gabriel said firmly, pointing toward the hallway. "I'm sure you could find it on your own. It's the one with all your luggage inside."

Knowing she'd been dismissed, Marion walked off in a huff.

"And if you don't need anything else, Gabriel and I'll be heading out as well." Sophie nodded at Michel, mouthed *good night* to Emma, and followed Gabriel out the door.

When it was just the two of them in the living room, Emma belatedly remembered that Michel had something to tell her. She turned to him and asked, "What did you want to talk about?"

"That is a conversation I would rather save for when we have true privacy." He pinched the bridge of his nose.

"Is it . . . it's nothing *bad*, right?" Nervousness fluttered in her stomach.

"Nothing bad." He reached for her hand and placed a tender kiss on her wrist. "I promise."

Emma nodded, sighing in relief. Michel never told her anything bad. It had shocked her to find out that he was a prince, but it wasn't necessarily *bad*. He was doing amazing things for his country. He was changing *the world*. No, it wasn't a bad thing at all. It was just irrelevant to their relationship.

Bruising pain gripped her chest, squeezing her heart like a stress ball. She couldn't stop herself from wanting an impossible future with him—a future she couldn't even imagine. But she knew nothing about the lives of royalty. How would she even fit into his life? The more she wanted to cling to him, the farther she wanted to run from him. She was being torn apart by her love for him. It hurt. And she wanted it to stop hurting.

"Thank you for tonight," she said with a determined smile, scattering the train of her desperate thoughts. "It was *magical*."

Michel chuckled at her cheesy joke. Honestly, it was impossible not to love a man who laughed at your cheesy jokes. She jumped to her feet. "I should . . . I should go."

His hand tightened around hers for a moment, then he sighed. "Let me take you home."

"Don't be silly." She headed for the front door in a quick hobble—her mermaid dress didn't allow her to take long, graceful strides. "I don't want to drag Sophie out again. Besides, I think she and Gabriel might be talking."

"And you approve of this?" Michel cocked his head.

"It's not for me to approve or disapprove." But she did approve. She realized Michel was right. They were good people who deserved a real chance. A real chance she and Michel would never get. She felt tears sting her nose. "I'll say good night here. If you follow me down, then Sophie will have to come, too. And I don't want to interrupt them."

He nodded a bit reluctantly, then leaned down to kiss her softly on the lips. "Good night, darling Emma."

Her toes curled in her high heels, and goose bumps spread across her arms. She *loved* it when he called her that. With a little growl of frustration, she pulled him down for a hard, searing kiss, then stepped out into the foyer before she could change her mind.

Sophie spotted Emma and snapped her mouth shut in the middle of a sentence, but Gabriel's eyes didn't leave her face, willing her to finish the sentence—as though his entire life depended on it.

Emma muttered a curse under her breath. She could tell she'd chosen the most inopportune time to interrupt. She rushed to the elevator, shielding her face with her hand as if that would make her invisible. "Don't mind me. Pretend I'm not here."

"I can drive you . . ." Sophie began, but her gaze drifted back to Gabriel. He looked at her like he missed her even though she was standing right in front of him.

"I'll be gone in a second." Emma poked repeatedly at the elevator button like she was trying to bring on the pain in a video combat game. Thankfully, the elevator arrived with a delicate ding before she could feel *really* awkward. She ran inside with a hasty wave and pressed the Close button. "Carry on."

Suddenly exhausted, she leaned against the wood panels of the elevator wall, letting her head fall back. She wished she could stay with Michel—it was the only way to keep her worries at bay these days—but her dad would be waiting up for her. He would pretend he fell asleep on the couch, but she knew better than to buy that.

"Ms. Yoon." The concierge hurried to her side when she walked out into the lobby. "Mr. Chevalier has requested that one of our drivers take you home."

Too tired to argue, she let herself be handed off to a kind-faced gentleman in a black suit and slid into a Lincoln Town Car just outside the hotel. She appreciated that the driver didn't try to engage in small talk and let her stare out the window. She couldn't believe it was only a few weeks ago that she'd thought it fortunate that Michel only had two months in LA. Now the thought of him leaving made every cell in her body hurt.

She had to remember that they had *nothing* in common. But a small voice insisted that their differences complemented each other's and made them better versions of themselves. *No.* They were practically a different species—a royal and a commoner. Maybe she was being unnecessarily harsh, but she couldn't forget how *ugly* falling out of love was. It wasn't just the fighting that she hated. Her parents' silence had been far worse—how they seemed to stop existing for each other. She wouldn't be able to bear that happening to her and Michel.

Emma could, however, admit to herself that there was no going back to *normal* when he left. And she sure as hell wasn't going on any more matseons. She would have to think of another way to preserve Auntie Soo's reputation. Even the thought of marrying a nice, compatible man—sharing her life with a man who wasn't Michel—made her stomach roil with nausea.

But she wouldn't be alone. She had her dad, her godmother, Jeremy, her friends, and her business. She would rebuild herself piece by piece if she had to. She would build a beautiful life for herself with jeongseong—with all of her shattered heart.

CHAPTER THIRTY-NINE

The commercial kitchen space was spotless, brightly lit, and as the name suggested, quite industrial looking with stainless steel appliances and surfaces at every station. But the large black-and-white ceramic tiles on the floor and the wide, open windows managed to keep the kitchen from feeling sterile.

Michel wistfully noted that it would satisfy Emma's need for order as well as provide a welcoming space for her students. Guilt surged up inside him, knowing he intended to ask her to give all this up for him. But he would do everything in his power to help her realize her dream in Rouleme somehow. He would find a way.

He had arrived a few minutes early with his two cousins and his royal guard, hoping to provide some assistance with party preparations. But Emma unsurprisingly had everything under control—mainly by bossing Jeremy around to set up each station with the requisite ingredients and tools. She had her hair in a neat bun and wore a V-neck sheath dress in black with a crisp white apron tied around her waist. She looked impeccably professional without giving up an inch of her femininity.

"Emma." He walked up to her and slid his arm around her

waist, tugging her close. He inhaled her scent—she smelled like jasmine and orange blossoms—and brushed his lips against her temple. "How can I help?"

She turned to fit her body against his even as she said, "We don't need any—"

"Yo, Chevalier." Jeremy jerked his head at Michel, commanding him to his side. "Don't listen to her. We need help setting out all the vegetable baskets at each station along with the color-coded cutting boards."

After stealing a quick kiss from Emma, Michel reluctantly left her side to stride up to the master station with the neat stacks of supplies ready to be distributed. "Why do we need multiple cutting boards?"

"Elementary, my dear Watson," Jeremy said with a smirk. "To prevent cross-contamination."

Emma rolled her eyes at her godbrother. "Less talking. More working."

"I came all the way from San Jose to *attend* a party," he grumbled, "not to be your kitchen maid."

"Come now, Jeremy." It was Michel's turn to smirk. "I'll help lighten the load."

"We'll help, too," Gabriel offered from the other side of the kitchen with Sophie by his side. They couldn't seem to stop smiling at each other.

Emma noticed and caught Michel's gaze with a happy grin. She raised her eyebrows in question, but he shrugged. He had no idea what was going on, but he was just happy that they seemed happy.

Marion didn't offer assistance, too busy dragging her finger across the stainless steel counter and glancing around the kitchen with a kind of horrified fascination. At least she wasn't getting in anyone's way.

Unfortunately, Marion had gotten in the way plenty of times

this past week. She'd walked in on every stolen kiss he shared with Emma with uncanny accuracy and interrupted any chance of a private conversation with a breezy *Oh, don't mind me.* Not that he would propose to Emma with Marion in the vicinity, but he had gotten into the habit of carrying his mother's ring in his pocket at all times in case the perfect opportunity arose.

Jeremy glanced around the kitchen, then froze with a carrot in his hand. He blinked after a moment and said out of the corner of his mouth, "You brought a Greek god to the party?"

"You mean Gabriel?" Michel chuckled. "That's just my cousin."

"*Just* your cousin?" Jeremy snorted. "I'm so glad I didn't bring Steven. I'd look like an ogre next to that man."

"Are all Korean ogres so good-looking?" Michel said dryly.

The other man laughed. "You're growing on me, Chevalier."

"Enough chitchat." Emma clapped her hands. "Let's go."

Michel and Jeremy jumped into action, laying out the ingredients. Gabriel and Sophie joined in to help. Marion glanced toward them as though considering offering her help. In the end, she meandered off to explore more of the kitchen.

With the preparations complete, Michel rejoined Emma at the master station and wrapped his arms around her waist from behind. Her busy hands stilled for a moment as she leaned back to smile up at him.

"Hi, Emma." Sarah Bae hurried over to them with a wide grin. "Hi, Professor Chevalier."

"Hello, Sarah." He dragged his eyes away from Emma and managed to return her smile. "It's good to see you."

"I'm so glad you could make it." Emma stepped out of his arms to give her friend a hug.

"This place is amazing," Sarah said, but stiffened when Gabriel's laughter rang out from across the kitchen.

Her eyes widened with shock as though she had never heard

him laugh before. It was quite possible the Sphinx did not laugh even though Gabriel did so often. His cousin leaned close to whisper something in Sophie's ear, who looked more amused than annoyed. That was a good sign.

"I assure you he'll be on his best behavior tonight," Michel told Emma's young friend to soothe her obvious unease.

"He has been unusually considerate to me at school lately, but I've never met him in a social setting before." Sarah grimaced. "Not counting that event at Town and Gown. But that was still a work function."

As though his cousin sensed he was the topic of their discussion, he glanced over at them. A flush crept up his neck when he spotted Sarah—Gabriel felt terrible about how he'd behaved at the mixer. He gave his TA an awkward smile with a nod of acknowledgment.

"I think Professor Laurent just smiled at me." Sarah waved limply at him. "I wonder if he's unwell."

"Don't be too shocked. Professors are human, too," Emma teased, then glanced at her mobile with a delicate frown between her brows. "I have another student who said she'd be here. Let's give her five more minutes before we start."

As if on cue, a young woman ran into the kitchen and skidded to a stop when all eyes turned to her. She made a little squeak and looked ready to run back out, but Emma said, "Jiyeon, you're right on time. You're in the front row here."

Michel took the station next to the newest arrival. He tipped his head in silent greeting with a polite smile. The woman blushed to the roots of her hair and ducked her chin. He didn't have time to wonder about her shyness because Emma clapped her hands for attention.

"Thank you for volunteering to be my guinea pigs tonight." She tucked a wayward strand of hair behind her ear with a nervous smile. But after a deep breath, she straightened her shoulders, standing taller. "Several of you are already pros at making Korean royal court cuisine, so please help out the novices if they seem to be having trouble following my instructions."

There's my Emma. It was bittersweet watching her in her element as he imagined what her life would be like if she stayed in Los Angeles.

"All right, let's get started." She clasped her hands together. "The dish we're cooking tonight is called sinseollo. There's a fancy story about a mountain god behind the name of the dish, but it's basically a Korean-style hotpot."

Laughter filled the kitchen. Michel couldn't take his eyes off Emma as she taught them to cook the various components of sinseollo with wit and patience. He was excited to learn how to make fish jeon, which was one of the ingredients for the hotpot. He could never forget the picnic she'd prepared for him at USC.

Emma made gungjung yori approachable and fun, but her cooking expertise was undeniable. She showed them how to make perfect rectangular slices of the various vegetables, her hands slow and steady as she demonstrated. But once she was certain everyone knew what to do, her knife seemed to fly over the rest of the ingredients, and they magically reappeared fully sliced and prepped.

She walked the kitchen to look in on her guests' progress, guiding them through the steps. When she came to his station, Michel's shoulders tensed. His stacks of vegetables—irregular and misshapen—looked nothing like hers. She put her hand on his shoulder, then let it slide down his back. He couldn't hold back a shiver in response, forgetting his embarrassment over his disastrous cooking attempt.

"That's impressive for your first time wielding a knife." She leaned close and lowered her voice. "But I've always known you were good with your hands."

"If you enjoy my hands"—he turned his head slowly and met

her eyes, her face only inches away—"then it might be a good idea for you to move on to your other guests before I chop off a finger. You're very distracting."

With a cheeky grin that made him want to slap her arse— and do a number of other things to her—she walked over to the station beside his.

"Jiyeon, that looks beautiful," she said, beaming at the young woman.

"Are you sure?" She chewed on her lip.

"I'm positive." Emma nodded for emphasis, then smiled mischievously. "Your mother was right. You do have the grace of a hippopotamus."

Michel's gaze snapped toward Emma so fast he must surely have gotten whiplash. Did he hear her correctly? How could she insult that poor girl in front of all these people? The whole kitchen had gone deathly quiet.

"Here." Emma took out her mobile while Jiyeon watched with a bewildered frown. "Let me show you something."

Within a few seconds, the young woman burst into tears and threw her arms around Emma. She returned Jiyeon's hug, patting her back.

"What is it?" Sarah chimed in. "I want to see."

"Of course you do." Emma shook her head with obvious affection. "I'll put it on the flat-screens."

It was a video of a hippopotamus swimming, its movements supple and fluid underwater. It was hard to believe an animal that likely weighed over three tons could move like a mermaid in a fairy tale.

"Aww," Marion fawned. "It's so beautiful."

"As you can see," Emma said kindly to Jiyeon, "we should all be so lucky to have the grace of a hippopotamus."

"You're right." The young woman sniffed and drew up to her

full height, newfound confidence in her stance. "The next time my mom compares me to a hippo, I'll just thank her."

Michel swallowed thickly. Wherever she went, Emma lifted people up, always seeing the best in them. Not only did she own his heart, but it would be a profound honor for his country to have her as their queen. Choosing Emma to be his wife was not a selfish decision at all. It was the best decision he could make for himself *and* his country—the only decision, really.

"Let's assemble the sinseollo." Emma drew their attention back to the task at hand. "Traditionally, sinseollo is made in a special pot that kind of looks like a wide-brimmed hat, where you put hot coal in the center and cook the food in the sunken 'brim.' But for the sake of building laws and general safety, we're going to assemble the casserole in a shallow saucepan.

"Alternating between each ingredient, we're going to line the pan to kind of look like a giant daisy—a pretty, multicolored one. Once the pan is filled with all the yummy goodness, we'll fill it to the rim with the beef broth and bring it to a boil on your stove. It only needs to cook for a few minutes before we move on to the best part of this party. Eating.

"I'd be happy to sample your masterpieces. And feel free to come up and taste mine to see if it's different from yours." Leaving her sinseollo to come to a boil, she came over to Michel and peeked at his dish. "Just look at that. Isn't it amazing what you could do with a little jeongseong?"

"Jeongseong?" He pulled her close and dropped a kiss on her temple.

"It means putting your heart—your very best—into something." She laid her head on his shoulder. "Didn't I tell you? It's my life philosophy. Everything worthwhile and beautiful in life requires jeongseong."

"I love that philosophy." *I love everything about you.* The ring burned in his pocket. It wanted to be presented to its rightful owner this instant.

"Ooh, I think your sinseollo is ready. Can I try it?" She picked up a small bowl and a ladle before he could protest. She blew on the hot broth and took a careful bite. A dreamy smile spread across her face. "Oh, Michel. This is delicious. I could taste your jeongseong in it."

"I had the best teacher to show me the way." He took her spoon and sampled some himself. His eyebrows rose up to his hairline. "Bloody hell. This *is* good."

Laughing with delight, Emma pecked him on the cheek and left to attend to her other guests. Spending time with her made him feel . . . weightless. She helped him stop walking the tightrope of duty and resentment, of gratitude and burden, and focus on just *being*. With her by his side, he felt whole—like *he* was enough, crown or no crown. She brightened everything she touched—including him.

Marion was family and he loved her. His cousin quickly warmed up to Emma, and she, his royal guard, and his girlfriend had made teasing him and Gabriel their favorite pastime for the last week. It was wonderful to see Emma getting along so well with the important people in his life. Even so, he'd been counting the days until his little cousin left tomorrow.

But he couldn't wait another moment to propose to Emma. His heart might burst from the hope and fear churning inside him unless he spoke to her as soon as possible. He would task Gabriel and Sophie with keeping Marion occupied so he and Emma could have his suite to themselves.

One way or another, the rest of his life would be decided tonight.

CHAPTER FORTY

When they reached the foyer of the presidential suite, Gabriel wrapped his arm around his sister's shoulders as Sophie sandwiched her from the other side and they bodily ushered Marion away from Michel's suite. Emma raised an eyebrow at Michel, and his brilliant smile made her knees weak.

Yesssss. She *finally* had him to herself. Anticipation coursed through her.

He held open the door for her, and Emma walked demurely into the suite. But as soon as he followed her inside, she slammed him against the door and crushed her lips against his. His hands found her hips and pulled her to him as he moaned into her mouth. He spun them around and pinned her against the door, his tongue tangling with hers in a desperate dance. He slid his palm down the side of her thigh, and she wrapped her leg around his waist, reaching for his belt buckle.

"Emma, wait." His voice was guttural and ragged as he gripped her wrist.

He didn't put up a fight when she shook his hand off and drew him out of his boxer briefs. She pumped her fist none too gently over him, and he hissed, his hips jerking helplessly into her hand.

"No." She smiled when he shuddered. "I don't think I'll wait."

Michel surrendered with a helpless groan, kissing her as though he was claiming her. He hiked her dress up with unsteady hands and tore off her lacy panties. She was too turned on to lament the loss of her pretty lingerie. In one rough motion, he lifted her by the waist and drove into her. She wrapped both her legs tightly around him and hung on to his broad shoulders. The hard ridges on the door jabbed into her back, but she couldn't have cared less. Having him deep inside her, filling her, stretching her . . . She needed this.

"Harder," she demanded.

Cursing under his breath, he hooked his hands under her thighs and carried her a few steps to the living room. He withdrew from her as he lowered her feet to the ground. Before she could protest, he turned her around and bent her over the nearest chair.

"Hold tight," he growled, and plunged into her just as she scrambled for a handhold.

She braced herself against the back of the chair as he pounded mercilessly into her. Her back arched as she lifted her ass, wanting him deeper. *More, more, more.* He cursed again and reached around to press the heel of his palm against her clit. They were lurching too wildly for more precision. But the pressure of his hand and his deep thrusts from behind sped her toward a blinding orgasm. She cried out his name as she came, and he pumped into her a few more times before he stiffened and shuddered against her.

As she drifted down from her climax, Michel's desperate hold on her hips loosened, finger by finger. "Are you okay?"

"Mmmfinoofke." Her face was buried in her arm, and she felt too limp to enunciate.

The silky lining of her dress felt cool sliding over her bare ass as Michel carefully set her clothes to rights. Then he lifted her into his arms as though she weighed nothing and carried her to his bedroom. He was still fully dressed in a dove-gray dress shirt and black slacks. She looked forward to watching him undress for her—slowly—once she got enough strength back.

After laying her limp body on his bed, he excused himself to the bathroom. Emma patted her hand on the nightstand and found a box of tissues for a hasty wipe down. She would clean up in the bathroom once her legs were fully functional. When Michel returned a few minutes later, she was already half-asleep. He sat down on the edge of the bed and tucked away a loose strand of hair behind her ear.

"Emma, darling." He lifted her hand and kissed her knuckles. "Gabriel and Sophie are going to do their best to keep Marion away, but I don't know how much longer we have."

She managed to pout without opening her eyes. "We don't get to go again?"

"We'll see what we can manage." Michel chuckled and dropped a tender kiss on her forehead. "But for now, we need to talk."

Emma finally forced her eyes open to find him studying her with an expression that made her breath catch in her throat. "Michel?"

"I never wanted a fling with you," he said as he studied her face with solemn, searching eyes. "You know that, right?"

"Right." She nodded hesitantly, not knowing where he was going with this. "A fling implies something purely physical. I don't think we're capable of that."

"No, we're not." He linked his fingers through hers and glanced down at their hands. "I never wanted this to be temporary either."

Her heart fluttered like the wings of a hummingbird, but she kept her mind carefully blank. She sat up on the bed and tucked her legs beneath her. "What are you saying, Michel?"

"Yes, whatever am I saying? I'm not doing a very good job of it, am I?" He dragged his free hand through his hair and huffed out a nervous laugh. After a deep breath, he met her eyes with his face stark and vulnerable. "I love you, Emma."

"Oh, Michel," she whispered and pressed her trembling fingers to her lips.

She wanted to tell him that she loved him, too. More than anything. But what did any of this mean when they couldn't be together? It would only make things harder when it came time for him to leave. Why was he doing this?

"I . . . I can't tell if you're upset or happy." His voice dipped nervously as his hand tightened around hers.

"Both. I'm both." Her eyes filled up with tears and the words she'd kept hidden deep inside tumbled out of her. "I fell in love with you despite my best intentions. I fell in love with you knowing that I could never have you."

"No, no, no." Michel reached out to cup her face with both his hands. "Emma, you can have me. All of me. I love you. I'd do anything for you."

"I don't understand." She blinked in confusion. "You would move to LA?"

"And leave Rouleme?" He drew back, startled. "No, I can't leave my people. I am to be their king."

"Then . . . what?" Fear and confusion sharpened her words. "What are you saying, Michel?"

"Marry me." The words rushed out of him like he'd been holding them back for a long time. "I want you to be my wife."

Emma nodded slowly like she understood the words coming out of his mouth, then scooted past him to get off the bed. She walked over to the bathroom and calmly locked herself inside. She pressed both her hands to her mouth as a warbled sound rose to her throat. It could've been a laugh or a sob. She couldn't tell for sure.

She stood in front of the sink, gripping the cold marble of the counter until her knuckles turned white. A *future with Michel*. The words resonated in her soul. She wanted it. So much that she couldn't breathe. She had wanted it desperately ever since she realized she loved him. She'd just never allowed herself to admit it. But in her heart of hearts, she'd wanted to sink to her knees and beg someone to let her *please* have a lifetime with him. She hadn't wanted to think about what it would cost her. She didn't want to think about it now. But how could she not?

Michel was a prince. There was no avoiding that fact. And she knew next to nothing about being a princess. *Me? A princess?* Hysterical laughter bubbled up inside her but faded away just as quickly. Why not? *Why can't I be a princess?*

She was a hard worker, and she could adapt to any situation life threw her way. She could learn to be a princess—a damn good one if she put her mind to it. Etiquette and decorum were her jam. Fashion? Forget about it. But more importantly, caring for people came naturally for her. She could learn to love the people of Rouleme as much as Michel loved them.

Emma had become a culinary instructor because she wanted to touch people's lives and make a difference. She loved cooking and teaching, but her passion lay in helping others nurture happiness in their lives. Couldn't she make a greater difference at Michel's side as a princess . . . as a queen?

But there was so much more than that. What about her dad? Auntie Soo? What about . . . *everything?*

Emma stared at herself in the mirror—at her dark hair, dark eyes, and the other features that made her decidedly not white. She didn't know much about Rouleme, but she was fairly certain that its people had never envisioned someone who looked like her as their princess . . . their future queen.

Even living in Los Angeles, she was no stranger to racism—from blatant slurs to constant microaggressions. Her favorite was when people asked her where she was *really* from. Because she couldn't *really* be from LA even though she was born and raised here. It was like they wanted to force her to acknowledge that she didn't belong in the US with the *real* Americans. She couldn't imagine what it would be like to be Asian *and* American in Rouleme, with no claim to their heritage or history, especially as their princess.

What could Michel possibly be thinking? Dating a young professor in LA was one thing. But marrying a prince in Rouleme was something else entirely. Did he know what he was asking of her? Did he expect her to leave everything behind to face an uncertain future with him? Someone who was different from her in so many ways? After everything she'd done to secure a safe, stable future? Her brain couldn't even process all the other impossibilities that stood between them.

"Emma?" There was a soft knock at the door. "Are you . . . are you all right?"

Oh no. She glanced frantically around the luxurious bathroom. What was she doing? Looking for an exit? Someplace to hide? The enormous clawfoot bathtub seemed like a good place. She scrunched her eyes shut. *Get a grip, Emma.*

"I have to pee," she yelled to buy herself time.

"Yes, of course." Michel sounded as though he wasn't sure whether he believed her. "My apologies for the intrusion."

She hated lying, so she sat down on the toilet. It was always a good idea to pee after sex anyway. She wouldn't want to deal with a UTI on top of this mess. Once she was done, she washed her hands for twenty seconds, humming a nursery tune under her breath. Even when she ran out of ways to stall, she couldn't make herself go out and face Michel. Especially since what she wanted more than anything was to throw herself into his arms and say, *Yes, yes, yes.* But that would be beyond unwise.

"Emma," he said in a soft, gentle voice after a few minutes had passed. "Emma, please come out."

"No, thank you," she said, facing the door with her palm pressed against it. She wanted to run to him . . . run from him.

"I don't think I handled that very well." He sighed. "I didn't even take out the ring."

"You have a ring?" She blinked back a rush of tears.

"Yes, it's . . . it's my mother's ring. It's rather old—passed down through generations—but I think you would like it. It's beautiful and unique. Like you."

"Your mother's ring?" she croaked, sliding down to the floor with her back against the door. "How do you have it with you?"

"I brought it with me from Rouleme . . ."

"Why?"

"Because I'm a hopeless romantic." His chuckle sounded sheepish. "Because I hoped that I would meet you. I think I *knew* that I would meet you, darling Emma."

"Michel?" she whispered.

"Yes?" There was a soft scraping sound. He must've put his palm against the door. Maybe right where she had hers a minute ago. "Tell me what you need."

She muffled a sob with her hand tight over her mouth. When she was certain she could speak without crying, she said, "Can you ask Sophie to come?"

"Sophie?" He sounded bewildered but quickly recovered. "Of course. Let me go get her. I'll be . . . I'll be right back."

Emma wiped her hands across her wet cheeks and blew out a long, shaky breath. Her heart was beating way too fast. She wanted to remind herself she needed to stay in America, her home, but it took more effort than she'd thought possible. All she could manage to focus on was that her dad needed her. But what did she need? She dug the heel of her hand into the center of her aching chest. She shook her head and composed herself the best she could.

"Emma, it's me," Sophie said from the other side of the door, her voice as soothing as a cool hand on a feverish forehead. "Are you all right?"

"I don't know." Emma forced the words past her sandpaper throat. "Is . . . is Michel there?"

"Yes, but . . ." Her friend sounded torn.

"Can you ask him to leave?" Emma turned her head so her cheek rested on the door.

There was a murmur of voices—Sophie's gentle and calm, Michel's confused and hurt—then her friend said, "He's gone now, but he's frantic with worry. It's hard to see him . . . and you . . . like this."

Emma somehow got to her feet, grabbing on to whatever she could, and opened the door. After one look at her face, Sophie gathered her into her arms. Emma made no attempt to stop the flow of tears. She wouldn't have succeeded anyway.

"He . . ." She hiccupped. "He wants to marry me."

"He does." Sophie rubbed her back, trying to ease her shivering. "He loves you, Emma."

"I know." She let her friend lead her to the sitting area and fell weakly into an armchair. "And I love him. I love him so much, but . . ."

"It's overwhelming," Sophie finished for her, tucking a blanket around her.

"It's too fucking much," Emma wailed.

"I can only imagine." Her friend settled on the opposite armchair, her brows furrowed in sympathy.

"I would be leaving everything and *everyone* I know behind." Fresh tears leaked out of the corners of her eyes.

"It's not an easy decision," Sophie murmured and reached across to squeeze her hand.

"And . . . and I'm Asian." Emma didn't know how to put all her apprehension into words.

"Yes, and they're so very white." A wry smile curled her friend's lips. "But the king and the rest of the royal family . . . they're good people."

"How about the rest of the country?" Emma asked, even though she remembered Michel telling her that they were an open-minded, hardworking people.

"*Most* people in Rouleme are fair-minded and progressive." Sophie didn't have to add the obvious—that *some* people were very much not. "The prince will not stand by and watch you get hurt. You'll have the entire royal family on your side."

Emma cradled her head in her hands. It was the vocal minority who always brought the vitriol, wasn't it? Hate was such a brutal weapon—it could wear down the bravest souls. But wasn't the love and support of the people who mattered stronger than hate? She covered her face with her hands. It was too much to digest all at once—maybe ever. She needed to think, but the tangle of contradicting emotions inside her overwhelmed her logic.

"Can you take me home?" she asked in a small, exhausted voice.

"Of course." Sophie hesitated. "I'll let Michel know. He's worried sick."

Emma grabbed her hand as she walked past her. "Please tell him I'm sorry. Tell him I just need some time to think."

"Don't worry." Her friend gave her a reassuring smile. "He'll understand."

Sophie was back in a matter of minutes to drive her home. But once they were in the lobby, she stopped to have a quick word with the hotel manager.

"No one goes in or out of the presidential suite," Sophie said in her take-no-prisoners voice. Emma scooted a few steps away from her. The woman was hella intimidating. "*No one.*"

"Understood." The pale-faced man nodded vigorously. "I will personally make sure of it."

Sophie was back by Emma's side in an instant and guided her to Michel's car in the parking lot. As her friend drove them out to the street, Emma looked sightlessly out the windshield. Michel and she loved each other. Despite their many differences, they *fit*. She could admit that now. But how could she trust her own judgment when she was so hopelessly, so *helplessly* in love with the man? And how could she turn her back on her life here? She couldn't leave her dad.

"How could he ask me to marry him?" Emma blurted, angry, confused, and frustrated. "How could he unload this on me? He spiked the ball into my court, and now *I* have to decide?"

"Would you rather he didn't ask you?" Sophie said in a sad, quiet voice that stopped Emma mid-rant. "I know it's bloody hard. But at least he's giving you a choice. Gabriel . . . he just left."

"Maybe he couldn't ask you to sacrifice everything for him." Emma placed a comforting hand on her friend's arm and wondered if sacrificing their love had been the kinder choice. "Besides, I thought you said your duty lies with your country."

"Yes." Sophie gave her a teary-eyed smile. "But my heart lies with Gabriel."

"Oh, sweetie," Emma whispered, her heart breaking for her friend. Sophie would've left Rouleme to be with the man she loved—she would've sacrificed everything for him—but she never got the chance. Maybe it hadn't been the kinder choice at all. "I don't know what to say."

"Say you'll think it over," her friend urged. "Say you'll make the choice that will make you the happiest."

The happiest . . . While she wanted to help people create moments of happiness in their lives, Emma had never thought about her own happiness. She'd been so preoccupied with building a secure, stable life for herself. But rather than settling for a *safe* life with *moments* of happiness, shouldn't she strive for a *happy life*, even with its ups and downs?

"I will." Emma swallowed the tears clogging her throat. "Thank you."

Soft classical music filled the car as Emma tried to breathe away her panic. She needed to think with a clear head, but a part of her wanted to stare blankly out the window and not think at all.

Despite her brief rant, Emma wasn't really angry at Michel. How could she be angry with him for telling her he loved her? That he wanted to marry her? She was just overwhelmed by his proposal. What normal human being wouldn't be after receiving a proposal from a prince? But overwhelmed or not, Sophie was right. Michel wasn't being selfish by asking her to choose. He was respecting *her* right to decide what she wanted to do with *her* life.

"Will you still be coming to Marion's farewell brunch tomorrow?" Sophie asked, pulling into the driveway.

"Oh . . . yes," Emma stammered, surprised to find herself home. "I'll be there."

And when she saw Michel tomorrow, they would talk and maybe . . . just maybe . . . they could figure out a future for themselves.

CHAPTER FORTY-ONE

♡

Michel paced back and forth in front of the elevator, waiting for Emma to make her way up. It shouldn't take more than a couple of minutes, but it felt as though it was taking an eternity for her to reach his floor. When the elevator doors finally slid open, all he could do was stare. She looked a little pale, with shadows beneath her eyes, but the soft smile on her face was radiant.

"Hi," she said with a little wave.

Christ, she was beautiful. He swallowed.

Emma took a step toward him and cocked her head to the side. "Michel?"

"My apologies." He quickly stepped aside, realizing he was blocking her path off the elevator. Then with a hand on the small of her back—he sighed in relief when she didn't flinch away—he led her toward his suite, where everyone waited. He cleared his throat. "How are you? Did you sleep well?"

"No, Michel." He knew it was a ridiculous question even before she arched an eyebrow at him. "I didn't sleep a wink."

"I couldn't sleep either," he said in a rush. "I was up all night . . . thinking about you. Worried for you."

"We'll talk . . . after." She glanced sideways at him with

tenderness and concern warring in her eyes. She huffed a sigh. "For now, let's go have some brunch."

When they reached the dining room, Gabriel promptly got to his feet and grinned at her. "Good morning, Emma. You look lovely as usual."

"Save the flirting for after brunch," Sophie admonished without much heat, then searched Emma's face. "But you do look lovely. Come have a seat."

Offering them a sweet smile, Emma slid into the chair Michel pulled out for her. "Thank you for coming to the party last night, Marion."

"Thank *you* for having me," Marion said with genuine warmth. "I had so much fun, and the food was absolutely sublime."

"Well"—Emma shrugged—"you're the one who made it."

"I *did* make it, didn't I?" Marion clapped her hands like a guileless child. Her lack of artifice was one of her best qualities.

"You sure did." Emma laughed with delight, and Michel couldn't help but smile. This was why she taught cooking—to give people joy and a sense of accomplishment. She added in a stage whisper, "Don't tell any of the other guests, but yours was one of the best in the group."

"You are too sweet." Marion actually blushed. "Oh my God, Emma. You *have* to visit me in Rouleme. My friends would *love* to learn to cook from you. And Isabelle could certainly learn a thing or two from you even though the future queen of Rouleme might not *need* to cook for herself . . ."

The fork Michel had been picking up clattered to his plate. It hit him all at once. He hadn't thought of Isabelle in the last few weeks. Not once. In his desperation to convince Emma to marry him, he'd forgotten that he had a fiancée. He and Isabelle never wanted to marry each other—they were too good of friends to pretend otherwise—but they would've been duty bound to see it through if Michel hadn't found Emma.

Coming to America to find his true love had been his best chance at avoiding a loveless, arranged marriage. He couldn't break the engagement—a long-held contract between their families—based on the mere *hope* of marrying for love. The elders would've been outraged at best. More likely, they would've laughed in his face for his childish ideals. He'd needed to find someone, a flesh-and-blood woman, to present to his father—to convince him that he was in love with her and couldn't live without her. Anything less would have been pointless.

Oh God. Why hadn't he explained everything to Emma? And now . . . He spun toward her to find her blinking at his cousin with a half smile, her head cocked to the side.

"Oh, for fuck's sake, Marion." Gabriel stood up with a rough push of his chair and dragged his sister to her feet. "I'm taking you to the airport."

"But . . . What did I say? Let go, Gabriel. I . . ." She gasped. "Bloody hell, Michel. I didn't mean . . . Emma, I'm so sorry . . ."

"Come on, Marion. Let's give these two some privacy." Sophie followed Michel's cousins out of the dining room with a worried glance over her shoulder.

All the blood drained from Emma's face as she watched them leave, and dread spread across Michel's chest. Still, she didn't look angry. The slight knit between her brows conveyed confusion more than anything.

"Emma . . ." he began, his heart pounding against his ribs.

What could he say? He wasn't sure what to think, much less what he needed to tell her to fix this . . . But did anything need fixing? Surely she would see that it was all just a terrible misunderstanding.

"Michel?" Her voice was small, childlike. She sounded . . . afraid. "What was Marion talking about? Who . . . who is the future queen of . . . of Rouleme?"

"I want *you* to be the future queen of Rouleme." He shut

down his panic and fear. Prince Michel, with his diplomacy and practiced detachment, took over. He heard himself say with cool arrogance, "I want you to be my wife."

Emma met his eyes, her frown deepening. "Then why did Marion say Isabelle was the future queen? Who's Isabelle? Wait . . . I remember that name. You said you had a friend named Isabelle once."

"Yes, Isabelle is a good friend." His spine felt stiff from holding himself ramrod straight—the posture of the future king. "We've been friends since childhood, along with Sophie and Gabriel."

"I don't want a walk down memory lane," she snapped, a flush staining her cheeks an angry red. "Why is Isabelle the future queen?"

"When we were mere infants, our parents decided that we would make an ideal pair," Prince Michel stated matter-of-factly. "Isabelle comes from a well-respected noble family with considerable wealth."

"Of course. A wealthy noblewoman from Rouleme. I assume she's white." It wasn't phrased as a question, but he still nodded in confirmation. Emma's mouth twisted into a cynical smirk. "Your parents weren't wrong. Isabelle is far better suited to be the queen of Rouleme than a middle-class Asian American like me." Even Prince Michel couldn't hold back a flinch. "Why did you ask me to marry you when you had the perfect fiancée waiting for you at home?"

"Isabelle and I have never been romantically involved. Neither of us ever wanted an arranged marriage. But we couldn't break our engagement on some vague hope that we might meet someone we love in the future." Prince Michel fought a burst of impatience. Why couldn't she see that he wouldn't have proposed to her if he didn't want to marry her? *Stop being an arse.* Emma's Michel broke through the surface. "I came to Los Angeles to find someone I want to spend the rest of my life with—someone I love with all my heart. My entire life has been ruled by my duty to Rouleme, but my heart . . . I wanted to choose the person I gave my heart to, Emma. And that person is you. I love *you*. I want to marry *you*."

"But what if you hadn't met me?" she choked out. "Would you have gone back to Rouleme and married Isabelle?"

"I . . . Yes," Prince Michel answered. He would've done his duty.

"What if . . ." Emma wiped away tears and took a shuddering breath. "What if I said no? What if I said I won't marry you? Will you go back and marry Isabelle?"

"Are you saying no?" Michel crumpled inside. "Are you saying you won't marry me?"

"Ans . . . answer me," she said through chattering teeth. "Will you . . . go home and . . . and marry your *fiancée*?"

"I don't know." Even Prince Michel felt too stunned to think. "I never thought . . . But my duty—"

"You didn't tell me." Her hands fisted on the dining table, their cheerful brunch cold and forgotten. "All this time, you were engaged to someone else and you didn't tell me." She brought a fist down hard enough to make the silverware clatter on her plate. "Yesterday, you asked me to give up *everything* . . . And all this time, you had a backup plan. You wouldn't have had to give up *anything*."

My God, I've lost her. Emma's Michel—his true self— scrabbled to take control. Fuck Prince Michel. *He* needed to do this. Michel had to fight for her with all his desperation. All his fear. All his love.

"*You* are my everything." It was a fervent vow. "My heart is yours and yours alone."

"Such pretty words." She rose abruptly to her feet. "But I'm done with your lies."

"Emma, please." He gripped her hand, but she shook him off with a violent jerk of her arm. "I love you."

The tears had dried, and only ice remained in her eyes. "Goodbye, Prince Michel."

His heart sank to his stomach. He *hated* hearing her call him that. He never wanted to be anything but Michel to her. But as she walked out of the dining room and the front door clicked shut behind her, he realized that she might never call him anything again.

CHAPTER FORTY-TWO

E mma parked her car in the driveway, unable to recall how she'd gotten home. Her head was filled with screams, and she couldn't form a coherent thought. It probably hadn't been a good idea for her to drive in the first place.

With her forehead pressed against the steering wheel, she forced herself to do some breathing exercises. In through the nose and out through the mouth. She couldn't fathom counting, so she just breathed slowly and methodically.

She didn't know how long she sat in her car like that, but the pressure in her ears began to fade, and she could hear herself think past the devastation sweeping through her. *Michel is engaged to another woman.*

"What the literal fuck?" She pounded her palm against the steering wheel in time with her rant. It made her feel marginally better, so she did it again. "Fuck, fuck, fuuuuuuck."

Emma decided to take advantage of her anger to get herself inside the house before she turned into a zombie again. But her hands were shaking so wildly that she couldn't fit her key into the lock. She kicked the door and started stabbing it with her key instead . . . because that was a perfectly logical way to get the door to open. She dropped her hand to her side and stared at her toes in shame. As she contemplated apologizing to the door, it opened wide to reveal her dad on the other side.

"What was that? I heard all these noises . . ." His confused frown morphed into alarm when he caught her expression. "Emma, what's wrong?"

He tugged her inside by her hand and led her to the living room. With gentle pressure on her shoulders, he convinced her to sit, then settled down beside her on the sofa. There wasn't much else to do except to throw her arms around his neck and redefine ugly crying. His arms came around her, one hand cradling her head and the other patting her back.

Her dad held her tight as though he wanted to hold her together and keep her safe—as though he wanted to absorb her pain so he could hurt for her instead. Ever loving and ever patient, he said nothing until her sobs became quiet hiccups—but only until then.

"Whose ass am I whooping?" he gritted through his teeth.

She laughed into his shoulder even though she knew he was dead serious. "No ass whooping, Appa. I don't want you to go to jail."

Besides, Sophie was duty bound to protect Michel, and her dad wouldn't stand a chance against that badass. Her laugh turned a little hysterical, so she pressed her lips shut.

"You're right. That won't do." Her dad smoothed his hand down the back of her head. "Who's going to take care of you if I'm behind bars?"

"Right?" She sat up and looked at him, her eyes blurry with unshed tears. "You're much too important for me to risk like that."

And she didn't really want to see Michel get hurt, because it would hurt her just as much. But thinking about him almost sucked her back into crying mode, so she glommed on to the traces of anger inside her. Michel lied to her. He was a liar. She was *angry* because he was a lying liar.

But did it really matter that he'd kept his engagement a secret from her? An engagement in name only? Until she realized she loved him, hadn't she planned on finding herself a perfect-on-paper husband once Michel left?

Would it have changed anything if he'd told her about his engagement? Of course she would've been shocked at first, but it would only have confirmed her stubborn stance that they were just passing through each other's lives. She probably would've convinced herself that she didn't care if he was formally engaged, because they were never supposed to have a future anyway. Maybe it wouldn't have mattered. *If* he hadn't proposed.

But he *had* proposed. He asked her to leave everything behind to be with him. That changed *everything*.

"I know you're worried, Appa." She squeezed his hand and stood up. "But I'll be okay. I just need a little time to myself."

"Let me know when you're ready to talk." Her dad let her retreat to her room even though she could tell it was hard for him.

Emma had hoped to cry herself to sleep, but no such luck. She paced the room like a caged animal, every instinct in her telling her that she had to run away. *Run away from what?* It didn't matter. Her muscles ached, taut and alert, and she was going to crawl out of her skin if she didn't *do* something. She had to cook. She needed to lose herself in it.

Time and distraction were all she needed. She would've lost Michel in two weeks anyway. That had always been the plan until last night. It wasn't the end of the world that it ended now instead. And no matter what, she would not think about his proposal.

$\sim\!\sim\!\sim$

"How long has she been like this?" Auntie Soo whispered to her dad.

They were both standing at the entrance to the kitchen, looking down at her crouched form with worried eyes. But Emma couldn't spare them more than a quick glance. She was busy.

Shaking her head to clear the fog from it, Emma returned to mixing the kimchi with both her hands. Her thighs burned from crouching in front of the giant stainless steel mixing bowl on the floor. You had to make kimchi on the kitchen floor. The massive mixing bowl barely fit on the counter, and it was hard to dig in your hands properly when the bowl was elevated. Her arms burned, too. She actually ached everywhere. She hadn't been sleeping. Or eating. Or feeling. Not feeling was her main priority. That required her not to think—which in turn required her to stay busy. *Busy, busy, busy.*

"Too long," her dad answered in a low, sad voice. "I thought she just needed some time, but this has been going on for three days now."

"Oh my. It's a good thing I stopped by." Auntie Soo stepped closer to Emma. "You need to stop cooking and cleaning, child. You're going to wear yourself down to the bones."

"Yes, baby girl," her dad added gently. "Why don't you go have a seat? You've been in the kitchen for hours. *Days*, really."

"Almost done." Emma clicked shut the fourth container of kimchi—this one was chonggak kimchi with little white radishes and long green stems. She'd already made baechu kimchi with napa cabbage, ggakdugi with squares of chopped white radishes, and oi sobagi with cucumbers and chives. "I just want to make sure we don't run out of kimchi for the next few months."

"You made enough to last us a year. Please be reasonable," her dad pleaded. "We don't have any more room in the refrigerator. Even the freezer is full from the mandu and bulgogi you made two days ago."

"You need to stop this instant." Her godmother towered over

her with her fists on her hips. Emma had enough sense left to be scared into compliance. "Your dad is worried sick."

"Let me just put this away," she croaked.

Emma had been determinedly cheerful as she cooked non-stop for the last three days. Every time she stopped from pure exhaustion, her heart beat out a frantic, erratic beat and panic built in her stomach. Her dad had been patient, giving her all the room she needed. But it seemed she had run out of time.

Emma put the chonggak kimchi in the kimchi refrigerator, pulled off her rubber gloves, and untied her apron. After folding the apron into a neat square and placing it on top of the counter, she trudged out to the living room and sat down on the couch. She stared blankly at the wall, fighting back feelings.

"Soo, thank you for getting her out of the kitchen," her dad said from the hallway. "I think I need to do this one on my own. I . . . I need to talk to my daughter."

"Of course, Jae. Please let me know how it goes." Her god-mother paused to sniffle. Was she crying? Emma only felt mild regret. "And I'm here for you and Emma anytime you need me."

"I know, old friend." His voice was thick with emotion, too. Had she made both of them cry? It was hard to take in, so she ignored it. After clicking the front door shut, her dad came to the living room and sat down beside her. "Emma, I know it's hard, but I need you to tell me what happened. This can't go on."

"Michel . . ." She forced herself to breathe. "We broke up."

"I gathered as much." Her dad dragged a hand down his face. "But there's more."

"Yes, a lot more," Emma agreed. "You know how I started going on matseons with the men that Auntie Soo handpicked for me?"

"Uh-huh."

"I thought letting her match me up with someone who has a lot in common with me—someone perfect on paper—was the key to a safe, stable marriage." She glanced down at her hands. "Marrying for love seemed like a foolish risk. I . . . I didn't want what happened with you and Mom to happen to me."

"Oh, Emma." Her dad tugged her into a hug. "I'm so sorry we made you think that way. I think your mom and I messed up by telling you we split up because of incompatibility."

"What do you mean?" She pulled back to look at him.

"Irreconcilable differences seemed like such a generic, *harmless* reason to give you. I realize now how much harm it actually caused." He shook his head, regret shadowing his eyes. "Emma, your mom and I were . . . What was it you said? Perfect on paper. It wasn't a lack of common ground that drew us apart, but a lack of unconditional love."

"I don't understand." Her brows knitted together.

"You and I . . . we never came first to your mom. When push came to shove, she chose her work over us without fail." Her dad sighed. "Her career had always been important to her. I married her knowing I would always come second—that I would never have all of her. But I loved her and thought it would be better to have a part of her than none at all.

"Then you came along, and I watched your mom make you promises she couldn't keep. It broke my heart to watch you search for her in the auditorium every time she missed one of your school recitals. Your mom and I fought more and more. I couldn't stand by while she hurt you time and time again.

"And it wasn't only you. I realized I was tired of being second best. I wasn't happy with having just a part of her anymore. I finally asked her to choose family over work—at least most of the time—but she just couldn't. Her career was too important to her." Her dad grasped both of Emma's hands. "We decided to tell you we were incompatible so you wouldn't think the divorce was in any way your fault."

Of course. She blew out a shaky breath as the puzzle pieces clicked into place and she saw patterns she'd refused to see before. It all made sense. If she'd wanted to, her mom could've had a real relationship with her instead of an obligatory annual Christmas call. It wasn't like she stayed away because she was *incompatible* with her own daughter. Her mom just had no space for her. Emma thought she'd come to terms with her absence a long time ago, but this clarity gutted her a little.

"Your mom loves you in her own way," her dad said gently.

"But she loves her career more," Emma bit out.

She tried so hard not to think about the heartache her mom caused her, but she had every right to be angry with her—hurt and angry. She needed to let it out sometimes. It didn't need to happen right away—this was a lot to take in—but it would eventually help her move on.

"It doesn't matter, though." And she meant it. She was grateful for the life she had. "You and Auntie Soo have more than made up for Mom's absence."

"I'm glad to hear that." Her dad sniffed. "God knows I tried."

"You did good, Appa." She squeezed his hands. "We both did."

"Now, my dear." He leveled a steady gaze on her. "Tell me what happened."

"Michel's engaged." She realized the second the words left her mouth that she had opened on the wrong note.

"I'll *kill* him." Her dad shot to his feet as though he intended to commit murder right that instant.

"Sit down, Appa. I thought we already talked about this. I don't want you going to prison." She tugged on the side of his pants. "And it's a bit more complicated than it sounds."

"He was cheating on his fiancée with you," he shouted. "That rotten bastard was *using* you. And what? Then he just dumped you?"

"Dad, you got it all . . . well . . . *mostly* wrong." She huffed out an exasperated laugh, feeling more like herself for the first time in days. "Sit down. Please?"

Her dad sat down beside her, his shoulders bunched and his hands in white-knuckled fists. Emma had never seen him so angry before. But at least he sat down.

"First, he didn't dump me. *I* left him." As expected, that appeased her dad by a smidgen, but it broke her heart to say the words. She *left* him. "And second, he wasn't cheating on her. They're just friends and neither of them want to marry each other. Their parents arranged the engagement when they were babies."

"Okay." He blew out a long, calming breath. "Emma, you're normally unnervingly frank. This roundabout explanation makes me think you haven't gotten everything figured out yet."

"I can't hide anything from you, can I?" Her lips curled into a wry grin even though her insides were quaking with nerves. Talking to her dad meant having to face all the things she'd been avoiding for the past three days.

"Why would you ever want to?" He smiled sweetly, his rare display of anger gone without a trace. "You're perfect."

"Am I?" She leaned her head on his shoulder, feeling undeserving of his praise. "From the moment I met Michel, I felt such a deep connection to him. But I fought tooth and nail against it because I was so afraid of falling in love."

"Did you win that fight?" he said with a skeptical arch of his brow. How did parents just *know* stuff?

"Not even close." Her throat closed up with tears. "I fell head over heels in love with him. And he fell for me, too."

"Then why did you break up?" A confused frown lined his forehead.

"Because Michel is the crown prince of Rouleme." She cringed, preparing herself for her dad's reaction. He choked on his own spit, and she pounded on his back until he was breathing normally. After a steadying breath, she added, "And he asked me to marry him."

"Wait. What?" Her dad cradled his head in his hands. "I need you to put this into chronological order for me. When did you find out he was a prince? A *prince*? Holy cow." He glanced up. "I'm so sorry, my dear. It's just a bit overwhelming. Please go on. When did he tell you?"

"Weeks ago," she confessed. If that was the real reason she broke up with him, then she would've done so long before this.

"You must've been shocked." *He* still looked shocked.

"I guess." She scratched at a stain on her sleeve. She must've splashed some kimchi on it earlier.

"You guess?" Her dad's voice rose with disbelief.

"I mostly pretended it didn't matter." She scrubbed at the stain with a bit of her own spit. *Eww.* What was she doing? "I told myself it didn't make a difference since we didn't have a future together anyway—we were already too different to begin with. So I stubbornly ignored the fact that he's a prince. I know. It's bonkers. You don't think I'm so perfect now, do you?"

"I just wish I'd talked to you about your mom and me sooner. That's all," her dad said, guilt marring his face. "Then what happened? When did you find out he was engaged?"

"Three days ago." She didn't want to think about that day. She wanted to shut down all her feelings and keep making kimchi. But her dad loved her too much to let her hide from herself.

Her dad nodded. "And when did he propose to you?"

"The day before I found out he was engaged." Her voice broke, the truth becoming harder and harder to ignore.

"Did you give him an answer when he proposed?" he gently prodded.

"No." She closed her eyes and shook her head. "I needed time to think."

"Did you have an answer for him when you saw him the next

day?" Her dad took both her hands and enveloped them between his own, lending his warmth and strength.

"I don't know," she whispered as tears rained down her cheeks. There was no more hiding from her thoughts. "I didn't want to lose him. I wanted to find a way. Then Marion let slip that he had a fiancée, and I got so angry. I couldn't believe he had a *backup* plan."

But she couldn't dredge up any anger. Was she even angry, then? Or did she just need an excuse to run?

"Kind of like *your* backup plan?" Her dad didn't pull his punch. He knew this was too important. "Didn't Soo have men lined up to meet you whenever you were ready?"

"That's beside the point, Appa. Do you realize what Michel was asking of me?" Her words took on a shrill note. "He was asking me to leave behind everything I know and love to move to another country—another continent—to be with him. He was asking me to give up *everything* while he risked *nothing*."

"So what you're really angry about is the fact that he asked you to marry him—not that he has a fiancée who he doesn't want to marry?" His expression was stern as he pushed her to face the truth.

"Yes." She jumped to her feet and paced the floor. "No."

"Or are you just scared, Emma?" He stood and held her by the shoulders, not letting her look away. "Because it's okay to be scared. I'd be scared, too, in your shoes."

Emma stopped breathing. She stared unblinkingly at her dad, blood pounding in her ears. He was right. She wasn't angry. She was scared . . . about everything. But most of all, she was scared of losing Michel.

"What if I leave everything behind to be with him in Rouleme and he . . ." She cried into her hands, unable to continue for a moment. She finally raised tear-soaked eyes to her dad. "And he stops loving me? What if he realizes I'm ordinary and . . . and boring and stops wanting to be with me?"

"Not possible." He gathered her in his arms. "You're extraordinary and always interesting."

A sound between a sob and a laugh broke past her tears.

"I've seen the way that young man looks at you—like his world begins and ends with you. That kind of love doesn't change as long as you both choose love above all else."

"Promise, Appa?" she whispered through trembling lips, tears coming down in torrents. "I'm so scared his love will fade. I don't think I can bear to lose him."

"Ask yourself this." He paused as though to emphasize the importance of his question. "Would you ever stop loving him?"

"No." She jerked back in surprise. She knew in the depths of her soul that her love would never change. "Never."

"Then why do you doubt his love for you? If you believe he loves you with all his heart, then love him back with all of yours." Her dad wiped her face dry with his handkerchief, snot and all. "*That's* the key to forever."

She let her dad's words sink in and realized what she had to do—what she should've done all along. "Appa, I have to go."

Emma would always love Michel, so she had to love him with jeongseong—generously, wholeheartedly, and fearlessly. If anyone deserved her very best—her everything—he did. And it started now.

CHAPTER FORTY-THREE

♥

*E*mma showered and changed in record time and marched down the stairs, not intending to stop until she was back at Michel's side. As she reached the living room—where her dad sat cradling a mug between his hands—the doorbell rang.

"I'll get that." Her dad put his tea down on the coffee table and squeezed her shoulder as he passed. A moment later, he said, "Emma, you have a visitor."

"Is Auntie Soo back?" She hurried to the front door, thinking she should've called her. But it wasn't her godmother who stood in the entryway. "Gabriel, what are you doing here?"

"I need to speak with you," he said in a low, tense voice.

Her stomach swooped to her feet, then clogged her throat. "Is he okay?"

"Yes, he's fine." Gabriel dragged a hand through his hair. "*Fine* isn't the right word. He's a right mess. Let's just say he's alive and unhurt."

"That's good." Emma almost sagged with relief. "Dad, this is Gabriel, Michel's cousin."

"Mr. Yoon, I'm sorry for barging in like this," Gabriel said with impeccable manners. "But I need to speak with your daughter quite urgently."

"Don't worry about it." Her dad clapped him on the shoulder. "Go on. You can talk in the living room."

Emma led him there with hurried steps. She took a seat on the sofa and waved her hand toward the armchair. Gabriel shook his head and paced instead.

"It might be a good idea for you to start talking," she said, her legs bouncing with nerves. "Since it's *quite urgent* and all."

"Michel left for Rouleme." He stopped in front of her, his hands clasped in front of him.

"He . . . he had more than a week left. He said . . . he said . . ." The blood drained out of her face, and her mind turned dull and empty. He left her. Without even a goodbye. But he loved her. Didn't he? "I see."

"No, I don't think you do." Gabriel knelt in front of her and took a breath to continue. "He—"

"Did Sophie leave with him?" She spoke over him, afraid of what he might say. Did Michel change his mind? Did he decide to marry perfect-on-paper Isabelle, after all? She didn't want to know. It felt safer to focus on her friends.

"She did, but"—Gabriel actually blushed—"she's coming back once she sorts everything out."

"Really?" Emma gasped. "So you finally came to your senses and asked her to stay?"

"Actually, she told me to stop being an utter wanker and to empty out her side of the closet." His wide, open grin made him look young and hopeful.

"Oh, Gabriel." Emma laid her hand on his shoulder. "I'm so happy for you guys."

"Thank you." He gave his head a sharp shake. "But Sophie will not hesitate to kick my arse if I mess this up, so let me explain everything."

"Okay." She had to be brave. No more halfways. She took a deep breath. "Tell me."

"Michel was . . . He fell apart when you left. I've never seen him so . . . It wasn't good." Gabriel's throat bobbed as he swallowed. "He loves you, Emma, and Sophie thinks he might do something very reckless to win you back."

"I . . . I love him, too." She pressed her fingers against her trembling lips. It took her a few moments to be sure she could speak. "But why did he leave? And what do you mean something reckless? What would he do?"

"He went to Rouleme to tell his father about his decision to . . ." Gabriel scrubbed a hand down his face. "To abdicate."

"What?" Emma shot to her feet and knocked the distraught man on his ass. "What in the literal *fuck* is he thinking? He loves Rouleme. He loves his people."

"He loves you more." His quiet sincerity came through even as he pushed himself off the floor. "But please don't make him choose."

"I would never make him choose," she shouted, too agitated to modulate her tone. "What is he *thinking*?"

"He's thinking that if you can't leave your life behind, then he'll leave his." He got to his feet and dusted off his slacks. "I told him to do whatever it takes to hold on to you because he would regret it for the rest of his life if he didn't. I had no idea the fool would go so far as to abdicate."

"We have to stop him." She fluttered her hands, eyes darting around the room. Even through her panic and outrage, her heart sang with happiness—with certainty that she came first to Michel. But abdicating was far too extreme for a grand gesture. She did *not* want that. "But how?"

"Ah, I'm glad you asked." Gabriel had the gall to wink at her. "I'm under orders—by the love of my life—to bring you to Rouleme as soon as humanly possible *even if I have to kidnap you.*"

"Sophie said that?" Emma crinkled her nose in disbelief.

"No, I added the last bit myself for dramatic effect." He grinned.

"Well, there's no need for kidnapping." She rolled her eyes. "I would be on my way to the hotel right now if you'd come ten minutes later. But he's not at the hotel, is he? He's in Rouleme to freaking *abdicate*."

"Which is why we need to leave right now. My car is out front." He glanced at his watch. "We can make it to the airport in half an hour if we hurry."

"But I don't have a plane ticket. And my passport expired ages ago, and I never got around to renewing it." Emma felt faint with panic. What if she didn't get to Michel in time? "Oh my God. What are we going to do?"

"Leave all that to me." Gabriel smirked and tugged her toward the front door. "All you need to do is come. Of your own free will, preferably."

Her dad jumped when they rounded the corner to the entry-way. Before Emma could tell him she had no time to explain, he said, "I heard everything. You need to hurry, baby girl. Stop that silly, wonderful boy from doing something he'll regret."

Emma gave her dad a rib-cracking hug before he practically shoved her out the door. She managed to say over her shoulder, "I'll call you as soon as I can. I love you, Appa."

She didn't even remember how she got in the car, but Gabriel drove like the *devil*. She hung on to the grab handle for dear life. "Do you always drive like this?"

"I did a stint in Formula One in my early twenties . . ." When he caught a glimpse of her pale face, he quickly averred, "It was a very brief stint. I can slow down. I'm just anxious to get on that plane."

"You bought my plane ticket ahead of time?" she asked, loosening her grip on the handle.

"No." He looked a bit sheepish. "We're taking a private jet."

"A private jet?" She swiveled in her seat to stare at him.

"It's not something the royal family does often, but this is an emergency. Sophie asked Michel's personal assistant to arrange it."

"I . . . I see," she said weakly, both impressed and flummoxed.

Emma had a lot of figuring out to do before they landed in Rouleme. Like coming to terms with the fact that the royal family had a private jet at their disposal—but more importantly that she might become a member of the royal family. No, she *would* become one, because she was marrying the crown prince.

"Oh my God." She looked down at the slightly rumpled shirt and jeans she'd thrown on. "Am I meeting the king? Wearing this?"

"Not to worry." Gabriel screeched into the airport. "Marion will have something suitable for you to change into."

"Something suitable for saving the future of Rouleme?" A faint smile lit her face. "I'm thinking the occasion calls for a cape."

"But please, no underwear on the outside," he deadpanned, pulling up in front of a sleek white airplane. "Underwear should be worn *under* the clothing even when the fate of a nation lies in your hands."

Emma burst into a fit of giggles fueled by nerves and anticipation. And she kept laughing as she and Gabriel ran to the waiting plane. She had to hold on to her aching side as she climbed on board—as much from the laughter as the unexpected cardio.

The opulent interior of the private jet lived up to the expectations created by TV shows and movies. But as the reality of the situation sank in, Emma felt too distraught to enjoy any of it other than to notice that her leather seat was really, really comfortable and that their flight attendant was super competent and nice.

With only two passengers, the plane took off in no time.

Emma stared sightlessly out the window as her stomach settled and her ears popped, her body adjusting to the altitude. Even though they were on their way to Rouleme as fast as humanly possible, she felt like a windup toy ready to snap with just one more creaky turn of the knob. She closed her eyes and prayed . . .

Please don't let me be too late. Please.

CHAPTER FORTY-FOUR

♥

Michel threw his dinner jacket on his bed and stepped out onto the balcony, facing the inner courtyard of the palace. The view of the elegant fountain surrounded by a neatly manicured garden usually relaxed him, but he couldn't draw a proper breath tonight.

He thought he would lose his mind when Emma left him. Her parting words had played over and over in his head, drowning him with shame, until he came to his decision to abdicate. Because she was right.

It was true he had asked her to give up everything while he risked nothing. In all his privilege and entitlement, he had never once thought *he* could be the one to sacrifice everything. Now he knew he would give anything to have Emma back.

But when he decided to abdicate, he realized that he truly *wanted* to rule Rouleme. He realized too late that he wanted to be a good king like his father. It would be a privilege to sit on the throne, not a burden. He loosened his tie with an impatient tug and ran his fingers through his hair. Leaving his people behind would be like ripping out a vital part of himself, but Emma was worth the sacrifice. He wouldn't be whole without his country, but he would be nothing without her.

Emma had been wrong about one thing. She'd accused him of keeping his engagement a secret as a *backup plan* when he never made a conscious decision not to tell her. In truth, he had been so focused on winning her over that he'd all but forgotten about his engagement to his childhood friend.

And she'd been wrong to suspect that he would've married Isabelle if she refused his proposal. He could never marry anyone else—duty be damned—because his heart would always belong to Emma. It wouldn't be fair to Isabelle, and it wouldn't be fair to him. He wanted to kick himself for not telling her that before she walked out of his hotel room.

But *God*, he hoped Emma would have him. He hoped he could prove to her that she would always come first for him. He would not have survived the last few days if he hadn't come up with a plan to win her back. Now that he'd decided to abdicate, he felt as though he was making his way back to her. The unbearable pressure in his chest had eased just enough to let him breathe. He wouldn't be whole until he was by her side again, but the hope of winning her back gave him enough strength to function—enough strength to carry out his plan.

Michel just prayed that it wouldn't kill his father to hear his decision. The longer he waited to tell his father, the more anxious he became, and he desperately needed to be done with it. But every time he tried to speak to his father alone, some peculiar obstacle would appear. It would usually be Sophie or Antoine with some urgent matter that needed Michel's immediate attention, which ultimately turned out to be a false alarm.

Their obvious interference was extremely vexing. Yesterday evening, he found his door locked from the outside when he tried to go to his father. When he texted Sophie, she came to his chamber without delay, then proceeded to apologize for nearly half an hour as she worked with Antoine to fix the allegedly broken lock. They ignored his suggestion to retrieve the palace caretaker and spent another half an hour saying *Almost there.* By the time they got his door open, his father had retired for the night.

With an aggrieved sigh, Michel turned his back on the court-yard and stepped into his chambers. Staring out into the night wasn't going to solve anything. He needed to speak with his father. As he steeled his nerves and reached for the door handle, a firm knock sounded at the door. His brows furrowed in confusion, but he finished opening the door as he'd intended.

"My . . . prince." Sophie seemed taken aback to have her knock answered so quickly, but gathered herself with a brisk shake of her head. "I mean . . . Do you have a moment to talk, Michel? As a friend?"

"Of course." It was his turn to be surprised, but his shock swiftly morphed into suspicion. This had to be another delay tactic. "Please come in."

He led her to his sitting room with the sky-blue wallpaper and dark wood trim. The soothing decor should make a nice backdrop for their *friend talk.* They sat down at the opposite ends of a long sofa. When Michel turned toward her and arched an eyebrow, Sophie cleared her throat.

"I don't know how to say this, so I'm just going to say it." She drew a deep breath. "It has been an honor to serve you and Rou-leme, but my place is by Gabriel's side."

His mouth fell open, and he sat gaping at his royal guard until she squirmed in her seat.

"Now would be a good time to say something, Michel," Sophie said dryly.

"My God," Michel murmured, finally closing his mouth. He reached across the sofa and clapped her shoulder. "You two have finally worked it out, then?"

"Yes." She ducked her chin with sudden shyness. His suspicion that this was another interference ploy evaporated. "I've already spoken with my parents. They are disappointed, of course. Our family has served yours for generations, but my happiness comes first for them."

"Did Gabriel ask you to move to Los Angeles?" For some reason, Michel held his breath as he waited for her answer.

"No, he didn't." Sophie deigned to roll her eyes, but a soft smile curled her lips. "That fool said he'd give up his tenure at USC to come back to Rouleme with me."

"He did?" Of course he did. His cousin was a better man than he was. But Michel intended to remedy his shortcomings as soon as he obtained the opportunity.

"Yes, but I wouldn't hear of it. What is he going to do in Rouleme? Resume his role as the tabloid's favorite international playboy? Like hell he is," she growled, her hands fisting on her lap. Michel leaned away from her out of self-preservation instincts. But she continued in a soft voice, "He built an amazing life for himself in Los Angeles. I was resentful at first, but I'm so proud of everything he's accomplished."

"But what about your accomplishments here? Are you at peace with uprooting *your* life?"

"Believe it or not, I find being your royal guard quite stressful," she said with a wry smile. "I'm excited to start a new life with Gabriel in Los Angeles. And I . . . I want to start painting again."

"I thought being a royal guard was your dream." He stared at her with wide eyes.

He remembered from their childhood that she was a talented artist. But her life seemed to revolve around preserving his own, and he'd conveniently assumed she had lost interest in painting.

"It was my parents' dream," his friend said without resentment. "I chose to follow that path because I wanted to make them proud, but now I realize they would rather see me happy."

"I'm glad you have a chance to follow your own dream now." He meant every word even though he would miss his dear friend. Sophie and Gabriel deserved a happy ending after a decade of heartache.

"Thank you, Michel," she said, squeezing his hand. But when her mobile buzzed, she shot to her feet, defaulting back to formalities. "I'm sorry, my prince. I have something to attend to. I thank you for your time."

Before he could ask her what was happening, his royal guard walked out of the sitting room at a fast clip, her thumbs flying over her mobile screen. He stayed where he sat for a dazed moment, digesting all that Sophie had shared with him. But he pushed off the couch, remembering he had to speak with the king.

He stepped out of his chambers into the burgundy-carpeted hallway with embossed white walls and gold-tipped sconces. The wing that housed the royal apartments had a warmer, more intimate feel than the rest of the palace. But tonight, it offered him no comfort as his insides quaked with worry and regret.

By the time he made his way into the main halls of the palace, his heart pounded in time with the echoing clack of his footsteps against the marble floors. The thought of disappointing his father and his people tore him apart, but Michel had to make a choice he could live with—and that meant choosing Emma above all else.

After a few inquiries, he discovered that his father was in the throne room, of all places. What was he doing there? The throne room was the most opulent, formal hall in the entire palace, meant to convey the strength and power of the royal family—of the country as a whole. They only used that room for formal occasions. But in some ways, it was fitting that Michel renounced the throne in there. He suppressed the nervous laughter bubbling up his throat and braced himself for what must be done.

The throne room was dimly lit, the gold brocade walls darkened into bronze in the shadowed evening light. It took a moment to locate his father, standing by one of the windows lining the grand room. He was as tall and broad as Michel, but his hair had turned silver, and his gray eyes were feathered with lines, etched by years of laughter and worries. The king now gazed wistfully at the dais and the single throne that sat upon it— the twin had been removed when Michel's mother passed away.

"Father." Michel walked up to him, his footsteps ringing in the nearly empty room. "Am I interrupting?"

"Not at all, my dear boy." His father smiled warmly at him and motioned him closer. "I was merely reminiscing as old men are wont to do."

"About what?" Michel followed the king as he strode toward the dais.

"The years I spent sitting on that throne." His father sighed deeply. "Wondering if I did my best for my country. For my people."

"Of course, Father. The people of Rouleme love you."

"That speaks more of the generosity of our people than of anything I have done to deserve their approval." The king chuckled. "Rouleme is not perfect, but it is a country I am proud to call my own. Our people are fair-minded and possess true decency. That is a great deal more than many countries can say about their own."

Michel felt his chest constrict with guilt. Rouleme was an amazing country, and the goodness of his people humbled him. And his father was a great king. He had often wondered whether he could be half the ruler that his father was, but now . . . he would never know.

He steeled himself and opened his mouth. "Father, I need to tell you—"

"My king. My prince." Sophie appeared at the entrance. "May I present to you Ms. Emma Yoon."

"E . . . Emma?" Michel breathed. Even as he doubted his

eyes, he drank in the sight of her, his throat tightening with tears. He hadn't allowed himself to wonder when he would see her again, but her absence had been gnawing away at his soul. He would've run to her if his legs hadn't felt too weak to hold him upright.

She was exquisite in a long-sleeved emerald-green dress that fell halfway down her calves, and her gleaming hair hung in artful waves past her shoulders. How was she *here*, looking so beautiful? Then again, she was always beautiful. His brain remained unhelpfully blank as he stared at her like she was his salvation.

Emma glided across the throne room with her innate grace and sank into a curtsy before the king. "Your Majesty."

And where did she learn to curtsy like that? It looked as effortless as though she'd been doing it all her life. Was that really the question he should be asking himself? He shook his head to clear it. Only then did he notice Emma's furtive glance his way. *Merde.* She couldn't get out of her curtsy. He finally broke free of his paralysis and helped her rise with a gentle hold on her elbow.

"Ms. Yoon," his father said, not unkindly, but shot a confused frown at Michel. "To what do I owe this pleasure?"

"Your Majesty." She cleared her throat softly. "I promised Michel . . . that is . . . Prince Michel, that I would be by his side when he told you about our engagement."

"Our engagement?" Michel repeated louder than he'd intended. He had no idea what was happening. What was she doing here? What did she mean *our engagement*? "Of course . . . Yes . . . Father, I need to tell you that . . . that is to say . . ."

He blindly grabbed Emma's hand, then lost his train of thought when he felt her ring scrape across his thumb. He glanced down—terrified and full of hope—to find that she was wearing his mother's ring. When he raised his gaze to her face, her eyes were shining with unshed tears, and she mouthed, *Yes.*

He wanted to grab her and kiss her until they both forgot what it meant to breathe.

"My son." His father's voice held a hint of reproach. "What exactly is it that you need to tell me?"

"Father, please allow me to introduce my fiancée, Emma Yoon." Strength infused his voice. Emma was by his side, and she had agreed to marry him.

"This is . . . highly irregular," the king said stiffly. "Please pardon me, Ms. Yoon. I mean you no offense, but I need to speak to my son in private."

"Yes, Father. We do need to speak. At length," Michel agreed readily. "But first, I need to speak with Emma."

"Michel." The look his father gave him would've withered him on the spot if he hadn't been exploding with happiness.

"I assure you, my king, the news I was about to share with you before Emma came would've been much worse than an unexpected engagement." Michel laughed. "Allow me to have an hour with my fiancée. I will come to your chambers and answer all your questions after."

"Michel." Emma glanced between him and his father. "Speak with your father. I can wait."

"Well, I can't." He grabbed her hand and ran out of the throne room in the most undignified fashion and didn't stop until they reached the privacy of his chambers. He pulled her inside and locked the door behind them, hoping it was in working order.

Their chests rising and falling rapidly, Michel and Emma stared at each other. When silent tears slid down her cheeks, he jolted into action. He gathered her into his arms, breathing in her scent and glorying in the feel of her soft body against his.

"You're here," he whispered, still afraid that he would wake from this wondrous dream.

"Yes." Her voice broke on the single word.

"And you'll marry me?" His arms tightened around her as his blood pounded in his ears.

"Yes." When he pulled back to search her face—checking to make sure she was really here—a watery laugh left her. "Yes, Michel. I'll marry you."

"How?" He enveloped her in another embrace. He quite literally never wanted to let her go.

"Gabriel and Sophie," she said simply.

"I don't know how to repay them, but I will try." He swallowed. "I can't believe they brought you to me. If it wasn't for them—"

Emma suddenly pushed him away, hard enough to make him stumble back, leaving his arms unbearably empty.

"What. Were. You. *Thinking?*" she shouted with such outrage that he cringed away from her.

"I . . . about which part?" He'd made so many mistakes, he couldn't figure out which one she was angry about. Maybe all of them?

"Abdicate?" she screeched. "How can you even *think* about abdicating? What about your father? What about your people?"

"How?" The tension and agony of the past few days combusted into anger in his veins. "How do you think? I thought I'd lost you. I thought it was the only way to win you back."

"For me?" She poked a finger at her chest. "You would've turned your back on your birthright? For me?"

"Yes," he roared. "I would've done *anything* if it meant I could have you back. You. Come. First." His anger seeped out of him. What right did he have to be angry? "Don't you see? Nothing matters if I can't be with you. *I* am nothing without you."

Emma's face crumpled, and he caught her in his arms as her legs gave out. He carried her to his bed and sat down with her in his lap. He gathered her against him, tucking her head under his chin. She was crying into his chest with sharp, broken sobs.

"Shh." He kissed her forehead. "Hush, darling Emma. I love you. Everything will be all right. Hush now."

"I . . . I love you, too." She hiccupped. "And I didn't . . . I didn't mean what I said about you not sacrificing anything. Love isn't about measuring how much we give up for each other." She cut him off when he tried to argue. "*It isn't*. Love is about being there for each other in the best way we can. It's about making sure that we are happy *together*.

"Getting angry at you for having Isabelle as your backup plan was just an excuse." She buried her face in his chest. "Who am I to judge you when I told you that you were just my 'break' from matseons?"

"I wouldn't have married Isabelle even if you wouldn't have me," he said in a rush. "You're the only one for me, Emma."

"And there is no one for me but you." Fresh tears filled her eyes as she gazed up at him. "I was so afraid of our love fading—so afraid of losing you—that I . . . I ran away. But I'll never run away from our love again. I belong to you as you belong to me. That will never change."

She cupped his cheek and looked into his eyes with such love that there was nothing he could do but kiss her. The soft, tender brushes of their lips soon became hungry and greedy. He drove his tongue into her hot, wet mouth and claimed her. *Mine, mine, mine*. And she claimed him right back to his great satisfaction. He was hers. All hers.

Michel laid her on the bed and covered her body with his, taut and aching. He needed to make her come. First, on his hand. Then against his tongue. He grabbed at her dress with fumbling fingers, but she clamped a hand over his. Stopping immediately, he rose onto his elbow and stared down at her flushed face.

"What is it, my love?" he asked, his breath coming in rough pants.

"Your father," she said, equally breathless. "You told him you'd go talk to him."

"Yes, of course." With great regret, he lifted his body off hers and lay down next to her. "But remind me. What was I supposed to talk to him about?"

"Tell him that neither you nor Isabelle want to marry each other." She explained his own mind to him with great patience. "Tell him you are in love with me, and you intend to marry me and no one else."

"Oh?" He turned his head to the side and grinned at her. "Is that all?"

"No, that is not all," she said primly, although she couldn't stop her dimple from winking enticingly at him. "You must also tell him that a brilliant botanist—namely, my father—will be coming to live with us in the palace."

"That's wonderful, Emma." He reached out to run the back of his fingers down her cheek. "Your father is agreeable to moving to Rouleme?"

She nodded with tears in her eyes. "I talked to him on my flight over. He said he would be happy anywhere as long as he had me and a garden to tend."

"He can have as much land as he wants," Michel said promptly, grateful beyond words to his future father-in-law.

"Actually, my dad would be a great asset to the organic farming initiatives you want to implement."

His eyebrows rose. "How do you know about my organic farming initiatives?"

"I eavesdropped on all your calls to Rouleme." She smiled mischievously. "Did you really think I had no interest in who you were?"

"I didn't know what to think." He tapped her nose. "I could only hope—hope that you would agree to be mine."

"You're making it really hard for me not to kiss you again." She crinkled her nose in an adorable scowl. "But you would never make it to your father's chambers in time if I did that."

"We could be quick." He grinned rakishly at her.

"Not on your life," she said sternly. "We're going to take our sweet time with our makeup sex. Now, shoo. Off you go. Go talk to your father."

"Anything else I should mention?" He grudgingly got off the bed and straightened his clothes.

"That's up to you." She sat up with her legs folded beneath her. "But at no time—now or later—will you *ever* utter the word *abdicate* in any shape or form. Understood?"

"Understood. Thank you, Emma." For choosing him. For not making him choose between her and his people. For loving him. All words he would save for later when he could properly express his gratitude. "Are you going to be all right while I'm gone?"

"I'll be fine." She grabbed his shirt and kissed him hard once before pushing him away. "Be gone, temptation. Sophie and Marion are going to be here in a minute to give me a crash course on palace etiquette."

He narrowed his eyes. "Did Sophie have to bribe my cousin?"

"No, she volunteered." Emma laughed. "Marion loves me, you know."

"Of course she does." He tucked a strand of hair behind her ear. "My people are going to love you, too."

"And I'll do everything in my power to deserve their love," she said solemnly. His heart felt as though it would burst with his love for her. "I don't know much about being a princess, but I will do my very best to be a good one."

"With jeongseong." His voice came out in a husky rasp.

"Yes," she whispered with a tender smile.

"And I will love you with jeongseong." He took her hand and kissed her knuckles.

"That's the only way I know how to love." Tears filled her eyes again, but her lips tilted up in a wobbly smile. "Maybe that was why I was so afraid to admit to myself that I loved you. I knew I couldn't give you just a piece of myself. But now, I trust you with all of me. I love you with everything in me."

"I don't know what I did to deserve you." He knelt at her feet and cupped her face between his hands. "But I'll spend the rest of my life loving you with all my heart."

"I'd like that very much." She pressed her forehead against his.

He blinked away tears of happiness. "Are you finally ready to admit that we are compatible despite our many differences?"

She threw her head back and laughed, light and joyous. "Yes, Michel. We are a perfect match in every way."

EPILOGUE

♡

ONE YEAR LATER

"I wish the Crones could see me now. My goddaughter, a *princess*." Auntie Soo placed her teacup back on the saucer with a dainty touch, glancing out to the gardens framed by the windows of the yellow sitting room.

Emma didn't remind her that those meddlesome matchmakers had definitely watched the wedding ceremony. They were much too nosy not to have watched when Emma and Michel's wedding was televised far and wide. Rouleme rarely made international headlines, but the media couldn't resist a royal wedding, especially when the bride was an Asian American commoner. The outpouring of support they received from around the world drowned the toxic bigotry into pesky squeaks. And her family, new and old, swatted even those away so vigilantly that the sharp digs didn't leave scars on her.

Even so, all the attention made Emma a bit weary. Michel assured her that it would soon fade and they would become old news. She hoped her husband was right. Thank goodness her

father-in-law had promised to push back his "retirement" and
continue his reign for a few more years. She would have time to
master this princess business before she had to learn how to be a
queen and become *new* news again.

But the king's motives weren't entirely altruistic. Based on
his pointed hints, he didn't want Emma and Michel stressed out
when they should be concentrating on giving him grandchil-
dren. Her dad was the king's staunchest ally in this endeavor.

"Though I must say," her godmother continued with a con-
tented sigh, "they have been much more pleasant to deal with
recently."

"I thought you wouldn't have to deal with the Crones once
you retired," Emma murmured, sipping her tea.

"That is precisely why I find them more pleasant." Her godmother winked. "Because I don't see them anymore."

"It's so good to have you here, Imo. I wish you didn't have to
leave so soon."

"Jeremy and Steven are good boys, but their wedding's going
to be a disaster if I don't take over the planning." Auntie Soo
reached out to pat Emma's knee. "Besides, I'll see you and Michel
at the wedding in a few months. Right?"

"Of course." Emma smiled. "We wouldn't miss it for the
world."

Unlike Gabriel and Sophie's wedding. Those assholes got
married in an LA courthouse without telling *anybody*. Emma
could've killed them if she wasn't so ridiculously happy for them.
At least she and Michel would be able to attend Sophie's first
exhibit when they were in town for Jeremy and Steven's wedding.

"Auntie Soo." Michel strode into the sitting room and bowed
from the waist to her. Then he settled a warm hand at the nape
of Emma's neck and pressed a kiss on her temple. "And how has
your day been, my darling wife?"

"Busy as usual," she said, letting her eyes soak up her handsome husband. "Auntie Soo and I attended the opening of the new community center in Halle."

"She means she spent most of her time in their kitchen," her godmother added with an affectionate eye roll.

"I spent *some* time in there." Emma pursed her lips. "It's a fantastic kitchen, by the way."

Michel's eyebrows drew into a faint furrow. He leaned down and whispered in her ear, "How are you feeling? Not too tired, I hope."

"I feel absolutely fine." Emma squeezed his hand. They had heard the baby's heartbeat for the first time a couple of days ago at her prenatal appointment. She was only eight weeks along, so it remained their secret for now, and she hoped to keep it that way for a few more weeks. "Don't fuss."

"Let me. Taking care of you is my privilege." Michel lifted her hand and kissed the inside of her wrist. She sucked in a sharp breath as a shiver ran down her spine. Her husband's wide mouth quirked into a knowing grin.

"Come to think of it," Emma said, rising to her feet, "I *am* a little tired. I think I'll go lie down until dinner. Will you be okay on your own, Imo?"

"Silly child. Didn't you know *I* am my favorite company?" Auntie Soo flapped her hand, shooing her away. "Besides, I promised to visit Princess Celine later today."

"Tell my aunt we said hello. And I'll see that Emma gets her rest," Michel promised gallantly even as his hand wrapped possessively around her waist.

Her godmother barely restrained herself from rolling her eyes again. "See that you do."

"Somebody's in a hurry." Emma had to skip to catch up with Michel's impatient strides. "Are you sure you don't have somewhere to be?"

"Antoine will cover for me," he said without slowing down.

"You're going to have to give him a raise for all the covering he's been doing for you these past few months," she teased.

"And whose fault is that?" Michel cocked an eyebrow at her. "If you're worried, you could try being a little less irresistible."

"Not possible." She grinned cheekily.

His gaze dropped to her mouth, and his hand tightened around her waist. They were nearly running by the time they reached their chambers. As soon as the bedroom door closed behind them, Michel's mouth was on hers, hungry and desperate.

"Have I told you today how much I love you?" he said against her lips.

"Maybe, but no one's stopping you from saying it again." She laughed when he swung her up into his arms and strode to their bed.

"I love you." He kissed her deeply as he laid her down on her back. "I love you so much."

"I love you, too," she said breathlessly.

"Are you happy, darling Emma?" He gently covered her body with his, holding on to her gaze. "Do I make you as happy as you make me?"

"Yes, Michel." This might not be the life she'd always dreamed of, but their love was everything that she could ever have hoped for. She smiled up at her husband with the brilliance of incandescent happiness. "You're the best decision I've ever made."

ACKNOWLEDGMENTS

Sometimes I think these acknowledgments sound repetitive after so many books. But it's actually really awesome that I get to thank the same amazing people over and over again because it means they've stuck by my side. I'm so very blessed to have them in my life.

To my agent, Sarah Younger, thank you for your seemingly endless patience, your fiery loyalty, and your overall awesomeness. I truly appreciate you and I can't imagine doing this without you.

To my editor, Mara Delgado Sánchez, I feel like we've grown together on this journey—this is our third book together, right?—as a writer and an editor. I believe *That Prince is Mine* shows our growth. And thank you for being my cheerleader and making everyone in your circle psyched to read this book.

To my critique partners, Christina Britton and Gwen Hernandez, your sage and honest counsel keeps me humble, while your support and gushing gives me the confidence to believe in myself and my books.

To my sunshiny friend Samantha Werner, thank you for helping me navigate my way around British English even when my questions were at times ridiculous. Your tutorial on "arse vs. ass" was truly priceless.

To LA's own The Last Bookstore, thank you for answering my panicked email asking whether your cooking section was on the first or second floor. I suddenly couldn't remember! I ended up taking some creative liberties with the layout, but I hope I showcased your wonderful store faithfully.

To my husband and my boys, thank you for making every effort to keep up with which book I'm drafting, editing, and promoting. I know I've written a lot of books in a short period of time, and it's not always easy to figure out which book I'm going on about. Thank you for listening and supporting me through everything. I love you, guys!

And, last but not the least, to my beautiful readers: every one of your smiles, your laughter and tears while reading *That Prince is Mine* is *why* I wrote this book. Thank you for joining me and staying with me on this journey. I hope this book is worthy of you.

ABOUT THE AUTHOR

Nichanh Nicole Photography

Jayci Lee writes poignant, sexy, and laugh-out-loud romance featuring Korean American main characters. Her books have been featured in O, *The Oprah Magazine*; *Cosmopolitan*; *Entertainment Weekly*; *The Hollywood Reporter*; *E! News*; and *Woman's World*. Jayci is retired from her fifteen-year career as a litigator because of all the badass heroines and drool-worthy heroes demanding to have their stories told. Food, wine, and travel are her jam. She makes her home in sunny California with her tall, dark, and handsome husband; two amazing boys; and a fluffy rescue dog.